The
LOGOS
_of_ Soul

A Novel on the Light and Sound

Kathryn Gabriel Loving

SoulJourn Books

ISBN-13: 978-0-9839838-0-4

For Souls Seeking Their Way

Note to the Reader

In this time of turmoil and uncertainty, people are seeking a modern, meaningful, and intimate connection with spirituality in increasing numbers. Meanwhile, the great religions, particularly Christianity, are being left behind often because they lack that contemporary intimacy and immediacy. Before discounting them entirely, it is worth a final examination for the mystic legacy they created and point to today.

Intriguingly, Jesus did have such a connection with his original disciples. The New Testament tells us that Jesus had two teachings. He taught in parables to the masses, those people who had neither the eyes nor ears to perceive the spiritual truths. But to his disciples it was "given to know the mystery of the Kingdom of God." In other words, to be shown the Mystery, an aspirant had to be initiated by Jesus in order to participate in a personal, direct, and frank exchange with him. One could only learn from Jesus in the flesh, and as the Bible says, he was the Word made flesh.

Jesus went on to say, "In my Father's house are many mansions ... I go to prepare a place for you" (John 14:2), and he also said, "The Kingdom of God is within you" (Luke 17:21). If the multi-layered mansions or heavens of God exist within the human being, and if such a master as Jesus is needed to navigate the soul there, then it stands to reason that both the student and the master have to be living while achieving such a feat.

This underscores so profound a conundrum that we might conclude that Jesus was not the man religion claims him to be. Oh, he was no mere mortal, but neither was he unique. Perhaps he did not die and resurrect to redeem all believers. Perhaps his mission only included those he personally initiated. But where does that leave the rest of us?

It is likely that Jesus belonged to a special class of divine beings known in modern terms as Light and Sound Masters. You might recognize the names of some other Light and Sound Masters, like Pythagoras, Lao Tzu, Socrates, Plato, Rumi, Hafiz, and Kabir. In fact, the Light and Sound Teachings have given rise to most of the religions throughout history.

How do we know that Jesus was a Light and Sound Master? Jesus primarily taught about merging the soul with the essence of God. The Teachings of Light and Sound refer to this no small process as God realization. The number one tenet of the teachings is that this journey is expedited by a living master.

Jesus said, "I will utter things that have been kept secret since the founding of the world" (Matthew 13:35). In the Hebrew context, a person who channels prophecies, parables, and allegories, as well as deciphers them, is known as a *Mara Ha-Davar*, or Master of the Word. Called the *Logos* in Greek and the *Memra* in Hebrew, the Word is also referred to as the *Shabda Dhun* in Sanskrit. The Word in contemporary terms is known as the Light and Sound, the "light" being the esoteric knowledge and the "Sound" being the palpable, vibrational love of the Divine Itself. In this context an exalted Master of the Word, also called a *Sat* or True Guru in Sanskrit, not only conveys the Light and Sound to his initiated disciples, he also helps the soul of each disciple to literally know and realize the mystery of the Kingdom of God in a very real manner. Most of the allegorical elements of the New Testament, therefore, culminate into a story about one's own potential birth and resurrection in soul. This is what Saint Paul called the "Logos of the cross."

Ironically, the religion that ultimately developed in Jesus's absence was based on the allegory and not on the secret teachings themselves. The entire New Testament, from manger to cross, is veiled in parable – the mysteries are never explicitly explained. We know from the writings of bishops in the early centuries of Christianity that many of the more esoteric gospels, labeled "*Gnostic*," were vehemently opposed and omitted from the Holy Bible. When these lost gospels began surfacing in the last century, there was an excitement that finally the secret teachings would be revealed, but they were even more cryptically veiled in near nonsensical mythology. Many are still looking for that definitive gospel that explains what Jesus taught.

I have written this novel for those of you who sense a deeper meaning in the New Testament but have been unable to get at it through the mountains of literature that attempts to decrypt it. This novel is meant to be a bridge between the Judeo-Greek traditions of Christianity and the Light and Sound Teachings. I was first raised a Catholic, and at age twenty I delved into metaphysics and so-called New Thought churches. I was initiated into one Light and Sound Path, called MasterPath, in 1993 at the age of thirty-seven. A journalist by training, I have written several non-fiction books on the archaeology and history of the greater American Southwest. Although it wasn't my intention to deconstruct the life and death of Jesus, for that task would be nearly impossible, it became necessary to separate truth from myth. I drew upon early Christian, Jewish, and Gnostic writings, along with the vast amount of scholarly speculation that now exists, particularly books by Elaine Pagels and Bruce Chilton. Three important works tying the Judaic-Christian-Gnostic mysticism to the Light and Sound Teachings include *The Gospel of Jesus: In Search of His Original Teachings* by John Davidson, *The Holy Name: Mysticism in Judaism* by Miriam Bokser Caravella, and *Light on Saint John* by Maharaj Charan Singh. But the major source for the Light and Sound Teachings comes from learning at the figurative feet of my own living master, Sri Gary Olsen, as well as from personal spiritual revelations and experiences.

Apart from the elusive Master Jesus, two of the most compelling characters in the New Testament are Mary Magdalene and Paul of Tarsus. Though her role has been downplayed over the last sixteen hundred years, and her appearance in the Bible short but sweet, she portrays profound spiritual symbolism. According to the gospels, Mary was the one whose seven demons were cast from her by Jesus, the one who sat beneath his cross as he died, the one who anointed his body for burial, and the one who was the first to see his resurrected spirit. In the Gnostic gospels, those writings that were censored from mainstream catechism, Mary was the one who Jesus loved the most, and the one he selected to carry on his ministry after his death. Her persona from whore to saint, however contrived, has inspired centuries of devotion as the iconic everywoman and everyman in spirituality. In the esoteric Gnostic religion, which only existed for two or three centuries beyond Jesus's lifespan,

Mary was metaphorically seen as the counterpart of Jesus. She was the proverbial bride and he was the groom, she was the disciple and he the Master, she was the soul and he the Sound.

Saul of Tarsus, who became Saint Paul, is equally compelling. Paul's letters to the churches within his ministry are part of the historical record. Unlike the gospels, which were composed, slanted, and edited for various political reasons, most of Paul's letters are authentic. Although Paul was a self-appointed apostle once removed, he testifies to the early politics of Christianity. Paul wasn't an initiate of the living Jesus; rather, he converted as a result of a vision. In his letters, Paul also describes a difference between his public speeches and his private, esoteric revelations. Since he wasn't a direct initiate of Jesus, he confesses that he invented much of what he preached, perhaps borrowing from his own training as a Pharisee priest in Jerusalem before his conversion as well as what he may have picked up later from the apostles or his travels. Despite his flamboyant distortion of Jesus's true teachings, this enigmatic figure nevertheless beautifully and uncannily expressed some of the more profound secrets of the Light and Sound.

The main part of this story takes place in Ephesus, Turkey, and is an ongoing *satsang*, a spiritual exchange, between Mary Magdalene and Paul. Nearly everything Paul says in this novel comes from his letters to the Galatians and the Corinthians in the New Testament, letters that were likely written in Ephesus. The events that unfold in Ephesus around Paul come from the Acts of the Apostles. The tension between Paul and the "Pillars of Jerusalem," namely Simon Peter, James, and John, comes from Paul's letters and Acts as well. For the sake of expediency, some biblical figures either have been omitted or merged in this novel. (Mary Magdalene didn't necessarily have a sister named Martha or a brother named Lazarus, for instance. In the New Testament, these siblings actually belong to a different Mary from Bethany.)

It is said that all roads lead to Rome, but there is only one royal road to heaven. Countless spiritual paths existed in Roman times, and to the unwary seeker, they must have all seemed equal in their methods of worship and their rewards for the devoted – much like today. Light and Sound Masters say that the path to God is not invented by man or woman, but is indelibly written upon each and every soul and eventually revealed to that soul by a living master. This novel brings to light some of the psychic rituals that existed in Ephesus and Jerusalem along with the rituals that scholars are now saying Paul may have contributed. The hope is to juxtapose some of these practices, which can be downright dangerous, against the Light and Sound Teachings to show what the Teachings are not.

Light and Sound Masters embrace the cultural concepts and vocabulary of the times to convey the principles to their initiates in a way they can comprehend. Although the teachings themselves are eternal and unchangeable, some of the practices are adjusted to fit their initiates. For instance, the Light and Sound Path originating in the Punjab, India, known as the Radha Soami Satsang, had to work through the cultural matrix of its immediate geographical area. The master we know as Jesus would likely have relied heavily on the Wisdom Literature of the *Tanakh* (Old Testament) for his Hebrew students, which contains evidence of Light and Sound influences. Incidentally, I purposely avoided the Judaic-mystic Kabbalah because it developed some seven to thirteen centuries after the time of Jesus, although Kabbalists may see similarities.

The Light and Sound Principles can be found in nearly every religion, spiritual path, or walk of life. Light and Sound Masters usually pass on the divine mantle of their ministry to a worthy successor, but when no one is ready to take the mantle, the line comes to an end. Often a new religion is given birth in its place, one which worships the original master, now dead, and focuses on his written teachings, now called "the Word," thereby reducing the Sound to just the light.

What complicates examination of the early Christianity that bubbled up in Jesus's absence is that it is a result of a fusion between Jewish mysticism and Greek philosophical traditions, which also has evidence of Light and Sound influences through Pythagoras, Heraclitus, Socrates, and Plato. For instance, the Hebrews lent the notion of the One God. The prophets of the Old Testament showed how ventures into the heavens are attainable by anybody who is aware. The Greeks, of course, contributed the ideas of an eternal soul and an afterlife, something the Jews hadn't yet grasped. Concepts such as these remain in the world for later generations of Light and Sound Masters to build upon.

To that end, I purposely used the Greek and Hebrew words to show the cultural evolution of some of these spiritual ideas. A glossary of selected ancient words is provided at the end of the book. Along those lines, Jesus, Mary, Paul, Simon Peter, James, and John are called by their Aramaic names here: Yeshua, Miryam, Paulos, Simeon, Yacob, and Johanan.

Bracketed around the Ephesus story in this novel is a story that takes place in the present involving a contemporary fictional character named Alyson Sego. Although the Ephesus story could stand on its own, the intention is to show how the Light and Sound is current and accessible to modern day seekers.

Finally, just because Mary Magdalene was seen as the leader of the esoteric Gnostic movement, while Simon Peter is clearly the proponent of Jesus's outer teachings of parables and allegories, it isn't my intention to champion a feminist cause. It is also not my intention to promote my own Light and Sound Path, for others do exist. Nor do I wish to denigrate Christianity or Judaism. On the contrary, my regard for these two profound religions has greatly increased, and they indeed helped an infinite number to yearn for the greater part of themselves and to ready them for that time when they set out to find their own Wayshower of the Mysteries.

Much gratitude to the following souls: Dennis Holtje, Carol Adams, Irene Swain, Deborah Malone, Robin Tawney, JoAnne Altrichter, Janet Gabriel, and Stan Byron. Their contributions, editorial assistance, satsanging, and friendship have been invaluable. A special thank you to Jessica Gabriel, whose site visit of the Ephesus ruins provided a spatial feel of the place. And finally much love and appreciation to David Loving for supporting my spiritual pursuits.

Ultimately, none of this is possible without the impetus and sustenance of the eternal Shabda. All glory to that Power.

May the blessings be,
KGL

Part One

The Logos Notebook
Denver, Colorado, 2003

Socrates: Now tell me, is there another sort of Logos that is brother to the written logos, but genuine? Can we see how it originates, and how much better and more powerful it is than the other?

Phaedo: What sort do you have in mind, and how is it generated?

Socrates: The sort that exists together with Knowledge and is written in the soul of the student, that has the power to defend itself, and knows to whom it should speak and to whom it should remain silent.

Phaedo: You mean the Logos of Knowing, alive and ensouled, of which the written logos may correctly be called an image?

Socrates: Precisely.

– Plato, *Phaedo*

One

For days the cats vied for dominion over the unopened parcel on Alyson Sego's dining room table. Stamped "fragile," the breadbox-sized package was from a Boston attorney, and to her that meant one of two things: Either it contained something from her recently deceased aunt's estate or, worse, it housed her actual remains. Whatever the case, she wasn't ready to face what her aunt's death represented to her, much less the urn of snowy ashes in her own life. The package became a fixture around which she ate, opened her bills, and wrote out her meager grocery list, and upon which the cats enjoyed sleeping. That was how she handled most things of discomfort these days.

"I can't believe you're not curious, Al," Evan Hartman said from beneath her kitchen sink one Sunday morning. "You're a reporter, for God's sake." As the apartment manager slash maintenance guy for a row of duplexes in downtown Denver where Alyson lived, Evan was installing a new garbage disposal, one she didn't necessarily need. He had accepted the package on her behalf and delivered it to her when she returned home from work. That was a week ago.

Alyson sat at the table with her coffee, reading the morning paper propped up on the box in question. She didn't actually read the paper, just scanned for typos out of habit. In-depth reading of the paper she worked for on her day off felt like a busman's holiday. Luce, the female gray and white cat, lay sound asleep on the box under the paper. Out of nowhere Noche, the male tuxedo cat, engaged his sister in a licking battle until she abdicated her cardboard throne to him. Having no patience for this feline sibling rivalry, Alyson tossed them both to the floor. They landed with indignant harumphs.

"I still find it hard to believe she's gone," Alyson said.

"Who?"

"Aunt Ruth. I think the box is from her attorney."

"Won't know unless you open it." Evan grunted, sounding like he was half listening as his wrench clanged against metal pipe. "Were you close?"

"Not exactly. Sadly, Ruth's career and then the Alzheimer's kept her apart from us, and I was too busy with my own life to go see her. But I admired her. Minored in anthropology because of her work as a contract archaeologist."

"But you ended up working for a newspaper."

"Columnist turned receptionist."

"A reverse career path," he chuckled. "I like that in a woman."

"It's a long story."

"Always is. Got a few to tell, myself." Evan Hartman pulled himself out from under the sink and lifted up from the floor, wiping his hands clean with a paper towel. He was a rather tall man in his late forties, medium build, blonde hair, mustache, striking topaz blue eyes that seemed self-luminous. All of his work shirts were endearingly embroidered "Evan" above the pockets. Well, she found it endearing. She could go for him, she thought, looking at him from above the reading glasses perched on her nose. He certainly found enough excuses to be in her tiny flat – he was working on a Sunday, no less. But she was through with relationships. Maybe not finished completely, but on an emotional sabbatical.

"Could be her last will and testament," he said.

"Might even be her, for all I know."

"You'll open it when you're through grieving ... or feeling guilty." He was flashing those eyes now, daring her.

"Ouch." Alyson exhaled loudly. He was right, though. She did feel guilty. Big sighs of surrender and she was out of her chair, fetching a knife from a kitchen drawer. She began severing the overly-taped seams and corners aggressively. Beneath several layers of Styrofoam peanuts, Bubble Wrap, and shredded newspaper, Alyson disinterred a dusty earthenware jar, brushing aside the nosy cats several times. A blast of energy hit her across the face, energy she interpreted as allergens mixed in with her own cauldron of emotions. *This is what I was afraid of,* she said to herself.

"Don't be afraid, Al. Your aunt's soul is not in this jar."

The comment startled Alyson. Coming from anyone else it would have been one of those platitudes mouthed at funerals. But he said it as if he *knew* it with certainty. He blushed and added more humbly, "I mean, they usually ship ashes in plastic bags, don't they? Nothing so elaborate that could shatter in the mail."

"The idea that this might be human ... ."

"Geez-o-pete, you're morbid. Just open it!"

Alyson lifted the jar in her hands to eye level. It was a plain earthenware jar, reddish in color, heavy, about eighteen inches tall, six inches in diameter at the ends, and bulging in the middle. The lid had been sealed with some kind of tar. "You're right. I don't think Ruth is in here." She turned the jar slowly in her hands. "In fact, I'd say this is no ordinary jar. Looks to be a thousand, maybe two thousand years old. We'll be hard put to break the seal without cracking the ceramic."

"What's this?" Evan pulled an envelope from the bottom of the box.

"Ah, maybe an explanation." She laid the jar back in its box, opened the envelope, and unfolded a letter. Not believing her eyes, she quickly spotted a check for $50,000 nestled in the letter's center folds. Rather than rejoicing, she felt her guilt intensify. Trembling, she began reading the letter silently to herself.

> *Dear Mrs. Sego,*
>
> *First of all, allow me to offer my condolences. Your Aunt Ruth spoke highly of you. As you may or may not know, I was her attorney and long-time friend.*
>
> *When Ruth first learned of her disease, she named me as her proxy and executor, and charged me with placing her in a nursing home when her health deteriorated. Difficult as it was, I kept my promise and liquidated most of her belongings and assets to pay for her prolonged care. The enclosed check was granted to you as the beneficiary of a small life insurance policy, and I am saddened to say, there was nothing left from her estate, except for this earthenware jar.*

The university with which she was associated retrieved everything of value from her years of archaeology. This jar in particular, however, had been stashed in a bedroom closet and forgotten about. She had found it in the open-air market on her last trip to Turkey, in the city of Selçuk near an excavation sight the locals call Efes. As you can imagine, merchants in foreign countries will try to hawk anything that looks like it has value, whether it does or not. Ruth, of course, had a trained eye and was able to bargain for it as casually as she would for a knock-off Persian rug. It wasn't long before she became profoundly ill, and she didn't explore the jar any further.

Ruth, however, did become quite lucid in her final hours. She barely weighed eighty pounds, she had a fractured pelvic bone and pneumonia, and she had stopped eating, but she woke up remembering details of her life with precise accuracy. She talked about her career at great length, and she remembered the jar for the first time in years. She told me it might be a significant find, but that opening it would be like opening a can of worms, or worse, Pandora's Box.

She specifically instructed me to send you the jar with the following caveat: The ultimate dilemma for any archaeologist is that in order to discover the truth, you must first destroy the thing holding it. Otherwise, you're nothing more than an art collector or grave robber. Her final words to me were: "Beware of answers, for they are a form of death." She passed on not too long after that. I think she died peacefully.

I hope the reason your aunt chose to give you the jar will become clear to you with time. Understand, there are antiquity laws regarding treasures from other countries, and there may be consequences for giving this to you. If you run into any legal trouble, please know you can contact me for assistance.

I was very fond of Ruth and I miss her deeply.

Warmest regards,

Eric Hall

Alyson clutched the letter and suppressed an overwhelming feeling to cry, just as she had suppressed her grief over the uncontrollable events in her life the past two years. If she allowed herself to hurl into an emotional upheaval, she was certain she would break into countless irreparable pieces, and no one could reassemble her. The feeling soon passed, and she began to breathe more easily.

Evan moved a step toward her and covered her delicate hand with his much larger one. "It is done." He retreated just as quickly, for he was, after all, just the apartment manager, and he didn't wish to overstep unspoken boundaries.

"Thank you," she said quietly, grateful someone was present, someone who didn't ask questions about mysterious letters. But having no one else to share this with, she handed him the letter to read anyway. She then lifted the jar from the box again and ever so gingerly sat it on end on the table to admire its rustic beauty. Just as she did, both cats jumped into the empty box with such enthusiastic force that it slid across the table and knocked the jar to the brick floor. The ceramic was too thick to shatter, but it did break into several pieces, inspiring a string of expletives to spew forth from Alyson's mouth.

"At least the decision to break the jar is no longer necessary," Evan said, without smiling.

Alyson nodded, fuming that the cats had forever destroyed the last vestige of her aunt's work. She squatted next to the scattered shards and carefully extracted the largest piece. Beneath it, a thick, curled stack of papyri emerged from the pottery chrysalis. "What's this?"

"Obviously the reason the jar was sealed," Evan said, squatting next to her. "Maybe it's the answer to everything you've been seeking."

"Hope not," she answered. "That would mean certain death according to Aunt Ruth." Within herself she wondered how Evan, or Ruth for that matter, knew she had recently started looking for answers.

Two

For the better part of two years, Alyson's natural curiosity had come into conflict with an emotional avoidance of truth. The avoidance began with "the accident" that stole Alyson's teenage daughter, husband, and her entire life out from under her. She called it an accident, but it was really a series of events that drove her daughter Kendra into oblivion and her husband Stan into estrangement. Drugs were the catalyst, though not the core issue. Called "red jackets" by their users, they were merely over-the-counter antihistamines under various brand names. Take a few at a time and you feel like you're ascending through multiple stages of a psychedelic heaven. Take sixteen of them and you "feel like God." Chase them with marijuana and crack cocaine, and you lose your mind.

Alyson could see Kendra's mental fitness deteriorating just before she disappeared. She had gone on about Siddhartha and seeking a kind of nirvana; the context (not the action) was seeded by required reading in high school English lit. The police called her drug-related disappearance a "mission" and said she would probably reappear in a week or so. Within just a day, however, Kendra resurfaced behind the wheel of someone else's Mustang. She wasn't driving it, exactly, just sitting there. The owner had left the car unlocked, so it wasn't as if she had broken into it. Already high from dozens of red jackets swallowed over a period of days and in no position to resist, someone had introduced her to crack cocaine. When the police arrested her, she was so incoherent and psychotic from the drugs, she could barely remember what had happened. She simply thought she would look cool in the car as she drove down the middle road in search of enlightenment.

"God," she told police when they asked for her name.

"Can you at least spell your name for us?" the officer asked, hoping to trick her.

"G-O-D," she answered. "Duh."

Ever the strict parent, Stan had refused to pay for a lawyer, and the overworked public defender was either too busy or too lazy to pursue mental incompetence. Drugs were not a defense for crime, he had told them. The judge suspended the charge, provided Kendra entered drug rehabilitation. She agreed.

When Kendra went into rehab, Alyson lost contact with her. All letters sent to her came back marked "returned to sender." No one would give Alyson information on her daughter's progress because at age eighteen she was, legally, an adult. The time for Kendra's release came and went without so much as a phone call from her letting Alyson and Stan know how she was doing or where she planned to go. Worried they'd lost their daughter to the streets forever, they took time off from work to search for her. But after weeks of endless inquiries of friends and incessant driving through questionable neighborhoods, Stan went back to work and suggested that Alyson do the same, saying Kendra would turn up again once she hit bottom. Alyson begrudgingly agreed, but she refused to give up entirely. Against Stan's wishes, she took an apartment on Emerson Street downtown, halfway between what she called Methville at one end and the student ghetto at the other. This way, she reasoned, she might run into Kendra.

Within a month or so, Stan served her with divorce papers. Perhaps he was tired of waiting for her, or perhaps he wanted to shock her into reality, or perhaps their marriage was simply not strong enough to endure the loss of a child – Alyson had no clue or wherewithal to fix it. Zombie-like, she signed the papers giving him their ranch-like home in the Ken-Caryl area south of Denver. It was just easier that way.

In retrospect, Alyson felt like she had allowed the accident to happen, even though there was probably nothing she could have done to stop the inevitable. Both Kendra and Stan had slipped through her fingers like water through a colander. It was like watching one's family get run over by a train, and being utterly helpless to stop the train or move the loved ones out of the way. Two imaginary gravestones marked the places where her relationships with both husband and daughter had once thrived.

After the divorce Alyson collapsed further within herself, refusing to accept all that had happened, feeling numb for weeks, then months. When the flames of separation threatened to singe her heart, she doused them with wine, good wine at first, but soon moved on to budget-conscious grocery store brands. Within weeks she realized she made a poor drunk, unable to physically tolerate the liquor any longer. The first glass reddened her face and squeezed her sinuses, the third glass made her sick to her stomach. It was a mixed fortune – she wasn't really cured of the desire to dull her senses, but the alcohol abandoned her to suck the life from a more apt victim.

Prior to the accident, she had been a reporter for the *Rocky Mountain News*, but lacking the mental edge she once had, she requested a transfer as copy editor on the city desk. Frankly, she just didn't have the energy to pursue stories she no longer cared about. But as copy editor she worked long hours, past the evening deadline for the morning news. Payroll discovered the overtime and asked her to stop – the *News* couldn't afford to pay for her need to drown her sorrows in work.

So, by daylight she had become a workaholic, meticulously adding commas where none were really needed, even crossing the line to rewriting leads. The reporters began complaining, and she was bumped to obituaries and soon put on the phones. The serial demotions had left her with more time to fill, busying herself like a manic receptionist – without the sculpted nails – meanwhile keeping her racing thoughts and emotions at bay. It wasn't long before she added the sculpted nails to complete the picture.

By night, when Alyson was alone, the anxiety returned, so she took up roaming the shopping malls, half hoping to spot Kendra working behind a counter or perusing the cheaper clothing racks or sitting on a bench begging for money. Little by little Alyson found herself dressing up, not in work clothes, but in the cheap high-heeled sandals, tight sweaters, and short skirts she bought in discount houses. She didn't look that bad for someone in her mid-forties, she told herself. When the malls closed, she haunted late night bookstores, catching the eye of lone male browsers, feeling as if she were still somebody when she caused heads to turn twice. But that's as far as she went. Sometimes she would ask herself why she dressed this way if she weren't interested in hooking up with anyone. Part of her knew what she was up to, the part of her that purchased the sexy undergarments and wore them for no one but herself. She never bought books either, for she wasn't able to concentrate long enough to finish a page let alone a whole paperback. She was trawling, but for what, she didn't know.

Then one rainy evening in the Tattered Cover bookstore she noticed a man following her from aisle to aisle. When she moved to the next floor, it wasn't long before he appeared there too. He wasn't entirely bad looking, though a bit too uptight looking for her tastes. He just seemed lonely, like her. She moved into the romance section. He trailed in behind her and selected a book from the shelf.

"You interested in romance?" she asked out of nowhere, surprising even herself.

He looked up from his reading, as if he had been unaware of her presence or was amazed someone actually talked to him. He scanned her from polished toenails to blonde highlights. It slowly dawned on her that he thought she might be soliciting him. She shook her head and pointed to the book.

"Oh," he said with some embarrassment and, yes, disappointment. "A friend recommended this novel. Said it didn't belong in this genre."

"What's it about?"

"Time travel. I suppose it's categorized as a romance because the heroine develops a heated relationship with a Scot in the period she travels to, but there's so much more than sex in the book." He blushed. "Or so I'm told."

"History is for romantics, wouldn't you say?"

He blushed again, shifted his glasses on his nose, ran a hand through his graying hair. "I'm Jerry. Can I buy you a cup of coffee?"

Alyson hesitated. Coffee with a stranger in the middle of the night? She didn't do that sort of thing, did she? "I don't know. It's kind of late."

He looked at his watch. "Half past seven."

"Oh, it's not that late, I guess."

"Just thought you'd like some company. At least I would." He glanced again at her short skirt a little too obviously.

"Well, I've been looking for something to read. Perhaps you can make some suggestions."

She accompanied him to the bottom floor and let him buy her a half-caf, no foam, skinny latte. He ordered a tall "regular" with room, naturally. That reminded her of Stan, who preferred gas station coffee over gourmet – too bitter. She stuffed that memory back where it came from and chose a table by the window where they could watch the rain before the sun drew the shades on the day.

Jerry didn't talk about books at all. He droned on about his dead-end job as an accountant, of his recent divorce, of his two girls he shared joint custody over. The monotony of detail matched the steady downpour outside. He never asked her about herself, something she both appreciated and resented. She didn't have much to say, anyway, and she certainly didn't want to show him up with her own list of tragedies and disappointments. On the other hand, she wasn't interested in another one-sided, self-absorbed man. At a point where she could break in, she stood. "I'm sorry," she said, searching for the way out of this awkward moment as well as the café. "I need to get home. Thanks for the coffee."

He was visibly shocked and a bit perturbed, but she turned and quickly shuffled toward the door, not really hearing his comments trailing behind her. Out of the corner of her eye she thought she caught a glimpse of him following her. She resisted running to her SUV in the adjoining parking structure – that might inspire him to run – but she walked very quickly, her spine broom-straight. As she approached her car, she shoved her hand into her pocket. No alarm key. She unzipped her tiny purse and fished around. The spare surfaced at last, and she speared the lock, climbed in, slammed the door. The noise the power locks made emphasized with finality her security and simultaneous isolation. When at last she built up the nerve, she looked around. No one in sight. It was all her imagination. She never saw the man again.

After that she took a long, hard look at herself. *Who am I kidding, dressing like I want men, not really wanting them?* she'd ask herself. She just wanted to relieve the pain, not create more problems for herself. There had to be something else she could do to occupy herself so she wouldn't have to think.

Managing Editor Frank Storey – and, yes, he was fond of the irony of his name – called her into his office one day. "Look, Al, I want to help, but I can't carry you forever. You need a professional."

"You know how I feel about therapists."

"Physician, heal thyself? Okay, so a lot of them come from dysfunctional families themselves, but there are a few who are legitimately good."

"I'll get over it, with time."

"You're a reporter, or at least you once were a damned good one. You could always research your way back to where you were before all this ... happened. Read a self-help book. *Something*!"

He had a point. She returned to the Tattered Cover, this time clad in jeans, oversized work shirt, and running shoes. She preferred the Tattered Cover in Denver's posh Cherry Creek neighborhood over the newer one in LoDo near Coors Stadium. To her, this bookstore wasn't just a bookstore, it was a five-story temple. No one religion was worshiped here, but all of them. Others had come here in a similar search, and she could see her pain reflected on their pallid, drawn faces. She was no longer just a patron, she was a seeker, but a seeker of what she did not know. To end the pain? That was fading. Her nightly quests had transformed from searching for her daughter and her next fix to searching for an answer. To death? No, she realized, to life. *That's a switch*, she thought.

When she looked at the self-help books, she felt she just couldn't face them quite yet, so she began roaming the aisles in search of anything that caught her eye. Soon she found herself in the romance novel section right where she had left off with the divorced accountant fiasco. *Maybe he was onto something*, she thought. She pulled the book he had been reading and was immediately drawn in. She purchased it and devoured it in less than a week. Every few days found her ravenously combing the shelves, pulling one book from its slot, turning it to scan the blurb on the back, then reading the first paragraph, then a random sampling. If the book didn't immediately settle into her veins, she would put it back and pull another. She was after brain candy, passion fruit, nothing heavy. Romance writers understood plot, a quick climax, a happy ending.

But soon she found the romance novels only reminded her of her own loneliness, and her vicarious sex life, adventure, and companionship through the characters left her feeling emptier than when she started. She passed up mystery for obvious reasons, not wishing to be reminded of her own loss, except Tony Hillerman's novels on Navajo cosmology. She envied the self-confidence of his hero, Officer Jim Chee, in his chosen spiritual path as a facilitator of Navajo ceremonies. Science fiction held her attention for a few weeks, especially the classics – Bradbury, Clark, and Heinlein. As she read *Time Enough for Love* and *Stranger in a Strange Land*, she almost forgot her own misery. No, the depression was still there, but it had grown into a deeper longing for something more fulfilling than temporary fixes. That much she *grokked*.

She moved from science fiction, though she appreciated their let-the-force-be-with-you kind of themes, and scanned the stacks of Christian inspirational fiction with little interest. She sensed the books would be about renewed faith, forgiveness, and black-or-white moralism, all of which would make her feel even guiltier than she already did. She didn't want to simply repent her sins for her failed marriage and botched parenting job to some entity she could barely relate to. That kind of purging would be a great relief now that she thought about it, but then what? Wait for the "rapture" and the "second coming" of Jesus? She wondered if anyone really took that stuff seriously. What about her own second coming?

The so-called New Age section took up an entire corner of the Tattered Cover, and the book titles glowed with their own hypnotic auras, beckoning her like sirens singing on the shore and promising a treasure chest of ancient secrets. She began with the classics. Didn't want to overtax herself mentally – just the feel-good, the sensational, the comfort food. In his day Richard Bach, the creator of *Jonathan Livingston Seagull*, was simple, fresh, fun. Shirley MacLaine projected an honest, gossipy, self-possessed persona, while psychic Sylvia Brown seemed uncanny. Carlos Castaneda on sorcery training was mystical fantasy. Jane Roberts, or rather, Seth, the Oversoul who allegedly and fantastically spoke through the author, was riveting, incredulous, and offered a tantalizing albeit outrageous alternative history to Christianity. She read a few metaphysical how-to books by contemporary authors and tried some of the exercises, then forgot about them. Finally, having tasted Spirit through the gateway drugs of pulp spirituality, she turned toward the hard stuff: Kant, Wilber, Watts, and even Blavatsky. The more she read, the more she sensed that her soul needed much more than chicken soup. She was dying here.

Eventually Alyson realized she was living a vicarious spiritual life through the metaphysical books, just as she had experienced relationships through romance novels. It was time to get her third eye wet. She pulled a few books on Buddhism, Hinduism, and other more obscure Eastern religions and mysticisms, but she didn't feel culturally equipped to sit in meditation on the floor for the decades required to reach cosmic consciousness, whatever that was. The books were full of images of malnourished, half-naked yogis with long beards and fingernails. That didn't seem like her.

The answer, she told herself, might lie in one of the cubbyholes of the wooden, altar-like shelving in the entryway to the Tattered Cover, where fliers and hand-out tabloids invited her to embark on various spirit quests. The metaphysical world lay at her fingertips: crystals, aromatherapy, yoga, tai chi, Tibetan meditation, past-life regression, law-of-attraction workshops. Her head whirled from this tempting spiritual smorgasbord. She didn't know what to try next.

Alyson's bookstore quest had taken the better part of a year, and she had come out the other end of it a well-read, miserable book junkie. Somehow she sensed that her addictive and attention deficit tendencies would spill over into her spiritual search and she froze, unable to make a decision on which way to turn. She could not venture down one aisle without the feeling that it would be too difficult to retrace her steps and start again on another aisle when the first no longer served her needs. Castaneda advised the spiritual aspirant to pursue a path until that path no longer had heart, but did she have the requisite attention span? She felt all of the choices closing in on her, and she suspected she was developing a kind of spiritual agoraphobia. What had she read? The teacher will appear when the student is ready, practically a mantra with most metaphysical authors. She decided to go cold turkey, to stop reading and stop searching and to wait to be shown what to do next. The anxiety did return, but she maintained her equilibrium. No longer distracted, she felt she might finally be ready to return to copy editing for the *News*. And, who knows, perhaps Frank Storey would eventually allow her to return to reporting the actual news for her column. Even her depression over losing her daughter had moved to the backburner of her mind.

That's when the package from her late Aunt Ruth arrived.

Three

"I'm sorry, I don't think I heard you correctly," Frank Storey told Alyson when she asked for a leave of absence the morning following the discovery of the ancient papyri.

"You heard me," she said, a little more boldly than usual.

Frank leaned back in his chair and rested a worn, well-polished pair of Tony Lamas on the edge of his desk. As the managing editor of the *News*, she thought he had been patient with her over the past two years, the way he had allowed her to demote herself from a high-profile columnist to receptionist. What was next, janitor? Alyson was beginning to suspect his patience had worn thin.

"As you know, my Aunt Ruth worked on a few archaeological sites in Jerusalem and Turkey." She didn't want to divulge much for fear it would make headlines in her own paper under someone else's byline, but she did feel she owed Frank an explanation after all he'd done for her. She might want to return to the *News* someday, and as a reporter, not as whatever it was she did now.

"Made quite a name for herself in those circles, as I recall."

"She died recently and left me her field notes. Some inscriptions and fragments I'd like to have translated, perhaps put together a posthumous book."

Frank raised his eyebrows. He was casual, yet shrewd. "Sounds interesting. Why didn't she have them translated herself?"

"Alzheimer's ended her career rather abruptly."

"Sorry to hear that." He sat up and rubbed the back of his head. "Thing is, Al, I'm having budget problems. I've kept you on because you were once one hell of a writer, and it would behoove the paper to get you back to your column. So I nursed you along for two years. Heck, after what you've been through, I was happy to. But if you leave even for only a month, I will have to replace you."

"I owe it to my aunt to complete her work."

"Can't do it evenings, weekends? It isn't as if your job is all that demanding. I hear you frequent the bookstores and libraries in your spare time anyway."

That made Alyson blush. She had the habit under control, but he had struck a blow to her ego. "I hear you frequent certain ... book stores as well."

A flash of anger spread across Frank's face. She had done it. If this bridge wasn't burned, it was at least dangling off the cliff. "You might want to take your stuff home to avoid moving it later." His eyes were cold steel now.

"Frank, I'm sorry. You've been very good to me. I have a feeling this work will save my life, maybe even my soul. I will let you off the hook and free up the job."

The phone rang and he answered it while avoiding further eye contact with her: "Storey here."

Summarily dismissed, Alyson returned to her desk in the newsroom. She sat down and fought the urge to cry in front of the other reporters. This job had been her one true safety net, and now she was unemployed. How long would Aunt Ruth's life insurance check last, six months, a year? The thought triggered the familiar anxiety. *Am I out of my mind for leaving my job?*

She returned her attention to Aunt Ruth's papyri, and the intrigue brightened her mood. The old woman on her death bed had left her with a mystery to solve – and a warning not to solve it. What did she mean, "Answers are a form of death?" Was that an omen, or just a general statement about life? At this point, Alyson wasn't even sure what the questions were. It almost didn't matter, for now she had a project to avert her attention from her own problems.

After the earthenware jar had crashed to the floor the day before, Evan helped her excavate the papyri from the sharp-edged pieces of broken ceramic using a paint brush and tweezers. He then swept up the shards and laid them in the Bubble Wrap inside the packaging the jar came in. Alyson vacuumed, then pulled clean bed sheets from the closet and spread them out on the floors throughout her apartment. Wearing cloth gloves Evan provided, they carefully separated the fragile papyrus pages and laid them out on the sheets in the order in which they had nestled together in the jar. The two of them then took a step back to view their unburied treasure.

The first page was just a scrap of papyrus the size of an envelope, but the rest were roughly the size and shape of modern letter paper turned sideways, a dozen in number. All of the pages except the first smaller one contained lettering on both sides. Considering their obvious antiquity, they were in remarkable shape with minimal deterioration around the edges.

"I'd say that page doesn't go with the rest," Evan said, pointing to the smaller piece.

"Unless it's a sort of cover page," Alyson offered.

"Maybe, hard to say. The rest of the pages look like they go together like a book."

"A codex, perhaps, without the stitching."

Evan smiled. "Archaeology 101?"

"Maybe 201," Alyson retorted, glad her undergraduate classwork finally served her. "I remember this because it was intriguing to me as an early form of publishing." She described how the Egyptians cut, peeled, and then stripped long strands of fiber from tall papyrus reeds that grew in the delta marshes. Workers laid the strips side by side horizontally on a flat, wet surface, and then pounded in a top layer of vertical strips. The dried sheets were pasted end to end, polished smooth by a sea shell or ivory, and then wrapped around a wooden rod. The Greeks called the scrolls *biblos* because they imported the papyrus through a Phoenician city by the same name. A biblos, or book, tended to be about fifteen feet long, twice that for a volume of books. Most volumes were about the height of a broadsheet newspaper, and a person would have to unroll a section of the scroll with the right hand and re-roll that section with the left hand as they read.

"Sounds cumbersome," Evan said. "Imagine trying to look something up."

"That's when they came up with the idea for the codex." She went on to explain that the Romans invented a writing tablet out of planks of wood covered in wax and fastened together to form a book for day-to-day notes and ciphering. They adopted the technique to papyrus and animal hide parchment, which allowed scribes to lay the pages flat and to write on both sides. "The Christians were the first to really use the codex form in abundance to distinguish their Bible from Jewish scripture or pagan literature."

"They're always the first to embrace new media technology."

"Anything to get the good news out," Alyson answered, laughing. "But this codex doesn't look like a formal book. The papyri look more like pages out of my reporter's notepad." She squatted near the first sheet. "Some of the lines are crossed out here."

"Yeah, the ink is smudged in some places."

"And that looks like a fingerprint." Alyson pointed to the margin of the first page of the codex.

"Now, isn't that interesting," Evan said, squatting next to her. "How often do you get such a clue?"

"If only Jesus had left an autographed copy of his teachings."

"Well, original manuscripts are called *autographa*, meaning written in one's own hand."

Alyson was taken aback. "Ancient Languages 101?"

"Even maintenance guys watch cable," he said with feigned offense.

"This looks too sloppy to be anything less than original. There's at least two languages. Greek and Hebrew?"

"Or Aramaic, the language of Jesus. Seriously, if I were you I would photograph these pages and then store them in a safety deposit box in whatever acid-free materials are appropriate. They're not only valuable, they're also fragile, and they haven't seen the light of day for maybe two millennia. If the light doesn't destroy them, the humidity will."

"You're right, of course. I'm not thinking. Still in shock."

"Understandable. Listen, what I have to do around the property is not that pressing. Why don't I help you photograph these so you can get them stored?"

When she agreed, Evan retrieved a camera, studio lights, and silver umbrellas from his apartment. Seeing Alyson's amazement, he said, "I was once a department store photographer. Must have taken a thousand toothless mug shots. This is film, though. Never went digital."

Alyson shook her head. "Never judge a guy by the name on his shirt."

"Ha, ha," he said sarcastically.

"Won't the lights bother the papyri?"

"I'm using low-watt Halogen bulbs and a slow shutter speed. It will whiten the color, but we'll get some good images without threatening the material." Evan set up his lights, silver umbrellas, and tripod over a low coffee table, pointing the lens of his camera straight down. Alyson shuttled the pages one by one to the photographing station, and after he shot a few frames of each one, she turned the page over so that he could shoot the other side. When they were finished, he packed the papyri into an airtight archival-quality museum box he'd purchased for the purpose. Evan's thoughtfulness impressed Alyson. Until now, he had just been little more than a passing figure in her life.

It didn't hit her until she unveiled the photos in the privacy of her car in the parking lot of the one-hour photo shop – the stroke of lightning, the light bulbs, the bells, and all other clichés went off in her head at once. Her career course, or what was left of it, had suddenly taken an unexpected correction. She would ask for a leave of absence from Frank first thing in the morning. In expectation of this moment, she could hardly sleep, and it was the first time she had something to live for in two years.

But Alyson did not anticipate getting fired. The top of her desk, the drawers within it, and her file cabinets were all bulging with clippings, notes, press releases, newswire articles. Boxing her personal belongings took about five minutes, but sorting through this mess would take at least a week on gallons of caffeine, she thought. She didn't have that kind of time or energy. She turned it over to a sympathetic intern and bolted. Frank was nowhere in sight, a painful but clear statement of his sentiment. He was tired of her, and with one blow, she had spiked their relationship the way editors killed stories.

By late evening Alyson sat at her dining room table sorting the prints in front of her. Evan's skillful photography had produced evenly-lit lettering.

Brilliantly, he had placed a tiny number in the frame of each picture so that the sequence of pages would stay in order.

How to proceed? She had no idea. Didn't Evan say he thought the languages were Greek and Aramaic? That reminded her of a college roommate who she'd heard had become a religious studies professor. She unburied her laptop, now an artifact of her former career, from beneath a stack of romance and science fiction novels. She jumped on the Web and, with a couple of clicks, she pointed the browser to an article about marriage and divorce contracts of the first century by Stephanie Johnson-Goodnight of the University of Denver. *Stephanie lives in Denver?* Alyson couldn't believe it. Better yet, she was in the phone book. She looked at her watch. Not too late to call.

"Alyson Stevenson, is that really you?"

"The same." Alyson recalled an image of her friend Stephanie as she was in college, a honey brunette whose individual facial features were plain yet, all told, culminated in what some might call classic beauty. By contrast, Alyson had a more roundish pixie look with a low center of gravity, as Stan had once described her.

"Haven't heard from you for, well, decades. Still hiding out in New Mexico?"

"No, I'm in Denver working for the *Rocky Mountain News.*" For expediency, she omitted information about being fired.

"Don't recall seeing your byline."

"Went by my married name, Sego. You?" She also decided not to mention the divorce.

"Married to Professor George Goodnight. Teaches classical languages at CU in Boulder. No children. You?"

"One ... out of the house." She wasn't interested in taking Stephanie down that memory lane either. Once the basic life status was logged between them, she turned to flattery. "I read about your work."

"Oh, really? I've been involved in a number of projects. Just published a paper comparing ancient marriage and divorce decrees to Paul's epistles."

"Yeah, saw it on the Web."

"Are you familiar with what Paul said about marriage in 1 Corinthians?"

"Not off the top of my head."

"He says marriage is not necessary to the spiritual life, but that it is better to marry than to burn with lust. He thought the world was going to end soon, so those who were already married might as well do everything within their power to avoid divorce, even if the spouse was not one of the members."

"Uh-huh." Stephanie could've been talking about the intricacies of a root canal for all Alyson cared, and she waited for a polite moment to break in.

"Thus setting the tone of morality for the Catholic Church in the centuries to come … ."

"Look, Steph, the reason I called … I just went on sabbatical from the paper to tie up loose ends on my Aunt Ruth's archaeological work. She passed away a few weeks ago."

"I remember Ruth Stevenson. My condolences. What's up?"

"She had a manuscript among her things that needs translating … ."

"Oh, Al, I don't really have the time."

"It is on papyrus."

"You have my attention." Suddenly Stephanie's tone changed. "Listen, I'm on deadline for a book, and I'm teaching three classes this term, but I have several grad students who can work on it. Will that help?"

"I'd rather you look at it personally."

Alyson heard a long exhale on the other end of the line. "I have some time before classes in the morning. Can you bring it by my office?"

"I had it professionally photographed. I'll e-mail you a sample image this evening. You can take a look and decide whether it's worth your while."

"Tell me, why didn't your aunt translate it herself?"

"Alzheimer's took her mind before she had a chance. It's very important to me to keep this a secret for now."

"It's probably nothing all that earth-shattering," Stephanie said, with just a hint of superiority.

Four

Alyson ran through a stone labyrinth of an ancient palace. The more she ran, the larger and more peculiar the palace became as she passed through a maze of rooms and grand halls and open-aired gardens that stretched out across pastoral hills and lakes. Slowly, she realized she was dreaming. That part of her that watched the dream was aware she was playing a life-sized board game, and the moves were determined by figuring out the clues on the papyrus scroll she carried with her.

One friend in particular appeared here and there to show her some short cuts. The friend was familiar to her, kind and gently loving, but ethereal almost, bathed in a soft, blue light. If this being had a gender, its energy felt masculine, but she couldn't be sure. She wandered from room to room until the being appeared to nudge her into a grand hall. The hall was empty except for a large, diamond-shaped mosaic embedded in the floor like a compass. One of the points of the diamond aligned with a diagram on the wall. The diagram was more like an emblem of an ornate symbol of a blue and yellow star. Facing it, she sensed that "home," the finish line, was just beyond the diagram. She felt an overwhelming sense that she was nearing the end of the game.

In the distance she could hear a bell gonging, pulling her toward the home stretch. She felt as though she could just lean into the sound of the bell, and she would be effortlessly absorbed into its vibration. She allowed herself to drift upward into wakefulness. Disoriented for a moment, she opened her eyes. The bell was still gonging, though her surroundings were not the ancient hall but her own bed. The beautiful gonging turned into the annoying, persistent ding-donging of her doorbell.

Alyson rolled out of bed, slipped on a robe, and reluctantly opened her front door to the apartment manager standing on her stoop.

"Evan, what are you doing up so early?"

"It's almost noon."

"Really? I rarely sleep late. Excuse me." She unlatched the screen and allowed him entrance.

"You must have needed it."

"Coffee?" She stumbled into the kitchen and poured water and grounds into her espresso machine.

"Usually go for regular joe, but I'll try whatever you're having."

A few minutes later they were both sitting on the back patio under a maple with cappuccinos in hand. Her apartment was half of a Victorianesque house, one of several in a row that Evan managed. This section of Emerson Street had undergone urban renewal, yet until recently she was too preoccupied by her life's tragedies to appreciate living here. After a few hits of the one and only drug she still allowed herself, she began to feel conscious.

"So, what's going on?" She wasn't accustomed to Evan's presence without a toolbox in hand and a mission to fix something. For that matter, he'd traded in the work shirt with his name on it for a beefy t-shirt. The denim tint set off his bright eyes and golden hair.

"Just wanted to see how you're faring after the big discovery."

"Well, I lost my job yesterday. Happened kind of strangely, sorta beyond my control."

"Nothing happens without our consent."

Alyson flinched at the triteness and simultaneous honesty of his comment. "I think I was a disappointment to my boss."

"How so?"

"Oh, you don't want to hear the details. Sounds a lot worse than it is." She took a sip as she couldn't help but look into his nonjudgmental eyes. "Actually, it is a lot worse than it sounds."

Surprisingly, Evan didn't ask to hear the story. "No wonder you slept until noon. How do you feel about leaving the job?"

"Sort of anxious and excited at the same time. I feel like I'm playing the game of my life. Why, just last night I dreamt I was very close to discovering a secret."

Evan's eyes twinkled. "You may well be."

"Have you ever had the feeling you're getting a call from your higher self, but there's no one on the line?"

Evan laughed. "Or it's a wrong number? I've gotten a few of those calls."

Alyson giggled as well, and it felt good. She thought of the codex. Did it contain the secrets she'd been looking for, as Evan suggested? "What do you suppose the codex might be?"

"Hard to say. In Egypt, just after World War II ended, some peasant farmers unburied a jar about three feet tall, just stuffed full of scrolls. Papyrus scrolls like yours, secret gospels and esoteric texts mostly written in Coptic, an ancient Egyptian language, more than sixteen hundred years old."

"I remember seeing something about this on the History Channel. The contents of the jar were collectively called a library?"

"Yes, that's right. The *Nag Hammadi* Library. Experts claimed that some of the codices were gospels that had been purposefully left out of the Bible. These texts were considered to be part of a Gnostic movement."

"Gnostic?"

"From the Greek *gnosis*, pertaining to knowledge of spiritual matters. Something the early church bishops tried to eradicate."

"You think Aunt Ruth's codex might be Gnostic?"

"Not out of the question. If it's an original text, it's probably closer to raw spirituality than later gospels had been and not as prone to censorship."

Alyson took another sip of her coffee and licked the foam from her lips. "What's the difference between what is considered Gnostic and what is not?"

"Simple. One is inner and the other is outer."

"What do you mean?"

"Gnostic texts, such as the Gospel of Truth, the *Pistis Sophia*, or the Gospels of Thomas, Mary, Philip, and Judas … ."

"Wait a minute. I knew Mary had a gospel, but Judas?"

"Yes, indeed. Anyway, Gnostic works tend to be more esoteric, focused on the symbolic aspects of Christianity, among other paths, while the canonized gospels tend to be more exoteric, more reliant on outward signs, miracles, and the flesh-and-blood details of the crucifixion."

"Outward signs?"

"Yes, for instance, the church promoted a bodily resurrection of Jesus as being a sign of his power to return at the end of days to save all those who believed and were baptized in his name. Gnostics believed that humans were born with a piece of God's spirit lodged within their own spirits, and if humans could turn away from the physical world and embrace the God-like qualities within themselves, they would be saved."

She wasn't sure she understood what Evan was talking about, but she was impressed. "So, you're no stranger to this stuff."

He smiled his golden-boy smile. "I've done a little extracurricular reading in the area. I can give you some books to read."

"I'd like that," Alyson said. "I've never been interested in the Bible except where my aunt's work was concerned. Guess it's time for a quickie education if I'm going to get into the business."

"You betcha," Evan agreed. "Last night I looked up the area near Selçuk, where your aunt's attorney said she'd purchased the jar. Its in the western region of Turkey near the coast of the Aegean Sea." He took some folded sheets of paper from his back pocket. "I printed out some information."

"And I'm supposed to be the reporter," she retorted, wishing she had thought of it. "What did you learn?"

"Selçuk is a modern town near the ruins of Ephesus, or Ephesos in the Bible, Efes as the locals call it," he said as he unfolded his print-out. "Popular tourist spot, especially among Christians. Many of the building facades still stand along marble streets, and the great theater is still intact. Had a latrine and a brothel as well."

"All the modern conveniences," Alyson said. "How old is Ephesus?"

"Let's see." Evan referred to his print-out. "First founded as an Attic-Ionian Greek colony about three thousand years ago, it fell under the reign of a number of civilizations over the first millennium, including Lydians and

Persians, the Hellenized Greeks under Alexander the Great, the Egyptians, and finally the Romans. A great temple built there to the goddess Artemis was supposed to have been one of the Seven Wonders of the World. Anthony and Cleopatra passed through Ephesus too. Had a population of several hundred thousand around the time of Christ, making it the second largest city in the Roman Empire."

"Hmmm. Never really heard of the place."

"Not many have, yet it's central to the development of Christianity in the first few centuries." He shuffled to the next page of his print out. "Paul spent several years in Ephesus two decades after the crucifixion, most likely in jail after burning books and inciting a riot among the silversmiths of idols as described in the Acts of the Apostles. Paul supposedly wrote some of his famous epistles while he was there."

"Like the letter to the Corinthians?" she asked, remembering her Bible lesson from her friend Stephanie.

"I think so. Next to Jerusalem, Ephesus was one of the most important early Christian centers of the times because of Paul. But that's not all. According to legend – and there's many legends surrounding Ephesus – the so-called Beloved Disciple mentioned in the Gospel of John took the mother of Jesus to Ephesus where she made her ascension to heaven. John is said to have been there later in that century where he supposedly wrote his gospel and the Book of Revelation."

"John the Baptist?"

"No. That John was beheaded long before the crucifixion. The traditional author of the Gospel of John is the son of Zebedee." Evan grinned. "Rookie mistake. "

Alyson blushed. "I really don't know the Bible at all."

"That's okay. It says here that a German nun in the eighteenth century had visions of a house on Mount Keressos near Ephesus where she believed the Virgin Mary lived. Missionaries found a stone building in an area that resembled the nun's vision. They've reconstructed a house there, and it is quite the pilgrimage spot for both Christians and Muslims today. Some legends place Mary Magdalene there as well."

She looked at him askance. "Are you a Christian, Evan?"

"Why do you ask?"

"You seem so ... interested."

He paused a moment as if to carefully choose his words. "I believe in what Jesus taught, but he wasn't the only one to master and share those same teachings with students throughout history. The Jesus we know today, and the religion that is practiced in his name, was created by the apostles and perpetuated and modified by Paul. Christianity later became institutionalized by the Roman Emperor Constantine and further amended by bishops and popes through the centuries. Some of the ecumenical councils were held in Ephesus, by the way. I believe that the gospels were heavily edited and not very close to what Jesus taught, although the essence was retained if one learns to read between the lines. How about you? Are you a Christian?"

Alyson flinched at the unexpected question. "Yes and no. My family considered themselves to be Methodist, a sort of middle-of-the-road denomination in my opinion. We were raised to be respectful of religions, and there was an unspoken belief in a higher power, a God, but no one insisted on going to church."

"Do you believe in the afterlife and the eternity of the soul?"

"Kind of a heavy topic for just getting out of bed." She thought a minute. "I don't know. Death seems so final, and it's hard to imagine one's life force – whatever it is – just ending. And if so, how can there be an afterlife without a beforelife? I don't think Christianity thought that one through, or else they suppressed it. If there is a beforelife, then it isn't too much of a stretch to ask why we would live only once. That's how I arrive at a cautious belief in reincarnation. But if you ask me if I believe in reincarnation, I'd say you're asking the wrong question."

"What is the *correct* question, then?"

"Ask me if I believe in the power of the single moment. It's eternal, everything's right in it, at least that's what I've read – I've yet to experience it. But I think it's more important than a belief in an afterlife or in multiple lives. I'd say trying to live life so you can get into heaven or into better circumstances next time around is deferred gratification. I mean, why bother?

I want instant gratification, I want it all right now. More importantly, I want to be liberated from all of the hellish moments I've had."

Evan studied Alyson, finally nodding as if he approved. She caught that. What did he know that she didn't? Did he have a big answer book? *Beware of answers*, she heard Aunt Ruth whispering from the Beyond.

"I never really thought about spirituality until recently." She wasn't sure if she should tell him about her near-obsessive excursions through bookstores and libraries, overturning every book in search of fresh morsels upon which her addictions and pain could feed.

"What was different about last year?"

"I went on a sort of, well, it was a mission." Alyson deliberately used the word in the way it had been used to describe her daughter's drug spree. "Let's just say certain ... traumas in my life caused me to go on a massive hunt on several different levels." Her face flamed up. Damn her Irish ancestors! She pulled back with a tinge of shame.

"Convention has it backwards," Evan said gently, as if he understood her reaction. "We are ashamed when bad things happen, as if we have any control over the random metering out of our own karma. But did anyone ever stop to think that the so-called bad things shape us and set us on the quest for the meaning of life? Bad things happen to good people because they are evolving, not the other way around. No one from the outside can judge a person for what is going on within their hearts."

She hadn't thought of it that way. Face recovered, gratefully, she continued. "If you ask me what I believe in or what doctrine I subscribe to, I couldn't really tell you. Once I read that Einstein had proclaimed himself a Mosaic, rather than a Jew. Now, that's someone who follows the laws of Moses. But when I read that about Einstein, I thought he meant that he had pieced together his beliefs from different systems and world views like a stained glass window. That's me, though, a mosaic of shards. Only a little bit here and there makes sense to me."

"Sounds like you've done a lot of soul-searching, Al. And at least with stained glass you have some light shining through."

Alyson was about to answer when she caught a flash of orange beyond the picket fence that separated her patio from the back alley. "Look, a fox!" It lifted its tail like a flag, chattered loudly for a moment, and darted away.

"That's Charlie," Evan said.

"He has a name?"

"That's what I call him. He's on the prowl for baby birds."

"How terrible."

"We don't live in a fairyland. When you say 'hell,' you're right. This is a warring universe. All forms of life feed on one another."

They both sat silent for a moment feeling the sun warm their faces. Alyson tried to remember how long it had been since the last time she'd had a discussion on spirituality with anyone. She was beginning to feel her brain warm up to a rosiness, and a sense of comfort filled her like chocolate-induced endorphins. Did talk of spirituality trigger these sensations? She hadn't really paid attention to that before, but she liked it. This could lead to a new addiction, or another stage of the old one.

"What about your Aunt Ruth?" Evan broke the silence. "What was her belief system?"

"Gosh, that's a good question. I think she was a Unitarian. To my understanding, that's not a religion so much as it is a book club. Ruth was curious, and she wanted to establish the Bible stories and the legends in the ground. Perhaps part of her wanted to believe in the story of the resurrection."

"Or maybe she wanted to disprove it."

"Maybe it was simply a matter of biblical archaeology being where the money is," she countered.

"Doubtful. Trying to work out excavations with governments in the Middle East is nearly impossible."

Alyson felt so comfortable around Evan, she toyed with the idea of telling him all that had happened to her, of crying on his compassionate shoulder. A telephone ring abruptly pierced the silence, saving her from further embarrassment, but she allowed the ringing to continue.

"You need to get that?" He pointed to the portable phone sitting on the little table next to her.

"It's probably just a sales call. Let the answering machine pick it up."

Once the ringing stopped, a disembodied voice called out from the machine inside the apartment: "Alyson? Al, are you home? I've had a chance to take a quick look at the text and ... is this some kind of a joke?"

"That's Stephanie, a professor of religious studies at DU," Alyson hurriedly mentioned before clicking the answer button on the portable. "Stephanie. I'm home. Joke, what joke?"

"Oh, hello, Al. Screening your calls?" Stephanie no longer sounded like the long lost friend she'd been the night before. She sounded perturbed.

"You mentioned a joke?"

"You know I'm something of an expert on ancient marriage and divorce contracts, right? Is that why you sent this to me?"

"I don't understand."

"Honestly, ever since *The Da Vinci Code* came out, everyone's been looking for lost manuscripts. The whole world has become smitten with the Mary Magdalene figure all over again and the idea of she and Jesus being a couple."

"Mary Magdalene and Jesus? What are you talking about?"

"The fragment you e-mailed me appears to be well-preserved, although it's difficult to tell from a scanned, compressed jpeg file. Some words are no longer legible, but from what I can make out, this is a last will and testament from the first century, by a man to a woman. It could be a *ketubah*, generally a marriage contract."

"A ... ketubah? How do you know this?"

"Hebrew for a 'written thing.' Marriage contracts back then were more like prenuptial agreements spelling out the terms of the marriage as a business partnership, what behavior was expected particularly from the woman, and what would happen to the marital property when the man died. A man rarely left a woman his belongings unless they were married or related somehow, but this contract is quite vague. It's in Aramaic, but I will translate: 'I, Yeshua ben Yosef min Natseret, give you, Miryam Binyamiyn min Migdal Nunya, my *talmidim* in the event of my death.' Jerusalem is stated as the place where the contract was written, and at the bottom, it says: 'I wrote this, Yosef of Arimathaea, the 19th year of Tiberius.'" Stephanie paused for effect.

"If this is a joke, I missed the punch line," Alyson said.

"That's because we know these people by the King James English – Jesus and Mary Magdalene," Stephanie said indignantly. "Joseph Arimathaea in the gospels is the one who put the corpse of the crucified Jesus in the private tomb on his land. The word 'talmidim' refers to students. In other words, Mary would inherit his ministry."

As soon as Alyson heard this, she was besieged by a wave of goose bumps, as if some invisible creature had danced on her scalp. She knew it to be true. And yet, it didn't make sense.

"Has that sunk in yet, Al?"

"Yes, it's ... it's quite unbelievable."

"It's highly unorthodox."

"But it sounds more like a will than a contract."

"It may not be a marriage contract per se, but if this is true, it does acknowledge some kind of important relationship between Mary and Jesus. Do you have any idea how earth-shattering that would be, what the implications are?" Stephanie's voice was becoming shrill.

"No, not really." Just the night before, Stephanie had said that the papyrus would probably be nothing momentous.

"This would mean that Peter wasn't Jesus's first choice for taking on his ministry after the crucifixion. Jewish rabbis tend not to bequeath their ministries, especially to women. But there were numerous pre-Judaic priestly sects back then, though Judaism itself hadn't yet congealed as a religion until well after the destruction of the Second Temple in Jerusalem. This ketubah would have thrilled the Gnostics, who held Mary Magdalene in high esteem in the centuries following the crucifixion."

Stephanie's explanation vaguely sounded like a plot right out of a novel, and that made her go into tough reporter mode. "Do you subscribe to the thinking that the Holy Grail, the proverbial cup from the Last Supper, is not the chalice that caught the blood of sacrifice at the crucifixion, but is instead the *sangreal*, the royal bloodline of Jesus and Mary's offspring?"

"You mean, as romantically described in pulp fiction and pop history books?"

"Yes, exactly."

"Very well. Jesus was, after all, a Jewish rabbi with every right to marry, but there is nothing to substantiate his marital status either way. If the ketubah is authentic, then I would consider putting a check in the 'yes' column. That said, sharing a bed with Jesus should in no way enhance or diminish her status as a powerful spiritual being in her own right."

Well put, Alyson thought. "Wasn't Mary Magdalene a prostitute? What does Jewish law say about marrying prostitutes?"

"All one needs is a dowry to marry. Prostitution would have to be proven. But, that's a myth about Mary Magdalene. You don't know your Bible, do you?"

She side-stepped the question. It was like asking if she reconciled her checkbook. "Okay, then, what if the ketubah is authentic? What do you make of it?"

"If it is real, and only if, I'd say that this find would confirm the Gospel of Philip."

"One of the Nag Hammadi texts," Alyson said tentatively, remembering the conversation she just had with Evan and hoping to make up for not knowing her Bible.

"That's right. Hold on, I have Philip's gospel right here." Alyson could hear Stephanie flipping through pages of a book. She began reading aloud: "'As for the Wisdom who is called the barren, she is the mother of the angels and the companion of the Savior, Mary Magdalene. He loved her more than all the disciples, and he used to kiss her often on her mouth.' Well, no one knows where he kissed her, because that one word is conveniently blotched out from the papyrus where this was written. It is presumed that Jesus kissed her on her mouth, though it could have been her forehead or her elbow, for all we know."

"What does that passage have to do with the Jesus contract?"

"Convention has it that John of Zebedee was the disciple who Jesus loved, not Mary Magdalene. In Chapter 19 of the Gospel of John, Jesus looks down from the cross and sees his mother, and his mother's sister, along with Mary the wife of Clopas, and Mary Magdalene. He sees his mother standing by 'whom he loved,' and he says to his mother, 'Woman, behold thy son! Then he says to the disciple, behold, thy mother! And the disciple took her to his own.'"

This is a lot to take in over the phone, Alyson thought. "I still don't understand how this all connects."

"To me, these passages show that the Holy Grail doesn't represent the bloodline so much as it represents the mantle. In the Gospel of Philip, Mary Magdalene is called Wisdom, which is a Gnostic concept they called the *Sophia,* the so-called Mother. In John, when Jesus asks the Beloved Disciple to take care of his mother, perhaps he is symbolically passing the Mother, the Sophia – perhaps the very mantle itself – to that Beloved Disciple. We know now that that person was Mary Magdalene, if the Jesus contract is authentic. The Gospel of Mary Magdalene, as well as some others, explicitly says that Jesus had asked Mary to continue his teachings."

"I don't get it. The Beloved Disciple in the Gospel of John is male."

"Yes, but that may have been a later edit in order to diminish women's ability to excel on a spiritual path. Besides, the Gospel of John doesn't name John as the Beloved Disciple outright; it is assumed that's him because the gospel is named after him. In fact, the gospel identifies Mary Magdalene at the cross in the previous verse. By the same token, she is traditionally portrayed as a prostitute simply because she is mentioned in an entire chapter following a sequence where a sinful, anonymous woman anoints Jesus's feet."

"So she is thought of as a prostitute by order of appearance but not as the Beloved Disciple by the same thinking."

"Doesn't seem fair, does it? In the Gospel of Thomas there is a great deal made about Mary Magdalene being a woman and how Jesus said he would make her male. Being 'made male' may have been a metaphor for spiritual transcendence of the mind over emotions, for all we know. It's hard to understand what was meant without projecting our own views onto them. What they called 'kissing' could have been symbolic of some kind of initiation, the transference of divine breath, the Living Spirit, the Word."

"Maybe it just meant that she was able to speak the Word of God, or in this case, the word of Jesus."

"Very good, Al," Stephanie conceded. "The Old Testament describes prophecies as being delivered from 'mouth to mouth.'"

"At any rate, does Jesus's last will to Mary remove the guesswork?"

"Not all of it, but it's the equivalent to a photo of a second Kennedy assassination gunman. Now, I don't know what you have against me, but I must say, whoever made this contract up sure knew their stuff. Of course, anyone handy in PhotoShop could forge their own contract."

"I assure you, this is not a prank, Steph. I have nothing but the utmost respect for you. We were roommates. Would I do something like this?"

Stephanie sighed audibly. "No, of course not. Perhaps someone is playing a joke on *you*."

"The papyrus was sealed in an earthenware jar that looked old. I'm no expert, but I think it is authentic."

"The contract was concealed in a jar, and you didn't tell me?"

"Didn't think it important to the translating."

"Where did your aunt find the jar?"

"A marketplace in Selçuk, Turkey. At least that's what Aunt Ruth's attorney thought. He sent the jar to me after she died. He was never really sure because Ruth was so far gone with Alzheimer's."

"And you've met this attorney?"

"Uh, no. I'd never heard of him before he contacted me."

"So, there's a possibility it's not legitimate. I can't believe you broke into the jar."

"There was an accident." She didn't want to tell her about the cat fight that knocked the jar to the floor.

"You, of all people, should've been more careful. What else was in the jar?"

Alyson hesitated. Should she tell Stephanie? She had to trust someone to help her. "The jar also contained a papyrus codex, a dozen or so pages written front and back."

"Why didn't you send photos of those pages as well?" She sounded angry for an instant. "But I suppose you had a right to test me."

Alyson exhaled to calm herself into a level of honesty. "To tell you the truth, I don't want to lose control over the story."

"Don't worry. Codices are traditionally named after their discoverers."

"I'm not after fame, Steph."

"Then, what do you want? Money? You'd have to sell this on the black market to get anything, especially if Turkey finds out about it, and they will."

"I just want to know what the manuscript says, and I want to write about the find. That's what journalists do – the pursuit of the story itself is the driving force."

"You will need experts to put it all together."

"That's why I contacted you."

"And you were correct in doing so. Have you had the papyri carbon dated? You know what that is, don't you?"

Alyson ducked the hint of sarcasm; she had minored in anthropology, after all. "Isn't that the rate that radioactive carbon decays in an organism once it has died? No I haven't had a chance to do that yet. I wouldn't even know how to go about it."

"This is what you do. Carefully, and I mean carefully, lay the pages out and cut samples from the top or the bottom in the margins where you are absolutely sure there is no writing. The pieces need to be about the size of a fingernail. Then wrap the samples in linen for mailing. Send them to the University of Arizona, not the University of Colorado, though it's right here. UA uses a tandem accelerator mass spectrometer, the same machine that proved that the Shroud of Turin dates only to the Middle Ages. Much more reliable than conventional carbon dating, and it can date much smaller pieces. It counts the atoms in carbon-14, rather than counting rates of disintegration."

"Didn't you say a date was mentioned in the contract?"

"The nineteenth year of Tiberius. That's 33 CE, the year most agree was the crucifixion. The C-14 dating will corroborate the authenticity of the contract."

"You said CE. Don't you mean AD?"

"A lot's changed since you were in college. The academic field prefers 'Before the Current Era' and 'Current Era,' rather than 'Before Christ' and 'After Death.' Not all cultures view Jesus as the beginning of modern times."

"I see." Alyson was embarrassed. "Doesn't the date in the contract establish the dating for the manuscript, roughly?"

"It will help determine whether the contract is a forgery," Stephanie said, no longer sounding quite so angry. "I also suggest you try infrared photography on the pages. It's a noninvasive way of making the illegible words pop out without exposing the papyri to air and UV light. I'm sending you to the West Semitic Research Project at the University of Southern California. When you get a good read, send it back to me."

"Can they be discreet?"

"In this day and age?" Stephanie laughed, almost forcibly. "Very little is private and nothing is sacred with the Internet."

Alyson changed her mind in a flash of inspiration. "There's time to do all that later. I'd rather get a translation now before turning it over to the academics. I feel the codex is only on loan to me for a short time, and it's up to me to make the best use of it while I have it. The photographic images are very clear. Is there any way you can do the translation from them?"

It was Stephanie's turn to hesitate. "Is it all in Aramaic?"

"I don't know languages like you, but I'd say only a few lines here and there. The rest looks Greek to me. Didn't you say you were married to a classical languages professor? Think he'd be interested?"

"Interested?" Stephanie laughed. "He'd be in both our debts for the rest of his natural life. I'll speak to him."

"Thank you for your help, Stephanie."

"No, thank you for bringing this to me. One more thing … ."

"I'm listening."

"I'm almost certain this is a prank. If it's real, however, it will create controversy. You can't reverse two thousand years of tradition and political control. There will be those who won't believe us. But others will. Change is slow to come in the Catholic Church. This is very exciting. I'll have George contact you right away." With that, dial tone.

Alyson hung up, barely able to speak. She wasn't so shocked that she didn't notice how Stephanie had started to take ownership of the project. She had gone a long way from thinking the contract was a prank to conspiring to reform the Catholic Church.

"Good news? Bad? I can't tell." Evan had been politely quiet until now.

"Did you get all that about the contract, Jesus willing his ministry to Mary Magdalene?"

"Fantastic!" Evan shook his head in disbelief.

"It substantiates a lot of theories for Stephanie, the Holy Grail being the mantle of Jesus's ministry. More coffee?"

"No thanks."

"I need another shot after news like that." Alyson hopped up, took both cups into the kitchen, and began making another cappuccino. Evan followed her as he continued talking. "I might agree with your friend, except I think it goes deeper than that. I think the Holy Grail represents the bestowal of divinity upon initiates of that spiritual path. It is a symbol for opening the third eye when, upturned, it's filled with the Divine Elixir."

"Wow, that was profound," Alyson said, visualizing a chalice where she imagined her third eye to be and feeling it fill with Godpower. She turned the espresso machine on and the noise stopped their conversation momentarily.

Evan picked up where he left off once Alyson silenced the machine. "Look, Mary's own gospel speaks of the vision she has of Jesus after the crucifixion and begins to lead the disciples. In John and Mark, she's the first to see the resurrection. In some teachings the resurrection is something that takes place in consciousness, *within* the disciple's own realm. One would really have to be devoted to see their Master Jesus inside themselves and, therefore, would be on one's way to becoming a master in their own right. It may be that the Holy Grail has been misrepresented all these thousands of years because it shows the availability of divinity to everyone. Well, at least for those souls who are ready to go home."

Alyson pulled a can of cat food from the cabinet. Luce and Noche came running as soon as they heard the lid tear off the can. She spooned the smelly gunk into separate dishes on the floor and then took a careful sip of the hot espresso. "What do you mean by *home*?" She leaned against the counter, giving him her full attention.

"I didn't think you were listening."

"I'm interested in everything you have to say."

He leaned against the counter opposite her. "Okay. All of Christianity is based on the single assumption of the truth of the resurrection. The resurrection proves the divinity of the Son of Man becoming the Son of God. Without the promise of Jesus being the mediator between heaven and earth and the one who died for our sins, there is no basis for Christianity. If Jesus had indeed passed on the mantle to Mary, or to anyone for that matter, then he is considered to be less than divine according to that single definition." He squatted to stroke the cats, and they took turns rubbing against his legs. "I'm not talking about the apostles here, which Jesus, according to gospel, sanctioned to carry on his teachings. I'm talking about a true successor who had the power to instill divinity within his – or her – students so that they could purify their own sins and resurrect themselves into heaven."

"Wow, you sound so sure. Is this what you believe?"

He glanced downward, shaking his head as if to quell his tongue by force. "It's a little of what I believe, but I am not ready to give you the whole story quite yet."

She felt slightly rebuffed, yet at the same time she admired his intimate and private attitude toward his spirituality. In a way, she was glad he stopped, because all this talk was making her head spin. She felt as if she were being sucked into a vortex of concepts, a vortex she had freely entered, though not completely of her own volition or making.

"Stephanie wants me to send pieces of the papyri to Arizona for carbon testing."

"Well, let's get on it," Evan said.

"I need to get out of my pj's first." Alyson sat her cup down, then seeing the cats licking their paws and washing their faces, she chuckled. "Stephanie said codices are usually named after their discoverers."

"The Luce/Noche Codex," Evan said, nodding. "I like it."

Five

The University of Colorado grounds in Boulder, with its northern Italian architecture set against the sharp-edged Flatiron Mountains, usually took Alyson's breath away. This trip, she barely noticed, as she drove into the visitor's parking lot and rushed across campus. She wanted to be prompt for her meeting with Stephanie's husband, George Goodnight. More pointedly, she couldn't wait to hear the translation of Aunt Ruth's codex. Forgoing the elevator, she flew up the stairs to the third floor of the new Eaton Humanities Building.

"Professor Goodnight just called saying he'd be late," said the young work-study co-ed sitting at the front desk of the Classics Department. Her hair was dyed neon pink and her eyes were outlined with black sludge. Her tongue piercing softened her consonants, making her sound like a toddler and making Alyson all the more irritated for having rushed.

"Did he say how long he'd be?"

The young woman shook her head. "You can wait out there." She pointed to a row of chairs in the hallway.

Without warning, doors flung open and a stampede of students spilled into the hallway from adjoining classrooms. "Could I wait in his office?"

"I don't have access." The girl stood and crossed to a photocopier, giving Alyson full view of her costume for the day. She wore a black sweater, a hot pink mini-skirt over black leggings cropped at the calf, and pink and black checkered Converse shoes. *She looks just like Kendra*, Alyson thought. Right down to the hair color. She even sported a similar red rose tattoo above her bare ankle. She had chided Kendra when she first got it: "Sure, it looks pretty now, but wait until you're pregnant and the swelling brings that rose into full, distorted bloom." Alyson's heart sank with the memory.

Dodging students in the hallway, she fell into the last empty chair, and settled into people-watching mode to take her mind off her lost daughter. For the most part, the students dressed normally, though she could never get used to seeing boxer shorts sticking out of jean tops prison-style. Every generation dressed for shock, she supposed. In her day, bell-bottomed, hip-hugging jeans were the great protest. That, and young women usually went braless.

Her first week of college in 1973, a woman on what would be the nation's final bra-burning circuit had come to the University of New Mexico campus in Albuquerque. Alyson watched the presentation from an upperfloor classroom of the journalism building overlooking Yale Park where it was held. That same week the National Guard flooded the campus in case the university staff's sit-in for higher wages got out of hand. Riots the previous years had taken their toll on the nerves of local government. But the staff sit-in came to naught, and campuses across the nation, after a few years of unrest, rested almost overnight. Well, they didn't rest; they turned to more important things, like partying and streaking. Toga!

Alyson was born at the peak of the post-World War II baby boom, and although she didn't hit high school until the early seventies, she knew a little about the ideology of the sixties, which by then had been mainstreamed into the popular culture. She was too young to protest the Vietnam War with any zeal, though she did ask her mother's permission to go watch the riots down around UNM during her sophomore year. Her adolescence was accompanied by a Simon and Garfunkel soundtrack. (Did silence really have a sound?) The walls of her bedroom, her sanctum sanctorum, had been decorated with posters that conveyed a yearning for freedom and merging with the cosmos, simply stated in psychedelic letters. It was a generation of few words, just enough to fit on a bumper sticker or into a measure of music: Peace, Flower Power, Make Love Not War. Her drug experimentation was limited to marijuana and a little peyote. What peyote buttons she could chew and swallow were not that fresh, but did open her mind to the more subtle and vibratory details of the physical world. Mirrors bearing lines of cocaine were passed over her head, LSD was never offered her. Perhaps everyone knew as she did that a little trip into alternate realities would mentally throw her off-balance, and she would be forever lost in the cracks between worlds. Not like today, not like Kendra, who did not have a healthy fear of drugs or the other side, and who ended up there for good, for all Alyson knew. Teenagers today had to go a long way to rebel against the previous generation.

One thing for certain, Kendra was a refugee of her times. Her teenage years would not be marked by bra-burnings and war protests. Nothing so romantic. Rather, she would open her yearbook and remember that the highlight of her junior year was the massacre at Columbine High School. Kendra attended a neighboring school just minutes away, but many of her friends went to Columbine. Every school in the greater metropolitan area went into immediate lock-down when news let out that students were being murdered in the library and halls on that cloud-cast day in April of 1999. It had felt like a day of siege with the helicopters flying over the neighborhood as events unfolded in real-time on television; there was no getting away from it. Alyson had covered the events for many weeks for the *Rocky Mountain News,* interviewing the wounded, the families of the victims, witnesses, anyone remotely affected by the tragedy. When it was soon discovered that the gunmen were two boys who had previously operated below the radar, parents in every sector of society wrung their hands and wondered if there, but for the grace of God, goes my child. Less than eighteen months later, on September 11, 2001, this inexplicable tragedy was eclipsed by terrorists crashing passenger jets into New York City's World Trade Center.

A few weeks after 9/11, Kendra laid on her belly in the intersection in front of their house to photograph a single-syllable headline she'd cut out of the newspaper: "War." Alyson thought it a brilliant commentary on how world events so intimately affected their lives, and how cathartic. Now she knew the photo may have been a cry for help, the drugs a form of self-medication from post traumatic stress syndrome. Alyson had missed all the signs.

Before she disappeared from Alyson's life, Kendra had started on a bedroom wall mural that had integrated mushrooms, cloud-like calligraphy, the yin-yang Taoist symbol, and pipe-smoking caterpillars in primary colors. At the time the mural looked like an innocent retro-seventies project. Later Alyson would assume that this marked the beginning of Kendra's drug trips, but now she wondered if they were also road signs along a spiritual vision quest. It was too late to ask. Kendra didn't live there anymore. Neither did Alyson, for that matter.

She wondered if spiritual yearning had crept up on herself the way mid-life had, with its hot flashes and reading glasses. Or had it been there all along, waiting patiently beneath the demands and details of life until the day came when trauma sprung it out into the open?

Alyson looked at her watch. *Just how much longer is he going to keep me waiting? I need that translation.* She shifted in the uncomfortable chair and reminded herself of the project at hand.

Aunt Ruth's papyri legacy, a mere two weeks in her custody, diverted her attention enough from her pain. She had resisted at first, not wanting to re-enter the reading binge, but she soon found herself absorbed and dizzy with the onslaught of facts and speculation regarding the life of Jesus and the Jesus movement. With the advent of the computer, Biblical scholars could now easily exchange silos of information, and it all lay at Alyson's fingertips. So many different angles to look at, it was difficult to decide whether to ignore someone's disparate opinion, or assimilate it with what one already believed was the truth. Indeed, she was caught up in the mystery, but more importantly she operated under the impression that if she could get through it all, she would be put in touch with her own spirituality. That made her feel guilty. Escaping from the reality of losing a child was one thing, but doing something for herself made her feel selfish. Why couldn't she have done this for Kendra? Survivor's guilt, she supposed.

"Alyson Sego?" A kind-faced, slightly-built man with thick, graying hair and beard stood before her, interrupting her stream of unconscious reverie. He wore the uniform of most college professors, the blue jeans and corduroy blazer with elbow patches that gave off an air of academic gentility while veiling self-importance.

"Y-yes," she stammered, standing up. "Are you Professor Goodnight?" He looked to be about fifteen years older than her friend Stephanie, and this would have surprised her except that he was quite handsome and no doubt talented. Stephanie had a good eye, and it was probably mutual.

He stuck out a hand. "Call me George. Stephanie's told me about your college days as roommates."

"I hope not too much."

The professor placed a hand over his heart as if to plead the fifth. "Shall we," he said, gesturing for her to follow him to his office. Inside was the typical ordered chaos of professorial life – shelves brimmed with books and mementos of world travel, in his case, Grecian and Roman locales. A bulletin board crammed with fliers promoted class field trips to Europe and a nine-week intensive to learn Greek or Latin for the joy of reading manuscripts in their original language. *I should've thought of that*, Alyson joked with herself. He showed her to the well-worn leather easy chair in front of his desk. After closing the door, he moved to his side of the desk piled high with open books, test booklets, and reams of test papers. He opened the oversized notebook containing the 11x14 photographs of the papyri in acetate sleeves – Evan's idea – which Alyson had mailed him the week before. He said nothing as he slowly flipped through the pages. She felt as if she'd been summoned for a critique on a paper she'd plagiarized.

She decided to break the silence. "Did Stephanie mention the results of the C-14?"

"Yes, dates to the middle of the first century CE." He looked up at her over his reading glasses. "Could be off by a hundred years. The age of a manuscript can be more precisely determined by analyzing script types, which change over relatively short periods of time. Paleographers look at whether letters are written in book-hand or cursive, if they are all caps and evenly spaced, or if they extend below or above the median line. The words in professionally-scribed documents at one point tended to be upper case and crammed together to save room on the expensive papyrus, for instance."

"Do you have a sense of the age of this codex?"

"I'm no paleographer. Except for a few Hebrew lines scattered throughout, much of the text is written it Koine, or 'common,' Greek, spoken during the Hellenistic period between 300 BCE and 300 CE. It's not the Attic-Greek of Homer."

"Well, that narrows it down to six hundred years." She added a tight smile to suppress her sarcasm and quickly moved on. "Isn't it significant that the C-14 dating of the papyrus itself is in the same ballpark as the contract Stephanie translated?"

"Yes, and if the C-14 results are accurate, then we possess the oldest known evidence of the New Testament."

"So, it's a gospel?"

"Not exactly."

"Then what, exactly?"

"I don't want us to get ahead of ourselves," he said crisply. "I'd like to introduce the material to you first before we jump to conclusions."

Alyson, against her journalistic instincts, resisted asking the next question: *Jumping to conclusions about what?* She sensed that he was either stalling or methodically building up to something big. "Please continue."

"The oldest fragment of the New Testament in existence, called P52, is a scrap from a codex that contains a few words from the Gospel of John as we know it today. It was written around 125 CE, and it's a copy, not an original. We have just about a hundred such papyri fragments from the early centuries, and they're all copies. That's it. After that there's tens of thousands of complete and partial copies mostly from the tenth century, and not one is an original."

"The original manuscripts were so well-read that they wore out?"

He shrugged off the question. "Humidity caused mold to destroy the fibers as well. That's why we see surviving papyri in the dry climate of Egypt. And every time a new copy was produced, mistakes were made, editorial liberties taken."

"A simple typo could change the meaning," she said, drawing parallels to her own editorial experience. "And what scribe couldn't resist little edits to make the words flow better?"

"Typographical errors and small edits go viral, as it were, and become truth. All told, there are nearly a half-million variations between biblical manuscripts. Ancient Jewish scribes, by contrast, developed practices to avoid mistakes in copying the *Tanakh*, right down to keeping track of the number of letters in a given line. To change anything was considered a sin, and the whole manuscript would be trashed. Maybe one error exists in 1,500 copies as a result."

"Impressive. What is the Tanakh?"

"Roughly the Old Testament of the Christian Bible. But what is labeled as the Old Testament in the Bible was taken from the Greek version of the Jewish Tanakh, called the *Septuagint*, which was already full of errors. It was modified to support the New Testament as the fulfillment of Old Testament prophesies."

"I thought the Jewish Bible was called the Torah."

The professor shook his head. "The Torah, meaning law or instruction in Hebrew, is just the first five books of Moses."

"I didn't know that," Alyson said. "What about this manuscript? Would you say it was an original or a copy?"

"Off hand, I would have to say that this is neither a complete manuscript nor a copy of an original text. Rather, it is a mix of both, more like a journal or a notebook."

"How so?"

The professor removed his reading glasses and folded his hands on the desk. "To begin with, on the first page are two names written several times in both Greek and Hebrew and randomly-placed as if for practice."

"And what are the names?"

"I'll get to that in a moment. I don't want to imply that these are the authors."

Alyson nodded. She understood the process now. "What makes you think of it as a notebook? That was my impression of it as well."

"It looks as though the authors were recording their favorite quotes from different sources. For instance, there are a few lines from the Tanakh written in Hebrew scattered throughout the codex, which is significant in and of itself if the notebook originated in the region of Turkey where you say your aunt found it. The language spoken by Jews at the time was Aramaic, and those living in the Diaspora, in exile that is, also spoke Greek and relied on the Greek Septuagint version of the Tanakh. Hebrew literacy outside of Jerusalem was rare."

"Interesting," Alyson said, *but please get on with it.*

"In addition to biblical quotes are excerpts from the philosophers Plato, Heraclitus, and Philo of Alexandria. That's unusual in this context."

"You said there is also original text?"

"Yes, from the New Testament, namely the Gospel of John."

"I don't understand. Original or copied?" *This is like pulling gum off the bottom of my shoe on a hot day*, she thought.

He exhaled audibly and ran his hands through his hair. "We've not seen the John verses exactly in this form, but it would appear that they were being composed as the author wrote them out, with word insertions and strike-outs, and the language itself is rougher. The quotations from the philosophers, on the other hand, are more precisely copied word for word."

"A first draft?"

He smiled almost sardonically. "That would imply that the author intended to compose a gospel. A proto-John might be the more accurate label, with the verses being appropriated later for that gospel."

"I understand that, except for the letters of Paul, most of the New Testament wasn't written until later in the first century, well beyond our target date." Thanks to Evan, she had scanned through the texts from the *Nag Hammadi Library* and the *Complete Gospels of Jesus*. "So, if the dating is dead-on, then that pushes the writing of John to the middle of the first century rather than at the end."

"You are correct. The Gospel of John is thought to have been written sometime after the destruction of the Jewish Second Temple in Jerusalem in 70 CE, because that gospel contains a passage that prophesies that Jesus will destroy the temple and then replace it with his resurrected body. But that verse is not in this codex."

"I see."

"There's not a lot to go on for dating the gospels other than historical inferences in the text and when bishops first mention the gospels in their writings in the first couple centuries."

"The selection of gospels was quite the drawn-out process, I read."

He nodded. "We assume that the gospels may have been first delivered orally by the apostles themselves and later by other members of the movement. The different membership groups then developed their own gospels to support the particular slant they preached. Eventually the stories were transcribed second or third hand in Greek, rather than the original Aramaic, and in this way included their Greek ideology."

"What about other languages?"

The professor began counting the number of translations on his fingers. "The Greek was soon translated into Latin, which was revised and recompiled by Jerome in the fourth century. Henry VIII had it translated into English in the sixteenth century, and the King James Version was completed in the seventeenth century."

"And each new translation was tweaked to reflect whatever nationalized values they wanted the public to follow," Alyson contributed.

"That's a fair assessment."

"I've read that there were more gospels than just the four."

"Oh, yes, a dozen more at least. But bishops and church fathers began promoting which gospels and epistles they wanted canonized as early as the second century as a defense against those works they considered Gnostic."

"Being Gnostic wasn't good, I take it."

"Depends on your point of view. Gnostics believed in the metaphor of the crucifixion, rather than the flesh-and-blood version, and that was considered heresy." The professor paused as if to recall his bible history. "Ironically, Marcion, the first theologian known to suggest a sort of bible, was excommunicated around 150 CE simply because he emphasized principles that tended toward Gnosticism. It took several centuries before it was determined which gospels would be canonized."

"How did they decide on the final four?"

"In the end they went with the fourfold gospels Bishop Irenaeus had suggested back in 180 – the *tetramorph*, it was called. Irenaeus had said that Mark, Matthew, Luke, and John would form the four-pillared foundation for the church, reflecting the four zones in which we live and the four winds of immortality, and also because these gospels promoted Peter as the chosen leader of the Christian movement. Irenaeus was wholeheartedly against Gnosticism, and what we know of the early movement we know from his negative criticism of it in his writings."

Alyson had looked up Gnosticism, but she could not get her head around it. From what she could tell, it was a potpourri of philosophy, esotericism, and dualistic symbolism from the Greek, Persian, Jewish, and Egyptian occults and mysteries in which everything alive was evil and everything good resided in a multi-layered and multi-ruled heaven. Christianity got into the mix as Gnosticism grew more popular. "This is all fascinating, Professor Goodnight, but I am mainly interested in what this codex says."

He stared at her almost disapprovingly. "Ms. Sego, not just one scholar examines the text, but many. The translation must be published and go through peer review, papers written to weigh its relevance and defended at conferences. I don't want to make any proclamations until I know more. Stephanie tells me you're a journalist, and I'd be remiss if I were to hand over the results prematurely only to see it appear in a headline crawl on Fox News."

"Please, give me a little credit to discriminate between what should be published and what should wait," she said, more defensively than she preferred. "You know this is my late aunt Ruth Stevenson's find, and it is, in effect, my property, which I am lending to you, and I have a right to know about my property."

"There are antiquity laws ... ."

"Yes, of course. I plan to eventually donate the codex to a worthy institution."

"Very well." George failed to conceal a triumphant grin, and Alyson realized he had what he wanted. As a team, this would make the careers for both George and Stephanie. That was fine with her. It's what Aunt Ruth might have wanted.

"You said there were names written on the codex. What are they?"

He exhaled deeply. "One name is Cerinthus and the other is Miryam."

The familiar chills ran through Alyson's nervous system once again. She had to ask: "If it is accompanied by the Jesus contract willing his ministry to a Miryam of Magdala, then is it safe to assume that the signature on the papyrus was also written by Mary Magdalene?"

"There were a lot of women named Miryam, or Mary, in the New Testament. The coincidence is hard to ignore, but inconclusive."

"All right. Mary Magdalene has a gospel of her own, as you know, discovered among the Nag Hammadi texts and elsewhere." Alyson again silently thanked Evan for giving her the books just a few days earlier, where she had read Mary's gospel with intent.

"That gospel was written in the second or third century, possibly to promote the leadership and standing of women in the church. And it was Gnostic. The style and content of the Magdalene gospel is not even remotely similar to the John verses in your codex."

"If not the Gospel of Mary, then what is it?"

"As I said before, the codex has some of the same stories and sayings as John, but the stories are written as parables attributed to an anonymous rabbi rather than miracles Jesus is said to have performed. No mention of his ministry, history, apostles, the resurrection. At the top are the traditional opening verses to John. You know ... 'In the beginning was the Word, and the Word was with God,' but the phrasing is different. The first line was written in Aramaic, and crossed out and reworded in Greek. Many of the quotes from the philosophers addressed the subject of the Word, or the *Logos*, in Greek."

"Interesting," Alyson said, not knowing what to think.

"It's what scholars have hoped to find," the professor said. "There has been so much back-and-forth about the origin of that opening passage, whether it was an homage to the Jewish or to the Greek heritage. It looks as though the author was grappling with the concept of the Logos throughout this notebook."

"Does this mean that Mary wrote the Gospel of John?"

"Or Cerinthus did, the other name on the papyrus, but we will have to leave that up to the handwriting analysts. I will tell you this: Cerinthus is a familiar name to us. Bishop Irenaeus said that Cerinthus was a Gnostic heretic teaching in Ephesus who was raised in the 'wisdoms of Egypt.' Irenaeus thought that John himself wrote his gospel to counter Cerinthus's Gnostic-like teachings, but Gnostics claimed that Cerinthus actually wrote the Gospel of John. Again, this is ironic because, of the four gospels, John is regarded as being the most Gnostic, particularly the opening passage regarding the Logos. However, none of the authors of the gospels are who they say they are, and speculation is wide as to who the authentic authors were."

"The gospels didn't have bylines in those days, huh?"

"We can't presume that either name scribbled on the papyrus was involved in writing the text, although it stands to reason. It is important to note that this is the first time we've seen actual names attached to gospel-like text without being part of the content itself. Epistles were quite different. Paul usually identified himself in the first paragraph of his letters, for instance."

There was very little left to say after that, and the conversation ended with Alyson promising she wouldn't publish anything without first consulting George and he promising to send her a preliminary transcript in perhaps two or three weeks. As she started down the hall, she turned back toward him. "If I donate the codex to CU, please name it after my aunt, Ruth Stevenson."

"Of course," he said. "Thank you for bringing this to us."

In her excitement, Alyson flew down the stairs and out of the building toward her car. Her mind was already busy churning up images of Mary Magdalene and Cerinthus writing about their spirituality. She couldn't wait to tell Evan the news, and she didn't know how she could stand waiting two or three more weeks for a definitive reading of the Logos Notebook. In fact she was so ecstatic, she barely felt her own physical body.

Later she would ask herself if she had tweaked her spinal cord at the neck as her boot heals hit the pavement, or if adrenaline had pumped more blood than normal into her brain, for something undeniable happened, and she had no words or physical explanation for it. Without warning, what seemed like her oversoul or expanded awareness, suddenly peered out through her corporeal eyes at her surroundings and immediate circumstances of her life, as if becoming awake for the first time. It was only a flash, the famous moment when everything comes together, but there was a vaguely recognizable feeling associated with this brief sense of extra-awareness.

Joy.

Your mosaic of shards is coming together, Al, she heard herself say. *And the light is beginning to shine through it.*

Part Two

Resurrection
Ephesus, 54 CE

... the Logos is, as it were,
the charioteer of the powers,
and he who utters It is the rider ...

– Philo of Alexandria,
The Migrations of Abraham

One

Miryam sat with eyes closed in deep inner *hakshavah* the way Rav Yeshua had taught her. As dawn broke over Ephesus, Miryam's inner landscape filled with blue and golden light. With a spiritual ear she listened to the divine melody softly lapping on the interior of her being. With soul's subtle power of sight she gazed on the radiant face of Ravi, the name she used for Rav Yeshua's divine presence within her being. He returned her gaze, yearning more for her than she for Him – if that were possible. No words or thoughts exchanged, just instant knowings emanating through her like raindrops on a still lake.

"Let me hear You all day, Ravi," she whispered. "For in You I trust. Let me know the way to walk, for I raise my *neshama*, my soul, to You."

Out of the early morning stillness a crow cawed, and a shadowy vision of a scarred-face man eclipsed the image of Rav Yeshua before her inner eye. Miryam challenged the aberration, asking, "Are you Ravi?" It vanished into a veil of black. Rav Yeshua had taught Miryam to shun any face she might see other than His own behind closed eyes. Though disturbing, she assumed the foreign face would be something to be revealed in its own time, perhaps as a vessel through which more of herself would be revealed to her – that was the *Orach Chayim*, the true Way of Life on a spiritual path. "Show me the Way of Life, where being in Your Presence is the fullness of joy and pleasures are eternal," she recited to herself.

The door to her room creaked open, causing Miryam to unfurl her attention from the folds of her *palla* of contemplation. Slowly her eyes took in the coarser lights, sounds, and forms of the external world. Martha stood before her with a cup of goat's milk. She was already dressed for the day in her freshly washed *tunica*. Her graying curly hair was combed and tied back with a clean rag. "Please excuse the interruption, Sister. There is a man out in the garden who would like to see us."

"*Ayn?*" Though the sisters lived in relative isolation on a mountaintop above Ephesus, it wasn't unusual for visitors to cross their doorstep. Miryam took the cup and drank. The tepid milk felt luxurious on her parched throat.

"He introduced himself as Paulos of Tarsus. Says he's a tentmaker who's been residing in Ephesus for the past few weeks."

Miryam didn't know of a Paulos from Tarsus. "Did he say what he wanted?"

"Only that he'd been told there were wise women from Galilee living on Mount Koressos he should meet."

"Wise, or just old? Do we qualify to offer the wisdom of elders? I've lost count."

Martha smiled. "You might have lived fifty years. I have not."

"But you're older, so if you're not fifty, then neither am I," Miryam rebuffed.

"Shall I send him away? Startled me at first, but I don't believe he means us harm."

Miryam focused her attention inwardly on the radiant face of Ravi. Pausing a second longer, she relaxed more deeply into His gaze, in the next few moments knowing they would receive the stranger into their home. "Could you ask him to come back this afternoon?" Martha nodded, but before she could leave, Miryam added: "Thank Cerinthus for milking the goat this morning."

Martha's eyes gleamed. "Nothing he wouldn't do for his favorite teacher."

Cerinthus was the son of their landlord who did odd chores around their property in exchange for tutoring in reading and writing scripture in *Ivrit*, the original language of Canaan deemed the Holy Tongue. The sisters taught the children of other exiled families to read and write in the Holy Tongue as well, for most could only speak *Aramit* or *Hellene*, the languages of their conquerors. The families paid the women in firewood, fruits, vegetables, grains, and some coin for taxes and shopping in the Ephesus agora for the scant staples of their modest lives. On occasion they were given used papyrus scrolls, which Miryam cut into smaller less cumbersome sheets and washed to remove previous writings. Using a mixture of soot and lamp oil, she copied lines of scripture onto the dried pages for her students to read.

Miryam and Martha's complex heritage involved thousands of years of migration, relinquishment, exile, and prophecy. As a result, the people were identified by many names. As descendants of Abraham, they were called Ivrit, meaning the "other-siders," because this scriptural paternal figure of Genesis had immigrated into Yisrael from the other side of the Euphrates River. They were called the Children of Yisrael after the tribes who flourished for a time in the Kingdom of the Pharaohs and were led to Yisrael by Moses. Shortly after King Solomon built the First Temple in Yerushalayim, Yisrael gave up its southern region to the Kingdom of Yehudah. After successive invasions by the Assyrians and Babylonians, among others, much of the population scattered and Solomon's temple was destroyed. The Persians officially imposed the Aramit language, which was eventually usurped by the Hellene language after the conquest by Alexander the Great. Under Rhōmaioi tyranny, the Holy Tongue became all but forgotten. In the end the people came to be called Yehudi because they maintained their faith and loyalty to the Second Temple at Yerushalayim in Yehudah.

What emerged from all of this strife and movement was the idea of the One Supreme Being. Those who followed the laws of Moses and Abraham were often collectively called *Am HaSefer*, the People of the Book. The Book was the *Tanakh*, a collection of the *sefers* of Moses and the Prophets. Aramit versions of the Tanakh had originated in Babylon, but copies were rare. Hellene-speakers had access to the *Targum Hashirim*, which had been translated from the original Ivrit by seventy-two elders in forced seclusion. Purists claimed the translations were so full of mistakes they were useless, and besides, if Yĕhovah had wanted the Tanakh read in Hellene, He would have provided one!

It wasn't common for Aramit speakers, let alone women, to read the Tanakh in the Holy Tongue, but Miryam's grandfather had been a *meturgeman* who translated the Ivrit verses from an ancient family scroll and recited them in Aramit from memory at synagogue; the trick was to look as if he were actually reading from the text in Aramit. Miryam had never understood why the people had to be protected from knowing the truth. The message was the same in any language. As their grandfather grew older, cataracts shuttered his eyesight, and he taught all three of his grandchildren – Miryam, Martha, and Lazarus – to read enough Ivrit to help him with his service. As a consequence, this act gave them a way to earn a living when they went into their own exile – an exile forced upon them because of what had happened to their Rav Yeshua in Yerushalayim two decades earlier.

"And ask Cerinthus to mend the garden fence. That goat is eating all my flowers."

"He has already taken the goat to join his family's herd while he works on the fence this afternoon."

"You're ahead of me as always, Martha. *Toda*."

Martha smiled slightly and left the room, causing Miryam to smile in turn. Martha was the competent one when it came to worldly matters, but Miryam was as headstrong as their goat when it came to matters of *ruach*, spirit. As young women, this had been a thorn of contention, but now it was just one of the many nuances that bonded them.

No matter where they lived, here in Ephesus, back in Migdal Nunya, or anywhere in Galilee and Yehudah, Martha was the lady of the house, and Miryam was her guest. She kept clean their simple, three-roomed house Lazarus had built on Mount Koressos, and that which is clean is next to Elah, she always said. Martha was the one who tended the fire in the central two-part fireplace. Sunk into the ground, the fireplace shared a short wall that helped to channel smoke upward through a hole in the ceiling, and provided each half of the house with heat and added a light source along with a few narrow, shuttered windows near the ceiling of each room. Under Martha's supervision, they prepared food and received their guests and students in the front room on chairs and benches at the long table. The back room was rounded and wider than the front room and was divided by a hanging rug – its brilliant red, yellow, and blue flowered patterns were threaded by locals. The women slept on one side of the rug and studied and contemplated on the other side where Lazarus slept whenever he returned home from his travels.

The room halves were each accessible by doors on either side of the fireplace. Martha made sure the floors were brushed out and that the divider rug was taken outside periodically for a good dust beating.

Miryam stretched her legs and back, thinking her middle-aged bones weren't quite so willing to sit for long periods as they once were. She lifted the cup to her lips again and drank the goat's milk Cerinthus had been thoughtful enough to provide. In doing so, she remembered their recent conversation about the opening verses of the *Bereshit* – Genesis. Cerinthus had been sitting at the table reading the book of Moses to himself from her grandfather's heirloom Tanakh when he lifted his head and said: "It is written that Elohim said, 'Let there be light and there was light.' Who was Elohim talking to when He said that?"

That is a very good question, Miryam thought. She had answered him by saying that, of course, Elah was talking to no one, that he'd simply thought about light and light appeared, and that seemed to quell his curiosity for the moment, but not hers. She tried to imagine an existence where there was no heaven or earth, no distinction between light and darkness. Did Elah create *E'Alma* – the heavens and worlds and all that exists – with His voice, and if so, why? She turned inward, chanting the secret words Rav Yeshua had given her upon immersion into the Way. Whenever she closed her eyes in contemplation, the darkness had turned bright blue and then golden, just as Rav Yeshua had told her would transpire with years of continuous practice. Because of her ongoing progress inwardly, she knew she would someday return to the true Bereshit, awakened as Rav Yeshua had promised. But it was something she could not fathom even after all she'd experienced.

Cerinthus's question presented a further conundrum to Miryam, for Rav Yeshua had taught that most of the stories about Elah were not accurate in their description of the True Father and the stories of heaven were not the True Origin. The stories of the Tanakh were meant to inspire one to seek deeper insight and service to Yĕhovah, and according to *Ha-Rav*, "the Master," the Tanakh described that which existed within one's own being, and so it wasn't possible to answer the question in a way Cerinthus would understand it. She wasn't even sure of her own understanding of it either.

Miryam would've forgotten about the question Cerinthus had posed, had it not been for the spice trader she'd met in the Ephesus agora the day before. Though the young man was from the Indus Valley, he could speak some Hellene, and their conversation quickly turned to Spirit. He told her that the heavens and earth had burst forth out of the Invisible with a sound like the utterance of speech. And then the dark-skinned young man with the red dot on his forehead said something else in his native language: "*Brahma vai idam agre aseet, tasya vag dvitiya aseet, vag vai paramam Brahman.*" As best he could, he translated it for her in Hellene: "In the beginning was Brahma, who was with the Word, and the Word was the Supreme Brahman."

"What is this ... Brahman?" Miryam had asked.

Wide-eyed, the young man answered, "Why, Brah-*ma* is the Creator, the Father of all things. And Brah-*man* is the supreme cosmic spirit, the pure unchanging consciousness."

Oy, Miryam thought, wondering if this Brahma was the same being as Abraham, the *abba-raham*, the Father of the Many, indeed the father of the twelve tribes of Yisrael. Abba, the Father, was a name Rav Yeshua had used most often, such was his familiarity with Elah, but he had said that Abraham wasn't the True Father, and perhaps neither was this Brahma. The True Father was much more powerful and much more ... distant from their understanding and interaction – much like Brahman.

"And what is this Word?" she had asked the young Hindu.

"The *Vak* is Aum. Aum is speech, man is speech, and so man is Aum."

"So, Brahma is one with the Word, and the Word is one with Brahman."

The young man's eyes sparkled. "One must meditate on that."

"What do you mean?"

"It is written in the *Upanishads:* 'One must meditate on the Aum to understand the laws that govern Creation, and also to feel fulfilled in all desires.'"

The Aum intrigued her because she experienced the *Shefa*, the Divine Flow, not as words exactly but more like a sound that vibrated throughout her body. The Sound began as a barely perceptible hum at first, which over the years formed into a gonging bell, then turned into a lowing conch shell that she couldn't hear exactly but felt within her being. And lately the Music had felt like a faint melody on a lyre. Initially, Rav Yeshua had given his students a word to chant, not "Aum," but "Hu," which he had said was the sound of Elah's name and the sum total of all sounds. Though the words were different, the Hindu concept was nearly the same as what Rav Yeshua had taught. "And what happens to the neshama when it becomes fulfilled of all desire?"

The man stared at her blankly. "Neshama?"

"Ayn, the part of Elah within us that never dies," Miryam said, first touching her breastbone with her right fist and then her forehead with her fingertips.

The Hindu's face flowed from furrowed brow to a sunburst of smiles as he finally understood her question. "Ah, the *atman*. One is reborn and reborn until the atman realizes it is identical to Brahman. Only then is it *moksha*, liberated from the wheel of rebirth." He then launched into a dizzying array of sacred texts he had called the *Vedas* and the *Mahabharata*, if she remembered correctly, and various gods and goddesses and rituals, and what he called *karma*, and some of the ancient teachers who claimed different interpretations. The young man's enthusiasm for his beliefs was infectious and Miryam was admittedly intrigued. There was much of what he told her that rang similar to Rav Yeshua's teachings, and she suspected that at the root of this religion long ago were teachers like Ha-Rav.

"Tell me, when you chant this Aum, do the heavens sing it back to you?"

The Hindu stared at her blankly. "I don't understand."

"Can you hear the Music with your inner ear, and in hearing it are you ... raised up?"

The young man shook his head. "Aum stills the mind so that we may eventually come into unity with all of creation," he explained. That was answer enough for Miryam. When she chanted Hu aloud, she could hear it repeated in the sounds around her. And when she chanted the secret words Ha-Rav had given her silently to herself, she felt herself being drawn inward and upward into ocean waves of joy filling her being.

She caught herself wanting to learn more, realizing that such a mission would clearly take a full lifetime. Yeshua's way was so much simpler and didn't require study and memorizations and worship to more than one deity. *Lo*, she would not take a bite of the apple from this tree, but she did see how a single divine seed of truth planted in fertile ground could become an overgrown orchard of knowledge that would waylay the soul's journey for a very long time. She would never leave the wheel of life that way.

The poetry and rhythm of the simple verse lingered, nevertheless: *In the beginning was the Aum.*

Miryam gulped down the rest of the milk, and as she did so, the effervescence within her began solidifying into words with increasing audibility and urgency. Pressing against the inside of her forehead, the words all but propelled her to her writing desk. Miryam picked up a sheet of papyrus where she and Cerinthus had practiced writing their names in Hellene and Aramit and where they had been recording verses of the *Bereshit*, along with the Hindu phrases she'd just learned in the agora. She flattened the sheet in front of her, weighing down the curling corners with candleholders, uncertain of whether she should obey the words pulsing through her, or obey the long-ago wishes of Ha-Rav.

Back when Miryam could still enjoy being in the company of Rav Yeshua, she so resonated with his words that she wanted to preserve them on papyrus. "You cannot write *davar* Elah until you become Ha-Davar Elah Itself," he once told her with a wink, referring to passages in the Tanakh in which the Word of the All came unto the prophets, from Elah's Mouth to their mouths. He was saying that she could not write about Elah until she embodied Elah's Word and became one with It. Rav Yeshua was fond of wordplay.

On the serious side, Rav Yeshua was adamant on maintaining the secrecy of what he'd called his *Sod Ha-Torah*, his secret teachings. "It is given to you to know the mysteries of the kingdom of heaven, but it is not given to them," Ha-Rav would say. When he spoke openly in marketplaces and near public wells, he spoke to attract the rare individual who was ready for the spiritual life, but he hid his truths in stories. He called these his outer teachings, those messages he presented *ayn b'gla*, "in open eye," which offered temporary upliftment for those who did not yet have "the eyes to see or ears to hear." The Inner Teachings would be like mustard seed on rock, pearls before swine.

That felt like lifetimes ago, and indeed it had been roughly half of her life since Rav Yeshua had left them – left her. She had his radiant *Shechinah*, His Divine Presence, whenever she turned her attention inward, but his actual teachings were fading. Out of desperation, she turned to scripture with ever sharper eyes. She read not to increase her knowledge of the world, nor to deepen her devotion to her heritage, but to search for Ha-Rav's words echoing within them, thereby strengthening her bond with his spirit. She began to see that some of the prophets in the Tanakh may also have been *Mara Memra*, Masters of the Word, deftly hiding their teachings in stories the way Rav Yeshua had disguised his teachings. She could see that even if spoken out loud in broad daylight, the secret teachings would stay buried to anyone who hadn't been initiated into them, for no one could ever grasp their depth and true meaning without the power instilled within them by an initiator of the Word Divine.

The Word would wait no longer. She dipped a split reed into a pot of lampblack and, hunching over the papyrus, carefully formed a phrase in a mix of Aramit and the Holy Tongue:

> *Memra haya bereshit, Memra haya Elah. Elah shĕva kol. La' kol haya yad Elah.*

> *The Word exists at the Source. The Word exists with Elah. Elah creates everything. Nothing exists that is not in the hand of Elah.*

Miryam sat in stillness, enraptured by the simplicity of what she'd just written. According to the Tanakh, Bereshit is the Source, the timeless beginning, the Great Void out of which Elah had created heaven and earth, night and day, the animal kingdom. He eventually created man, Adam, out of the dirt as his name implies, and from his ribs, *Chavah*, meaning "breath of life." Elah created all this with the very act of His voice: *Elah memra haya 'owr, 'owr.* "God *said* let there be light and there was light."

Miryam found it interesting that she'd written "Memra" rather then "Davar," because both meant nearly the same thing. Davar referred to the words, sayings, laws, or instruction of Elah, but Memra referred to the Voice of the One, the Utterance, the Sound of Elah the All, the very *act* of Divine Speech as the source of Creation. *Memra bara 'owr*: The Word, the Utterance, the Sound, manifested as light – and everything else.

Miryam thought about the names her ancestors had used to describe the One – there were seventy in all – names deemed so awesome and so powerful that few spoke them for fear of misusing that power or bringing terrible consequences upon one's head and household. There evolved a tradition of creating abbreviations for these names for the Elah, the Awesome One, by dropping the vowels out of written words or reducing a string of names to their first letters and then creating a new name out of just these letters. The Holy Name of the Unutterable, YHVH, was a word that transcended meaning because it could not be pronounced, so appropriate for a Creator who could not even be imagined. These cryptic words themselves began to assume a power of their own. Rav Yeshua had said that the Supreme Deity had no name at all.

Ever since humankind could write letters, there was the sense that letters in and of themselves contained their own divine utterance and power. All through the Tanakh, Elah's voice, word, and instruction became allegory for omniscient power, creation, and sustenance. Indeed, initiates of Memra, the Word, entered the realm of the All upon Yĕchezqel's chariot, chanting their sacred words their masters had given them. And just as the person who delivered a king's message was to be treated as if the messenger as well as the message were the king himself, Elah, the Word, and the Master of the Word were one in the same and thus interchangeable.

Miryam waited for more to come, her stylus poised midair as she listened within herself with a hundred ears. She tried not to strain, hoping to receive the Memra, the Word, rather than to demand it, although she could not contain her impatience. She looked up from her desk to find Martha standing before her, and Miryam had to restrain herself from becoming cross with her for interrupting her concentration and first communion with the Word.

"Our mystery visitor has come back," Martha said. "Are you ready to see him now?"

"So soon?"

"Where does one wait on a mountain? After thrashing about in the garden, he went for a walk, then returned shortly to say he could wait no longer. Patience may not be his better virtue."

Nor mine, Miryam thought. She nodded in resignation, knowing there was so much more to receive and explore. "Very well, please invite him in."

Martha started to go, then hesitated.

"What is it?" Miryam asked.

"You're covered in lampblack," Martha said, pointing to Miryam's forehead and then to a strand of her long, thick, graying black hair.

"I've got it on my hands and clothes too." Agitated, she tried to rub the smudges off her tunica without much success. Martha brought her a bowl of water and a rag to dab at the smudges on her forehead and hair.

"It's not coming off," Martha said, half giggling. "Oy, Saba would roll over in his grave if he saw the shape of your work."

Miryam looked down to see a black fingerprint marring the right-hand side of the papyrus. Indeed, such clumsiness would have rendered an entire copy of the Tanakh invalid, and it would have been destroyed. "I should have known better. At least tied my hair up first." She wrapped herself in the palla, a long rectangular cloth, thereby covering up the black smudges on her dress. She hoped the stain could be scrubbed out without shredding the threads. "Let's not keep the man waiting any longer."

Two

Nothing in Miryam's life prepared her for meeting the visitor who called himself Paulos. He looked familiar, yet he didn't look like anyone she'd ever seen before. He wore the typical garb of all citizens of the empire, an elaborately-draped toga over an ankle-length tunic, both white. Whereas the toga of a senator or equestrian class might be bordered with purple stripes, his garments boasted blue stripes. *How brave*, Miryam thought. In Yerushalayim, men sewed blue tassels into the hems of their garments to remind them to keep the commandments or to display their devotion, and she wondered what Paulos was trying to convey.

Paulos was about the same age as herself, of medium height and fit-looking perhaps from a life of travel. In contrast to his physique and meticulously-styled clothing were his injuries. His leathery, dark-complected skin was scarred as if he'd been pushed down a rocky cliff or two, or worse, beaten and stoned. His eyes, the most startling, were swollen and the skin around them red raw with open sores. Miryam didn't know whether to fear this man or to feel sympathy for all he'd obviously encountered and endured.

Paulos, meanwhile, first took in Miryam's face, perhaps noticing the black smudges there. Then, as he quickly scanned the contents of her writing table and sheet of papyrus she was working on, a slight look of surprise crossed his face. Surprise mixed with what – disgust? Just as quickly the expression slid behind a tight smile, too late hidden from Miryam's discerning eye.

"Do you know letters?" She instinctively addressed him in Aramit, which would be native to his homeland of Tarsus despite the cultural integration his clothing and mannerisms suggested. Blending the two cultures was the nature of the *galut*, those living in exile outside of the homeland, especially those allowed Rhōmaioi citizenship. Even she and Martha had abandoned the traditional heavier, multi-colored flaxen garments for the light-colored woolen fabrics. She checked the ink on the papyrus for dryness and decided to wait a moment before rolling the scroll so as not to smudge any more than she already had.

"I write many letters," he said with a sardonic crinkle of his lips. "That is, I do not write them personally, for as you can see I suffer from weakness of flesh." He presented his hands so she could see the scars. "I am of a means to hire scribes now, but I do not wish to boast."

"I sense you don't approve of literate women. You'll find that here in Ephesus some women of the upper classes know how to read."

The expression showed again on Paulos's face, and Miryam predicted it to be a sign of future exchanges. "There is neither male nor female, for all are one in the body of the Lord," he answered solemnly, then switched his tone. "Women are commanded obedience under the law. Let them ask their husbands at home if they have questions."

"A traditionalist," Miryam declared. "Is it not true that the Tanakh is ambiguous on raising daughters to read? I wasn't aware of it written on Moses's stone tablets." *Even if the Torah specifically spelled it out that women weren't allowed to read, Ha-Rav never excluded women from his teachings*, Miryam thought with some indulgence of pride.

"I am justified by faith and not by the works of the Torah."

"I'm not sure I understand what you mean."

"It is a long story, Maria Magdalana." Paulos looked at her wryly. "Or should I say Miryam Magadan, to use the Aramit pronunciation?"

This declaration took her aback. She and Martha lived in Ephesus in what they'd hoped was obscurity. "Both pronunciations of my name are acceptable. But most people call me by my abba's name, Binyamiyn. How do you know of me, of my birthplace?" More to the point: How did Paulos know Rav Yeshua had called her "the Magadan" to distinguish her from others called Miryam? It was no secret that he'd poked fun at her strength of mind while reminding her to apply the same resoluteness to some of her weaknesses by naming her after the unique fish storage towers in her hometown village of Migdal Nunya.

"When one travels as widely as me, one hears stories."

"What stories, exactly?"

"That he drove seven demons from your body, that he loved you the most of all his disciples."

Miryam stood in silence and shock. She'd never been spoken of so blatantly, and these so-called stories twisted the truth while both flattering and insulting her. Not quite knowing how to respond, she chanted the secret words Ha-Rav had given her in order to stay as solid as a tower.

"Some say you went to Gaul. I have passed through Ephesus before, but it wasn't until recently I heard you might be here."

"My sister and I settled here years ago." She didn't want to give this stranger the details of their lives and travels.

Paulos smiled as if hitting his intended target, then changed the subject. "Are you just learning to write?" he asked, subtly gesturing to her accidents of ink.

"One would think so."

He took a couple steps toward the desk to scan its surface. "What are you writing?"

Miryam promptly rolled up the papyrus on the off-chance Paulos could read Aramit upside down. The stiffened sheet crackled as she rolled it. She placed the scroll in a stack of papyri while considering what to do with this man. Part of her wanted to send him away, but the other part, perhaps the higher part, wanted to hear what he had to say. *Or was it the other way around?*

"I haven't properly greeted you." She walked around the desk and crossed to him with arms extended in a gesture of welcome. "*Barukh haba,*" she said. "Welcome."

Paulos stepped back as if to duck her embrace and instead grabbed her hands in his. "*Shlama,*" he answered in Aramit. "Peace be with you."

"Please, please join me by the hearth." Miryam showed Paulos to one of two simple wooden chairs facing the fire where the sisters usually sat and contemplated. "The air is a bit crisper up on Nightingale Mountain than down near the harbor. I like to curl up like a squirrel here in the late afternoons." She sat in a chair opposite his.

"I see you've adopted the Hellene style of dining."

"Rather than a rug on the floor? We had tables and stools in my abba's house, but, ayn, there are some civilities here that are preferable and easier to manage at my age. I apologize for not having a couch to recline on."

Martha appeared in the room with steaming handbowls on a tray and sat it on the small table between the chairs.

"Martha is a much more gracious hostess than I."

"The water was already boiling when our visitor arrived," Martha replied as she sat the tray down on a table by the hearth and added a log to the fire.

"I saw the natural spring flowing from beneath the house," Paulos said, reaching for a bowl.

"We were fortunate to find this spot. We can fill our buckets through a hole in the floor without having to go outside."

"Clever." Cradling the bowl in the palms of both hands, Paulos sniffed the fragrant liquid, and then blew off the steam, greeting his first tentative sip with a smile. "Bitter yet sweet. What is it?"

"Leaves from the *t'u* tree imported from Chang'an," Martha said.

"My sister likes to experiment with infusions of spices and fruits."

Paulos poised the bowl beneath his hooked nose and again sniffed. "It's interesting with the milk and honey, but what's the spice I smell?"

"Cardamom, from Hindustan," Martha answered. "The *agora* near the harbor is full of all sorts of exotic spices. I'm glad you like the t'u. Very healing."

"Healing?"

"Tumors, abscesses, chest congestion, other infirmities. It's the closest we have to the Divine Elixir on earth!"

"Keeps you awake all night if you drink it too close to bedtime," Miryam added.

"I could use a barrel of it, if that's the case," Paulos said.

"For healing or wakefulness?" Martha asked.

Paulos gestured toward the sores around his eyes. "Both."

"I can make a poultice for that," Martha offered.

"I've tried everything. Even petitioned *Kyrios* three times to remove this thorn from my flesh, but he gave it to me so that I don't exalt myself too high." He lightly touched the sores around his eyes. "I take pleasure in my infirmities because my strength is made perfect in my weakness, and the power of the *Christos* may rest upon me."

"Very well," Martha said, careful not to react to his strange declaration of piety. She stood at the doorway and waited for a signal from Miryam to leave.

Miryam sipped from her own warm bowl, drinking in the presence of Paulos for a moment. He didn't seem all that threatening. She nodded to Martha, letting her know it was safe to leave her alone with him while she gardened. If Paulos had noticed, he didn't indicate it. He seemed more preoccupied with his pain, and Miryam felt it best to put his mind on other things.

"Here at Ephesus, where the Silk Road meets the sea, so many new things come in with the wind, like the t'u leaves," she mused. True, Ephesus was the modern-day tower of Babel, a paradigm of diversity. As an ancient shipping harbor, it served as a lively intersection between the Qin and Han Dynasties and the extensive *Imperium Romanum*. Whatever humanity could invent, including all manner of deity and worship, it all flowed from the far corners of the earth into Ephesus and mixed in the agora along with tangible trade goods. It suddenly occurred to Miryam that this might be the man she'd heard had been rejected by the local galut. "Tell me, Paulos, what brings you to Ephesus, besides lecturing in the synagogue?"

"Implying that I, too, blew in with the wind?" Paulos chuckled uncomfortably at his attempt at humor. "I have been, as you say, lecturing. You are well informed."

"I keep a regular place in the public bathhouse. What do you teach?"

Paulos straightened proudly in his chair and announced, "I am *Ethnos Apostolos*, or, if you prefer the Aramit, *Shikha l'Kapa*."

"I don't understand what you mean by 'apostolos.'"

He frowned at her ignorance. "I was appointed to be messenger of the *euaggelion*, the *sevarteh d'Meshikha*."

Miryam found it interesting how Paulos so easily and frequently shifted between Hellene and Aramit. These were not compatible languages. Hellene was the language of coin and politics across the empire. Aramit speakers found Hellene (or *Yonaya*, as her people called it) difficult to pronounce. Miryam and her siblings had learned a little of the language in order to help manage the family's fish packing business in Migdal Nunya and to pay Rhōmaioi taxes. Their knowledge of it had allowed the siblings to relocate to Ephesus, where they became more fluent over the years. Gratefully, Miryam could follow Paulos in his odyssey of strange words. "The euaggelion?"

He pointed upward. "The gospel, the triumphant Memra, the Word of Elah."

The Memra. Miryam's neck hair bristled. This odd man just echoed the subject of her morning contemplation. "And what is this Word of Elah?"

"As it is written, there shall come out of Sion the Deliverer who will turn Yisrael away from ungodliness."

"You are a long way from Yisrael."

"Not all who are descended from Yisrael are Yisrael. That is to say, not all who are descended from Yisrael are true Children of Elah on the inside, and not all Children of Elah are Yisrael."

"Who appointed you to spread this Word of Elah?"

"It comes not from men but from the Kyrios Christos unveiled within me and from *Theos* who raised him from the dead."

Miryam noticed that Paulos used the Hellene word Theos to mean Elah, though the Hellene did not believe in the One Deity – they worshiped a whole slew of deities. "And who is this Christos?"

"Why, your Yeshua, of course." Again, her ignorance seemed to surprise Paulos. "We call him Iēsous."

"Excuse me?" Miryam was so caught off guard, she nearly choked on her hot t'u. She didn't know how to unknot what Paulos had just declared. Rav Yeshua ... messiah ... raised from the dead? "I have passed my prime, but I still remember many things, and I don't remember you. Were you an initiate of Rav Yeshua?"

"Ah, so you *are* Miryam the Magadan!" Paulos looked like he'd just unburied a lost treasure. "That's Martha out there, but where is your brother, Lazarus?"

There was no use safeguarding her identity with him now. "My brother is on a ... journey." She wasn't about to offer further explanation and returned to the more pressing subject: "Do others refer to Ha-Rav as Christos?"

"Christos, the Anointed One, is how he is called among the *pisteuō*, the Faithful. In Antioch the Hellene called us 'Christianos' as a jeer, but it is an honor to carry the brand of the Christos. We are all anointed in him through *baptisma* in his spirit."

"I see." She did not see. Everything this curious man said was foreign to Miryam. She wouldn't have encouraged a non-initiate to refer to Ha-Rav as messiah, the anointed king. Certainly, Rav Yeshua would not call himself that. The miracles Ravi performed within her own being might warrant such a title, but the general public, which hadn't been initiated into the Shefa, the Divine Flow? Lo! And the baptisma Paulos spoke of – the *tevilah*, the immersion – had Paulos been initiated into the Way? Who among Ha-Rav's students had risen high enough within themselves to initiate new followers?

"Why do you call Rav Yeshua the messiah?"

Paulos looked like he'd been abruptly shoved from behind by a donkey. "You of all people should know."

"Lo, I don't know."

"He was crucified and raised from the dead." He spread his arms and raised them toward the ceiling. "I call it the *anastasis*."

Miryam was bound by a vow not to discuss the circumstances of Ha-Rav's passing, especially not with a stranger. Surely, this anastasis Paulos spoke of, this resurrection, was a misunderstanding. "My family and I escaped Yerushalayim soon after Ha-Rav left us. Ephesus is so far enough removed, we rarely hear news from the city, and we never hear of stories involving Rav Yeshua's teachings or what might have happened to his other students."

"That's reasonable," Paulos said, though he seemed skeptical that she knew as little as she did. "The Word spreads slowly."

Miryam was aware of a few veiled references to the idea of resurrection in the Tanakh. The book of *Daniel* said: "Many who sleep in the dust of the earth shall awake, some to everlasting life, and some to shame and everlasting contempt." Though an allegory about spiritual growth to Miryam, the idea of the resurrected soul had provided comfort for those who lost loved ones through Rhōmaioi tyranny. "This anastasis of the Christos, can it be verified?"

Paulos nodded enthusiastically, and for the first time since his arrival, Miryam detected a light in his eyes. "Christos died for our transgressions, was buried and raised on the third day when he appeared to Simeon Kephas – who we call Simon Petros, the Rock – then to the twelve. Then he appeared to more than five hundred brothers at once, most who remain until now, but some have also fallen asleep. Then he appeared to Yakob, then to all the apostles, and last of all, as to the child born at the wrong time, he appeared to me."

"In the flesh or as a vision?"

"Whether in the body or out of the body, I do not know."

Miryam frowned. She could not compare these events to her own experience. According to the Way, one's master could appear to initiates in a dream or as a bright star seen inwardly, as if the sun were shining brightly on the inside of one's own forehead. After years of rigorous practice and purification, the disciple could see the face of Rav Yeshua in place of the star. In her experience, these visions did not occur outside the body and certainly not as a public expression for all to share. But who was she to judge how Ha-Rav had chosen to move among his own? On the other hand, absent the living master to school their minds and keep them on the straight and narrow, the students may have invented stories that strayed from his teachings. "Can you elaborate, Paulos?"

"I am not so attached to the signs as those in Yerushalayim are. I am only interested in the second coming of our Kyrios at the end of days. But perhaps it will help to tell you of this long journey from the beginning."

"By all means, I'm curious now."

He cleared his throat. "I was born Saulus in the city of Tarsus in the country of Cilicia, a member of the people of Yisrael, of the tribe of Binyamiyn as you are, Ivrit born of Ivrit, circumcised on the eighth day." Paulos sang this as a litany, polished by the tongue that had glossed over it so often. "I was educated in Yerushalayim at the feet of Gamaliel, grandson of the great sage Hillel ... as to the Torah, a Pharisee."

"Important lineage," Miryam remarked.

Paulos raised his voice, for he obviously didn't appreciate being interrupted. "As to zeal, a persecutor of the faithful of Christos, as to righteousness under the Torah, blameless."

Talking with this man is like chasing a jackass around in circles, she thought. "Didn't you just say you were an apostle? Now you say you yourself blamelessly persecuted the believers!"

Paulos lowered his head contritely. "I ruthlessly hunted them down and ravaged them."

Miryam cringed. This news meant that the students Ha-Rav had left in Yerushalayim had become a threat to the temple, and that was contrary to what he would've wanted.

"When I studied at the temple to become a Pharisee priest, I advanced quickly for my age. Obsessed as I was with mastering the teachings of my ancestors, I paid little attention to anything outside of my ablutions. We were not even aware of the son of Theos while alive, nor of the crucifixion. But when Simeon and the apostles started creating disturbances in the temple, we began to take notice. There were many wonders and signs and stories about Simeon's healing powers and ability to speak in tongues. Nearly three thousand souls received baptisma from Simeon in a single day."

"Do you mean all those people received tevilah?"

"They were not immersed in the so-called 'living water' of the temple but in the spirit of the Christos."

Paulos explained that fear came down on every soul, and many sold all their possessions to live and eat and study communally near the temple. Bolstered by a new confidence, Simeon and Yakob entered the temple and taught every day. Multitudes of men and women from Yerushalayim and other cities crowded around the apostles on Solomon's porch, hoping Simeon, by his very passing shadow, could heal them of unclean spirits. This caused great alarm and perhaps some jealousy among the Pharisees, particularly the high priest. They seized the apostles and put them into public custody. But the next morning, the apostles had somehow escaped their prison and resumed their usual place on the porch, teaching to scores of new believers. This inspired further stories of the power of Christos working through Simeon. The guards eventually escorted the apostles before the Sanhedrin, the high council of religious law in the temple. The high priest asked the apostles: "Did we not strictly charge you with refraining from speaking the name of your deceased rav? You have filled the city with his teachings, and you will bring his blood upon us." To which Simeon responded, "We must obey Yĕhovah, rather than the men who killed His son. Yĕhovah raised His son to give repentance to Yisrael and remission of our transgressions."

"And what was their reaction?" Miryam asked.

"Some priests wanted to have the apostles killed, of course. But my teacher, Gamaliel, was a wise man who wrote many letters on the torah of Moses. He cautioned the council to be careful of what they did to the apostles, because if their work was Yĕhovah's will, the council would not be able to overthrow it, and in fact they would be fighting against Yĕhovah Himself."

"Did the priests agree with Gamaliel?"

Paulos shrugged. "The apostles were still beaten, warned never to speak the name of Yeshua again, and set free. But the apostles never stopped speaking his name, and they never stopped teaching in the temple. Meanwhile, a dissension arose between the Pharisees and the Sadducees. The Sadducees did not believe in angels, spirit, or the resurrection, and the Pharisees did believe in them."

Challenging the high priests and counsel sounded like something Simeon would do, Miryam thought. He had beseeched Yeshua for a return to the laws of the Torah, for building a resistance against Rhōmaioi influence in the temple, and for the liberation of Yisrael. But she wondered how much of the story about Simeon's "miracles and signs" had been embellished. "Were the apostles punished for continuing to defy the council after that?"

"The number of disciples soon multiplied. Even a few Pharisees became obedient to the faith. Tensions increased nevertheless, and opposing Pharisees were too afraid to do anything."

"Were you taken in by the stories?"

"Despite the tolerant Gamaliel being my teacher, I aligned myself with the high priest, who wished to persuade the Yehudi to conform to the Torah."

Paulos paused to sip more t'u, appearing to be slightly reluctant to convey the next part of the story. "One man in particular, Stephanos of Hellene heritage, was brought before the council for saying that Christos would destroy the temple. He was stoned to death outside the city." Paulos drew in a deep breath and continued, obviously with great shame. "By custom, the men who carried out this punishment stripped themselves of their outer garments, and placed them at the feet of a young man named Saulus to guard. A great persecution arose against the assembly in Yerushalayim that day. Saulus ravaged the assembly, entered into every house, and dragged both men and women off to prison."

"And who was this Saulus?"

"The man sitting in your presence today."

Remaining perfectly still on the outside, Miryam imagined this odd man beating, imprisoning, and assassinating her fellow spiritual aspirants, and she felt great sadness for them. She turned her gaze inwardly to the radiant face before her inner eye. Inhaling deeply, feeling the eternal, effervescent love within, she returned her focus to the man in front of her. "Should we be frightened of you?"

"In Aramit there is an expression: *mitheelidh min dresh*."

"To be renewed or reborn in one's habits? How did this renewal come about?"

"Christos asked me to stop persecuting his students," Paulos said matter-of-factly.

Miryam started to ask how Rav Yeshua could have made the request as a crucified man, but Paulos put up a hand and continued. "I was on my way to Damascus with papers calling for the arrest of some followers of the Way. We stopped for the night and camped near a roadside shrine where I performed the ceremonial rights of a priest of my standing. There I was suddenly blinded by a bright light that seemed to come from everywhere. As I fell to the ground I heard a voice say, 'Saulus, Saulus, why do you persecute me?' I asked, 'Who's speaking to me?' The Voice responded, 'I am Yeshua, the one you persecute. Get up and enter the city, and you will be told what to do.'

A man named Ananias came to me and baptized me. If I had been blind to the Savior, I could now see, as if fish scales had been removed from my eyes."

Did Rav Yeshua himself actually approach this man and ask him to stop killing? She shook her head at how unbelievable that sounded. *And what of this Ananias?* Toward the end, Ha-Rav had some seventy students and a man named Ananias was one of them. She didn't know by what authority he could initiate new students. A living master was requisite for an initiation to hold true, and staying in constant contact with such a rav was needed for the Shefa to do its work – at least in the beginning. Otherwise, the teachings could be misinterpreted and the student could either become confused and deranged, or make himself out to be a messiah himself. To her knowledge, Rav Yeshua had passed on the mantle to only one disciple who would have the authority to initiate new aspirants, but that person hadn't yet accepted the responsibility.

Paulos took another sip of his t'u and, in doing so, the hand holding the ceramic bowl began to tremble. Careful not to spill the contents, he sat the bowl down on the table next to him and cradled his shaking hand with the steadier one. Miryam took note of the affliction, wondering if it was due to the disease around his eyes or the ecstatic rituals that often caused a disease of the mind. His vision of Ha-Rav may have even come from this affliction. She'd heard of Pharisee priests performing such rituals as fasting and chanting to induce visions, rituals so dangerous they were kept secret. She wondered if Simeon had been aware of these practices and if he was teaching them to some of his apostles. Whatever the case, Paulos did seem to believe the story he told was the truth.

"The vision on the road to Damascus was your call to become an apostle?"

"That is where it began. I am the least of the apostles, unworthy to be called an apostle because I persecuted the followers. But by the grace of Theos, I am what I am. His grace that was bestowed on me was not futile, for I worked more than all of them; though not I, but the grace of Theos."

"And this is why you are now called Paulos, rather than Saulus."

"The Hellene name honors my rebirth, while it also allows me safer passage. The name shows that the Christos Way is not reserved for just the Ivrit."

Interesting, Miryam thought. Surely he knew that *paulos* was a Hellene word for "small." Perhaps he had purposely chosen it to further emphasize his humility while also diminishing the horror of his former life as judge and executioner. "And Rav Yeshua's *original* students taught you about the Way?"

"What I preach does not come from flesh."

"If you were not an initiate of Rav Yeshua himself, and you didn't learn from the apostles, then where do your teachings come from?"

"I neither received the Word from man, nor was I taught it, but it comes to me through *apokalypsis* from the son of Theos within me."

"What do you mean by this?"

"I will explain. When it was the good pleasure of Theos to call me through His grace and unveil His son in me that I might preach the son among the *goyim*, the nations of the uncircumcised, I didn't immediately confer with flesh and blood. Rather, I spent a few years in the desert. Later I met with the Pillars, those respected in Yerushalayim, but of the other apostles I saw no one."

"When you say you met with 'the Pillars' in Yerushalayim, you mean Simeon and Yakob?"

"And Johanan, but what they are does not matter to me, for Theos shows no partiality."

Miryam detected tension between Paulos and the Pillars. "Were you amiable toward one another?"

"At first Simeon would have nothing to do with me because I had called myself a fellow apostle. But a man named Barnabas intervened, explaining how on the road I had seen and spoken with the Christos, and how I had been baptized, and how I preached that Iēsous Christos was the son of Theos. We met occasionally over the course of two weeks until they sent me to set up an *ekklēsia* in Tarsus. I helped Barnabas with his ekklēsia in Antioch, and we later traveled together quite extensively preaching the gospel."

Miryam understood an ekklēsia was like the Ivrit *kehillah*, a religious gathering of like-minded participants, and it didn't concern her that the uninitiated were meeting to talk about Ha-Rav. She was more concerned that Simeon and Yakob had assumed leadership over Rav Yeshua's talmidim and were allowing others to teach his Word in these ekklēsia. She felt certain that Rav Yeshua would not have approved of such a far-reaching enterprise without himself at the reins. "Tell me again … what is this gospel you preach?"

"Simply, that Christos will return to redeem all believers."

Miryam raised her eyebrows at the grandeur of such a prospect. "Is that what Simeon believes?"

"Don't you?"

Miryam shook her head ever so slightly. She did not believe that Ha-Rav died to redeem all those who worshiped him after his death. Rather, he guided his own students toward liberation within themselves *while he was alive*. She sighed and studied Paulos. He was more zealous than Simeon ever had been. But was it appropriate for her to be the one to set the man straight? She would have to investigate further. "How do you know that Rav Yeshua has risen?"

"The visions, of course, and the fact that Simeon and Yakob discovered his empty tomb."

Paulos spoke the truth for once. These two men had indeed discovered that Rav Yeshua was missing from the sepulcher. "For Simeon and Yakob, the empty tomb and the signs and miracles would enhance their stature as leaders, would they not?"

Paulos shrugged. "That would stand to reason, but they say Christos appointed them."

Is that true? "Did you have other encounters with the … Pillars?"

"Barnabas and I went to Yerushalayim fourteen years later regarding the issue of … ." Paulos finished his sentence by snipping the air with an invisible tool held between his thumb and forefinger.

Miryam had no idea what he meant by this gesture.

"It's performed on young male infants."

"You mean the *brit milah*?" She was incredulous.

The apostle nodded and his eyes flashed with just a hint of anger. "By this time it was decided that Yakob would remain at the temple in Yerushalayim, while Simeon would baptize all those who believed in Yĕhovah yet did not participate in the covenants of Abraham – the God-Fearers outside of

Yerushalayim, that is. Simeon argued that to be saved by Christos, one could not be baptized unless one were circumcised."

What does circumcision have to do with entering the Kingdom? Miryam asked herself. Rav Yeshua's male followers, born of Ivrit women, were probably already circumcised before they met him. And being raised on this *mitzvah*, these men thought the ritual would help them in attaining eternal life. Miryam always wondered where that left female spiritual aspirants. Ha-Rav exposed the misconception that all those who were circumcised would be guaranteed salvation. He said: "If circumcision helped you reach heaven, then you would have been born circumcised. Only the true circumcision in spirit is useful." Miryam had taken that to mean that snipping off one's attachment to and desires of the physical world brought one closer to the gate of heaven within the initiate. Clearly, Simeon did not understand this point in Ha-Rav's teachings – or else he ignored it.

Paulos continued. "Yacob decreed that we follow all the laws of cleanliness. In Antioch, I confronted Simeon for eating with a man who ate unclean meat, yet Simeon demands that all should be circumcised. I told him that the grown men of Antioch and Galatia did not care to be circumcised, and they are not bound by the covenants of Abraham. I am convinced by the Kyrios that nothing is unclean in and of itself. Something is unclean only to the person who considers it so."

"Rav Yeshua taught the same thing. But I suppose a thousand years of honoring the covenants of Abraham cannot be undone so easily, although I am surprised by Simeon and Yakob's mandate in light of the teachings."

Paulos nodded. "I heard that Christos called some of the priests hypocrites because they would clean the outside of the cup and platter, while inside they were full of greed and self-indulgence. He said that if they would first clean the inside of the cup, the outside would be clean also, for He who made that which is outside also made that which is inside."

Miryam stopped short of adding that the spiritual kingdom was inside the human vessel, for she wasn't sure how much he knew about the Way. "What happened when you protested the rite of circumcision?"

"I presented the Pillars with a different gospel, one that requires a circumcision in spirit only."

"Can you elaborate?"

"It is *kryptos*, secret. Only for the mature, the few, the elect. But I can tell you this: Abraham gave the covenants of cleanliness to his seed to help ward off misconduct. Now we have a savior who has died for our wrongdoings and will return to reunite us with Theos. We no longer need the law. I struggle to explain this in the letters I write to the ekklēsia."

"Was your gospel accepted in Yerushalayim?"

Paulos nodded. "We were given the right hand of fellowship. It was decided that I would go to the goyim – the uncircumcised – and Simeon and Yakob would go to the orthodox."

"Sounds like a fair compromise. I'm surprised they allowed you a mission at all."

"It was Yakob ultimately who made the decision. But it was never their plan to minister to the uncircumcised, only to bring them under the tabernacle, the big tent."

"A fitting job for a tentmaker."

Paulos nodded slowly at Miryam's joke. "You're beginning to understand me."

"And what did they ask of you in return?"

"That we maintain the torah of cleanliness as I explained earlier, and that we remember the poor. But circumcision isn't mandatory."

Remember the poor, Miryam repeated to herself. "Do you mean you were asked to send *mammon* to them?"

"I told them I was willing to send offerings from the ekklēsia."

An interesting trade, shekels for foreskin, Miryam thought. This was another area in which the students in Yerushalayim differed from Rav Yeshua. He never asked for offerings. Granted, Miryam and her siblings had used their inheritance to fund Rav Yeshua's journeys in the search and gathering of his own marked sheep. She followed him because she could not bear not being near him. They purchased room and board where available and often slept in the homes of students in exchange for an evening of discourse, but they certainly weren't beggars. He did suggest to some that they sell all their belongings and give their mammon to the poor because wealth was encumbering. Once one began to feel the Shefa, the Divine Flow, filling their beings, material things seemed to fall away. "Be envious of the desireless spirits," Rav Yeshua had said. "They will inherit the *Malchut Hashamayim*, the Kingdom of Heaven." But he never expected offerings be given to him and certainly not to the temple. "What do you receive in return for your ministry, Paulos?"

"Let the students share with their teacher in all good things," he answered, indignantly. "I assure you that I have suffered, and I have been comforted for the benefit of the ekklēsia."

What Paulos asks of his ekklēsia is his own business, she reckoned. *But Rav Yeshua's teachings are my business.* "I am still puzzled by the way you divide your students. Earlier you said that you have two gospels, one for the immature and one for the mature. Am I to understand that you teach the uncircumcised differently from the way you would teach the circumcised, that these are the mature?"

"You're taking this too literally. The uncircumcised include the Hellene, who have a long tradition of studying many different philosophies." Paulos glanced at Miryam, reading what she assumed was a look of confusion. "This has nothing to do with foreskin and everything to do with the ability to comprehend spirit. My teacher, Gamaliel, grouped his students into four different schools of fish."

"Fish?"

Paulos ticked off the kinds of fish on his fingers: "Filthy fish from poor parents who understand nothing. Clean fish of rich parents who can learn and understand everything. Fish from the Jordan River who can learn anything yet do not know how to respond. And fish from the sea of the Hellene who can learn everything and do know how to respond."

Interestingly, Miryam thought, the Hellene held the same attitude toward those who did not speak their language – barbarians all! "What kind of fish are you?"

"I am obligated to all fish. You see, the group from the Jordan River seeks signs that Christos was the prophesied messiah. The group from the Hellene sea seeks wisdom. I provide both the signs of prophecy and the wisdom."

"Let me see if I understand," Miryam said. "To the immature you preach ... ?"

"I preach righteousness through the story of the crucifixion and resurrection, that he died for our misconduct and will return in the flesh to redeem us."

"And to the mature ... ?"

"To the elect," Paulos interrupted, "I preach the secret gospel. The many call upon the Christos's name and receive his teaching outside of themselves, while the few are called by him within themselves."

"And the elect are ready to hear the gospel?" she asked.

"They hear it and understand it. But the immature can be transformed from the slavery under the laws of the *kosmos* to freedom as well. And, of course, the mature can fall asleep at any time and forget all they have learned."

"Does Ha-Rav rise from the dead and return in the secret gospel as well?"

"He returns to release the mature spirit from the elements and powers of the kosmos and reunite it with Theos. That is the wisdom given to me in revelation. I can tell you no more."

Despite his misconceptions, Paulos's perspective of Rav Yeshua's teachings intrigued Miryam. Either this was what Simeon and Yakob were teaching, or this self-appointed prophet had uncannily stumbled across a speck of Ha-Rav's hidden teachings. He, too, had both an outer teaching for the crowds of people that came to hear him speak and an inner teaching for his initiated disciples who were, indeed, mature in spirit ... or at least striving for maturity. Moreover, a master of the Word would assist in releasing the matured spirit from the elements and powers of the kosmos to reunite with Elah ... but while living. She sighed audibly, worried that Paulos had crafted all this to his own distorted understanding.

Miryam stood and bent to stir the dying embers in the fireplace. She realized her strange visitor was making her feel weary. "This has been enlightening, and I appreciate your coming to tell me about all that has transpired since we left Yerushalayim. But I don't think that's why you came here today. Is there something you want from me?"

"I have just one question." Paulos sat forward in his chair. "Are you mature or foolish?"

Mature ... or foolish, Miryam repeated to herself. Paulos had asked the question without shame or malice, and so she didn't feel purposely insulted. "I sometimes wonder that myself," she said with a smile. "You realize I'm a fish from the Jordan. In fact, my family was in the fish business."

"But you've relocated to the sea of the Hellene."

"I am still a fish out of water. I've yet to arrive in the Ocean of Elah."

"Who is being kryptos now?"

"Paulos, you said some priests seek outer praise for their rituals of devotion. But spirituality is a process of inner revelation, not of outer acknowledgment by others."

"Of course," Paulos responded, not to be intimidated.

"Simeon's miracles and signs not only seem contradictory but also unbelievable to me."

"Perhaps you can believe this: My two gospels have something in common ... both are based on the law of *agape*. Could not this world use more morality and love?"

"Ha-Rav himself would have embraced that point, especially in this time of gruesome Rhōmaioi pleasures and debauchery," she said, nodding deeply. "Have the Yehudi in Ephesus accepted either gospel?"

Paulos replied with a simple shrug of the shoulders.

"I'm not surprised," Miryam said. The Yehudi enjoyed a tenuous autonomy in Ephesus, unlike their kin in Yerushalayim. Their annual half-shekel offerings were allowed to go directly to *Beit HaMikdash,* the temple in Yerushalayim, without interference from the Rhōmaioi. They would not want that relationship broken by one self-proclaimed apostle. "How do the Hellene accept you?"

"Much more favorably. There are many *Yiray-Elohim* living here, those God-Fearers who admire the One God of the Ivrit yet reject the laws of purity. My friends from Korinthos have settled here and have opened their villa to an ekklēsia. That's good for the established Faithful, but without being welcome in the synagogue, I'm left with shouting on the steps of public forums to engage newcomers."

"Has that tactic been useful in other provinces?"

"I've been stoned, exiled, and put in bonds more times than I can count in the name of the Christos."

In the name of Christos. The only task Ha-Rav would have his students undertake in his name would be to break out of the bonds that had their souls chained to the world. "I would caution you to keep your enthusiasm in check here," she warned Paulos. "Hundreds of thousands of people squeeze into Ephesus like ants on over-ripe fruit, and indeed they come in search of some kind of nourishment for their bellies, minds, and spirits. It's a free polis, open to new ideas. Most of the locals themselves are dedicated to one idea or another: the goddess Artemis, the rituals of Dionysus, the mysteries of Demeter, the fire cult of Zoroaster, and Egyptian deities I've yet to investigate, not to mention schools of ancient philosophies and the formal worship of various Rhōmaioi emperors during the games."

"I understand."

"Do you? It's as if Ephesus is a cart piled high with different kinds of fruit, and if you come along and toss a melon on it, the cart will tip over. You might feel like it's just one piece of fruit, one small voice in a crowd, but if Ephesians feel their livelihood is threatened in any way, they will not hesitate to crush you like a grape."

"I've had worse things happen to me."

"Indeed." Miryam said, having no doubt that Paulos had rubbed many the wrong way. "The Rhōmaioi have a great admiration for the ancient culture of the Hellene. They allow different ways of worship to coexist in order to work together for the good of the polis as long as there is an understanding of who's in charge. In return, funds pour into the area for paved roads, aqueducts, and construction projects that provide work for all. No one wants that put in danger."

"This is the wealthiest polis in the region, and I can create quite a foothold here for the Way. But you are right. No one will be interested in sacrificing their well-being if made a spectacle of. This is why private homes for worship and study are less of a threat to both the seekers and the authorities. You might consider allowing us to meet in your home."

Miryam wasn't expecting that suggestion. "Opening myself to scrutiny would indeed make me a fool, would it not? Or have you already judged my spiritual aptitude?"

Paulos shook his head.

"Paulos, I don't share your vision," she said. "Rav Yeshua had his followers while he was alive. Besides, my sister and I have enjoyed anonymity here. Yeshua was persecuted, remember?"

"You must forgive my urgency. Christos's return is imminent, and I don't feel there is much time to spread the gospel before he appears."

"Paulos, Rav Yeshua won't be returning. At least not in the way you preach." As soon as she said that, Miryam knew she had gone too far, for the statement unnerved him.

Frustrated, Paulos swiftly drank the remains of his t'u in one gulp and then stood suddenly, sending the bowl to the brick floor where it splintered into many pieces. As he bent to clean up the mess, he cut his finger on a shard.

Martha appeared in the doorway, but Miryam shook her head as she knelt next to Paulos. She took the shards from his hand and carefully scooped the other fragments into her palla. She transferred the pieces onto the tray and then wiped the trickle of blood from his finger with a corner of the same palla. As she did so, she began to understand something of Paulos's nervousness.

Paulos accepted her attention, and then they both returned to their chairs without wholly acknowledging what just happened. He sighed deeply. "You were the one he loved most, or so say some of the apostles. Some say you were the first to see Christos after he rose from the dead, and not Simeon."

Miryam shook her head. "You continue to surprise me with your foreknowledge of me and your special words and your stories of raising the dead like magic." She lowered her voice to just above a whisper so as not to rattle the man's state of mind any further. "I don't know who told you that, but it isn't as one might think. Along the way of spirituality, there are certain ... junctures ... and I'm afraid these are often interpreted as real-life, bodily events."

"Ah, the *logos* of the cross," Paulos said in agreement.

"Logos?" She knew the Hellene word, but didn't understand it in this context.

Paulos nodded. "The cross is the means by which Christos died and resurrected. I teach the wisdom of the cross. What is folly to the godless, is divine power to those of us who are saved." He was on familiar ground now and looked much calmer than a moment earlier. In fact, he was almost smiling.

Logos of the cross, Miryam repeated to herself. Of everything Paulos had said, this concept intrigued her most.

Paulos must have caught that, for he said, "I would like to submit my gospel to you."

"Why? For my approval? Have you not told me everything?"

"Let us just say an exchange might be mutually beneficial. I have so much more to tell you."

An exchange? Was he implying that she would have something to learn from his revelations, or had the well run dry and he was looking for ways to replenish the water and make it come alive again? Miryam turned inward to Ravi: *What would You have me do?* When no immediate answer came, she knew she would have to wait and contemplate the matter. "I have a feeling you're a man of many contradictions. That is a sign of ... depth." She wanted to add "of much inner turmoil" to her assessment, but selected the more diplomatic approach. Honey was more successful than vinegar in matters of spirit.

He stood and approached her, taking her hands into his but more gently this time. "You cared for the son of Theos." He turned the hands over and politely kissed them as if she were royalty, intimately known to him. "And now you must care for his legacy."

Miryam gingerly withdrew her hands and led him to the door. "I will let you know when I've made a decision."

"Shall I come to you?"

"I will meet you in Ephesus. I suspect you won't be too hard to find."

"I am staying with my Korinthos friends, Aquila and his wife, Priscilla. They are also tentmakers and live in the Embolos on the Mount Pion side. Ask for directions in the rug shop closest to the agora."

Miryam was impressed. The Embolos was the merchant's sector and home to much of Ephesus's upper class. "One more thing, Paulos, before you go." Miryam held him lightly by the elbow.

"What is that?"

"If, as you say, Rav Yeshua is the messiah, why had you not heard of him when you trained in the temple at Yerushalayim? I should think such a great man would be familiar to everyone."

Paulos was speechless, for once. He recovered quickly. "My time to hear of him was not until later when I met him on the road to Damascus, as I explained."

"I think the reason why you hadn't heard of him was because Rav Yeshua was a humble master to just a few students. He said that only those who have the eyes to see and the ears to hear would know the Kingdom of Elah."

"I would agree with you. I have seen the Light and have heard the Voice."

"Light has replaced Might with you. You once wished to purge all believers from the world, and now you want everyone to become one." Miryam raised a hand. "This will keep until we meet again. Do be careful."

He nodded and followed Miryam through the door. Martha was waiting for them in the garden and handed him a muslin bag full of herbs. "I've made you a poultice of t'u and the roots, petals, and leaves of several plants. Steep it in a cup of boiling hot water. If you hold it against your sores, it should draw out the infection."

Paulos accepted the bag with some embarrassment, bowed his head to both women, and exited down the path.

Once he was gone, Martha turned to Miryam for her opinion of Paulos.

"He drives two teams of horses at once," Miryam said without hesitation. "He has one foot in each chariot, and it may split him in half." She seated herself on a stone bench in the garden and placed her head in her hands for a moment. "Yet he seems to grasp some subtle spiritual principles, as if someone has been teaching him."

"He was a Pharisee, after all," Martha said.

"But he has started his own Way, while trying to also pay allegiance to the Pillars in Yerushalayim. None other than Simeon, Yakob, and Johanan. Did you hear?"

Martha sat next to her. "Ah, the Rock and the Sons of Thunder, as Ha-Rav called them. Why do you suppose Paulos calls them the Pillars?"

"Maybe that's what they call themselves."

"He could be referring to the Three Pillars of Righteousness: Follow the Torah, serve Yěhovah, and perform acts of loving kindness."

Miryam shrugged. "If that's their mission, then I endorse it, but I am more appalled by what Simeon and the others have done to the rest of Ha-Rav's teachings. As for Paulos? He clearly loves the *idea* of Rav Yeshua, even if he does not know the full truth, but I sense danger in him and for him."

"Nothing can be done about it now," Martha said. She stood and headed for the house. "I'm having another cup of t'u."

"I'm right behind you."

Three

Early next morning, Miryam and Martha walked through the woods on the hillside path that afforded tree-framed views of the sea to the west. Even after all these years, the sight caught Miryam's breath because of what it promised to represent as the Source of Elah. But now she was preoccupied by the strange events of the previous day: the contemplation on the Word, the verse she'd written on papyrus, and the visit by Paulos. She realized the vision she'd had in her morning contemplation of a scarred-face man may have been Ravi's warning about Paulos. Was there a spiritual lesson she had missed? There were few chance events on the inner Way.

And what a striking contrast it was between the pure, direct, immediate commune with the Word and Paulos's worship of a man he never knew, of a man now long gone, however heartfelt that worship and feeling of closeness it was to Paulos. Miryam wished this spiritual intimacy for everyone, while understanding how crucial baby steps toward the All were. For without learning to devote oneself to a spiritual way, and then losing that devotion when the illusion of that way was revealed, would the neshama – the soul – yearn for Truth. Only then would the true way appear in all its glory.

Martha, naturally a talkative woman, kept silent. Miryam appreciated Martha's intuitive company, her uncanny sense of knowing just when to engage in conversation on spiritual topics, when to discuss the weather or shopping in the agora at Ephesus, and when to say absolutely nothing. What Miryam admired most about Martha was the natural charm and grace she had on people and her undying service to others. There was a time when Martha may have resented her sister's devotional following of the Word, that is, until she began to feel it for herself.

Paulos troubled Miryam. His undying service was of a different nature, almost compulsive, frenzied, breathless. He was also self-consumed. In Ivrit the word for vanity was *havel*. When Kaïn killed his brother Havel, he was figuratively killing his own vanity. Miryam liked the Hellene word for it – *hubris* – and Paulos's hubris was overt. She did not understand Paulos's need to gather converts and to do so over such an enormous territory as the Imperium Romanum.

More troublesome was what Paulos represented. Without him knowing it, he had shown Miryam the current status of the teachings and how they had evolved into something quite different from what Rav Yeshua had taught. What's more, the idea of Yeshua as an accomplished master had turned into something quite different from who he truly was – as if what he was wasn't enough! She hadn't seen Simeon or Yakob for so long, nor had she seen any of Rav Yeshua's other closest students for that matter. Clearly, they had continued teaching and recruiting new initiates in Yerushalayim, but did they go along with Paulos's scheme of converting *everyone*? Rav Yeshua had left strict instructions to spread the seed of hope and tolerance into the world bereft of morality but not to bring any new students into the flock, unless his successor was ready to do so. Other readied souls would have to seek out other masters. Did Simeon truly understand this, the major point of the teachings? Had he returned to traditional covenants? Was he indeed insisting on circumcision, to which Paulos so intensely objected?

Miryam didn't have to travel to Yerushalayim to find out the answers to these questions because it all sounded so familiar. She recalled how Simeon continuously challenged Rav Yeshua on these subjects, especially during his daily talks with his disciples. One day in particular stuck out in her mind. This day was significant, for everything changed after that.

Some twenty men and women of various ages sat around Ha-Rav on a craggy hillside overlooking the Sea of Galilee, enjoying the sun and his wisdom. He suddenly stopped mid-sentence and stared at Simeon. Everyone turned their heads toward the student in question. "Do you have something to add to what I am saying, Simeon Kephas?"

Simeon had yet to say a word, but Rav must have perceived some confusion, some kind of longing in his young face. These interludes, these interruptions in the master's discourses, were always striking, and the students knew something significant was about to be revealed. They all knew that when he referred to his young student as "Kephas," the Rock, in response to his given name "Simeon," meaning "to hear," he was implying that although he heard the master's instructions, he failed to understand them.

Simeon stood, his head bowed, his eyes downcast. "Behold, the days come, says Yĕhovah, that I will raise unto David a righteous branch of fruitfulness and plenty, and a king shall reign and prosper, and shall execute judgment and justice on earth."

"You can recite the sefer of Yirmĕyah. You are to be commended. Didn't we put this subject to rest the last time we discussed it, if not the time before that?" Rav Yeshua stood before Simeon with hands on hips, smiling his smile of warning not to pursue this challenge further.

But Simeon wasn't to surrender on this his favorite subject. "In His days Yehudah shall be saved," he continued reciting. "And Yisrael shall dwell safely, and He shall be called our Lord of Righteousness."

"The prophet Yirmĕyah expressing a yearning for the return of the dynasty after being usurped by invaders," Ha-Rav responded. "I'm not descended from David. Isn't that required to fulfill the prophecy?"

"Behold, the days come, says Yĕhovah, that I will make a new covenant with the house of Yisrael and with the house of Yehudah." Tears were now streaming down Simeon's face as he defied his teacher.

Rav Yeshua's usual joviality vanished, and in its place a paternal sternness exuded from his expressions and posture. "Yirmĕyah on the broken covenant Abraham had made with Yĕhovah. The scriptures tell of many pledges Yĕhovah has made with the people, requiring certain conduct from them in return. To Noah, He promised that He would never again destroy the earth with a flood. He promised Abraham that he would father a great nation, provided Abraham sealed the covenant by circumcising all males of that nation. To Moses, Yĕhovah promised that Yisrael would reach the Promised Land, but they must obey hundreds of commandments in return. Through Yirměyah, He made an everlasting covenant with Yisreal, forgiving all transgressions, provided they never depart from Him. Tell me, Simeon, what promise would I negotiate with you, and what outcome would I procure in return?"

Simeon didn't hesitate, not that he was undaunted by Ha-Rav, but that he already had some ideas. "That we would resist dominion over us by the Rhōmaioi, and that we go back to obeying the traditional torah of Yisrael."

"And what will you get out of returning to tradition and obeying the torah?"

"Eternal salvation at the end of days." Simeon was looking Yeshua straight in the eye, not quivering like a rabbit, but challenging like a goat with horns ready to butt.

"I *am* giving you eternal salvation." Ha-Rav was clearly not pleased. He'd dealt with Simeon's misunderstandings before. "Do you think following all 613 commandants will get you into the Malchut Hashamayim?"

Simeon nodded.

"Then, you have missed my teachings. Only by following Ha-Rav's instructions can you enter the Kingdom. Why don't you just go live with the Essenes? I believe you will find them more aligned to your way of thinking."

Simeon flung his arms in exasperation. "Rav Yeshua, you know I was with them at Qumran for five years."

"Then, why did you leave them?"

The students continued to take in the exchange, turning their heads this way and that as if watching a Rhōmaioi game. Ha-Rav had been down this road before with Simeon, but for Simeon it was always the first time, and it would continue to be until he understood the nature of Rav Yeshua's teachings. Simeon could not answer his question.

Rav Yeshua answered it for him: "Because despite the community's strict adherence to traditional laws, to their vows of celibacy, their reputation for miracle healings, and their trance-inducing rituals that make them think they are riding chariots across the heavens ... you didn't feel filled. Isn't that correct?"

Simeon hung his head and nodded, then revived quickly. "We could restore Yehudah's power and tradition, and have eternal salvation for all!"

"Yisrael has been without a king and without sovereignty for centuries. Why now?"

"Because of taxes, the rich are getting richer and the poor, poorer. No one can even enter the temple without paying a tax to the high priest or without buying a lamb to sacrifice on the altar."

"And so now you wish to sacrifice your master?" Rav Yeshua's voice boomed as he finally understood the essence of Simeon's request.

Simeon shook his head. "Lo, of course not."

"That's what will happen. If I were to lead an uprising, I would be executed. I am not a leader or a warrior." He crossed to Simeon and put a hand on his shoulder. "Your devotion is apparent but misplaced. Lift your eyes unto the hills, Simeon, not unto me. Broaden your view so that you can see yourself more clearly. I appreciate your enthusiasm for helping with Abba's mission, but I will not have you encouraging my disciples to become zealots. I know the Yehudi are living under the heavy arm of the Rhōmaioi. The Beit HaMikdash, which should be a refuge for worship, is under constant struggle between the elite Sadducees who administer it at the pleasure of the Rhōmaioi and the Pharisees who are working to reform it. I know there are rebels from all factions who mean to deliver the people from Rhōmaioi tyranny. Behold, the days come, when I deliver your neshama, your soul, to Malchut Hashamayim. Not the people of Yisrael, nor Yehudah. Yours! Now sit down."

But Simeon continued to stand, trembling now. "Moses and Yĕshayah were also reluctant prophets."

"My mission differs from theirs."

"You have always said you come not to bring peace, but a sword."

Rav Yeshua turned his back to Simeon again and paced in front of the group, then suddenly turned and spoke so abruptly, it made all of the students thankful they weren't being held at this sword's edge – at least not this time. "With this sword you will cut off your own head so that you will enter the Kingdom. That is my covenant, Simeon Kephas! That is the cup I drink from."

Miryam saw the resolve in Simeon's face and the spiritual fury in Rav Yeshua's eyes. Was Simeon foolish enough to think he could convince Ha-Rav to lead a rebellion?

"Simeon, be zealous, ayn, but be zealous about the Memra, the Word, calling you from within." He turned away from Simeon and faced the group. The wind played in Ha-Rav's short, thick brown curls, the sun glinted in his brown eyes and deepened his olive complexion. "Please understand, I do not care about earthly taxes and politics, only the politics of returning the neshama back to its original glory. I am not the Essene Teacher of Righteousness wishing to reform the temple to the Torah. Abba is not the Yĕhovah of history like Abraham. He is the Yĕhovah of eternity. His only interest is in placing you on your own throne, but only when you are matured." He stopped and faced Simeon again. "I took you as a student because you said you were ready. Now you're telling me that you want to liberate the Yehudi from the Rhōmaioi and reform the temple. The only temple you should be interested in is that of your own body and what lives inside it. Worship that. Reform that. Liberate that."

Defeated at last, Simeon finally sat down, but Miryam knew the issue wasn't resolved for him, nor would it be resolved any time soon. In her experience, such concerns were brought to the surface so that the student could see one's own flaws and then turn water into wine, as Ha-Rav was fond of saying; that is, wash the impurities in the intoxicating elixir of the divine Shefa.

"This is why I say this to you, that you must know yourselves," Ha-Rav said, continuing his discourse before Simeon's interruption. "For the Malchut Hashamayim is like a bushel of grain that sprouted in a field. And when it ripened, it scattered its fruit and, in turn, filled the field with more grain for another year. Be zealous to reap for yourselves a bushel of life in order that you may be filled with the Kingdom. Now, how do you become filled with the Kingdom?"

Miryam spoke up: "Through *zakar*, *devakut*, and *hakshavah*."

"Ayn," Yeshua said. "Let's take them one by one. Zakar is remembrance. Remember Ravi and repeat your secret words in sweet anticipation. Constantly practice feeling Ravi's Shechinah, His Presence, while repeating your secret words. Yĕshayah says, 'In the Way of Judgments we have yearned for Yĕhovah; the desire of soul is for the Name and remembrance of Yĕhovah.' Or from *Psalms*: 'I call to remembrance my Song in the night. I commune with my own heart, while my spirit searches with diligence.' And what is devakut?"

This time Martha rose before Miryam had a chance to answer. "Devotion, to cling, to cleave, to dwell on the Word with the Inner Eye. From *Psalms*: 'I rise early at dawn, and cry. I dwell in Your Word. My eyes stay open during the night, and watch that I might commune with Your Word.'"

Ha-Rav raised both hands palms-up, from his waist to his face. "Once you have touched the Shefa and feel it welling up within you, you must stay with it for as long as you can. Devakut comes from the word *davak*, which means glue. Stick with the Inner Rav in the way that Yob's bones stuck to his skin, and you will stay alive. Do this in remembrance of the Inner Rav so that some day you will come *panim El-Panim*, face to Face with Him. This is what Yakob called it when he rose to face Elohim, and his 'neshama was preserved.' This leads to the third stage."

"Hakshavah," Simeon muttered into his chest, perhaps to show that although he was still sore from the confrontation, he knew the teachings. "Listening to the Word."

Ha-Rav nodded matter-of-factly, refusing to placate him. "Dwell in the garden with the Comforter until you can hear His Voice. Hakshavah means to listen intently and with all of your attention so that you can hear Ravi's instructions."

The disciples were silent as they imagined the stages of coming face to Face with Elah. He'd told them about the spiritual practices of remembrance, devotion, and listening many times, but it always sounded different. All that could be heard were some goats bleating in the distance and a breeze blowing through surrounding olive tree leaves. Rav Yeshua seated himself on the ground in the center of the group, but spoke directly to Simeon. "You may remember that Yĕhovah told Yirmĕyah to stand at the gate of Yĕhovah's house and hear the Word. The scriptures say that Yirmĕyah was told to proclaim this commandment to all of Yisrael who enter there to worship, but there is a secret meaning. The gate can refer to an ornate palace, a temple, or even heaven itself." Yeshua placed the tips of his fingers on his forehead, between and just above his two eyes. "The ancient ravs say in truth that the sacred gate is here, and it is not ornate, but plain and narrow like a wicket gate. Few be there who find it. To enter through here, you must devoid yourself of all vanity by concentrating upon the Word of Elah. As you do this, you will raise your powers and begin to feel His love and sense His instruction. After many years of this, you will begin to hear His divine melodies and rise through all of the palaces in His house. You must do this every day in order to become mature. I will tell you this: It is easier to thread a needle with a *gamal* than for a rich man to enter the Malchut Hashamayim."

The students howled with laughter at Ha-Rav's sudden joke. "Gamal" referred to either a camel or a ship's braided rope, depending on how it was pronounced. He was saying that neither a rope nor a camel could be shoved through the eye of a needle, nor could a man buy his way through the wicket gate, nor could a smart man reason his way into heaven. The only way through the narrow gate of heaven was *ahab*, the love of one's rav. Everything Ha-Rav said always contained at least two meanings – the fruit above the earth tender for plucking, and the roots hidden in the dirt for which the students had to dig deep.

Many times over the years Miryam wondered why events had unraveled as they had, and so rapidly. One day Rav Yeshua happily basked with them in the holiday fervor of *Pesach* in Yerushalayim, and nearly the next day he was gone. There was a ruckus in the temple, something about overturned currency exchange tables. The Rhōmaioi later arrested Rav Yeshua for the crime, but he hadn't committed that crime. Miryam knew that the rebels had used Rav Yeshua as a scapegoat to promote their cause. Ha-Rav would be the anointed king, the *melek* of Yisrael, who would drive out the Rhōmaioi, or so this radical faction had thought. Even if they could be convinced that this dream of Yeshua as a divine king wasn't true, they could still persuade others to believe it in order to stand up to the Rhōmaioi.

Could the Rhōmaioi possibly be threatened by a single teacher and his band of students? Miryam had wondered. There were many such religious fanatics wandering the streets of Yerushalayim, and even the Pharisees were splintered into this or that house of interpretation of the Torah. Surely Rav Yeshua's popularity to ever-growing groups of people wasn't a threat to Augustus Caesar's monolithic legion, power, and wealth. Rav Yeshua never voiced an interest in conquering the Empire with his small army of disarmed men and women followers, neither in public nor in private, and if Simeon had just stopped to think about it, he would see that the idea was preposterous. Leave to the world that which belonged to the world and all human endeavors it encompassed, Ha-Rav often said. He was only interested in matters of the spirit.

Miryam and her siblings knew that the arrest, though unfounded, would put Rav Yeshua's talmidim at risk because their group was now out in the open. They would always be watched by soldiers for any hint of wrongdoing. Even if he were released, he would always be under suspicion. A true master crowned by Elah could take care of himself, or he was nothing. It was Lazarus who said it first: If Rav Yeshua were to teach among current attitudes, he would invite danger to his flock and defeat the purpose of his mission. Something had to be done.

The evening of his arrest, Rav Yeshua had met with his disciples on *Har Zayith*, the Mount of Olives, for what would be their last time together. Rav Yeshua warned them that his time with them would be short. "As long as I am with you, give heed to me and obey me," he had said. "But when I am to depart from you, remember me. And remember me because I was with you before you even perceived me within yourself."

This had been his only mandate – zakar. The students did not pay as much attention to this instruction of remembrance as it deserved, considering that it was to be his final instruction, for when it came right down to it, Ha-Rav had been saying this all along. Remember me, not Rav Yeshua the person, but

Ravi, Ha-Rav within. Die? Even if the man died, his Spirit would never die within his disciples. That was Abba's promise of the Word.

The spiritual grace that had come to them that evening on the Mount of Olives was palpable, a strong, inner vibration of love. Each student present was so completely immersed in the ocean of Shefa that the Rhōmaioi could have descended upon them, and no one would have been bothered, for it wouldn't have seemed real next to that which was growing within them.

The Rhōmaioi soldiers did come late that evening and arrest Rav Yeshua at the place where olives are pressed at the foot of the mountain.

Miryam was not present for the arrest, for she and Martha had already retired to their sleeping quarters, but when she heard of it, she collapsed to the floor in interior zakar – white-knuckled zakar – keeping the wolves of her own worry and fear at bay to make room for the larger transfiguration on high. To her wonder, a miracle occurred; she did not plummet to the depths of despair. Something was transpiring within her, and wondrously she had no trouble reconciling that with the terrifying, tragic event that was taking place in the world outside of herself. All she could do was go in, go in. Miryam was vaguely aware of people checking in on her, periodically bringing her small meals of bread, milk, and fish, but the force that kept her inside herself was just too strong to be pulled out for social amenities, bodily needs, or even tragedy. Time was no longer of concern either, though she was aware of the morning sun's first light streaming through the boarded windows, only to recede in the evening. The air in the room became rare from the candlelight vigil that someone, probably Martha, held for Ha-Rav. She continued to sit in the corner, wrapped in a black shawl like a raven in deep slumber, yet she felt more awake than any time in her life.

At last she heard Simeon's voice in the hallway, no doubt come to be consoled about Ha-Rav's imprisonment by the Rhōmaioi. She heard the door creak open and closed. She could sense his presence, sense him staring at her, perhaps deciding whether to disturb her contemplation or not. She wondered that herself. She opened her eyes but remained seated cross-legged on the floor. "Simeon," she whispered. "We have been expecting you." She beckoned him closer.

He approached and knelt in front of her cautiously, as if she were far more delicate than she knew herself to be. "Martha says you haven't eaten for days. You don't look as pale and wan as I thought you might, being cooped up in here so long." Simeon could not conceal his disapproval.

Miryam smiled wryly. "Would you rather I be conspiring to free Ha-Rav? What can I, a mere woman, do?"

"That's not what I meant. We are concerned that you have taken it too hard."

"I have never been more healthy and content in my life. The Shefa is all the food and sleep I need."

This took Simeon aback. "Do you not fear for his life?"

"He is Ha-Rav." For disciples, no further explanation should be needed, and yet Simeon never understood the reach of Rav Yeshua's power. "Tell me, Simeon, how are you faring?"

"I'm heartbroken. We all are." He held his face in his hands. "Yakob and I have been nosing around the Temple. The high council refuses to try the case because it is a holy day and have turned the matter over to the Rhōmaioi. Miryam, the gossip is that they will execute him."

"This is partly your doing, is it not?"

Simeon shook his head. "There are those who believe he is truly the prophesied messiah. I thought I believed that too, but if he were, how could he allow this to happen to himself?"

"Simeon, have you not felt the Shefa just as he promised?"

Simeon shrugged and nodded.

"Then, how can you believe that there is not some greater purpose being served by what he is undergoing, by what we are all undergoing? He is just a teacher for a chosen few, those of us who are willing and ready to accept and abide by his teaching, but he cannot continue teaching as long as zealous men desire to force him into leading a rebellion."

"And what is wrong with that? What is wrong with Rav Yeshua liberating the Yehudi from Rhōmaioi power? It would take a charismatic leader like him to unite our efforts."

All Simeon could see were the colorful threads that had been woven into a grand illusion, Miryam thought. He could see the designers who plotted to put Rav Yeshua in power, but he missed the larger tapestry of the divine Power that promised to some day place a laurel wreath upon his own soul. "Hasn't he always told us that he is in this world, but not of it? He has no desire to participate in politics, as callous as that sounds. He is here only to help us liberate ourselves. But this political strife may tear him in half, and then where would we be?"

"I can't believe that as loving as Rav Yeshua is that he wouldn't want to help Yisrael." He stood and paced the room. "Look, I've spoken with a few friends who say they can help free him from the guard."

"Stop right there. That's not a good idea. Simeon, you must learn to consider the effects of your own actions. Such a rebel group would be killed almost immediately, or, if successful, wouldn't the Rhōmaioi come after all of us? They'll brush us off like flies. Or worse, execute us on display in one of their stadiums."

"Ayn, you're right. What about your brother, Lazarus? He has friends in high places. Can't they bribe someone to speak to Herod?"

"And then Yeshua and Lazarus would be indebted to Herod. How would that be perceived? Oy, Simeon, do you not see?"

Simeon was red with anger, barely able to contain himself. Clearly, he hated being told that he couldn't see. He could see, all right. He could see that the Rhōmaioi were about to kill his beloved master, and it might be his fault. She wondered if he was regretting his political ambitions.

"Are you afraid for him or for yourself?"

Simeon had no answer, and she expected none. From within, she heard the words, "Speak to Simeon the truth." It wasn't that she heard it, so much as she felt it like a breeze of awareness. "Simeon, I must tell you. Ha-Rav will not be returning to us here."

"How do you know that?" Simeon looked incredulous. "So you think they will release him? Are you certain of this?"

"I know nothing with any certainty, except Rav Yeshua's love for each of us."

"You speak in circles. If they don't execute him, then he will return to us, correct?"

Miryam shook her head as if to console a child, and Simeon subtly resented being treated in such a way. Of all the students, Simeon thought himself to be the most astute, and that was his downfall, she thought.

"We have become too dependent on him," she said. "We have never understood his teachings. He must leave us to save us." She didn't know how she knew this truth, but she was convinced of it.

Confused, angered, Simeon fought the eruption before he lashed out at her. "Miryam, the lack of sleep and nourishment has made you weak. You're talking nonsense."

Miryam stayed neutral, something that would otherwise be impossible if it were not for the Shefa keeping her buoyant. "Rav Yeshua has told us many times that he lives within each of us, that the kingdom is inside us. We have become too attached to his face, his touch, his company to ever see him within ourselves."

"Miryam, he is facing execution, and all you can talk about is the spiritual."

"Simeon, how many times has he told us that he who has the ears to hear and eyes to see will understand? What do you think he means by that?"

Miryam watched the angered Simeon turn and leave the room. He did not understand, she thought, and she could empathize with him. As usual she was two people: Part of her sensed that whatever was happening to Rav Yeshua was for the betterment of his students, and the knowledge of it allowed her to rise above it. The other part of herself felt victimized and sad that her world was about to change. It was difficult for even her to see the larger scheme. Ever since the guards arrested Rav Yeshua in the garden, she had been in deep contemplation petitioning for clarity.

Ha-Rav had repeatedly taught her to sit quietly every day with eyes closed, her attention on the shepherd's gate in the middle of her forehead. He had told her that with constant and consistent practice, she would no longer see darkness; she would see a blue star, orchards of light, a sun, a moon, and, finally, his radiant glory. She would eventually hear sounds, like a big bell gonging or a conch shell moaning, and these sounds would lead her through the wicket gate. If she couldn't hear the sounds, she would certainly feel them with her innate spiritual senses.

What Rav Yeshua had promised her was beginning to come true. The blue star had appeared on her inner horizon behind closed eyes. She could see – or sense – an eternal flame glowing within her, which seemed to set her on fire and illuminate her inner worlds. And lately she saw Ravi – Rav Yeshua's inner form – within herself, his golden brown eyes so close to her own eyes that she mistakenly thought he was actually present in the flesh and peering at her. Since her initiation she had occasionally felt an ocean wave of love, pure love, and though that periodic love had grown steadily stronger, it wasn't until recently that she felt that love every time she allowed herself to feel it. It wasn't like the love she felt for Yeshua the man—that was complicated. Lo, it was like being loved from the inside out, like wearing veils of soft drum beats, like being drunk on wine, like the very act of creation itself in which one's own self completely and joyously evaporates in the vapors of pure Love. That was Shefa, the Divine Flow, and the Memra, the Divine Word.

At last she was indeed developing the spiritual ears to hear and the eyes to see.

Martha entered the room and closed the door behind her. Miryam stood, crossed to a wash basin, and splashed water over her face with cupped hands. "Simeon is truly afraid for Rav Yeshua. There's already talk of an execution." She toweled her face with her palla and turned toward Martha.

"Lazarus was just here. He's heard from Yosef." Yosef of Arimathaea, a secret follower of Ha-Rav who was also a Pharisee and a member of the high council, had developed a plan. He would try to persuade his friend Pontius Pilate to release Rav Yeshua as a favor, but to time the release on the same day that they crucified prisoners so that he could disappear during the commotion. In return he would promise that Rav Yeshua would leave the region, never to take up residence or teaching in the province again. "The Rhōmaioi authority has agreed to the plan," Martha said glumly.

Miryam's heart skipped a beat. Would there be a glimmer of hope that they could all return to their studies and practices before this incident? "And Ha-Rav has gone along with this?"

"Apparently the authorities are convinced he is not interested in becoming king and leading an impossible political takeover."

"I hope so, Martha. I am not ready to live without him yet."

Martha turned to Miryam and put her hands on her sister's shoulders, looking her squarely in the eye. "His life will be spared, but he will be leaving us, and to that you must surrender."

Ayn, ayn, she knew she had to let him go.

The sisters didn't have long to wait. Simeon returned to the house the next morning, grief-stricken and out of breath. "There's word in the streets that the Rhōmaioi plan to stage a crucifixion today!" he exclaimed as Miryam led him to the hearth. For the ruse to succeed, it had been important to keep the plan a secret to everyone but Miryam's family. She ladled water for him, and when he refused it, she drank it herself.

"Is Rav Yeshua ... ?" He was not to be put to death, but she wasn't sure she could trust the Rhōmaioi to keep their word.

"I tried to find out, but no luck. Soldiers are embedding a new post on Golgotha right now."

As she felt herself succumbing to the fear, she began silently chanting the secret words of her initiation, the process by which she regained her senses. "The Rhōmaioi usually don't crucify for lesser crimes, just slaves and enemies of state they mean to humiliate."

"And rebels. Why wouldn't they want to humiliate Ha-Rav?" he asked indignantly, as if she of all people should understand their master's status and threat to the empire.

She couldn't let herself go down the path of argument once again with Simeon, but even her own *nefesh*, her mind, began having the same argument with herself: *But what if Simeon is right? Lo, not possible.* As much as she loathed doing so, she suggested they go and watch the execution to confirm whether Ha-Rav was the one to be crucified – or not.

Miryam, Martha, Simeon, and other students pushed their way through the crowds to the streetside in time to see a broken-down, bloodied man slog past them carrying a solid wooden beam across his shoulders. Whether or not the man was Ha-Rav, despite the reasoning telling her differently, she didn't want to look, for she couldn't bear to have the image seared in her mind for eternity. She forced herself to look, anyway. The man was the same build and height as Rav Yeshua, but he was unrecognizable from the disfiguring flagellation he'd received earlier. Simeon and the others called to him as he passed by. "Rav Yeshua! Rav Yeshua!" The man never looked up as he tried to protect himself from a barrage of stones.

Spellbound, the students and the sisters were carried along the streets to Golgotha by the moving crowd. Fear and grief consumed Miryam – all inner sight and comfort from Ravi disintegrated by the immediacy of this violence before her physical eyes. Once on the hill, the crowd spread out. The students watched in horror as the soldiers centered the crossbeam on the post and then pulled the broken man upward onto the apparatus by ropes. Standing on scaffolding, the soldiers lashed the prisoner's arms to either end of the crossbeam and then lashed his feet to the post. Though unrecognizable, the agony on the man's face was nonetheless apparent even from this distance. It was all Miryam could bear. She crumpled to her knees and wailed uncontrollably.

Martha wrapped a robe around Miryam's shoulders and drew her to her protective chest in one movement. "It isn't Ha-Rav," she whispered. She could hear Martha say to the others, "Leave here now. We can do nothing for this man. Go find a quiet corner to grieve and focus on Ravi at the inner gate within your beings. Soon, soon, we will talk."

Martha's statement snapped Miryam's attention back to center, and she pulled herself up from the ground, now recomposed. She looked at the stricken faces gathered around them, their shoulders hunched over in despair. "Ayn," she chimed in. "Ha-Rav told us to remember him, remember him because he knew us long before we could perceive him within ourselves. How can that kind of power die? It can't. Go and witness it birthing inside you."

Miryam and Martha returned to their contemplative vigil at Yosef's house to remember and to await their next step. Their wait was not long. With a quick knock on the door, Lazarus walked into the room. "It is done," he said, bowing his head.

"Rav Yeshua – he is safe?" Miryam had to ask.

"Of course, he is safe. Now comes the most difficult part."

Miryam stiffened. She knew what was coming next, and she didn't think she could bare it. "We must anoint the body."

"It is important to maintain the prisoner's secret identity, and we owe it to him for using him in this way. I've arranged to have the body brought to a private tomb on my property."

Martha stood first. "Come along, Miryam."

They followed Yosef into the grotto to attend to the corpse while Lazarus stayed with the guards at the tomb's opening. The bloodied carcass had been stretched out on a stone bench as best as could be managed. Martha tried removing the man's loin cloth, but it was stuck in dried blood. They filled bowls from a barrel full of water and poured it on the skin to rid it of as much of the blood as was possible before wrapping the body in a long sheet of white linen dipped in a mixture of myrrh and aloes. Though they had dressed their grandfather, father, and Miryam's young husband for burial, nothing prepared them for this gruesome task. At the same time, Miryam was reassured that Ha-Rav was not physically present in this cave, though his glorified form exuded from every pore of her own body. The sisters returned to their quarters in Yosef's villa and collapsed into a deep sleep.

Miryam arose at dawn the next day and walked through the garden, finding a boulder where she could sit and re-center her attention, but she could not help but cry.

"Woman, why do you weep?"

She turned toward the sound of Rav Yeshua's voice to see a hooded man standing before her. So ecstatic to see him alive, she threw herself at him. He wrapped his strong arms around her shoulders and back, placing her head on his chest. He felt very much alive. "Why do you weep?" he whispered.

"My mind plays tricks on me. I know you are alive. I can touch you, but I know you are also dead to me. I will never see you again."

"Go ahead and grieve. Part of you has died, the part that is attached to your physical being and mine. If you remain attached to the flesh, your spirit will never rise to me. That is the message of this crucifixion, only it is *your* lower vestige that is being crucified, not your master's." He tilted her face upward and gazed into her eyes in the way only he could gaze. It was not Yeshua the man looking at her, but the power of Elah gazing at her through the man's flamelit eyes.

"Where will you go?"

"You know I can't tell you. It is dangerous for all of us now. The Rhōmaioi have only so much patience. They were willing to release me as long as I promised to leave Yehudah. I will tell you this ... this business will not stop Elah from searching for His marked sheep. I will continue traveling and teaching and telling stories – under a different identity, of course."

"Why can't we go with you?"

"Some of the students are not ready for the Way of Truth. I know that now. They will just start this trouble over again."

"But why can't Martha, Lazarus, and I go with you? Are we not ready?"

"If we all travel as a group and gather new students together, we will draw attention. Lo, you would do best to stay in one place and continue with your practices and your devakut. You have everything you need inside you."

"Should we stay in Yerushalayim or go back to Migdal Nunya?"

"It might not be safe anywhere. There is much tension welling up in the entire region. You could consider going west."

"West? Where?"

"Ephesus, perhaps?"

She had never heard of Ephesus. "Why there?"

"It is on the coast of the Aegean Sea, where the Rhōmaioi are not so strict on the Yehudi as long as they remain discreet. You will be happy there, you will learn much about the Way, and you will continue to grow." He placed his fingertips on her forehead. "Remember, I am always here." His lightning-flash touch felt as if it had physically unknotted a rope at the front of her skull; she could all but hear the popping sound as it unraveled. "You have climbed the ladder to this gate here, where you see me in my Shechinah, my glorified body. Stay here with me at all times. There are many more worlds to transcend beyond this gate. Talk to me constantly, for you must know that I am always with you – always. I am the Light that will prepare a place for you ahead. Walk always in that Light, and you will never stray from the path. One day you will merge with my ruach, my spirit, and you and I will be one. You will then go to Abba and become one with Abba."

She felt enveloped in a world that included just the two of them. She felt so light she thought she could fly past the treetops and float on a cloud, or that she could walk on water.

"Someday this will all pass." Ha-Rav removed a scroll from his robes and handed it to her. "When it does, and when you are ready, I want you to walk in my footsteps. I want you to carry on the talmidim with new initiates and to any of my matured students who have understood what has transpired and have the eyes to see, the ears to hear. This ketubah, signed by Yosef, proves that I have willed it."

Miryam took the scroll in her hands as if it were a precious, fragile treasure. "I can never walk in your footsteps."

"Ayn, you will, when you feel yourself to be ready, when you *know* that you and Ravi have merged. Teach my other sheep to walk with me as well."

"What if they will not follow me?"

"Then they will not reach the Kingdom." With that, he kissed her on the forehead, turned and moved away. He then stopped and turned back. "I have planted seeds here. Stories about me will sprout, and the teachings will grow in ways you will not recognize. Some will try to lead these teachings in my absence. Do not be concerned about this. Abba has a plan. The world is going through its own initiation in a way, readying souls for their own masters for many, many years to come."

Rav Yeshua stepped into the dense woods. Miryam watched her beloved master disappear from her life, but the effervescence of love and joy remained even without his presence. She wanted to wrap herself in the glory and hide from the world forever, but the sudden appearance of Simeon and Yakob running up the path toward her interrupted her bliss.

"Miryam, Ha-Rav's body is gone!" Simeon yelled when he saw her, both men gasping to catch their breath.

"What do you mean, gone?" She hoped they hadn't seen Ha-Rav talking to her just now.

"At day break we went inside to see him one last time, but the body was no longer there – only his grave cloths neatly folded on the ground."

"What possessed you?" Miryam was shocked by the audacity of their actions.

Simeon grabbed Miryam by the arms. "Are you not hearing us?"

Wisely Yosef must have moved the corpse in case the disciples sneaked in and saw that the man was not their master, she thought. "Perhaps somebody stole it," she said. "No matter. Rav Yeshua is no longer in the body. His spirit is with Abba."

Simeon dropped to his knees. "Or maybe it's a sign, as prophesied in Yĕshayah." He began reciting: "'Surely he has borne our misery and carried our sorrows. We considered him stricken, smitten of Yĕhovah, and afflicted, but he was wounded because of our transgressions, he was bruised for our iniquities. The punishment of our peace fell upon him, and with his stripes we are healed.'" Simeon drenched himself in a cauldron of sorrow mixed with elation – sad that his beloved rav was gone forever, and almost jubilant that the absent corpse promised a miracle. "'So shall he startle many nations. The kings shall shut their mouths at him, for that which has not been told them they shall see, and that which they have not heard they shall understand.'"

"Still believe in the rebellion, do you, Simeon? Rather than having a teacher, you now have a martyr, and you have completely misunderstood Ha-Rav's teachings." Clinging to the scroll Ha-Rav had just given her, she said, "Gather all the disciples that are still around. We will meet this afternoon on Mount Olives." Miryam began walking away without looking back, though she could feel their stares upon her. And so it begins, she thought.

Miryam, Martha, and Lazarus waited for the other core disciples on Mount Olives, but the disciples did not come, as Miryam had half expected. They barely even accepted her as a fellow student. "Why do you love her more than us?" Simeon had once asked Ha-Rav. "Why do you think I don't love you as much as I love her?" he had answered. All were equals in Ha-Rav's eyes. Once the three siblings realized the other students weren't coming, they decided to make their own plans to leave Yehudah and head west across the sea. Weeks later, they arrived in Ephesus and rented a small plot of land on top of Mount Koressos with what was left of their family's fortune.

Half a lifetime had passed since the successful deception of Ha-Rav's death. Although Rav Yeshua had survived and disappeared, he evidently had still been turned into a deified martyr for the rebellion. Miryam was not at all sure that the movement had achieved its original purpose of reforming the temple and ousting the Rhōmaioi. She wondered if Simeon was satisfied with the outcome, for which he so ardently campaigned Rav Yeshua's participation. Or did he have any regrets? From Paulos's description of Simeon and Yakob's doctrine, he hadn't reformed the temple but had created a new sect within it, further entangling the covenants and laws. Nevertheless, the memory of Rav Yeshua had been transformed into something that struck a deep chord in the hearts of many people who had never even met him. Perhaps that wasn't all bad.

Miryam still missed Ha-Rav's person, his electric touch, the poised movements of a dancer not dancing. Mostly the eyes she missed. Those golden brown orbs that looked into one down to the quick of the soul. He placed little worth on the outer vestige of the body. A person was all-neshama to him, and he was desperately in love with that neshama, so much so that he would risk everything to take it to its true Home. All that he required of the student was to risk everything too. "Whoever will save his life shall lose it," Rav Yeshua had once said. "And whoever will lose his life in the name of Abba shall find eternity."

Tears welled up in Miryam's eyes. *Forgive me, Ravi, but I still resent them all for taking Rav Yeshua away from me.* The response was instantaneous, a wave of love that bathed her senses and calmed her nerves, brought her attention to center and raised it another rung on Yakob's ladder to heaven. *Ayn, it was necessary. All the more powerful You have become now that I see You so clearly within the realm of my own inner worlds.* And this was true. Ever since that final week of the crucifixion, she was a different person, no longer concerned about all the mundane worries that can assail one on a daily basis, no longer fearful of even the cataclysmic events of life. Although Yeshua the man was not present in the flesh, Ravi the Comforter was present every moment of her waking day as well as her dream life, carefully guiding her through dark tunnels of her nefesh, her mind, and into the light.

But no matter how far one travels in the quest to know oneself, no matter how much one sees about the self, there is always another layer yet to be revealed. Paulos's arrival in Ephesus exhumed the feelings she thought she'd laid to rest, after all these years since she'd left Yerushalayim. She thought she felt safe and secure. But now this single man managed to dredge up new worries and fears. What was to transpire, she didn't know, but she felt he was a harbinger of change.

Miryam stopped suddenly in her tracks. Martha, who had entered her own world of contemplation on foot, returned her attention to Miryam and stopped as well. "You look resolute, Sister."

"Ayn. I now know I must spend some time with Paulos before all this slips away from us irretrievably."

Martha nodded and gazed over the sea. "The people of Ephesus say that the river backfills their man-made harbor with so much silt that it pushes the sea further and further away. The people must dig the harbor out again, for without the harbor, there is little industry to keep the polis alive. But someday there may not be enough labor, strength, and money to dig out the harbor, and Ephesus will be abandoned. Paulos is the river that fills the harbor with dirt. You know the people name their rivers after their deities – that's how much power the rivers have. We may not have any control over the build up of silt, Miryam, but we might be able to divert some of its damage."

"And channel it for the good of humanity," Miryam added. "You are wise, Martha. Very wise. Come along. Let's go find Paulos."

Four

Cerinthus harnessed Pegasus, the sisters' aging donkey, to a cart that amounted to little more than a large wooden crate on large wooden wheels, both weathered and full of splinters. The boy would watch the donkey while the women visited Paulos at the home of his Korinthos associates. The slender, dark, curly-headed adolescent climbed into the floor of the cart enthusiastically, eager to spend the day with his teachers. Martha sat on the cross bench in front and took the reins. Miryam rode beside her.

Ephesus lay in the valley due north of their rolling mountaintop home, and traveling down meandering shepherd's paths that circumnavigated the hills would normally take several hours were it not for the nearby Rhōmaioi logging road. As soldiers marched, the road extended just over a league down the mountain and, like all Rhōmaioi roads, it was straight as an arrow and on a steep grade. The donkey-driven cart saved ankles from twisting on the way down and hearts from giving out on the way back up. Because they were starting out early enough in the day, they could be home by sundown.

As they descended the mountain, they began to glimpse views of the ancient, beautiful polis cradled between the shallow Mount Pion and their own Mount Koressos. The all-white temples, mansions, public buildings, and open theaters and agoras sparkled in the sun beneath rust-colored terracotta tiles. Many times over the years Miryam had asked herself why she lived in such a place, and the only answer that emerged was because it was her ardent desire to honor Ha-Rav's suggestion. As it turned out, Ephesus was the perfect place for the sisters to continue their contemplations. Apart from the balmy coastal climate that suited their aging joints, the pleasant solitude of their mountain that suited their spirituality, and the bounty to be purchased in the

agora that suited their appetites, however diminishing, Ephesus did not have
to bear the pall of oppression that Yerushalayim lived under. The Rhōmaioi
were very much present, and everyone was mindful of the emperor's violent
and perverted whims, especially when they spread to his outliers, but they
were easily forgotten in the streets of an economically and intellectually
blossoming polis. One could sit on a mountaintop only so long, and doing so
didn't make one any more spiritual. Rather, it was Ha-Rav's way to hone the
soul by having it bathe and shop and eat with humanity.

At the bottom of the mountain, they pulled into traffic – a steady stream
of pedestrians, chariots, and wagons traveling in both directions. Men and
women carrying loads of produce and fish in baskets on their backs or bearing
goats strapped around their necks walked toward the triple-arched Magnesia
Gate to make their way to the stalls at the open agora. No one paid much
more than a passing glance to the two plainly-dressed women driving their
crude cart through the gate.

Once inside the city wall, they headed toward the polis proper along a
declining road. It was always exciting to go into the polis, even though they
had just shopped in the agora mere days earlier. With so many sights and
sounds pulling one's eye this way and that, it was such a contrast to the
solitude of their remote home. At the same time it was draining, for all of
the bright colors, tastes, music, and foreign visitors enticed the senses and
lured one away from the inner fountain. Miryam wasn't sure she could face
that today, if it weren't for that force from within driving her to find Paulos.

Ephesus was divided into four sectors that followed the natural contours
of the niches between the foothills of Mounts Koressos and Pion. Three
major boulevards underscored the first three prominent sectors; each street
was long and straight and wide enough for chariots to race along their course,
provided they could negotiate the heavy two-legged and four-legged traffic.
State buildings and monuments occupied the slopes closest to the Magnesia
Gate. Next came the wealthy commercial sector, followed by the public
sector encompassing the theater, agora, and harbor trades for the masses. The
common folk lived, played, and worshiped in the ghettos in the fourth, less-
defined sector that occupied the valley between the harbor and Mount Pion.

Martha drove the cart into the vicinity of the state agora and its complex of administration buildings, an area where the sisters rarely ventured. Statesmen assembled in this paved enclosure for meetings and religious ceremonies, sharing space with a necropolis and a monument to Isis. Abutting Mount Pion on the far side of the agora stood a magistrate building, a theater seating as many as 1,400 *boules*, or council members, a town hall housing the holy fire of the hearth goddess Hestia, and a temple to the imperial cult of Julius Caesar. Closely-spaced columns topped with bull heads decorated the facades, and statues of prominent individuals and deities stood between the columns.

Passing through Ephesus always reminded Miryam of how intertwined religious and public life were to the citizens of Ephesus. Most of the buildings served the double purpose of government and one religious sect or another. Even the shops catered to both customs. Ephesians never completely got rid of the deities they outgrew; rather, they simply erected another layer of stone, another statue, another temple over or next to the older religious structures. To Miryam, the city reflected how the neshama is entrapped by layers and layers of old beliefs and desires. What's more, the Hellene devotedly set their deities in stone in an effort to humanize them, and meanwhile chiseled their own elite into statues as if to put them on equal footing with their divinity. Yet the builders, rulers, and commoners who moved beneath these statues and structures remained oblivious to the divinity of all people and to the means for tapping into that divine fount that would not only put them on equal footing with the deities but would also place them far above them.

The tendency to erect monuments and sculptures to the gods was a direct affront to most anyone raised on the Torah because they violated the second commandment of Moses: "You shall not make for yourself an idol, whether in the form of anything that is in heaven above, or that is on the earth beneath, or that is in the water under the earth." But Miryam was not at all bothered by them. The longer she walked among the stone deities of Ephesus, the more she began to see how they portrayed all of the unsavory traits housed in the human being. In listening to the stories of the gods, she was always amazed by how mischievous, greedy, lustful, and jealous they were, and how they toyed with the earthly beings as if they were pets or game pieces. By contrast to the Pantheon, the One Elohim of Abraham was much more paternal and stern, one who must be obeyed with countless acts of outward purity and sacrifice, or suffer the consequences. Ha-Rav's Abba was neither of these extremes; rather, a disciple would purify one's own pantheon of lower bodily, emotional, and mental attributes in order to merge with the One, the Absolute, the All-Love.

The fountain house across from the state complex was one of Miryam's favorite resting places. The Rhōmaioi called the house a *nymphaeum*, so named because such structures typically surrounded a natural spring and were consecrated to water nymphs. In this case, the nymphaeum was fed by an aqueduct from the Marnas river, and was filled with plants, fountains, and sculpture. The nymphaeum reminded her of the water house they had on their property in Migdal Nunya, although the Hellene version was considerably more ornate than the austere Ivrit structure at home. This trip they had no time to stop and soak up the water, despite the fact that women would have the house to themselves at this hour.

Martha drove the donkey onto Market Street, which cut diagonally across the polis grid and steadily descended downhill. This sector was called the Embolos because it was wedged between the foothills of Pion and Koressos like a bird's beak. Covered colonnades stretched along both sides of the street, offering protection from the sun and rain for customers as they visited the shops. Tombs, monuments, and statues of patrons who funded various construction projects studded this sector marked by expensive peristyle houses terraced up the slopes on both sides of the road. She'd heard that some of the villas exhibited marble or mosaic patterned floors and frescoes painted into the walls. An earthquake several decades earlier had hit this sector hardest, and so much of the construction was new here.

As instructed by Paulos, Miryam entered the last rug shop on the Embolos to ask for directions to the house of his friends. But the shopkeeper informed her that they'd stopped in that morning before setting out to the temple of Artemis and said they'd be gone most of the day.

"How peculiar," Martha said when Miryam returned to the cart. "What business would Paulos have at the Artemision?"

"Maybe he plans to recruit new believers as they lay an offering at her feet," Miryam answered.

"I'd laugh if I didn't think it true."

"Should we go to the agora first, or head straight to the temple?"

"Your choice," Martha said.

Entrance into the great commercial agora at the bottom of Market Street was just a few minutes away, but once they entered it, meandering from stall to stall and dodging thousands of shoppers and hundreds of sellers as they hawked their wares could consume the rest of their day. From the sounds of roaring crowds coming from the grand theater across from the agora, they assumed hundreds more would be pushing their way into the market all day long. "I'd like to track down Paulos before we lose him."

"The temple it is," Martha said, turning Pegasus around. It didn't take long to retrace their way past the state agora and exit the polis gate. They headed northeast along the Sacred Way through the suburbs and farmland around Mount Pion to the Artemision a mere half-league away. On flatter, less populated terrain and little to negotiate besides crossing two rivers via wooden bridges, the women could talk. Pegasus's ears laid backward on the sides of his head as if listening to the sisters' conversation. Cerinthus would also be listening from the back of the cart, though feigning otherwise out of respect for his teachers.

"I hardly agreed with anything Paulos said when he visited us, but I have to admit, he *knows* things," Miryam said.

"What does he know?"

"He understands there is a difference between an inner teaching and an outer one. He acknowledges that spirituality takes place within one's being, although I'm not sure he understands it. How could he know such things?"

"Perhaps from Simeon and Yakob themselves."

"But Paulos admitted he avoided them for many years. And when they finally met, they disapproved of his teaching against the covenants. Did you hear about the gospels he's preaching?"

"What I could make out is that he preaches one way to the Yehudi and another way to the Hellene. He called the Yehudi fools and the Hellene the mature." Martha paused a moment, then giggled.

"What are you laughing at?"

"Are the Yehudi fools because they don't understand Paulos's teachings, or does he consider them fools because they choose to ignore him?"

"You have a point, Sister. But both of his teachings are wrong. For the immature, he teaches that Ha-Rav rose from the dead, having died for the sins of the world. And for the mature elect, the crucifixion means a personal death to the flesh and reunion with the Father through Christos. For the immature, Christos returns in the flesh, and for the mature, he returns in what sounds like a vision, but both happen after death. And neither have a living guide to lead the way."

"Ayn, both ways lack a living master."

"I am more concerned about Simeon and Yakob. To them Ha-Rav is dead. They didn't know that he wasn't crucified. Instead, they have turned the story into a *nevuah*, a prophecy, which is what Simeon wanted in the first place."

"Amazing how quickly the story of Ha-Rav rising from the dead has spread as truth," Martha said.

"Do you think that Simeon created the story to promote his plans of liberating Yisrael?"

Martha shrugged. "I don't believe that Simeon meant for Ha-Rav to be killed, and I don't believe he intended to lead a rebellion himself with the martyred master as his staff. Ha-Rav warned you that stories like this one would spread, did he not?"

"Ayn, and he said there would be a purpose in it."

"And that divine purpose would no doubt be much larger than Simeon's ambitions."

"May I ask what you're talking about?" Cerinthus was on his knees in the bed of the cart, poking his head and shoulders between the women on the bench in front, his dark eyes bright as if illuminated from within. He rarely interrupted their private conversation, but he looked as if he could actually contribute. "Unless it's secret," he added with a dip of his chin.

Miryam glanced at Martha, who shrugged. "One's education in spirituality should encompass what spirituality is not."

Agreeing, Miryam turned sideways to face Cerinthus behind her. "Yesterday, a visitor told us a story about our spiritual teacher in Galilee that was greatly exaggerated."

"What story?"

Miryam sighed. This wasn't easy to talk about. "That he was executed in a horrible way, that he ascended into the heavens alive, and that he changed into a being capable of taking away the transgressions of all believers in him when the world is destroyed."

The boy's eyes grew even wider. "Is this true?"

"Lo, it is not true."

"How do you know?" Cerinthus asked his questions with the innocence of a child and the wisdom of an ancient soul.

Miryam hesitated. Even after all these years she felt she could not betray her rav, though telling this boy, this young man, the truth would be of no threat to Ha-Rav now. But how could she predict the outcome of any action? "I know because I know, Cerinthus." She and Martha exchanged further glances.

"Sounds like the story of Osiris."

"What do you mean?" Miryam asked.

"In my homeland of Egypt, Osiris was son of the sun god, Ra. There are many stories about him, but basically he was killed, he traveled through the underworld where everyone goes after death, and then he was brought back by his wife, Isis, through a ritual, and he became lord of the dead. All those associated with him are said to have eternal life."

"Interesting story," Miryam said.

"We're Ivrit and so we never practiced the rituals of Osiris, but dead grain is planted during the festival of Osiris, and it is reborn in the spring. Doesn't all life go through cycles? The crops die in the winter and are reborn in the spring, the sun sets to rise every morning, and perhaps we are reborn after we die."

"Cerinthus, you never cease to amaze me," Miryam said, laughing and exchanging eye contact with her sister.

"Don't forget about the emperor becoming a shooting star!" he exclaimed.

"That's right," Miryam said. She'd learned from her students that Octavian, the son of the assassinated Julius Caesar, observed a star as it blazed across the sky over a game being played in honor of his father. Octavian saw it as a sign that Julius had achieved *apotheosis*, that he had joined the ranks of Zeus, as if he himself had resurrected. Indeed, there wasn't a statue, building, or gate erected, a game played, a song or dance performed without homage being paid to the *Sebastoi*, the emperors. Even festivals honoring Artemis carefully included acknowledgment to the emperor as the *Huios Theos*, the son of God. As far as Miryam was concerned, it made it easier for the Rhōmaioi to collect more taxes – in her judgment the main reason the empire existed in the first place.

Martha drove Pegasus through farmland filled with melons and olive trees, and reached the rows of shacks and villas in various stages of squalor or comfort that surrounded the Artemision. These housed the beggars, infirm, and hangers-on, the artisans and merchants who crafted and sold likenesses of Artemis, and the personnel who served her in the temple. They tried not to gawk at the poverty that lived alongside the richness supported by wealthy Ephesian benefactors.

The red-tiled roof of Artemis's marble temple soon glistened up ahead, and as usual the sight always impressed Miryam. Since it was outside of the polis and on the far side of Mount Pion, the temple wasn't something that was visible on regular trips to Ephesus. A person had to make a concerted effort to head directly to the Artemision unless passing en route to regions beyond it, and for Miryam and Martha there was almost no occasion to go there. They had toured it when they first arrived in Ephesus years ago, but Miriam could remember revisiting it only a handful of times since then.

Miryam understood Artemis to be an ancient deity already thoroughly established by the time the Hellene and then the Rhōmaioi arrived over many centuries. She'd learned that the goddess' original name was Cybele, the fertile earth mother, and seeing familiar traits in her, the Hellene transformed her and merged her with their own Artemis, the huntress, the sister of Apollo, daughter to Zeus and his human wife, Leto. Keeping the Hellene name, she became the Lady of Ephesus, with qualities of fertility and abundance unique unto herself.

Statues of Artemis depicted the lower half of her body encased within a tapering pillar, with her bare toes peeking out from the bottom as if to emphasize her human half. To Miryam the effect resembled that of an Egyptian sarcophagus, as if to say that life is made possible through death, and that might have been the original intent. Strangely the casing over Artemis's lower half was decorated with bulls, perhaps to symbolize one of the myths surrounding Artemis. Similar to the story of Isis and Osiris, Cybele had resurrected her son, Attis, after he had castrated himself in an ecstatic ritual, inspiring a new rite of castrating bulls in his name.

But the most interesting and, to some, repelling part of Artemis was her upper half, perhaps her divine half, the multiple rows of golden orbs that covered her bodice. These may have represented bull's testicles in honor of her ritual to her resurrected son, or eggs, a honeycomb, or breasts, all meaning the same thing: the perpetuation of life. Miryam was repulsed the first time she saw the orbs, but over time she began to appreciate the significance of such an archaic display.

Miryam and Martha may have lived on a mountaintop in daily contemplation with their inner rav the last two decades, but even they were aware that Ephesians believed their recent prosperity had come directly from Artemis. So in awe of her warrior spirit, they placed a statue of her on a platform in front of the temple, depicted in her Hellene aspect wearing a helmet and riding a chariot pulled by black serpents. They also housed the more ancient form of her image within the inner vault of the temple, protected by a forest of gigantic, evenly-spaced columns. From the front of the temple Miryam could see her peering through the columns around her vault like a lioness peers through the bars of a cage. In this form she was not free like the naked statues of deities in the polis, but trapped and chastened in marble and stone, stoic, wise, and detached. This deity, this Ancient of

Days, was worshiped and adorned by throngs of dedicated rulers, priests, virgins, eunuchs, and citizens who lay sacrificial offerings at her feet, hoping to perpetuate their own wealth. In doing so they fooled themselves into believing they tamed the lioness, as if they could tame Nature herself, as if they could contain their own animal urges. Miryam almost felt sorry for her, and for the people for not lifting their eyes to the sky and yearning for something more.

"There are one hundred twenty-six columns in all surrounding the vault," Cerinthus offered as they drove up to the temple. "I counted them once. Three rows of eight columns at the front of the temple, two rows of nine columns in the back, and a double row of twenty-one columns along each side. I could almost wrap my arms all the way around one of them."

Miryam wondered if the guard allowed children to play around the temple. Certainly not in Yerushalayim.

They quickly spotted Paulos sitting on the temple steps in deep conversation with an elegantly dressed man and woman in the shadow of the statue of the warrior Artemis on her chariot. The sisters jumped out of the wagon, giving Cerinthus the reins. The boy turned the donkey toward the river for water and grass, while the women climbed the steps toward Paulos. But he did not notice their approach, and Miryam didn't know whether to interrupt him or wait until he finished talking.

"Oh, foolish Galatians," Paulos suddenly shouted. "Who has bewitched them?" Clearly agitated, Paulos leapt up and slapped his thigh. "Whoever persuaded them to go back to accepting circumcision should cut their own foreskins off themselves!"

The woman sitting on a step near Paulos gasped. "That's rather harsh."

"I am afraid I have wasted my efforts on them, and that I am going through labor pains all over again. They used to understand the meaning of Christos's death, as if I'd drawn a picture of the crucifixion for them, and now they wish to observe the holy days and the torah of purity? Who has been talking to them? I am shocked that they have so quickly deserted the one who called them by the grace of Christos for a different gospel, which is really no gospel at all. Someone is throwing them into confusion and is perverting my gospel."

The woman companion noticed Miryam and Martha approaching and alerted Paulos. He turned quickly to glare. As soon as he recognized them, he composed himself and descended the steps toward them with outstretched arms. "Miryam, Martha, please forgive me. I am having trouble with my ekklēsia in Galatia."

"Not at all," Miryam said. "Where else to speak of circumcision than on the threshold of the mother of castration."

Paulos's forced smile dropped into a frown. "I don't understand."

Martha tapped Miryam's shoulder in a subtle gesture of censorship. "My sister tells a joke at the expense of Artemis."

"What?"

Half smiling, she pointed upward toward the statue of Artemis with the bulls decorating her stone skirt and the testicle-like orbs adorning her chest.

"Oh, I see," Paulos said with a harumph and a quick dismissal. He turned red briefly, but Miryam was glad to see the sores on his face didn't look quite as angry as they had the day before, presumably because he'd applied the poultice Martha had given him.

"What are you doing here, Paulos? Preaching isn't allowed at the temple, especially against Artemis."

"We are simply touring the local landmarks, Atta Miryam," he said. "Come, I have some people I'd like you to meet." He ushered the sisters up the steps as the male companion stood promptly. The man towered over Paulos in stature, and he was several times thicker around the middle. "Allow me to introduce Miryam and Martha bar Binyamiyn of Migdal Nunya," he said solemnly.

The man stood, gently tugging his woman to her feet. "Shlama."

"Peace be multiplied to you." Miryam answered.

"These are my friends from Korinthos I told you about," Paulos said with a rare smile. "Aquila and his wife Priscilla have been kind enough to open their homes to me, here in Ephesus as well as abroad."

"We are deeply, deeply honored to be in your presence." Aquila bowed before her as if she were a dignitary. Priscilla nodded her head and smiled, as a lady of her stature would. While her husband's girth matched their obvious wealth, Priscilla's slender physique kept hidden any appetites she might have.

But something about Aquila's mannerisms alerted Miryam. She caught Paulos by the elbow and drew him aside. "You didn't tell your associates about us, did you?"

Paulos looked as though he had been caught gossiping.

"You must keep our identity a secret and you must not exaggerate our image," she whispered. "No one in Ephesus knows about our ... past."

"Forgive me, Miryam. These are the only two I've told."

Miryam had no choice but to believe him. She approached Paulos's perplexed friends. "Do not believe everything Paulos says about us," she said.

"Paulos did say you were a humble woman," Aquila responded.

Miryam thought she detected a Rhōmaioi accent. "Are you originally from Korinthos?"

"My wife and I fled to Korinthos after Claudius Caesar threw all Yehudi out of Rhōmē."

"Claudius died recently, I hear," Martha said. "It's all the talk in Ephesus."

"That's right," Miryam added. "Poisoned to death, rumor has it. Why haven't you moved back to Korinthos?"

"The situation could still be unstable for the Faithful living there," Paulos said. "Nero is just as bad, if not worse, than Claudius. But I may have burned bridges in Korinthos bringing the Christos to the synagogue there."

"Were they receptive?"

"Some were. Others?" Paulos shifted nervously. "Others blasphemed Christos. I finally said to them, 'Your blood is upon your own heads. I am clean.'"

"What happened?" Miryam asked.

Aquila picked up the story thread. "Paulos was summoned to court with the charge of trying to persuade Ivrit to worship Christos against the torah. The deputy of the province threw the case out of court before Paulos could speak for himself, saying that if it were a matter of wrong or wicked lewdness, he would have agreed with the Ivrit. But since it was a matter of words and names and beliefs, he would not judge such matters."

"Sounds fair," Miryam said. "What did you do next?"

"The three of us eventually sailed here," Paulos said. "I left them to set up a home here, while I sailed at once to Yerushalayim in time for the feast of the *Pentēkostē*."

Miryam had allowed the holy day to come and go without notice, so far had she strayed from the rituals of her childhood. Pentēkostē, or *Shavout* in Ivrit, occurred on the "fiftieth day" after Pesach, or Passover, and was the second of the three great harvest festivals, Pesach being the first. "Why is this feast day so important to you, Paulos, that you had to attend it in Yerushalayim? Shavout is celebrated here as well, though quietly." He was contradicting himself, Miryam thought. He'd just admonished the Galatians for observing the holy days, but he went out of his way to participate in religious activities himself.

"As I told you, I was asked to remember the poor."

"You were asked by Yakob to offer sacrifices from your ekklēsia, ayn, I remember."

"Before I did so, I took the vow of *Nezirut* and offered my hair along with the funds we raised."

"Why?" The vow of Nezirut meant he kept his hair long and followed all the laws of purity for at least a month, then shaved his hair so that he could offer it in the temple. That explained why his hair was so short now, but it was another in a growing list of incongruities.

"Yakob, as the brother of Rav Yeshua, is widely respected in the temple for his adherence to the vows of the Nezirut and laws of purity, and that is why he is allowed to remain in the temple and teach of the Christos. You of all people should understand the significance of taking the vow before the Pentēkostē."

Miryam shrugged her shoulders and shook her head. Then it dawned on her. When he spoke of Yakob at her house the day before, she assumed he meant the son of Zebedee and brother of Johanan, not Rav Yeshua's own brother, who hadn't been interested in his mission at all. But now it seemed Rav Yeshua's brother had become leader of the Christos movement. *Incredible*, she thought. "Tell me, Paulos, of the significance of the holy day."

Paulos exhaled audibly to show his disappointment in her, then launched the story: "It was Simeon and Yakob's vision for the temple to become the house of prayer for all God-Fearers, not just the Ivrit or Yehudi. And on the Pentēkostē – the Shavout – this vision became a reality. Seven weeks after the death and rebirth of the Christos, the apostles gathered on the Pentēkostē. While they were praying, a sound of rushing wind suddenly came from heaven and filled the house where they met. What was described as a Presence appeared like cloven tongues of fire and set upon each of the apostles. As the apostles became possessed of the Spirit, they began speaking in tongues."

"Paulos, did you witness this event yourself?"

"It is a story told by the Pillars. Remember, my time to receive the Word did not come until I traveled to Damascus."

"Wouldn't the sight of cloven tongues of fire have caught the attention of everyone in Yerushalayim?" Just as she posed this challenge to Paulos, an elderly couple climbing the steps nearby turned their heads. From their tattered robes, she assumed they were peasant farmers in the region come to pay homage to Artemis.

Paulos saw them as well and switched to Hellene as he raised his voice. "At this time, there resided in Yerushalayim many devout people speaking many different languages from every nation under heaven. Each person heard the Word in their own native tongue and was amazed and perplexed by what they were hearing. Others who did not hear the tongues mocked them, saying everyone was drunk on wine."

Paulos, Aquila, and Priscilla turned to the sisters for some kind of affirmation or response, but both women were speechless by this account. They returned their stare of incredulity at Paulos. The elderly woman stopped in her ascent to Artemis, flinging her arm when her husband tried to grab it to drag her up the steps, obviously caught by Paulos's story.

"The apostle Simon Petros stood before the masses and lifted up his voice." Likewise, Paulos himself stood and began acting out his words, his speech booming in an orator's cadence. "Men of Yehudah, and all who dwell at Yerushalayim, listen to my words. These people have not been drinking.

They are overcome by Spirit. In his last days, Iēsous the Christos promised that he would pour his spirit on everyone, even the slaves and servants, and all would have visions and dreams. He would perform miracles in the sky above and wonders on the earth below. There would be blood and fire and thick smoke. The sun would turn into darkness and the moon into blood before that great and notable day when the Christos returns. Whoever calls out the name of Christos shall be saved."

Paulos paced across the temple steps, swinging his arms as if he were the one giving the speech to the mob instead of Simeon, and indeed his shouting had now drawn a growing crowd of onlookers. Everyone on those steps that day had come to the temple to worship Artemis, not to listen to a story of a redeemer. The elderly woman drawn in by Paulos's voice was now standing beside Paulos, watching him in awe. Her husband stood behind her, ready to pounce on Paulos at the first sign of danger.

"Christos's divine authority was clearly proven by the miracles and wonders and signs Theos performed through his son. Theos raised him from death because it was impossible for death to hold him prisoner. He was not abandoned in the underworld of the dead; his body did not rot in the grave. Theos raised Iēsous from death to sit at his right hand. Simon Petros said, 'What you now see and hear is his gift pouring through me.'" Paulos paused for effect, then continued, "Three thousand received baptisma that day."

The middle-aged woman interrupted Paulos, asking, "Who is this Christos?"

"Why, he is your savior!" Paulos shouted to the woman.

To Miryam's surprise, the woman seemed to accept the answer without hesitation. "And what is baptisma?"

Paulos moved to stand in front of the woman. "Simon Petros told the masses, as I tell you now, that you should be baptized so that the Christos will take away your *hamartia*."

"*My* sins?" the woman asked, placing a hand on her chest.

"All the times you might have gossiped, lied, stolen ... lusted."

The woman looked at Paulos as if he had peered into her being, and she began to weep. "Will you give me this baptisma now?"

"Where do you live?" Paulos asked the woman.

"Magnesia," her angering husband answered gruffly for her. He tried to shove her along with his body, but she stood steadfast in front of Paulos. Clearly, he wasn't interested in his wife being baptized by this verbose and quite possibly demented stranger.

"Magnesia is not far. I will begin speaking at Tyrannus Hall in Ephesus soon. Perhaps you can come hear me speak, and after a period of study, if you want baptisma, it will be so."

"We are only here for the day," the husband barked. "It would be difficult to return anytime soon."

The woman looked disappointed. "If not baptize me, can you heal me?" She lifted the hem of her robe to reveal a swollen leg wrapped in bandages. "This is why we brought an offering to Artemis." She sat on the step to unwind a length of the bandage and uncovered some of the infected skin.

"Oy," Martha said as she sat beside her. "Soak yarrow and echinacea in hot water, then wrap it in cloth, and hold it against the sore. Do this as quickly as possible, for if it turns green, you will die." She patted the woman on the shoulder. Too late consoled, she broke down in sobs.

The woman's husband would have nothing of it. "We're on our way to the *asclepieion* in Ephesus," he shouted at Martha. "They'll cure her."

Miryam cringed at the thought of sleeping there with snakes crawling under the beds. Based on what dreams the snakes would inspire, a priest would prescribe a bath, a tonic, a romp in the gym, or yet another snake ritual. Considered sacred, a doubled-forked staff of intertwining serpents marked the house.

"Paulos can heal you in the spirit of Christos," Priscilla offered.

The woman looked up at Paulos, tears streaming down her chin, eyes hopeful.

Paulos stood over her looking mighty, hands on hips, feet spread. He considered a moment and, glancing toward the temple, said, "It is not that simple. You must first understand that the things you sacrifice to Artemis, you sacrifice to the *daimonion* and not to Theos. I would not be in partnership with demons, if I were you."

The woman's face turned pale white. The color red spread in her husband's cheeks. "You mean to insult her, not heal her."

"Not at all," Paulos said. "Let me ask you: When you die, where do you go?"

The woman trembled. "Hopefully not Tartarus where the terrible go, though maybe not Paradise either. Probably the Fields of Asphodel. That's where most folks go."

"The Fields of Asphodel, that peaceful place where the souls of the masses roam aimlessly in the underworld for an eternity?"

She nodded, her eyes distant at such a prospect, which for all she knew was imminent if her leg didn't heal.

"What if I were to tell you that the Christos promises eternal salvation in the *Basileia Ouranos*, the heavens above, and all you have to do is believe in him and be baptized in his spirit."

"That's what I asked you to do. Give me baptisma."

Paulos shook his head, no. "I cannot. You must first learn more. I will cast out the demon from your leg if you promise me you will consider joining us at Tyrannus Hall."

When the woman nodded agreement, Paulos lifted her to her feet. She stumbled a bit and leaned against her husband. Paulos opened his arms to the sky, taking all of the invisible power he imagined to be there into himself, then laid his hands on the top of her head and closed his eyes as if in deep concentration. "In the name of the *Hagios Pneuma*, the Holy Spirit, of the Christos ... deliver this woman from Satanas's destruction of the flesh, so that her spirit may be saved in the day of the Kyrios Iēsous. May Theos crush Satanas beneath his feet." With that, Paulos pushed hard on the woman's head for extra measure, and she fell backward into the arms of her husband. "It is so," Paulos said. "Come back and hear more about your Lord and Savior." Her man lifted his bewildered wife to her feet. She nodded feebly and stumbled down the steps, leaning heavily on the glowering man.

The entire episode stunned Miryam. Rav Yeshua would never have manipulated an aspirant with such acts of magic. He didn't perform public healings, he didn't even bless people at their request. Rather, he gazed into the eyes of a sincere soul with all of Abba's Shefa passing through him, and if that person happened to recover from an illness or misfortune, that was none of Rav's concern. Sometimes, Miryam noticed, a person who was blessed enough to be gazed upon by Ha-Rav did not experience a miracle but instead fell into hardship, not out of punishment, but through a quicker fulfillment of whatever was written on that person's tablet for this life.

Entering into discipleship was a deeply personal exploration not to be taken lightly. The initiation itself was sacred and required a period of fasting beforehand and a long period of probation afterward, during which time the student would undergo soulful searching of their sincere longing for a spiritual teaching and a deep, lifelong commitment and devotion to it. This woman had been won by the sheer charisma of a masterful storyteller. She would add the idea of this "savior" to her kitchen shelf of religious icons for safekeeping and for keeping her safe against all eventualities. She knew nothing of Rav Yeshua's teachings and of what they offered her. Would she come to hear Paulos speak? That would depend on how well her leg healed. Then again, she might forget about it.

As for the story Paulos had told that attracted the woman in the first place, Miryam could see that someone, if not Paulos, had carefully crafted it as evidence of prophecy. Although it had no bearing in truth, it must have had roots somewhere. "Is this story part of the gospel being taught in Yerushalayim, as you were telling me yesterday?"

Paulos nodded.

"For the mature or the immature?"

"Both, but for different reasons."

"And that woman – you consider her a fool?"

"Wouldn't you?"

Miryam didn't answer, but she was beginning to see how Paulos operated, at least in public. The event of speaking in tongues he had described that allured the woman reminded her of the story of the spirit of prophecy that visited Yĕchezqel. According to scripture, Yĕchezqel saw a whirlwind of fire unfold out of a great cloud. Divine visitation was often described in such terms of fantasia, and perhaps no words could otherwise explain inner-worldly experiences. Rav Yeshua had told his disciples that many would-be mystics concentrated on the passages of Yĕchezqel's vision to evoke their own visions, aided by days of fasting and chanting and contorting oneself into odd physical postures. Simeon would've learned such rituals while he lived with the Essenes at Qumran. Were Ha-Rav's students practicing and teaching these rituals in Yerushalayim?

Truth be told, the event Paulos had described could have applied to any time the students were in the company of their Rav Yeshua. The Shechinah, the Inner Presence, was always amplified – some experienced Its warmth throughout their bodies, some experienced It as a flame dancing on the crown of their heads, while still others heard the sound of wind blowing as if from heaven but inside one's own skull. It was something that was very real and yet indescribable and personal, intimately felt within their own beings, and no two experiences were alike. Initiates would experience the Shefa in their own way, but it wouldn't have been as dramatic or as outwardly expressed as speaking in tongues like Paulos had just described. Not being a student of a living rav, Paulos must have heard the story from Simeon or Yakob, for who says the students didn't convene during the holy days after her family had left Yerushalayim? Then Paulos may have embellished upon the story for his recruits, the immature seekers who sought signs.

"What story do you tell the mature seeker?"

Paulos started to answer when he was interrupted by shouts coming from the top of the temple steps.

"Hey, stop what you're doing right now!" Everyone turned and looked up to see an angry temple official rapidly descending the steps toward them with his guard in tow. He squared off in front of Paulos.

"Phylaktos, have you come to hear the Word?" Paulos asked smugly.

"I've asked you before not to peddle your savior here." The robust elderly man, draped in a violet toga, was red in the face, as much from his anger as from the exertion of carrying so much weight. His small band of temple guard wore yellow togas. The colors were exclusive to temple garb, and not typical of Rhōmaioi citizenship. To Miryam, the color violet enhanced the overall joviality of the man, in love with the company of people as well as his food, despite his current outrage with Paulos.

"You've trespassed on these temple steps before, Paulos?" Miryam was again aghast by his hubris.

Phylaktos nodded. "And you should leave before the *megabyxus*, the high priest, hears about this. He is very jealous of who or what is presented in his temple of Artemis."

"Please excuse us. We mean no disrespect to Artemis or to the megabyxus." Miryam wanted to add that she neither condoned nor subscribed to Paulos's gospel. She held her tongue, not knowing how Paulos would react.

"Respect Artemis?" Paulos asked incredulously. "I could never respect any deity with more than two breasts, and I should think neither could you, Miryam!"

"Artemis is the most ancient and venerated of all deities," the guardian snapped. "Artemis is the daughter of Zeus Most High. As sister of the sun Apollo, she is the moon that watches over Ephesus and keeps us safe in darkness. Her temple has been destroyed by earthquake, fire, and the hands of men, yet each time it has been rebuilt – that's how powerful she is!"

"This is the way for Ephesians, Paulos, as it has been for thousands of years," Miryam added.

The temple guardian nodded emphatically, but Paulos wasn't convinced. "Artemis is carved out of stone and smithed out of silver." He pointed to the booths across from the temple, where Artemis's likeness could be purchased as small silver statues. "Temples and trinkets can be destroyed and rebuilt, but Theos is not made by the hands of men."

"Smithing is their livelihood," Phylaktos said. "The followers of Artemis have the right to take home a token of their visit here, so that they may remember her and beseech her for protection and prosperity."

"Turn from the worship of these foolish things," Paulos shouted, his voice carrying up to the temple and echoing between the columns. "Pray instead to the Lord Almighty who made heaven and earth and the sea and everything in them. No animal or human sacrifices are made to Christos.

Instead he sacrificed himself to take away the sins of the world. And he will soon return to take back those who have been baptized in his name. Can Artemis do that?"

Phylaktos remained silent, stumped.

Seeing that he may have beaten the elderly man, Paulos continued. "Of course, she can't. Artemis is just an idea in stone. Christos is real!"

The guardian had enough. "I ask you one more time to leave. And if you return, I'll have you arrested."

When Paulos didn't budge, the guardian nodded to two of his larger men. They moved to Paulos's side in an instant. No contest for their strength, they lifted Paulos under his arms, dragged him down the steps, and threw him to the dirt. Aquila picked Paulos up quickly and started to slap the dust from his toga, but Paulos threw off his help with a fling of his arm. "See what I have to go through in the name of Christos, Miryam?" He shook a fist in the air. "You were of no help!" He turned and stomped away angrily and with his usual bravado.

Aquila ran after Paulos, while a mortified Priscilla stayed behind, clearly searching for something to say. "He means well," she said to Miryam. "Come to our ekklēsia someday, and you will see him at his best when he is among his own. We meet at our house on the Sabbath." Before Miryam could respond, Priscilla descended the steps and ran after Aquila and Paulos.

Miryam turned to the guardian and took a deep breath. "My name is Miryam, and this is my sister, Martha. We can't vouch for Paulos or his words." Miryam didn't want to become an enemy of the temple or a person of contempt with the citizens of Ephesus, wishing to stay here to her dying days.

"I don't blame you, but he'll cause you much trouble if you continue to associate with him. He is such a *spermologos*."

"A what?" The word sounded foreign to her.

"A scavenging, talkative crow. Crows are messengers of the gods, but they usually bring bad news – that's why Apollo turned their white feathers black. From what I've been able to glean, Paulos has traveled so broadly he's picked up all kinds of ideas and tries to put them together into one idea. That's a crow, a spermologos."

Miryam laughed at the image of a black bird hanging around the agora, pecking the ground with abandon for every last seed scattered from sacks with holes in them, or rummaging through garbage for dead rodents or rotting scraps of meat. "I only met him yesterday, but I agree with you. He has some interesting, yet contradictory ideas. I can't promise he'll stop challenging you or Artemis. This is his life's mission, and he's traveled the Imperium Romanum to do it. But he misinterprets ... truth."

"It will probably be the death of him." He stopped a moment for consideration. "This Christos must be a very powerful being."

"The man he speaks of was a teacher of the Mysteries. I suspect he'd never endorse the things Paulos says about him," Miryam said.

"You might tell me about him someday."

"Someday, perhaps."

Phylaktos smiled. "Something tells me you were a student of this great man, such is the light in your face and the wisdom of your words." He studied Martha a moment. "Your sister was also a student."

Before Miryam could respond, Cerinthus drove the donkey cart in front of the temple steps. "Our chariot," Miryam said to Phylaktos. Martha lifted her tunic high enough to climb up the footpegs in the cartwheel and settle on the bench.

Just as Miryam started to take her turn up the wagon, the guardian tugged at her arm. "Who is the young man?" he asked in a low voice, eying the boy.

Miryam glanced quickly at Cerinthus, who seemed too busy reining Pegasus to hear the question, not that he'd understand the subtle danger of making friends with this temple guardian. Taking young boys into the temple was an aspect of Rhōmaioi-Hellene society she neither understood nor accepted. The price to their manhood was too high, and for all she knew the guardian himself had been castrated in order to serve the priestesses, called *melissa*, who served Artemis like honey bees around a blossom. "He is a student of mine, and he's Ivrit at that. Not interested in Hellene temple life."

"No, of course not," he said. "But he is interested in ancient literature, is he not?"

Cerinthus heard that. "I most definitely am."

"Let me introduce myself," the guardian said to Miryam, suddenly perky, his anger with Paulos forgotten. "My name is Phylaktos. I'm the head of the guard and somewhat of an amateur of history. Do you and the boy have time to come into the temple with me? I have something that might interest both of you."

"What is it?" the boy asked.

"Oh, some scribbles of antiquity from a man of great wisdom," he said to Cerinthus. "Your teacher must give permission." He turned to Miryam with a wry smile.

"Can we see them, Atta Miryam?" Cerinthus's butterfly attention was netted.

Miryam was leery, yet admittedly intrigued.

"Go look," Martha said with a wave of the hand. "I'll stay with Pegasus, but mind we aren't caught off the mountain after sundown."

Five

Phylaktos stopped Miryam and Cerinthus at the top of the temple steps and waved an arm in a single sweeping gesture. "Five hundred years ago, the historian Herodutus wrote that the Artemision was a *themata*, one of the seven must-sees of the world. Antipater of Sidon wrote a poem about the Seven Wonders of the World." Phylaktos drew in a breath and began reciting:

> *I have set eyes on the wall of lofty Babylon on which is a road for chariots, and the statue of Zeus by the Alpheus, and the hanging gardens, and the Colossus of the Sun, and the huge labor of the high pyramids, and the vast tomb of Mausolus; but when I saw the house of Artemis that mounted to the clouds, those other marvels lost their brilliancy, and I said, 'Lo, apart from Olympus, the Sun never looked on anything so grand.'*

Phylaktos boasted that the temple was one hundred fifteen strides long by fifty-five strides wide, making it nearly three times larger than the Parthenon in Athens. The cypress doors were seasoned for four years before hanging, and the cedar roof was covered with terracotta tiles. Scenes depicting mythological stories Miryam didn't recognize were carved into the bases of the marble columns and eaves of the roof. Phylaktos explained that the temple had been destroyed and rebuilt seven times, the first temple having been erected thousands of years ago. A man who wanted infamy burned down the temple on the day Alexander the Great was born. Alexander, at the age of twenty-two, offered to rebuild the temple, but the megabyxus of the time declined, saying it was inappropriate for one deity to build a temple for another deity. Alexander sent his architect anyway.

Phylaktos led Miryam and Cerinthus through Artemis's inner chamber. In addition to the grand rendition of the goddess standing at the far end of the hall, a number of smaller, more ornate wooden Artemis statues stood with several statues of her parents, Zeus and Leto, and twin brother, Apollo, all draped in gold and jewels and laden with blossoming, smoldering, or decaying offerings at their feet. The ethereal melissa priestesses dressed in violet or yellow tunics tended to the votive activities.

The three of them slipped silently into a torch-lit hallway within the vault walls. Phylaktos didn't need to explain to Miryam what she already knew, that the temple through the centuries had served as an administrative center and more recently as a treasury for Ephesus, as it had begun to prosper again under its latest civilization cycle with the Rhōmaioi. She assumed the treasury was hidden in rooms abutting the hallway, or perhaps in underground chambers beneath the temple.

The guardian stopped in front of one door and, looking up and down the hallway for witnesses, unlocked the door and escorted them inside a musty, windowless room. He lit a torch inside the room with one from the hallway, thus revealing floor-to-ceiling shelving stuffed with papyrus scrolls. Miryam immediately sneezed several times.

Phylaktos pulled a golden box from the shelf and opened the lid. Inside were dozens of papyrus fragments. "Each shred of papyrus in here conveys a different saying," the guardian said with a wide smile, as if he were showing magic to a child. "The author was Heraclitus, an eccentric philosopher who lived in Ephesus nearly six centuries ago. He threw away his inheritance of political and religious office for a life of contemplation and dice-playing here in the Artemision. The temple *cuertes* priests called him the Dark One, the Laughing Philosopher, or the Weeping Philosopher, some for his snobbery and some for his legendary madness that led him to die of suicidal exposure in the forest."

Cerinthus reached toward the box, only to have his hand playfully slapped by the guardian. "Wait for my word," he scolded good-naturedly. "Very fragile."

Cerinthus withdrew his hand but did not cower, his brown eyes dancing.

"Now, Heraclitus pondered the order of the universe, scratched his philosophical riddles onto papyrus, and stuffed torn-off scraps into the nooks and crannies of the temple. The priests would secretly pull the pieces out of the walls as soon as he left them there and add them to the collection in this box. Many scholars have come to the temple over the centuries to copy the sayings, but these are the originals. This box has been passed down from megabyxus to megabyxus, and all have carefully guarded it. These writings have survived everything that destroyed the temple, and the priests believe Heraclitus must have been a protected son of Artemis and his sayings to be his offerings to her."

The box of papyrus pieces glinted in the lantern light like gold leaf. Cerinthus again reached into the box to finger the scraps, but stopped to check for permission. "Go ahead, boy, but be very careful not to tear," Phylaktos said.

He randomly selected a fragile fragment and carefully held it to the lamplight. Though the dialect was extinct, the alphabet hadn't changed much through the centuries, making it easy to sound out the words, "ὁδὸς ἄνω κάτω μία καὶ ὡυτή." He looked to Phylaktos for approval and translation.

"'The way up and the way down are one in the same,'" Phylaktos interpreted.

Cerinthus thought about it a moment. "I don't understand."

"Neither do I, entirely, but this is a prime example of the seemingly nonsensical things the Weeping Philosopher wrote about. As we read on, you will see certain themes emerge. Try another one."

Cerinthus was already reaching for another piece, clearly enjoying the game of plucking the oracles from the box. Again he sounded out the words and looked to the old guardian.

"'Eyes and ears are bad witnesses to men having barbarian *psychē*,'" Phylaktos translated, laughing.

"Psychē?" Miryam was unfamiliar with the word.

"Neshama," Cerinthus translated for her. "Soul."

Miryam nodded. "So, Heraclitus was considered arrogant because he thought most men had barbarian souls? Paulos would agree with that."

"Paulos is also arrogant," the old man said.

"My teacher might have interpreted the statement to mean that not all souls have the eyes and ears to penetrate the truth. Perhaps that is what Heraclitus meant."

"That makes more sense." Phylaktos pulled a scrap from the box. "Ah, one of my favorites: 'You could not discover the limits of the psychē, even if you traveled by every path in order to do so; such is the depth of its meaning.'"

"True, no one can know the psychē by any means on earth," Miryam acknowledged.

Phylaktos eyed her a moment, then continued. "Heraclitus has much to say about the psychē that is not so easy to understand right away, such as: 'Psychēs are vaporized from what is moist.'"

Miryam laughed, and deep within her she thought she heard Ravi laugh as well.

"Heraclitus had some ideas about fire and vapor being keys to the kosmos. The word 'psychē' comes from the word 'breath,' which is a kind of vapor that can't be grasped by human hands or minds."

Cerinthus scrunched his brow. "Like the steam rising above a pot of boiling water?"

"Something like that," Phylaktos answered, shrugging.

"The word neshama also means breath," Miryam added.

"Some ideas are universal. Heraclitus says, 'The psychē takes pleasure in becoming moist ... we live in the death of them and they in our death,'" Phylaktos continued. "Then in another fragment he says, 'A dry psychē is wisest and best. The best and wisest psychē is a dry beam of light.'"

Miryam thought about this a moment. "Perhaps he means that when a psychē becomes human, it becomes moist, but then as the psychē becomes disciplined, it turns to light. My teacher used to say, 'The lamp of the body is the eye. When the eye becomes single, the whole body fills with light.'"

"Would this be the same teacher Paulos was preaching on our steps?"

Miryam flinched. She hadn't intended to give away her association with the very object of Paulos's zealousness. She remained silent.

Phylaktos smiled. "Don't worry. Your secret is safe with me. Time for one more?" When Miryam nodded, Phylaktos pulled out another slip and read: "'Listening not to me but to the Logos, it is wise to acknowledge that all is one.'"

Miryam felt her scalp tingle. *Logos*. Paulos had mentioned the word logos in regard to his personal philosophy about Rav Yeshua or, rather, the resurrected Christos. Now here was the word in a different context. The saying reminded her of what the Hindu had told her at the agora just a few days ago: *One must meditate on the Aum to understand the laws that govern Creation, and also to feel fulfilled in all desires.* Miryam knew that logos could be loosely translated as davar in Ivrit, meaning speech, words, thoughts, reason, but did logos have a greater meaning, a spiritual meaning, just as Memra is the Utterance, the Voice, the Word of Elah? "Tell me, what does logos mean to you, Phylaktos?"

"The philosophers, the lovers of wisdom, have discussed the logos at great length over the ages since Heraclitus coined it. Some have thought that logos means reason in the highest sense, but to others logos means universal order or pattern. To me, Heraclitus's logos is much more complex. He said, 'Although the Logos is common to all, most men live as if they each have a private intelligence of their own.' He also said, 'Logos holds eternal, yet humans always prove unable to understand it.' His Logos was a circle in which the alpha and the omega are the same point. His Logos was in the unity of opposites: day and night, winter and summer, war and peace, youth and old age. And yet he suggested that we must listen to the Logos to know that all is One. To listen to the Logos implies it is some kind of faceless, overriding power that steers all things through all things, as opposed to the Pantheon of many deities. This was appalling to the priests, but they completely missed the instruction to 'listen' to the Logos, *logizomai*, maybe because the Logos is a wisdom that can be heard. He challenged men to know themselves, and perhaps the way to know oneself is to listen to the Logos."

Well put, Miryam thought. "In Ivrit we have a similar word, hakshavah, meaning to listen with attentiveness." She was beginning to suspect that legends about Heraclitus, the Weeping Philosopher, had grown up around him like weeds around a tomb of misinterpretation. Heraclitus was more than a philosopher; he might have been a disciple of the Logos, if not a master himself. And the life of those who pursued the Logos could never be understood by outsiders.

Phylaktos considered what she said a moment. "Plato wrote somewhere about listening to the Logos. Just a matter of remembering which biblos it's in." He reached into a cubbyhole and checked the tags tied to the handles of several scrolls. "*Phaedo.* This is it," he said. He pulled the scroll from the shelf and placed it on a nearby slanted table. With a hand on each of the two wooden rods holding the scroll, he began unrolling one end and re-rolling the other at the same time. "It's about a conversation his teacher, Socrates, had with students and friends on the day before his execution. He said the psychē is the invisible, divine, incorruptible part of the disciplined philosopher, which doesn't vanish after death."

"Who is Socrates, and why was he to be killed?" Miryam asked.

"Socrates was a great thinker," Cerinthus jumped in to explain.

"His life began just as Heraclitus's life was ending," Phylaktos added. "He was killed for refusing to believe in the Athenian deities."

Miryam winced at the familiarity and what could have happened to Rav Yeshua. Life was hard on the great teachers.

"Ah, here is what Socrates said." Phylaktos began reading:

> *The soul will calm passion by listening to the Logos within and by always being in it and by beholding what is true and divine and not the object of opinion.*

"Listening to the Logos ... just like Heraclitus," Cerinthus said.

Phylaktos nodded and continued:

> *And being nurtured by it, the soul will seek to live in this way for as long as she lives, so that when she dies, she will enter that which is kindred and similar to her own nature, and be freed from human ills.*

"My teacher taught that it is paramount to listen to what you call the Logos to enter into 'that which is kindred' before dying," Miryam said.

"While alive? Now, that's something I would have to look into."

"Truly? If I were to tell you, would you store what you learn in this dusty library? Because if you were to become interested, you would have to consider leaving the temple to follow the Way. You cannot serve two masters at once. Unlike Paulos, my teacher would not have recruited you for the sake of recruiting you. You have to be ready to seek salvation."

Phylaktos looked at Miryam a moment, his jaw slightly ajar at what she'd so boldly stated. He started to say something, then thought differently, clearly stumped. He slumped and sighed. "You're correct. I can't leave the temple. I'm wedded for life."

"And you seem content here," Miryam said.

"Content, yes, to continue studying all beliefs while remaining devoted to temple life." Phylaktos smiled, and then changed the subject. "Since we were speaking of the crow earlier, you might be interested in this passage where Socrates likens the soul to the swan." The old temple guardian began reading dramatically like a poet:

> *Swans, when they feel they are to die, sing most and best in their joy that they are to go to the gods whose servants they are. But men, because of their own fear of death, misrepresent the swans and say that they sing for sorrow, in mourning for their own death. No bird sings when it is hungry or cold or has any other trouble, not even the nightingale or the swallow or the hoopoe. I do not believe they sing for grief, nor do the swans; but since they are Apollo's birds, I believe they have prophetic vision, and because they have foreknowledge of the blessings in the other world, they sing and rejoice on that day more than ever before. And I think that I am myself a fellow servant of the swans, and am consecrated to the same gods and have received from our master a gift of prophecy no whit inferior to theirs, and that I go out from life with as little sorrow as they.*

Miryam felt her soul caught up in the word breezes and transported to some distant land. It was as if Socrates was speaking directly to her. Though she was not on the eve of her death, a part of her was dying, and although she herself sometimes grieved for the retreating world as it simultaneously fought to keep her in its talons, she also rejoiced with great exaltation in the promise of the world to come as a fellow servant of the Elah.

"So both the crow and the swan belong to Apollo?" Miryam asked.

"All birds belong to the deities, for they fly closest to their home on Olympus, much like your angels."

"We consider all water fowl to be unclean birds and unsuitable for eating," the boy said.

"One of our many cultural differences," Phylaktos responded.

"You have given me much to ... listen to, Phylaktos." Miryam was beginning to feel an invisible tug from Martha out in the cart to end this trek into literature, as uplifting as it was. "Thank you so much for showing us these treasures. You are well-educated yourself."

"Temple life is infused with scholarship," he said, with a nod to the boy.

"We need to return to my sister." She pulled her young student toward the door. "Again, thank you, and I apologize for the earlier ruckus on the temple steps."

"We are all dyed in the hue of the company we keep," the guardian said.

"You mean *I* am a scavenging crow by association with Paulos," she joked.

Phylaktos laughed. "Maybe he is becoming a swan through his company with you." He started to show them out of the room, then hesitated a moment. "If you're interested in gaining more insight on the Logos, I have something that might help."

"More?" Miryam was already quite full from this visit.

"You'll appreciate these biblos," he said, winking at Cerinthus. "Now, where is that scroll? He began pulling papyri out of their cubicles one by one, quickly unrolling the scroll just enough to read a section, and re-rolling and re-shelving each reject. "It was a volume of scrolls. My memory isn't what it used to be." In a moment, his eyes brightened with remembrance. He leaned a nearby ladder against the shelves and climbed to the top, feeling around until he found a large leather container, long and round in shape. "Ah, here it is." He slapped the dust from the container and turned it to read the engraving along one side: "Julius Philo Alexandrinus."

Once on the floor again, the guardian pulled the cap from the case to reveal a mass of tightly wound scrolls snuggled within it. "Until construction on the Celsius Library in Ephesus is completed, the Artemision is serving as a library. Philo deposited this case en route to Rhōmē some ten, fifteen years ago. If I recall, he told me he'd sought to build a bridge between Hellene philosophy and Ivrit wisdom. His writings didn't find a home at the synagogue among the Ivrit, and it isn't of much interest to our temple, but I did promise to safeguard it. Perhaps you might like to borrow it for a period. I assume no one will miss it."

"I'm from Alexandria," Cerinthus exclaimed. "I'd love to take a look at the manuscripts, Atta Miryam."

Miryam scowled. She wanted to decline for the boy's sake, not wishing him to be drawn in any further, but she was just as curious as he was. Rav Yeshua had trained in Egypt, and perhaps the writings contained further clues to the Mysteries. She took the scroll case and put it under her palla. Then the two of them followed Phylaktos down a less attended passageway to a discreet exit out the side of the temple.

"If I change my mind about what we discussed earlier, where can I find you?"

"We live near the top of Mount Koressos," she called back, knowing their conversation would continue to haunt him for a long time. She and the boy scampered to the cart where Martha sat with pursed lips, no doubt chanting her secret words to keep from scolding their tardiness.

Six

"I found it!" Cerinthus exclaimed. For the past week, he and Miryam had been pouring over the works of Philo of Alexandria after morning chores. "The answer to the question I asked you not too long ago: Who was Elohim talking to when He said, 'Let there be light, and there was light.' Remember?" Here's what Philo wrote: 'While He spoke the Logos, He did at the same moment create. He did not allow anything to come between the Logos and the deed – His Logos is His deed.'"

"So, His voice creates everything," Miryam responded, amazed that Cerinthus found the phrase in such a vast forest of words, let alone understood it. More than a dozen volumes were stuffed into the leather case, and each scroll was so long it could only be spread out on the meal table a length at a time. Sometimes they stretched the papyri across the room over chairbacks, with Martha helping to keep them from touching the floor.

Philo's writings were completely opposite to those of the Weeping Philosopher the elderly guardian Phylaktos had introduced them to at the temple. Heraclitus's sayings on scraps of papyrus were brief, to the point, and provocative, while Philo took his time to explore each subject so thoroughly, Miryam nearly forgot what she was reading about. It was easy to get bogged down in the writing, but she found some real gems there. In a way, unburying the treasure was not much different from pulling a riddle by Heraclitus out of the storage box at the temple. Both were equally random, yet seemingly guided by the hand of Elah.

"That verse from Genesis can be interpreted differently depending on whether one reads it in Ivrit or Hellene," Miryam told Cerinthus. She liked to challenge her young student, but now they challenged each other. "In Ivrit,

Elah created with His Memra, or Voice, but in Hellene He creates through Logos, or wisdom and reasoning."

"I think Philo meant it both ways, and some ways of his own," Cerinthus said, scratching his head. "Philo says many things about the Logos. For instance, he says that the voice of mortals is heard by human ears, but the Voice of the All is seen and not heard. Here, I wrote it down: 'The Voice is not an impact of air made by the mouth and tongue, but radiating splendor … seen by the eye of the soul.'"

"Ah!" Miryam said, knowing the very truth of that statement because she lived it personally every day. "Then, not only is light something that emanates from the sun, it is also the Voice, which is both the action and wisdom of Elah," Miryam said.

Cerinthus nodded agreement. "In another place, Philo writes that the Logos 'descends from the fountain of wisdom like a river to wash and water the celestial garden of virtue-loving souls.'"

"Beautifully put. Can you help me read this section here?" Though Miryam could speak Hellene with little trouble, she still could not read it that well. Not only did she have to get used to a whole different set of characters, she also had to learn to read from left to right rather than from right to left. She would sometimes scan the text until she found a word or two that looked familiar, and then ask Cerinthus to help her. This often led to some profound statement she was sure Ravi himself had inspired her to find, such as this passage from a book on dreams:

> *And who can pour over the happy soul, which proffers its own logos as the most sacred cup, the holy goblets of true joy, except the cup-bearer of God, the master of the feast, the Logos, not differing from the draught Itself, but being Itself in an unmixed state, the pure delight and sweetness, and pouring forth, and joy, and ambrosial medicine of pleasure and happiness, if we too may, for a moment, employ the language of the poets.*

Miryam swooned and her neshama soared like a dove above her head, not only from the poetry of the writer, but also because of the truth she knew and lived and could hardly contain. Philo presented the Logos as the Living

Power that It is, transcending the idea of the Logos as being cold, dry reason. Philo was clearly a master of words, but was he also an initiate of *the* Word, the Logos? Some passages indicated an influence by the things of Spirit, such as this one: "The Logos is the charioteer of the powers, and he who utters it is the rider who guides the charioteer with a view to the proper guidance of the universe." *How did Philo know that, unless he'd been initiated?*

When the moment passed, a moment that took her to places unknown even to herself, her senses returned to the kitchen, and she found Cerinthus studying her. "That is what the Logos feels like to you," this ancient youth declared. "You don't have to tell me, if it is private."

Not knowing what to say or what she should say, Miryam opted to say nothing for the moment. Later she would contemplate a proper response for Cerinthus thoroughly with Ravi. In the meantime they continued studying Philo.

From what she could gather, Philo applied what he knew about Hellene philosophy to the Ivrit stories in the five books of Moses. The Hellene philosophers talked about the Logos, the *Nous* of understanding, the Divine Mind that exists alive in every human being. To Philo, the ordered Creation that came from the Reasoning Power of the Logos or the Voice of the Memra were the same in either language, for he regarded them both as Wisdom, called the *Sophia* in Helene and the *Chochmah* in Ivrit. Clearly, Philo was enamored with the thinking of the Hellene philosophers, and he did try to wed their ideas with the prophecies and guidance of Ivrit scripture, whether they were compatible or not.

In fact, Philo considered Moses to be the "summit of philosophy," and he figured a Hellene philosopher named Pythagoras to be a student of Moses, but Cerinthus thought that Moses had lived a very long time before Pythagoras. "Every schoolboy in Ephesus knows who Pythagoras is," he informed her. He was a mathematician and philosopher who described the celestial bodies in the night sky as moving together precisely like the strings of a lyre. *Harmaronia universalis*, they called it, the Music of the Spheres. Apparently the idea came when Pythagoras heard blacksmiths hitting hot metal on their anvils, and the sounds were so resonant and harmonious and uplifting that to him they could only be expressed by number. *The Logos is the Music of the Spheres*, she thought as she reveled in this newest layer of description.

Miryam was beginning to appreciate a universality of the concept of the Logos that even her own master hadn't disclosed to her. The principles of the Memra/Logos seemed to remain the same no matter where they manifested, she was noticing, but each culture they encountered added a fresh vocabulary and understanding to them. If Logos existed before the light and darkness and heaven and earth existed, and nothing else existed but Logos, then the Logos Way must also have pre-existed Creation. Rav Yeshua's teachings did not originate in his homeland or by his hand – the teachings were eternal.

Just as Philo helped to enlarge Miryam's understanding of the Logos, he also enhanced her understanding of soul's return journey to its origin. Philo described the soul as "having descended into the body as into a river, carried away and swallowed up by the voracity of a most violent whirlpool." After so much time in the whirlpool, the soul "strives with all of its power to resist its impulsiveness, at first swimming on the top of it, and afterward flying back to the place from where it started." He wrote that these superior souls "have been taught some kind of sublime philosophy, some meditating, from beginning to end, on dying as to the life of the body in order to obtain an inheritance of the immortal and eternal life, which is to be enjoyed in the presence of the unmanifested and everlasting God." Philo never wrote about the soul living more than one lifetime, but he implied it with this passage.

Philo went on to write that those souls who are swallowed up in the whirlpool of human existence, "have disregarded wisdom, giving themselves up to the pursuit of unstable things regulated by chance alone ... rather than to the dead corpse connected with us." In other words, most people would rather pursue all of the things the world has to offer, which is the dead image, rather than pursue the live image of the soul.

Rav Yeshua would have agreed with Philo. Indeed the bulk of humanity did not care about *philosophía*, the love of wisdom, or about swimming above the torrential whirlpool of physical life. Even the spiritual initiate floundered in the whirlpool and sometimes drowned in it. Just as Philo wrote that it was the body that was dead, Ha-Rav also taught that all people were the walking dead. "Let the dead bury the dead," he would say to his disciples when they wished to attend the burial of a family member. He would criticize the priests "who lie in unmarked graves, and everyone walks over them unknowingly," and for all their training and praying and rituals, the priests were no more "alive" than the masses. Some of his disciples "would not taste death until they experienced the power of the kingdom and shall be as angels in heaven," and that the time would eventually come for them to hear the Voice within themselves. "Abba is not the God of the dead, but the God of the Living," he would say. "Why seek the living among the dead?"

The prophets beseeched Yĕhovah to let their nefesh, the spark of life, out of the grave because the corpse stays there and decays. "Deliver my nefesh from the sword, my beingness from the dog of death," as it was written in *Psalms*. But there was a different sentiment in verses about the neshama, the soul, the spirit of the Divine. From *Proverbs*: "The neshama is the candle of Yĕhovah searching for the innermost parts of the Womb." To Miryam's understanding, that was neshama's prime desire, to return to the Womb of the One, not to re-enliven one's body rotting in the grave.

Philo described how some souls ascend as if by a ladder reaching to heaven through the contemplation on scripture. When elevated to a high enough level, these devoted beings would be instructed indirectly through a vision of the Logos as the *dēmiourgós* of the One, an "artisan of the kosmos," the lesser power or co-worker of the Divine that becomes clearer as one ascends. To Philo, "the most universal is God, and next to Him, the Logos of God, the perceptible order of all things." The Logos was at once the first-born power as the son of God and the creative power of the kosmos. In other words, Philo understood that the Logos was a mediator between soul and heaven, and without such a mediator or guide, the soul would never return to the Womb of the One, its primordial origin. That rang true with Miryam.

She was so inspired, she began to experience a quickening deep within herself. *The Word is stirring*, she thought. When Cerinthus reluctantly left at the end of one day, Miryam unrolled the practice papyrus where she had previously scrawled her first verse on the Word in Aramit:

> *The Word exists at the Source. The Word exists with Elah. Elah creates everything. Nothing exists that is not in the hand of Elah.*

Guided from within, she drew lines through the verse. On another page, below where Cerinthus had recorded their favorite excerpts from Heraclitus and Philo, she rewrote her verse in Hellene, substituting Logos for Memra, which to her contained the fuller meaning:

> *The Logos exists at the Source, and the Logos exists with the One, and the Logos is the One, and the One is the Source. The One makes all, and nothing exists that is not in the hand of the One. From the One comes life, and the life is the Light of the world.*

As she wrote this, she realized the verse had expanded a bit with her newfound understanding of the Logos as described by Philo. The Logos is not just the message and the creative power of the Divine, she thought. It is also the very Essence and Redeemer of the Divine. Since the One was too unimaginably great to exist within His own creation, He had to send down a power that could live within all of life. For without that power, the Logos, nothing could exist.

Miryam felt a new verse form in her head:

> *And the Light shines in darkness, and the darkness comprehends it not.*

She sat back and reviewed the new sentence she just penned, admiring how simply it explained how the One power at the Origin became Two interplaying yet opposing powers in the lower world, a phrase that was inspired, perhaps, by Heraclitus. The Logos was One, the unlimited, unfathomable, immeasurable, invisible, unutterable, unnamable, and eternal. The Logos became Two, the Light and the Darkness, the Adam and the Chavah who fell into the world and became the first Father and the first Mother, Thought and Wisdom. These two equal powers remained at constant odds with one another for all eternity. The description reminded her of a riddle she heard the men chant as they gambled over a dice game on the Temple steps: "First there was One, then there were Two, then there was One again." For without the merging of the two powers within one's self, the soul could not enter the Kingdom.

Miryam thought about how the divided powers became unified. Philo had written that the Logos was the Cupbearer, that the soul needed someone to behave as an advocate on its behalf before God. Another phrase knocked at her inner door. As the stylus began scratching on the papyrus once again, she immediately saw how Logos was now transformed into an even higher truth:

> *The Logos is made flesh and dwells among us, and we behold His glory, the glory as the son of the One, full of grace and truth. In Him is life, and the life is the Light of all souls.*

Ah, how true, Miryam thought. This is Rav Yeshua, the Master Divine, the Logos made flesh, the unifier of the two powers. He embodies the Logos and instills it in His disciples. He is half divine, half human. Not Yeshua the man, who had two human parents, but Yeshua who was also initiated into the mystery of the Logos and mastered It and *became* the Divine. No, Paulos and Simeon, Yeshua did not die and then resurrect, he rose before death. He achieved apotheosis. He merged with the One so that He could appear within His initiates in His glorified body and aid them in realizing the same divinity within themselves. He is the Light of the world, and the darkness can never comprehend him. He illuminates the path to the One within our beings as we follow in His footsteps to achieve our own apotheosis.

Rav Yeshua taught that every living being had within them both powers, the nefesh *and* the neshama, the mind and soul, though neither power was aware of the other. The neshama is the invisible divine part that is capable of knowing, being, and seeing the All. The nefesh is the mind, the part that allows one to think, to have appetites, passions, desires, emotions. The nefesh stays in control of the individual, while the neshama slumbers until that glorious day when initiation into the Logos begins the awakening and ascending and merging. Moses may have parted the Red Sea, but it is the master, the Logos made flesh, who reunites the dual streams of creation, the light and the darkness, the Adam and the Chavah, the nefesh and neshama within each initiate, who then rides the unified stream to the All in spirit. The multiple layers of Creation and the Logos of the One, heard and seen inwardly, are all embodied in and conveyed to the initiate by and through the Living Master.

Just as Rav Yeshua is the Logos made flesh and the Light of the world, so too is the disciple, she thought. She repeated Rav Yeshua's words to herself: *When your eye becomes single, your whole body will fill with light*. And Rav Yeshua was the light, or rather Ravi, the Radiant Form of the Logos, was the light! Therefore, if the disciple could make the inner eye single, Ravi would appear.

It was the task of every disciple, to become familiar with one's thoughts, memories, words, actions, and deeds brought on by the two physical eyes, with the purpose of making the inner eye singular through persistent concentration on the Logos so that one stayed buoyant in the whirlpool of physical life. She knew from personal experience that, miraculously, Ravi fills the initiate with light through the Logos, thus illuminating all of the lower parts that are not the soul and flooding one with the Living Water. Being flooded as such, the initiates could rise within themselves. Upon seeing the radiant form of the outer rav through one's singular eye, the student's soul is then elevated by the Inner Rav from the unmarked grave of the physical body in order to lead it through subsequently higher realms of heaven toward the Nameless One.

If she could have a frank conversation with Paulos, she would tell him that a spiritual rising was not a release from the body when someone suddenly awakened from death and floated up to Christos in the sky. A spiritual "rising" was an interior progression, a blessing after many, many years of following a true, living rav, the Logos made flesh. The student died inwardly to their worldly attachments and desires and vanity only to experience their own spirits rise within themselves through the portal of the single eye to meet the Rav Within – and then the real journey through a spiritual landscape began! Just as the body is the tomb that traps the soul, it is also the temple of the Divine.

Rav Yeshua had taught that the Logos is eternal. It always wears the face of the current living master made flesh so that the Inner Rav could be recognized by the disciple. For students of other true and living masters, the Logos would bear the face of those masters. It was true, Miryam had seen the risen Ha-Rav – Ravi – in His glorified form. She held Him in her third eye in every moment, and yet she was not the first among her fellow students to see Him. Her brother, Lazarus, had been the first to rise from the dead in spirit. She wondered if Simeon and Yakob could also view the Radiant Form of Ha-Rav within themselves, as suggested by the stories told of being shown his Glorified Body on the mountain? She would never know.

This much she knew for certain: Rav Yeshua was born into this world to bring only his own readied students back to heaven. "I am the good shepherd," he would say. "I know my own, and I'm known by my own; even as the Father knows me, and I know the Father." Everyone would eventually meet their own master, who would transform each in spirit so that each could reunite with the Nameless One.

As new ideas poured into the overflowing cup of Miryam's nefesh, thoughts of Paulos still plagued her. He remained an enigma to her, and she knew he was not going to go away quietly. With his propensity to challenge religious authority, serious trouble was inevitable for him in Ephesus, and the silence was like waiting for a flower bud to open and then wilt. In the end, the blossom always dried up and blew away in the wind.

Seven

Miryam and Martha continued their daily routine. They rose before daybreak, lit the fire they had prepared the night before, and settled in chairs near the warmth to commune with Ravi within. They focused their attention on what Rav Yeshua had called the shepherd's gate, the inner *tera*, the portal between and above their outer eyes. They chanted the five secret words Rav Yeshua had given them upon initiation into the Logos, chanting not with the tongue but with the heart of neshama. They smiled on the radiant face of Ravi, listening to and immersing in the sound of His love drawing them ever inward to His bosom. Here, in this inner sanctum, there were no intellectual pursuits, no problems, no darkness. Only the golden light and the sweet, pining harmony playing to neshama on the lyre of the Divine.

For Miryam, it was crucial to turn away from thinking about the Logos, and continue the daily practice of becoming the Logos. Philo had understood that it was one thing to get drunk on the Shefa, the True Wine, but then it was important to mature one's wisdom through the power of the Logos to identify the passions and illusions that kept them in the grave.

It was as Socrates had written: "The soul calms passions by listening to the Logos." And what were these passions, the human ills that the soul would calm? They were not sins exactly, as Paulos had told the peasant woman at the temple, but persistent tendencies that kept the soul trapped: anger, lust, greed, attachment, and vanity. It is through these tricks of the mind that enslaves the soul to illusion, when in truth the mind is the servant of soul. Paulos had erroneously stated that the resurrected Yeshua would wash away the sins of the baptized believer. A master would have to be the size of Atlas to shoulder the weight of all the sins of his disciples let alone those of the world. But in a sense, a master did take up the debts gathered over lifetimes of existence and then meter them back to the initiates in perfect order so that they might learn about themselves and set about unleashing the soul from the power of the mind.

So, listening to the Logos was a daily process of looking at a given situation, observing one's reactions to that situation, and then realizing the reactions are of the mind and not the soul. During hakshavah, the practice of listening inwardly, one presents all that one has observed and learned about the self to the Inner Ravi. Rav Yeshua called the process "turning the other cheek." When someone hit you on one cheek, he taught to show them the other cheek. He didn't intend for his students to allow the enemy to hit them twice, as some of Miryam's fellow students had erroneously thought, but to baptize one's reactions to it. Turn water into wine. Turn pain into love, anger into forgiveness, but do so inwardly with the herculean strength of Ravi. That's how the sins of the devotees were transfigured and redeemed.

On this day, Miryam's inner sight filled with light brighter than the sun, and she spiritually swam in it. But it wasn't enough. She wanted to go higher, to once and for all receive permanent relief from this intriguing yet punishing, unbearable *sheol* of a world. Craving more sights and sounds, she allowed her senses to push just a bit harder. The radiant form of Ha-Rav abruptly gave way to Paulos's sharp-featured face. Where once beamed the enrapturing eyes of Ravi, Paulos's reddened eyes now seared her forehead.

Miryam instantly opened her physical eyes, exasperated. This was the second time Paulos's image had abruptly stopped her contemplation. Clearly, she still had work to do.

She turned her gaze to Martha, who was still engrossed in her own contemplation. With eyes closed, head tilted toward the ceiling, the corners of her mouth turned upward in a slight smile, she looked like an angel in contrast to the image of Paulos that had just assaulted her senses. She wondered if Martha was ever troubled. Miryam's older sister rarely discussed her problems with her or expressed any fears or dissatisfactions. She may have been that much more adept than Miryam ever had been at taking her problems before Ravi, seeing the lesson within them, and then releasing them to rise higher within herself. Martha was the lady of her own house, quietly going about her business, her problems as well as her spiritual gains kept in their proper place. Miryam was the magadan, the tower as Ha-Rav had teased, bold and obvious. *Indeed, the taller and stronger the mind, the more difficult it is to overcome*, she thought. She sighed and quietly stood to take her contemplation outside.

The crisp mountain air was a welcome respite to the stifling images of her mind. The sun's first rays were beginning to peak over hilltops, revealing some of the unwanted growth in their garden. Miryam shooed away the crows perched on the fence, then dropped to all fours alongside a row of onions and began tugging at one weed in particular, but it resisted her pull. *The tap root of this one must run deep*, she thought. How had it become so entrenched before she or Martha noticed it? "You sow what you reap," she suddenly remembered Rav Yeshua saying once. He also said that your enemies weed your garden without payment, and your reward is discovering your own flaws. A soft giggle came to her lips and she sat up. *Am I so resistant, Ravi?* She yanked on the weed with both hands, and fell backwards when it finally gave way, landing her squarely on her rear end. *Oy!*

Miryam stood triumphantly with weed in hand and slapped away the dirt from the back of her night tunic. One of the crows, which had quietly returned to the fence while she weeded, fluttered at the outburst. Again she laughed inwardly, remembering Rav Yeshua's lesson on this annoying bird. "The raven neither sows nor reaps nor stores its food, yet Abba still feeds it." In other words, "seek first the kingdom and all else will be added unto you," he would say, implying that soul's ascension was natural and spontaneous. Applied to the moment, all of her concerns were probably not that serious in the scheme of things.

In the past few weeks her nefesh was like a waterwheel, constantly circling through all the things she knew about Paulos in an effort to find an answer. When no answer came, she pushed the wheel around again. *Not this time*, she resolved within herself. This time she would lay all the things that concerned her about Paulos in a basket at Ravi's feet. She drew a deep breath and chanted her secret words. Releasing and relaxing, she felt ready to begin again, but this time from her soul and not her mind.

All right, she admitted to Ravi, Paulos was becoming all-consuming. Despite how she liked to think of herself, accepting of everyone, Miryam had to concede she didn't like Paulos. She didn't like how he had misrepresented Ha-Rav, how he misrepresented Ha-Rav's teachings and his students. She didn't like how he trumped up the use of magic – signs and wonders and mighty deeds he called them – to convince people to become baptized. She didn't like how he used Ha-Rav's name to promote his own cause, whatever that was. She didn't like how he seemed to promote himself in the name of "Christos." She didn't like how he seemed to model his own life after the Christos stories, as if he, himself, were the martyr wounded in much the same way.

Miryam had only been in Paulos's presence twice – once in her home when they first met, and again on the Artemision steps. Yet Paulos, or Miryam's reaction to Paulos, or something within her that Paulos represented, was somehow blocking her entrance into the higher circles of heaven. What that something was, was still unclear to Miryam. She realized she had been pulling and pulling at the roots of this weed, trying to figure out why he disturbed her so much. She knew that once she presented the weed to Ravi, He would miraculously make it disappear – in His own time and whenever He felt she had gathered as much of the nourishment she needed from this weed. Ayn, in spiritual growth, there were only two sources of nutrients: the Shefa from the inner Ravi, which shed light on the weeds, and the weeds themselves, which contained within them bits of one's own energy. She needed that energy to get back to the source of the Living Water.

Miryam exhaled a long, deep breath while chanting her secret words. She would wait patiently for Ravi's miracles. After all, it wasn't her task to fix this problem, but to turn it over to Him. Her only task was to see that she still had some lingering misunderstandings, and these were embodied in Paulos as a mirror. In that surrender, an overwhelming wave of love flooded over her.

Grateful to finally gain approval of Ravi within her, she stood and turned toward the house, but before she could open the door, she heard footsteps coming up the path. Paulos entered her garden. *Speak of my daimonion*, she thought.

"Shlama," he said.

"Shlama, Paulos. What brings you here so early?" Miryam wasn't used to unannounced visitors at this time of day. Thankful she had grabbed her palla before coming outside, she now pulled it tightly across the front of her night tunic.

"You never gave me an answer about whether you and I could have an exchange."

"There's more to say? Haven't I already received a fair amount of your gospel?"

"There's so much more," he said.

"After what happened at the temple, you're not angry with me?"

"I do become passionate about the Christos, and I'm amazed you are not." He raised a hand before she could respond. "I also understand your need for anonymity, and I apologize if I put you in danger. After all, we are all persecuted."

Paulos would always view himself as a cohort in promoting and defending what he thought to be Rav Yeshua's mission, Miryam thought. She was about to dismiss him when she felt a sudden blast of Shefa within her skull, and in that instant was reminded of the grander plan Ha-Rav had long ago mentioned that was now unfolding before her eyes. This was Ravi's way of calling her attention to something important. *Gnothi seauton*, as the Hellene were fond of carving on their temple walls. "Know yourself." Sometimes the only way to know oneself was through encounters with others. Sighing, she surrendered to the resistance of this weed in her garden. "Swear upon your Christos you will tell no one of our visits?"

Paulos lifted a hand from his heart skyward.

"Our names must never cross your lips or be written by your hand. Do you understand?"

Paulos nodded. "Of course."

"Martha and I are baking this morning, and we have our students coming this afternoon. Tomorrow?"

"Why not now?" He tilted his head downward in an unprecedented sign of reverence. "Or are you able to bake and talk at the same time?"

Miryam wasn't surprised or offended by Paulos's persistence, for today he seemed more sincere than usual. "Let me speak with Martha, and then give us a moment to prepare."

Paulos sat down on the same tree stump where she'd just sat and contemplated her annoyances with him. The wilting, uprooted, stubborn weed that had given her a flash of insight mere moments earlier lay near his feet. Miryam took it as a further sign of the inner work she must do. *What do I need, a burning bush?* She laughed before catching herself.

"What's so funny?" Paulos asked, a bit defensively.

"Nothing. I will call you in when we're ready."

Martha was already dressed for the day when Miryam entered the house and changed her own clothes as she explained her arrangement with Paulos. "I gathered as much when I heard his voice," Martha said.

Cerinthus soon arrived with firewood, and after stacking the short logs outside, he brought a few inside to help Martha build a fire. "Atta Miryam, I'd hoped to read Philo's writings this morning, but I see you have a visitor. Do you mind if I sit at the table and read? I won't get in the way."

Miryam wasn't sure how far the conversation with Paulos would go, but Cerinthus could most likely benefit from whatever she would say to the evangelist. A glance from Martha told her she approved. "As long as you're quiet. If I ask you to leave, please do so quickly and politely, knowing it isn't out of punishment but out of a necessity to speak with the visitor alone. We'll set Philo aside for now. Don't want to get flour on the scrolls."

"Toda." He took a seat at the end of the table, his eyes gleaming.

Invited inside at last, Paulos sat opposite Cerinthus, giving him a questioning look. "This is a student of ours, Paulos," Miryam said.

"I asked for a private exchange," he answered, folding his hands, perhaps to calm his tendency toward agitation.

"I believe you will find Cerinthus to be quite ... mature."

"Ah," he murmured, raising his eyebrows and smiling slightly as he studied this new, albeit young, prospect. "I am called Paulos, apostolos."

"I recognize you from the temple steps," Cerinthus said, pinching off a chunk of the barley loaf Martha placed on the table. Obviously, at least to Miryam, Cerinthus already knew who Paulos was when he saw him in the garden, and he had asked to watch out of curiosity.

Miryam began mixing flour and water for the bread, while Martha stoked the fire. Like Cerinthus, Paulos was quiet, his countenance open like a rose in full bloom, poised to take in everything Miryam had to say, thereby imparting his own message in the meantime. Paulos wasn't necessarily a pleasant-looking man by her eye, but in this light and with this posture, he looked quite attractive. Miryam wondered how long his serenity would last if his beliefs were challenged.

"Cerinthus, do you know the words neshama and nefesh?" Martha asked casually.

That cut right to the heart of it, Miryam thought. By testing the boy, they could test Paulos's understanding of spiritual principles.

"In the *Bereshit*, Yĕhovah formed man from dust and breathed into his nostrils, and man became a nefesh *chayah*, a living creature," Cerinthus recited. "The breath of Yĕhovah is similar to the leaven that will make this dough rise. I like this saying from the book of *Yob*: 'My neshama is in me, and the ruach of Yĕhovah is in my nostrils. There is a ruach, or a spirit, in man, and the neshama of the Almighty gives them understanding.' In other words, the neshama is a spark of Yĕhovah's spirit."

Miryam was pleased that her student could sense the subtle differences between the Ivrit words, which all meant the same thing: breath. Did Paulos understand the differences as well? "Paulos, would you translate nefesh as *anemos* in Hellene?" Martha asked. "Or *animas*, as the Rhōmaioi might say?"

Paulos considered this a moment. "The Hellene use psychē to describe both our worldly and our divine parts. But I use the word psychē to mean nefesh, which is the worldly part of ourselves. I prefer the word *pneuma* to describe our spirit, or soul, whose understanding is inspired by the Almighty."

"So, you would say psychē for nefesh and pneuma for neshama in Hellene?"

"Roughly." Paulos nodded. "In my gospel, the immature are the *psychikos* and the mature are the *pneumatikos*."

"What determines whether a person is one or the other, mature or immature?" Martha asked.

"They are chosen at birth."

"Indeed? How do you know this?" Miryam asked.

"I am writing about this very subject in my letters. It comes from Scripture." Seeing a teaching opportunity, he turned to Cerinthus. "Abraham had two sons, one by the slave woman, and one by the free woman. The son by the slave was born according to the flesh, but the son by the free woman was born through promise. Now, this allegory represents two groups." He held out his left palm. "The psychikos below, being born of the cosmic powers and elements, live under a curse and worship the rulers of the cosmic powers and elements." He raised his right palm over his left one. "The pneumatikos are from the realm of spirit above, and they are free to worship in spirit and truth, praising Wisdom, the Sophia, the mother of all."

Miryam nodded her approval. Perhaps Paulos did understand the subtle distinctions between the nefesh and neshama in the way Ha-Rav had taught, or in this case the psychē and the pneuma. In an odd way, Rav Yeshua might have agreed with Paulos's assessment of the condition under which all people lived. As he had taught, until the soul is ready to return to heaven, it is cursed to live out a life, indeed many lifetimes, subject to the cosmic elements and powers. "Please continue," she urged, hoping Paulos was finally imparting his secret gospel.

Paulos smiled. "Before Christos, when we were children, we were all held in bondage under the weak and impoverished elements of the world. But when there came the *pleroma*, the fullness of time, Theos sent down his son to collect Abraham's seed according to promise, and to also redeem those who were born in bondage so that they could become heirs by adoption. The Hellene are included in the free group because they are born of a free woman."

No, Paulos doesn't understand, Miryam said to herself with some disappointment. What's worse, Paulos had mixed this key teaching of Ha-Rav's with biblical allegory into his own twisted concept. She needed to hear more.

"Are you speaking in terms of one people over another, of those who would be regarded as the 'chosen'? Aren't wars started on lesser grounds?"

"This is only allegory, for there is neither Ivrit nor Hellene, there is neither slave nor free, there is neither male nor female – all are one in Christos. All are children of Theos through the Christos. He reveals himself to the elect pneumatikos, who then proclaim his glory to the psychikos."

Miryam placed a cloth over the balls of dough she had formed to give them time to rise. "But Paulos, do not all humans have both a psychē and a pneuma, and is it not the task of each to transform the lower to the higher, from the spark of life to realizing the spark of spirit?"

"Ayn, but every being is more closely associated with either his psychē or his pneuma, and I use these two distinctions to help identify who is who. It is much easier for the elect to mature and ripen and then, out of love, help the immature."

"And maturity is determined either by birth and revelation or through the help of someone more mature?"

"Certainly not through circumcision!" Paulos suddenly reddened in the face, and Miryam could see this was still a sore topic with him.

"I didn't say anything about circumcision," Miryam said. It amazed her that Paulos could balance himself on a delicate branch like a bird, and then fall off the branch with the slightest breeze.

"Forgive me. Some of my brothers in Galatia wish to return to the old covenants, and they've missed the point. I'm afraid they've fallen away from grace." He covered his face with his hands and rubbed it vigorously. "The Galatia ekklēsia was doing well until someone interfered. Anyone who believes in such laws are debtors to the law, and Christos will profit them nothing for it." He pointed to the dough. "A little leaven leavens the whole loaf. There is so much to do before Christos returns to save us."

"If not through the covenants, how does one ripen?" Miryam hoped to take his attention off the worries of his mission and bring it back to the kitchen – and truth.

Paulos shrugged. "Baptisma." The answer was clear to him.

"Ayn, baptisma seems important to you," Miryam said, seating herself opposite him. "I'm not sure I understand it fully."

"Flesh and blood cannot inherit the kingdom. The Tanakh shows the soul being trapped in the grave of the earth and suffering a great deal. Its material nature is prone to passions and appetites that weigh it down."

"This is true," Miryam answered.

"The chosen are buried with the Christos by baptism into his death," Paulos answered.

"You've said that before. What do you mean?"

"Through baptisma we are symbolically buried with the Christos as a sort of covenant. All of our sins are removed. At the end of days, we are also raised from the dead by his glory. Raised, we walk in newness of life."

Philo had presented similar concepts in the biblos she was reading. "When we are alive, our spirit is dead and buried in our body, as if in a tomb," Philo had written. "But if we were to die, then our spirit would live according to its proper life, being released from the evil and dead body to which it is bound." The similarities made her wonder if Paulos, in his broad travels, had met Philo or had studied under the same influences as Philo. She wondered if Rav Yeshua had also encountered the same influences.

"That, and no more? Once the chosen are baptized, are they now free to live however they wish until they are redeemed when the Christos returns?"

"Of course not. Those who belong to the Christos nail the passions and desires of their sinful nature to his cross."

"This is heartening," Miryam said. "But it is not so easy."

"Now, the passions of the flesh are obvious." Paulos began to tick them off on his fingertips: "Adultery, sexual immorality, uncleanliness, lustfulness, idolatry, sorcery, hatred, strife, jealousy, outbursts of anger, rivalries, divisions, heresies, murders, drunkenness, orgies, and things like these." He pulled a piece from the barley loaf and popped it into his mouth. "I've had problems with the ekklēsia of this nature in Korinthos," he said, chewing as he spoke. "They've had *porneia* among them, for a man is having his father's wife. The body is not for porneia. The body is the temple of the Kyrios."

"Porneia?" Miryam did not know the Hellene word.

"*Zanah*," Cerinthus said in Ivrit, half giggling.

Miryam also wanted to laugh out loud, but Martha looked a little shocked, not expecting to hear about sexual scandal at her kitchen table. "Paulos ...," she whispered.

"I told Atta Miryam I wanted to speak with her privately. Anyway, I call these transgressions hamartia – sins."

"Hamartia?" Cerinthus asked. "Doesn't that mean 'missing the target' in Hellene?" To Miryam he added as an aside. "That's *chata* in Ivrit."

Paulos nodded at the translation.

"Paulos, you can resist committing hamartia, even lead an exemplary life, and still be left in the grave," Miryam said.

"Death has reigned over the kosmos since Adam," Paulos said. "Even those who never break a commandment die anyway."

"What does Adam have to do with hamartia?"

"Sin entered the world through the first man, Adam, who brought death and sin to all people."

"So, you are saying that death is for all people because of this sin, and the Christos will redeem all people of this sin of death at the end of days so that we can have eternal life?"

"As long as they are baptized."

"Why not those who are not baptized?"

"They continue to live under the law of the kosmos."

Miryam thought for a moment, trying to decipher what Paulos was saying. "Baptisma carries a power that resists sin?"

"The first man, Adam, was made a living psychē. Christos, who was the last Adam, was made a quickening pneuma. The material spirit is in opposition to the divine spirit, and the divine spirit is against the material spirit. But those who receive baptisma must also walk in the divine spirit. He who sows to his own flesh will from the flesh reap corruption, but he who sows to the spirit will from the spirit reap eternal life."

"What would you sow in spirit?"

"Love, joy, peace, patience, kindness, goodness, faithfulness, gentleness, and self-control. The law can be fulfilled in one statement: 'Love your neighbor as you love yourself.'"

"One does reap what one sows, Paulos," Miryam said. "Rav Yeshua would say that you don't get barley from planting wheat, or by sowing weeds for that matter. But Rav Yeshua's teaching on sin was a little different."

"How so?"

"He likened sin to *chowb*, or debt." There was a truth to what Paulos was saying, Miryam thought. But he was looking backwards at a passing messiah, rather than a living, current, true master. An initiate's transgressions accrued over lifetimes, and one could not ascend in spirit until it was depleted. Ha-Rav, as the Logos made flesh, took much of it into his own body, while using the rest to polish the patina of soul. "Let me explain what I mean by debt this way: One of his disciples once asked him if they should pay tribute to Caesar. By way of an answer, he asked the student whose picture was on the coin."

"Caesar's," Cerinthus answered.

"Precisely. Ha-Rav instructed his disciples to give to Caesar what belongs to Caesar, and give to Elah what belongs to Elah. He told us that we will never get out of this prison until we pay every last *dēnarion* we owe. We must always pay our tribute money for the bounty as well as the weeds we let grow in our gardens, our misjudgments and transgressions. We always carry forth the balance of our debt into the next life, and the payment is precise: an eye for an eye, tooth for a tooth, life for a life."

"You speak of the Code of Hammurabi, the law of retaliation," Paulos said, frowning.

"It is the law of Elah, not of man, and it's not about revenge. It's about one's actions. Rav Yeshua instructed his disciples to resist evil, but when your enemy slaps you on the cheek, turn the other cheek. Don't create new debt by hitting them back. *Proverbs* says, 'Whoever digs a pit shall fall into it, whoever rolls a stone will have it return to him.'"

"The great teacher Hillel once saw the head of a man he recognized floating on the water and said to it, 'You have drowned because you drowned others.'"

Paulos was happy to contribute to the conversation, she thought, but did he actually understand the principle? She decided to move to a different subject, his primary claim that Christos redeemed the baptized. "Why do you feel that only Rav Yeshua can raise us from the grave, and no other master?"

"Not Iēsous the man, but the resurrected Christos. Again, I take it from the Tanakh."

"I'm not aware that the Tanakh says anything about baptisma."

"You are correct. The Prophets do not speak of being released from pain despite pleadings to the Theos," Paulos argued. "So I say that the stories prophesied Christos's coming and that all instruction and guidance were given to the people in the interim until the Savior arrives."

"Perhaps none of the prophets talk about being raised from the grave because the way is secret," Miryam said. "The Torah shows that Yĕhovah wished to lead Yisrael onto a road out of the trackless desert so that they might see Yĕhovah. As it is written in *Yĕshayah*, 'a great road does exist, the Way of Holiness, and only the pure can travel it.' Why would the Tanakh say a way exists without there also being a Wayshower?"

"There is a Wayshower. Christos."

"But don't you find it interesting that passages like these existed long before, as you say, the fullness of time when the Christos lived and died?" She felt exhilarated herself as she sensed the Logos sounding through her now and saw where it was going. At the same time, she didn't want to go too far, for she didn't know what Paulos's reaction would be, so invested was he in his mission. Nor did she wish to reveal too much of Yeshua's teachings – they were for the initiated. But something inside her, Ravi perhaps, was nudging her forward.

Miryam stood and spread flour on the table to knead the puffed-up dough a second time. "When Yob said, 'My neshama is in me, and the ruach of Yĕhovah is in my nostrils,' I believe he was saying that the breath, power, and wisdom of Elah is within us. Rav Yeshua taught that if the spirit and voice of the All is within us, then it would follow that the Kingdom of Heaven is within us as well. He used to say that if heaven were in the sky, then the birds would already be in heaven. In other words, when we die, we don't rise to the heavens in the sky. Instead, heaven is within us, and we must realize it while we are alive because the road out of our own desert is also within us."

"I would ask, then, if the spirit and the kingdom of the Almighty is within, why aren't *we* already in heaven?"

"That's a fair question, Paulos. And maybe we are already in heaven, but we just don't know it. Let me ask you a question: Do the Faithful assume that you rise in your physical body after death? You yourself just said that flesh and blood cannot inherit the Kingdom."

Paulos frowned. "Many ask how we are raised, and what kind of body we will have. I answer it this way: When a seed grows into a plant, it no longer looks like a seed. So it is with the resurrection of the dead. What is sown is perishable and decays, what is raised is immortal. We are sown a physical body and raised a spiritual body."

"Ayn, but it isn't the body that transforms as it is raised from the grave, it is the neshama that is raised within us."

Paulos sat silent, concealing his reaction from Miryam.

"Take the sighting of the resurrected Christos by the disciples. If Rav Yeshua ascended into heaven in spirit, as you say, then it would not be possible for people to see him with their physical eyes, correct? They would need spiritual eyes to see a spiritual body."

Paulos shook his head, looking bewildered. "I've had more than one experience, whether in the body or out of the body, I do not know."

"So, if we view through our spiritual eyes, then we must do so through our own spiritual body, our neshama."

"That's what I was saying. I did not know whether I saw the Christos in my body or out of my body."

"What I am saying is that all of this occurs within our own body."

"I don't understand."

Miryam placed the loaves back in the bowl to rise again. Something like a breeze blew in her ear and she suddenly had an idea. She scattered more flour on the table, then drew a large circle in the flour with her finger. "Allow me to be simplistic. This circle is our physical body, the *soma* in Hellene."

She drew a small dot in the center of the circle. "This is the seed of the Divine, the neshama. The physical body is formed out of the earth, as you have said, but our spirit is a spark of Elah."

Miryam then wiped away the outer circle, leaving only the dot in the middle. "After death, we lose our physical body but keep our spirit body." She then drew lines radiating from the center of the circle to form a wheel, remembering the Wheel of Life the young Hindustan spice trader had told her about at the agora. "Each spoke represents a different lifetime, maybe as a male or female, Hellene or Ivrit, wealthy or poor, ruler or slave, until all aspects of life are experienced. The spirit continues to be reborn again and again like a chariot wheel that never stops turning."

Paulos gulped, and it was almost audible.

Miryam wiped away the wheel sketch, scattered more flour on the table, and redrew the circle. "This is the kosmos. It contains the earth, the sky, the stars, the sun, the moon, all the animals, birds, fish, and insects, and all the people. It corresponds with our physical body." She drew a series of four interlocking circles just above the first circle, each stacked one upon the other. "Ha-Rav said, 'In my Father's house are many palaces.'"

"By palaces, you mean heavens," Paulos said. "As described by the prophets."

Miryam nodded, hopeful he was following along. "Those stories of angels escorting the prophets upward to ascending levels of heaven are allegory for what occurs within us. Ha-Rav told us that there are five palaces or levels of heaven to Creation, and for each level there is a corresponding body. The final level is the realm of the All, the Nameless One."

Paulos sat perfectly still, as did Cerinthus, the former being appalled and the latter enraptured.

Miryam dared to continue. "The neshama is also from the fifth heaven but it is unaware of heaven itself. As the *Bereshit* states, Adam and Chavah took a bite from the fruit on the tree of knowledge – *etz daat*."

"Gnosis," Paulos said, contributing the Hellene translation. "Knowledge."

"The fruit represents the taking on of the physical body and mind and emotions – everything in E'Alma, the lower worlds." She drew a line straight down the center of the circles. "Like Adam, our neshama journeys through all the levels so that it can experience the entire creation. This was Elah's plan, for neshama to mature. As we descend through the heavenly realms, we take on a new body of each realm like a robe, but invisible. That is, the neshama takes on the attributes of each realm. Finally, we take on the physical body."

"Those of us who have been baptized in Christos are clothed by him," Paulos said.

Miryam sighed within herself. She wasn't getting through to him.

"I believe what Atta Miryam is saying is that there are many different spokes on the chariot wheel, many different garments, many different lives," Cerinthus explained to Paulos with all the respect he could muster.

"Ayn, and everyone is on the wheel of life," Miryam answered.

"Beginning with Adam and Chavah?" Paulos asked bristling at being interrupted by the youngster.

"Well, on the wheel, there is no beginning or end," Miryam said. "But, ayn, the story of the first man and woman is an allegory for each person's journey from heaven. Chavah was created from Adam's rib, meaning that Chavah and Adam are two parts of the same being. Adam is the neshama, the divine part of our beings, and Chavah is the nefesh, the material part."

"Christos was the last Adam," Paulos interjected, repeating himself.

"If you mean that Adam was the first to descend from heaven and Ha-Rav was the last to descend and the first to return, we are all the first and last Adam, Paulos."

Paulos shrugged. He would have to think about it.

"It is a matter of uncovering the Adam within us," Miryam continued. "And taking a bite from the inverted Tree of Life in order to return to the Garden of Eden within us."

"By receiving the Gnosis through Christos," he said resolutely.

"By receiving initiation from a *living* rav. The master has to be alive, not dead and risen – that's very important. You can still have knowledge without the power and guidance to return to heaven."

Again, Paulos stiffened. He was beginning to look uncomfortable.

"But it doesn't happen right away," Miryam pressed on, against her better judgment. "After many, many lifetimes each neshama has experienced just about everything there is to experience, and it next begins to mature through the various kinds of religions and cults."

"Ayn, I've noticed that different religions appeal to different people," Cerinthus said.

"In Tarsus where I was raised, the people worship a deity called Tarku and burn him in effigy every year to ensure better health or prosperity," Paulos said. "The Ivrit have their rituals and laws as you know, the Hellene theirs, and so on."

"Exactly," Miryam affirmed.

"Some religions make sacrifices and rituals to the sun and moon," Cerinthus interjected. "And some make sacrifices of the flesh."

"And some sacrifice the pleasures of the flesh itself," Paulos added.

"Yet none of these things will get one to the fifth circle of heaven. It takes many, many lifetimes to cultivate one's maturity. Finally, a lifetime comes when one's neshama yearns to return to its origin and to That which sent it. This is why you have observed different levels of spiritual maturity and interests. Everyone seeks and understands according to their spiritual station on the wheel. Now, in order to return to the origin, it is the commission of the 'mature' student to expose each invisible garment we've donned, by rising and merging with the next higher level by degrees, as if riding a wave of the Logos." She tapped each circle drawn in the flour from bottom to top. "But hear this, Paulos. Everyone will eventually know themselves directly as their neshama. Everyone."

"Even the psychikos."

"Even the young in soul, but perhaps not in this lifetime. Now, to awaken in one's soul while alive, there must be a quickening, as you mentioned."

"Through the risen savior."

"Lo!" Miryam said emphatically, frustrated at having to repeat herself. She immediately calmed herself and whispered, "Through a living master who is already risen while alive and in the body." She let that sink in, and then continued. "Ha Rav said, 'I will go and prepare a place for you ... that where I am, so shall you be. I am the way, the truth, and the light.' A living master must be able to teach his initiates in the flesh as well as in the spirit. That is to say, he must be able to sit face to face as we are now while also being able to appear to the disciple on the inside." She waved a hand in the air. "But he doesn't appear to us as a vision outside of our bodies." She placed a hand on her forehead. "He comes to us in here. He descends through all of the circles of heaven and waits for us here on the threshold to the first heaven. But only if he first initiates us in the flesh."

"I have dreamed of Christos. And I've certainly experienced him in a vision. And I was caught up to the third heaven."

"But you didn't learn from Rav Yeshua in the flesh, didn't sit in front of him during one of his lectures. You didn't experience initiation by his hand or feel overwhelming love by his mere bodily presence. Both forms are needed – his physical body *and* his spiritual body."

Paulos paused a moment, frowning. "So when Iēsous comes again, we will rise together alive and meet him in the air ... or in spirit?"

"Neither. Remember, the kingdom is *within* and Ha-Rav is *within* and we meet Him *within*. To do this, we have to be alive."

"Does he appear as in a dream or a vision on the inside?" Cerinthus asked, as if spellbound.

Miryam questioned the wisdom of allowing Cerinthus to stay. In many ways his level of spiritual maturity exceeded Paulos's, and the distinctions she was trying to make were for Paulos's benefit. On the other hand, Cerinthus did allow Miryam the opportunity to correct some of Paulos's misconceptions without confronting him directly. "A living rav can appear to an initiate through visions and dreams, but such a rav is needed to help determine whether the vision or dream is real or an illusion. The nefesh plays tricks. I'm talking about a persistent Presence, one that through practice can eventually be experienced every moment of the day."

Miryam glanced at Martha from the corner of her eye. Martha was alert, still as a mouse watching a hawk about to attack. Miryam took that as a warning to be careful with Paulos so as not to trigger his anger and fear again. She lowered her voice and continued. "Paulos, at the Artemision when you said that the Almighty raised Rav Yeshua from death to sit at his right hand, this was true. But it isn't the physical body that is raised from the dead, it is the spirit. Ha-Rav's spiritual body was already raised while he walked across Yehudah. All Masters of the Logos are the Logos made flesh. When they initiate a student, they re-enliven the Logos here." She touched her forehead again where the inner gate would be. "The ritual of immersion in natural running water represents initiation into the Logos within, but natural water in and of itself has no power." She paused, then added, "Neither does the idea of initiating in a dead master's spirit."

Paulos's left hand began to quiver. "He will return to save the righteous from their sins."

Miryam shook her head and lowered her voice even more. "He will not be coming back for anyone he did not personally initiate himself. Yob, Yirměyah, Yěchezqel – they all had their own initiates. There will be other ravs to come."

Paulos stared at Miryam in silence, both hands clasped to still the shaking in them. After a moment, he repeated, "But I was baptized by Ananias, and I was caught up in the third heaven fourteen years ago."

"Paulos, there are many things of the Spirit that are mystery and cannot be explained." Ha-Rav had warned his disciples that the nefesh itself could rise on its own without benefit of the Inner Rav, and would become drunk with power. Such a thing may have happened to Paulos. She kept this to herself.

"I have died to the law, that I might live in Theos," Paulos said. "I have been crucified with Christos, and it is no longer I that lives, but Christos living in me. That life which I now live in the flesh, I live by faith in the son of Theos, who loved me, and gave himself up for me. If this is not true, then Christos died for nothing!"

"I do not share in your view," Miryam whispered, and she had to admit that the symbolism of being crucified so that one's master could be viewed within the initiate was an accurate description of the process, but she had no more words to convince Paulos of the subtle difference between the reality of it and his own interpretation.

"And I do not believe your explanations." Suddenly he stood and inadvertently knocked over his chair. He fumbled to aright it. "I must leave now."

"Very well." Both Miryam and Martha stood, with Martha rushing to hold the door open for him. "Wait, Paulos." Miryam touched Paulos's arm, and he stopped reluctantly. "Much of your gospel is true."

Paulos smiled feebly.

"We are all temples of Elah. What you are doing may be helpful in readying the neshama within many people for the time when they are to meet their true rav." Miryam thought a moment. "But I am curious. How do you convey your gospel of inheriting Abraham's seed to those who were not raised on the books of Moses?"

"I don't understand," Paulos answered.

"How do you convince the Hellene that Christos is the fulfillment of prophecy if they don't believe in, or even know about, the prophecies in the first place?"

"That is a good question," Paulos said, regaining some of the composure he had shown earlier. "If you come to ekklēsia this Sabbath, I will show you. We meet at the home of my friends from Korinthos, Aquila and Priscilla. You met them at the Artemision. You will know the house by the symbol of the *ichthys* over the door." Paulos picked up a twig and bent to draw two intersecting arcs in the dirt, the lines on the right side extending to resemble a fish tail. "Come just after daybreak and come hungry." With that, Paulos tossed the twigs and turned his back without waiting for a response to his invitation – such was his confidence they'd accept. He disappeared quickly down the path.

"He is persistent, if nothing else," Martha said. "I think we should go to the meeting."

"Ayn, you are right. It would prove interesting."

Cerinthus stood and quietly pushed his chair in under the table when the sisters re-entered the house. He looked at each of them, as if considering what to say. "Atta Miryam, Atta Martha, will you tell me about your teacher, Rav Yeshua? I want to know everything."

Eight

"The reason Rav Yeshua is so appealing to Paulos and his followers may be because he is human," Martha said, as she bent to pluck a tomato. Their students had left for the day, and this was the first opportunity the sisters had to discuss their meeting with Paulos that morning. "The Faithful might prefer a savior they can worship, a deity who first walked the earth in their sandals."

Miryam accepted the tomato from Martha and placed it in her basket alongside other newly harvested vegetables. "He is not another stone face in a marble temple, and he doesn't expect sacrifices made to him."

"I admire Paulos's devotion to his mission and the strength of will to take it across half the known world at his own risk and expense," Martha said.

"That's because he believes he will have everlasting life when his savior returns," Miryam replied. "I gather he thinks that time is near."

"And yet, how utterly empty and alone he seems. Waiting for your own death to unite with the Christos is not the same as having Ha-Rav right now, while alive."

Miryam nodded agreement. Rav Yeshua had also been consumed by his mission. He radiated Spirit, always confident yet modest. As he became familiar to the disciple, the disciple began to sense within him unfathomable depths of heaven. That was because upon initiation, Ravi's Shechinah waited at the inner wicket gate for His disciples, drawing them closer to Him, whispering to them all day of His love, reminding them to release their troubles to Him. Paulos may have had several visionary and inspirational events, but their effects couldn't last without the Ravi within.

"Are you going to tell Cerinthus about Rav Yeshua, Miryam?"

"I wouldn't know where to start."

"Simple," Martha said as she walked into the house. "Start at the beginning."

All day long memories of Miryam's first meeting with Yeshua rained down on her, and she mused over the precious moment when the neshama reunites with Ha-Rav after lifetimes of separation. Her meeting was some thirty years earlier, and although so much had since transpired, the rich images and feelings still flooded her senses whenever she called upon them.

Miryam first met Yeshua when he traveled to her small fishing town of Migdal Nunya on the western shore of the Sea of Galilee. After spending most of the day working the ledgers for the family fish-salting business, she had decided to take a break and walk to the well house across from their villa. Used by the locals for personal water collection, meetings, ritual, and prayer, the well house was a pleasant place to quietly sit and lose oneself in the sound of the gurgling water as it ran in open channels throughout the building.

Though similar to a Hellene nymphaeum, the well house was much more austere and simply constructed as appropriate to their tastes. In the main room, seven columns supported three of the basalt stone walls, and the fourth wall was lined with stone steps stacked five high for seating. Water from an underground spring rushed through clay pipes between the colonnade, which represented *mayim chayim*, the "living" water. The water fed a flagstone-lined pool, or *mikveh*, in the center of the room used for the tevilah, the rite of immersion and purification.

When Miryam entered the well room, she saw a man speaking to a dozen fishermen sitting around him in various positions on the benches and flagstone floor. She thought nothing of it; men in her village gathered at the well to gossip more than women did in her estimation. They were blocking access to the water, but she figured they would naturally shift aside once she came closer. Yet they didn't notice her, so drawn were they to the speaker's words. If bodies could talk, these were disagreeing with him, but it was as if they were listening to a musician and were simply, perhaps even deeply, enjoying the very sound of the words as they rolled off his tongue.

The speaker's back was to her, but he sensed her approach and turned. As soon as he saw her, he crossed over and clasped both her hands in his. "I have been waiting for you," he whispered with a smile of recognition.

She was speechless. His forwardness should have been offensive and sinful, but his gestures were as gentle as an old friend greeting the other after an eternity of separation. Yet this wasn't even her first response. She was immediately taken by the depth of his glistening brown eyes, with the shaft of light that seemed to dance on his head, and his alone. He waited patiently, gazing into her eyes, piercing her very being. She felt herself lift inward and upward as if hovering above herself, though she was still quite conscious of her body, still viewing through her two corporeal eyes. The feeling was like being intoxicated on her father's wine, though nothing had passed her lips.

"Have we met?" Her trembling, small voice sounded like it was coming from the bottom of the well and not her own vocal chords.

"It was a very long time ago." He seemed to be drinking in her countenance almost as much as she his.

"Are you quite sure? I would have remembered you."

"Someday you will learn everything." He pulled on her arm. "Come sit with us."

She was very busy with the family's business. Her father had been ailing recently, leaving his son and two daughters to pick up the slack. Some of the workers hadn't come in that day. In fact, she finally noticed, they were here listening to the storyteller. The other men she recognized as fishers and sailors from around Migdal Nunya. She wanted to decline, yet she asked herself: *How could I explore this stranger, who is not a stranger, if I do not stay?*

It wasn't as if she had a choice. She was two people – one who wanted to flee, and the other who felt compelled to sit beside this man forever. She obeyed her inner prompting and sat cross-legged on the ground beside him, completely oblivious of the floor's dustiness.

"I was just telling these men a story about a woman drawing water from a well such as this."

"Please continue." She nodded, surprised at the patience of these men to listen to a story about a woman.

"I will start at the beginning. A stranger traveling through Samaria stopped at the local water well. A woman approached him, and he asked her if she would be kind enough to give him a drink. As you can imagine, the woman was surprised. She said, 'You ask me, a Samarian, for a drink?' The stranger told her, 'If you knew who asks, you would ask *him* for a drink, and he would have given you Living Water.' The woman replied, 'Where is this water?' To which the stranger told her, 'Everyone who drinks this water will thirst again, but whoever drinks of the water He gives them will never thirst again. The water He gives becomes in them a well of water springing up to eternal life.' The woman was confused. She said, 'Our fathers worshiped the water spirit in this mountain, and the Yehudi say we must worship at the temple in Yerushalayim, yet the priests say we must pay to become purified in their living water. Now you are saying I can have salvation by simply drinking the water at this mysterious well? Sir, give me this water so that I may never thirst, and so that I won't have to come all the way here for water.'"

The speaker stopped telling his story and gazed at his small audience in the wellhouse. Whether or not the men believed the story, they definitely wanted to hear about the source of the Living Water. Miryam knew she did.

He continued the story: "The stranger said to the woman, 'Believe me, the time will come when you will not make sacrifices to the Father in this mountain or in the temple in Yerushalayim. The Father is spirit, and those who bow down to Him must do so in spirit and truth. True worshipers worship what they have knowledge of, and they are who the Father seeks.' The woman asked the stranger. 'How can I gain such knowledge?' He told her to go and bring back her husband, but the woman shook her head, saying she had none. 'Does this mean I cannot drink of the living water if I'm not married?' The stranger said, 'In truth you have five husbands.' To which the woman asked, 'Are you a prophet?'"

One man, leaning against the post, arms crossed, asked, "Why would the stranger ask a Samarian woman with five husbands for water? She is unclean in three ways."

A giggle burst through Miryam's lips, and everyone including the speaker turned toward her waiting for an explanation. She shrugged. "Excuse me, but with so many husbands, she doesn't have time to worship at the temple, in the mountains, *or* at the well."

The speaker smiled as the group of onlookers laughed self-consciously. "That is precisely the point," he said.

"I wasn't trying to make a point, just playing with the story."

"What is laughter but truth, what is play but divinity?" he said.

Miryam blushed. Now that she thought of it, she *was* being truthful. After her own husband died in their first year of marriage, she hadn't found the time to remarry.

"Within each of us is an eternally-flowing river of my Father's love and grace." The speaker knelt and scooped up the well water with cupped hand, brought it to his mouth, and quickly sipped what did not slip away. "These so-called living channels are hand-made, not God-made. The water is elusive, and though it temporarily nourishes the body and cleans the flesh and lulls the senses with its noise, it can never sustain the neshama and deliver it to its rightful throne. Earthly water is symbolic at best, but I'm here to tell you that you do not have to climb the mountain like Moses to see the Father and hear His commandments, you do not have to go to the temple and be purified by water that has never been touched by human hands. You need only find a living master such as the one at the old woman's well to taste the elixir of eternal life."

"If there is a well within me, why do I not experience it already?" Miryam asked.

"You are all prohibited from drinking this water by your five husbands. You need only one bridegroom to lead you to the well."

"That applies to women," one man spoke up. "But what about men?"

"You all have husbands."

"Hey!" the man exclaimed indignantly.

"Not trying to insult you. Merely trying to explain the reason why you cannot tap into your own well. When you marry someone, you are pledging yourself to take responsibility for that person. And in doing so, aren't you expecting something in return? Doesn't the responsibility seem like a burden sometimes? The husbands represent the obsessions of the nefesh, the mind, that sit around the rim of the well and block entrance to the bride."

"Who are the husbands?" Miryam asked.

"Anger, lust, greed, attachment, and vanity – all is vanity, Scripture claims."

"And who is the bride?" she asked.

"Another good question. That is your very neshama."

He speaks as if *he* is the prophet, Miryam thought, yet she was suspicious. Scripture had many prophets, but they all lived in antiquity. Tradition had it that a prophet would be marked by overt events of great magnitude. "Can you give us a sign that you are a true prophet?"

"How vain of you to ask," the speaker said sternly. "What would convince you? Bring back the dead, heal the sick, cause a well to follow you around? Force the Rhōmaioi to lay down their swords as Samuel predicted the seed of David would command? Create a kind of paradise on earth? Abba doesn't care about such things. If I were to perform miracles and magic tricks, I would draw crowds of spectators and cause pandemonium. What would that achieve? Lo, the signs you seek can only be proven within yourself."

That was a good answer, Miryam thought, frowning. She remained suspicious of the stranger.

"I am not a prophet," the speaker continued. "Stories of prophets arise out of a strong yearning for liberation from oppression on behalf of one's people. Here, in this world, oppression will always exist. Such masters as the one at the Samaritan well are here to liberate the neshama from the unmarked grave so that it will know itself and then go on to know the Father."

"You are the bridegroom," Miryam said, not as a confirmation – because how could she know? – but as the final progression of his parable.

"Not me," the speaker answered. "The rav in the story is the bridegroom."

The man who stood against the wall with his arms crossed burst out laughing. "Your story smells like rotting fish." With a wave of a hand under his nose, he stormed out of the well house with all of the other men in tow. Their bellowing echoed as they walked through the anti-chamber.

But the speaker remained unaffected by the outburst. He stretched both hands to Miryam still seated on the flagstone, and when she took them, he pulled her to her feet and gazed into her eyes. "You and I are inextricably connected," he said quietly yet resolutely.

Miryam was taken aback. Which part of her was it that trembled and which part swooned? She didn't know whether to run from the insanity of being with a stranger, dangerously alone in the well house with him as she was, or linger in the arms of this long lost lover with the well-deep eyes and the powerful touch.

She ran. She did not stop running until she reached the wharf. At the sea's edge, she sat on a log bench and rested her head in her hands. She wanted to cry but could not, still feeling both inebriated and scared. A group of men cleaned fish nearby, tossing entrails to the gulls as they flew overhead. She swore the squawking birds mocked her, but she rested in the familiarity of the smells of the sea breezes.

Suddenly, she felt a hand on her shoulder, and her head snapped upward. It was the speaker, backlit by the setting sun.

"Please, forgive me for startling you, then and now. I wasn't trying to take advantage of you or trick you with magical talk."

Miryam wanted to stand, but her legs felt weak. Instead, the speaker sat next to her, keeping an appropriate distance between them. "I am Yeshua ben Yosef min Natseret. I am a laborer with a penchant for storytelling. I do not wish to claim special powers of superiority, nor ingratiate myself to you. I have traveled far, and I cannot help but share my experiences and show others the way. I will go away if you wish, but I would prefer not to leave until I've finished the story."

"There's more to the story about the woman at the well?" Against her better judgment, she felt compelled to hear him out. Or was staying her better judgment? She no longer knew.

"This is a different part of the story. Will your duties permit you to stay and listen?"

She nodded. "I have a few moments."

"Imagine a tribe of people who live in a desert and have never seen the ocean," he began.

"That would be far from here. Our land is on the sea, and it's all I've ever known."

"Well, imagine a vast desert far away from the sea, surrounded by more desert as far as their most enduring camel could travel. After a hundred generations of living in the desert, a lone trader appears on the horizon and enters the camp of the desert nomads. He tells them about a body of water that is more infinite than their desert, with waves larger than sand dunes and swimming animals larger than camels. He tells them there is more life in the ocean than grains of sand in the desert and that the ocean provides the people who live near it with everything they would ever need to survive for generations. He gives them sea shells they can put to their ears and listen to the ocean waves, and he feeds them dried fish so that they may taste the salt of the sea." Yeshua paused and gazed out over the water a moment.

"The ocean is unfathomable to the tribesmen," he continued. "But they believe the trader. They have known water when it rained or bubbled up all too infrequently, and so they think they know the ocean. They reason that the ocean is so powerful that they begin to invent stories about it and make rituals to it, eventually turning it into a deity they could worship. Seeing all this, the trader tells them to stop what they are doing, because for all the stories, rituals, and adulation, they would never know the ocean. He tells them that the only way they would ever know the ocean is to see it for themselves. He warns them that it would be a long trip, that it would take a lifetime, and that the traveling would be met with many challenges and tests."

Yeshua paused for effect, then began again more quietly. "There was only one person, a man, who accepted the trader's offer. No one else was interested in leaving their families, comforts, and the goods they had accumulated. Nevertheless, the trader was pleased, for it was a rare person who would be willing to take the risk, so deep was their yearning to see the ocean."

Miryam thought about this a moment, spellbound by the story and the images he had created for her. "What set that one person apart from the others that he was willing to give up everything to search for the ocean? Was it just adventure?"

"Ah! That is a very good question. This young man was already a seeker. He had turned over every stone in the desert, had ridden every camel, sipped water from every well, smelled the scent of every woman, and prayed at every shrine. There was nothing in the desert that he hadn't been consumed by and then disappointed by. And yet he was still filled with such a burning desire that he couldn't quite name the object of his desire. He sensed that the ocean the trader described was the answer to his despair. Secretly, he prayed to the god of the ocean to be shown what it was that he yearned for."

Yeshua let her steep in this moment. Finally he asked, "Do you hear whispers from the ocean's shore?"

"Ayn," she answered without hesitation. Later, she would wonder why she said that. More importantly, she would begin asking herself if she had overturned every stone in her desert. Had she even thought about such a search? She was happy, was she not? Her family enjoyed a thriving living on their fish-packing business. But all she knew was loss. As the youngest of her brother and sister, her mother had died giving birth to her. She had been raised by her older siblings, her father, and her grandfather. She had married at a young age soon after her grandfather died, and then almost as quickly her new bridegroom died when his fishing boat overturned in a storm, leaving her childless. That had been two, three years ago. Ayn, all she had known was loss and disappointment. Desire? That was something she hadn't begun to feel until this stranger with the dancing light around his head showed up and reminded her of her emptiness.

On each passing day, Miryam left her bookkeeping early and met Yeshua down by the wharf. They went for long walks along the shore, and he began to tell her about what he called the Living Water. Miryam could see that Yeshua was not just an itinerant worker, and though not a prophet either, he was a teacher and obviously a holy man. She knew this because he inspired her imagination, awakened her latent yearning, and her nerves felt bubbly around him, not giddy like a girl in love (though she did feel that way), but like she was encircled by Love Itself.

"Where did you learn these stories you tell?" Miryam asked Yeshua one evening when he had finally stopped his long discoursing to her to allow her to absorb his messages. "How did you become so wise? Who showed you the ocean?"

He stopped and studied her face. "I'm not sure you would understand."

"I might not, you're right," she decided. "How many stones did you overturn?"

"My desert was quite large." He laughed deeply and with his whole body. "For as long as I can remember, I've traveled widely and have sat at the feet of many teachers." His eyes became distant as if in remembrance, and she realized he would tell nothing more about his past.

The first time she called him "rav" was quite inadvertent, and she was as surprised by it as was he. "Why did you call me that?"

She did not hesitate with an answer: "I believe you've seen the ocean and that you can take others there."

He looked down at his hands, speechless for the first time. It suddenly became clear to Miryam that this young master was not sure about his mission.

It was also clear to Miryam that Yeshua, Rav Yeshua, might need work to support himself, and that he would soon leave to search for his next job. As much as she couldn't put her finger on her own yearning for the distant shore, she knew she would feel emptier if this guide left her. It occurred to her that he could do carpentry repair work on the family house and fishing business in exchange for room and board. This way she could be certain to continue hearing his stories and absorbing their lessons for as long as he cared to stay.

Martha and Lazarus weren't so enthralled by the thought of the traveling storyteller's presence in their house. Miryam found them in the fish house, aproned and elbow-deep in the fish-cleaning tub. "The boys told me about the woman at the well and all those husbands," Lazarus said with a smile. "They think she was a whore." He tossed a cleaned fish into the bucket of salt water.

Martha kept silent until she could no longer contain herself. "I think you're infatuated by him, Miryam. But we can't have this beggar telling bawdy stories in our house with Abba on his sick bed."

"He's not a beggar."

"What would you call him?"

"He travels from village to village looking for work and for people willing to listen to his stories."

"Homeless and shekel-less," Martha said. "That's what I would call him. What if he robs us? Or worse...?"

Miryam shook her head. "I don't think that will happen. Wait until you've met him before you judge."

"Let me talk to him." Lazarus wiped his fish-scaled hands on his apron and headed for the door.

"I'm coming along," Martha said, running after him.

"Wait, both of you," Miryam said. "I haven't invited him to work for us yet."

"We won't mention that part until we've made our decision."

"You don't know where he is. Why don't you let me invite him for a meal, and I'll introduce him to you both?"

Martha remained tight-lipped. Lazarus sighed. "What do you see in him?"

Miryam shrugged. "He has seen the ocean."

"We all have. We live right on the sea."

"That's not the one I mean." She turned and walked away to find Yeshua.

Martha prepared a simple meal of fish, lentil soup, figs, and barley bread for their guest. She brought three small loaves to the table, handing one to Yeshua. He tore off a chunk and placed it on his plate. "Ah, manna from heaven," he said as he sopped up some lentils.

"Wait until you try it before you decide its divinity,'" Martha said.

Lazarus tore off a portion of bread and chewed as he spoke: "Can you imagine that sticky tamarisk tree gum falling on the people every night for forty years as they wandered in the desert? I don't believe it is a true story."

"The Ivrit accept it as affirmation that they are the chosen, but there is a deeper meaning." Yeshua's eyes twinkled as he baited Lazarus.

"Moses told them to only take what they could eat in one day," Miryam said. "To me it is a story about being too greedy."

"It goes even deeper than that," Yeshua said. "As I remember from scripture, manna was prone to decay. All living creatures need physical nourishment, but we cannot live by bread alone, cannot be nourished by earthly things. Spiritual sustenance does not decay." He dipped another piece of bread in the stew and said, "Daily, we must eat of Abba's bounty." He popped the bread in his mouth, smiling.

Miryam noticed both Lazarus and Martha had stopped eating and were already spellbound by this stranger, and only a few moments had passed since his arrival. "Please, tell us more, Rav Yeshua," Lazarus said.

"Rav, is it?" Yeshua raised his eyebrows.

"Her word, not mine," he said, nodding to Miryam.

"Very well, Abba's kingdom is like a woman who took a little leaven, hid it in three measures of meal, and shaped it into large loaves. Of course, we've already devoured one of Abba's worlds." He smiled his boyish smile.

Martha passed another loaf to her guest, thinking he was still hungry. "Whatever do you mean by that, Yeshua? When you speak of your father's kingdom, do you mean to imply that you come from royalty?"

"Lo, Martha, his family is not royal." Miryam giggled. "Or is it?" She was enjoying their quick acceptance of Rav Yeshua and his wisdom.

Yeshua shook his head. "My kingdom is not here in this world."

"He says things like that all the time, Martha. You'll grow to love it. Rav Yeshua, when you say that Abba's kingdom is like three loaves from one small piece of leaven, is it similar to what you've said about Abba's house having many palaces?"

"You can see we live in cramped quarters here," Lazarus said, taking the bread from Yeshua.

Yeshua looked around him. "This beautiful villa is much larger than it looks from the outside. Ayn, Miryam, Abba's house is equally an illusion. It is like three loaves or worlds in one. The world we see, hear, feel, and touch, the world of our emotions, desires, and thoughts where we also go between lives, and the world that is Abba. The worlds all exist at once."

"Between ... lives?" Lazarus asked.

Yeshua smiled. "Ayn, we all have many more than the one life."

True to Lazarus's upbringing, he did not judge Yeshua's answer or his belief, he did not even flinch. "And the leaven?"

"The leaven is Abba's love that runs though all the worlds. The leaven is also the neshama, which can experience any world any time it chooses."

Lazarus looked at his beaming sister and nodded. "After our meal, I would like to introduce you to *our* abba. He is resting in his private room. If he consents, I would like you to stay and work for us."

Yeshua considered this offer for a moment, though he did not seem surprised by it. "Ayn, I would be grateful for the accommodations and would gladly return the favor with whatever carpentry or repairs you might need."

"Then, it's settled," Lazarus said.

Miryam clapped her hands, and Martha remained silent. Miryam knew Martha would eventually come around. It was her nature to take her time getting to know people, possibly the reason why she had yet to marry.

In the ensuing weeks, Miryam followed Rav Yeshua everywhere like a dog trailing the one who fed it, to the point of embarrassing him and aggravating her siblings. Martha came to him one day and complained that Miryam was neglecting her duties. Rav Yeshua answered: "Martha, Martha, you are worried about many things, but only one thing is needed, and that is to take heart in your spirituality. Miryam has chosen the better part, which cannot be taken away from her." But Rav Yeshua spoke to Miryam, suggesting that she tend to her chores. "You must live the life," he told her. Before long, all three siblings were following their new employee and teacher, and Miryam became somewhat jealous that he was paying more attention to them than to her.

After several weeks of Rav Yeshua's company, Miryam looked up from her bookkeeping to see him standing in front of her, his simple belongings wrapped in a small blanket roll. "I must go."

Miryam felt the world end. "Lo," she said quietly, knowing that Yeshua was not a man to be persuaded against his will.

He crossed to her and cradled her small hands. His skin was dry and callused from his carpentry work, but warm and gentle. "The love you feel is not for me but for my Abba through me."

"Then, introduce me to your Abba so that I might love Him directly."

Yeshua visibly melted, his eyes softened. "That is more difficult than you could know."

Before he could say anything, Miryam continued. "I believe you to be a rav in the highest sense. Not a scroll-reader, but a master who can somehow connect a student to the Source. I don't understand how this can be done, but I sense it is true."

Yeshua shook his head. "I think you confuse my storytelling skills with magic the sages speak of."

Miryam's brother and sister entered the room. Lazarus took one look at Yeshua's traveling clothes and stated the obvious: "You are leaving us."

"I must. I cause strain between the three of you. I am feeling called elsewhere."

Miryam continued. "You come to me in my dreams, and not just to me. I suspect you come to Martha and Lazarus as well."

Martha nodded. "I hear you in my head all day long, instructing me in ways to see myself more clearly than ever before."

"Tell me, if you are not a rav, a true master, then why do you feel compelled to travel around and tell people your stories about Abba?" Lazarus asked.

Yeshua had no answer. He put his traveling pack on the floor and sat on a wooden stool.

"How did it happen for you?" Martha asked. "Were you initiated into the Mystery by a great master?"

"Ayn, I was initiated by a man named Johanan who lived in the woods and cleansed devotees in the Jordan river so that they wouldn't have to pay to be cleansed in the elaborate pools of the Great Temple."

"Johanan saw the Ocean?"

"I cannot say one way or the other. He was one teacher. I had others in lands far away from here. My true teacher was Abba Himself."

"Could you initiate us?" Miryam asked.

"What good would it be for me to fulfill your request, for you will experience nothing without the daily discourse of a rav's teachings."

"Then, stay and teach us," Miryam pleaded.

Rav Yeshua sat a moment, then slapped his chest and laughed sonorously, eyes rolled upward. "I see I can no longer avoid this mission." Miryam felt that the comment was not made to them, but to the Abba who Yeshua spoke of so frequently. He then became serious again. "This is what I want you to do. For three days, I want you to fast. You will have no food; you will drink nothing but water. You will purify your bodies, your minds, and your hearts. We will meet on the third day in the well house before dawn. Dress in a clean tunic."

With that, Yeshua left, traveling roll and all. The siblings did not see him again during those three days, causing them to wonder if he would return. They followed his instructions carefully, being prudent not to fuss with each other. Surprisingly, the fast was not as difficult as Miryam had dreaded. Oy, throughout the first day, Miryam craved for a mouthful of bread or a shred of dry fish, something to crunch on, but by the end of the second day, she was feeling quite intoxicated and remarkably full.

The day came when the three of them rose before dawn and made their way barefoot to the well house in the dark where they could be initiated in secret. Each wore their white sleeping tunics, which they had scrubbed clean. As promised, Yeshua waited for them next to the well, his image flickering in the light of the torch he had lit. He gestured for them to sit on the marble steps facing the well, and they complied. Miryam was chilled by the cold stone, but her excitement warmed her core.

"You have asked for initiation with great sincerity, and that cannot be denied. With this initiation you will embark on a long journey that will ultimately lead you to my Abba, as those before you have done. You must understand the gravity of initiation, for as soon as you accept it, you will be taught, challenged, and tested. The initiation is not the end of the journey but the beginning, and the journey will culminate with the maturing of your neshamas, and that may take your entire lives. Do you have the ears to hear?"

Miryam, Martha, and Lazarus each nodded that they had understood, though they knew they had no way of knowing the reality of Rav Yeshua's words.

"Let us chant," he said. "*Hu* is the sound for the All. As you chant the word, lose yourself in the Shefa, the Divine Flow." Yeshua took a deep breath, then, in one long, deep note, he sang: "*Huuuuuu.*" The note echoing in the chamber was astounding and uplifting to Miryam, as if a slumbering entity within her being was stirring. When he ran out of breath, he inhaled again and repeated the note. He did this several times as they joined in, singing the Hu until the sound of the note began to take on a melody of its own, palpably yearning for the Divine. Even when silent, she could still sense the vibration of the Shefa.

After a moment, Yeshua continued. "Now, in the tradition of the temple, the priests immerse all devotees in what they call the living water. But the living water is only an outer symbol of the river of love you will begin to feel in growing degrees within your own being. I will not ask you to go into the pool as they would." Yeshua leaned over the pool and filled a wooden cup with water. He then stood in front of each of his new students and, one at a time, dipped a finger into the cup and pressed a drop of liquid onto the middle of their foreheads, each time saying: "In the name of my Father, I immerse you into the Mystery of the Living Water. I will give you what eye has not seen and what ear has not heard, what has not been touched, and what has not yet arisen in the hearts of most humans. Swear, each of you, that you will never divulge the Mysteries to anyone."

Miryam nodded agreement, by now feeling warm and expansive.

Finished with the formal part of the initiation, Rav Yeshua sat cross-legged on the floor in front of them. "The Hu is a chant we do when we are together. I will give you five secret words that correspond with the five levels of heaven for you to repeat softly to yourself during your morning contemplation, and throughout your day whenever you are idle. Do so in remembrance of me."

With that, Ha-Rav poured the remaining drops of water back into the pool and faced his first talmidim. He looked into the eyes of each student for an eternity. To Miryam, it wasn't Yeshua the man looking at her. She was locking eyes and hearts with Abba himself!

"The initiation is over. Please sit quietly and take this in. You are free to leave at any time, but I encourage you to remain alone until your duties draw you back into the world. It is necessary for you to allow the initiation to quicken and take hold. Whenever you feel yourself separate from Abba, just chant your secret words quietly to yourself a few times and all will be well again. This is your task: Constantly remember the purpose of your initiation. In a few days, I will begin discoursing on the Mystery, direct from Abba's mouth."

Miryam did not know how long she sat in the humidity of the well house. At first, she had been disappointed by the simplicity of the initiation. She hadn't known what to expect, but she had expected a lot more show and, ayn, some magic. But when she chanted the Hu and, later, her five secret words, and felt the Divine Presence, she surrendered all lower expectations. When Rav Yeshua touched his wet finger to her forehead, it was as if he had touched her with a hot ball of metal. In the blackness of her closed eyes, a blue orb swirled in the middle of her forehead. She felt immediately calm yet exhilarated, drugged by some magical potion that never touched her physical lips. All the while an Invisible Source beckoned her: *Come to me, come to me, come to me.* The Love that had encircled her whenever Rav Yeshua was around had now moved within her!

Months passed, then a year, and the dawn came when it was time for Yeshua to leave. This time there was no argument to stop him. Miryam could see that as he slowly accepted the mantle, he saw his three students open like rose blossoms. Of course, they were not his only sheep – they all knew there had to be others. As they stood in the courtyard of the villa to bid farewell, Lazarus and Martha stayed dry-eyed and sober, yet it was Rav Yeshua whose eyes glistened. She could see that teaching meant as much if not more to him than to those being taught. The sensation was like feeding a baby on the breast, he once explained to them. The more milk that was needed, the more was created as long as the mother remembered to feed herself. If the baby suddenly went off the milk, or if the mother were out in the field unable to feed the baby, the breasts would fill painfully until they felt like they would burst. That was the way of the Shefa the masters channeled to their students like rushing water. Miryam knew there was a never-ending supply, and that as he conveyed the Shefa, he himself penetrated deeper levels of heaven within his own inner worlds. The depth and reach of Ha-Rav was unfathomable to Miryam.

The siblings were heartbroken, yet Miryam took it the hardest. How could she live without him, how could she go on feeling such bliss with her beloved Yeshua gone? Miryam dropped to her knees and wrapped her arms around his ankles. He sat down on the ground and cradled her in his arms. "It is not separation from Yeshua the man you feel," he whispered, pushing back the hair from her wet eyes. "It is the ancient separation from Abba you feel. I am always with you, and I will be with you until I re-introduce you to Abba. That is Abba's promise and therefore my promise to you."

When it looked as though Miryam's storm had eased, Lazarus lifted her to her feet, allowing Rav Yeshua to stand. He sighed heavily, giving them each a look of compassion. "In time, you will know what to do," he said, and without further explanation, he turned and left the courtyard.

Within a few weeks, the siblings's father died, having grown weaker over the past year while his children grew stronger in spirit. Not one to follow the custom of the land, the one that said that women did not inherit, their father had left them each with an equal portion of his modest fortune. They sat around the table after the traditionally hurried funeral, staring at one another; each knowing what was in the other's heart without saying anything. They knew what they had to do: Sell the villa and the business so that they could spend more time with Ha-Rav. Though rare, none of the siblings were married; they had no ties to Migdal.

Another month and it was done. The house and most of its contents sold. The three gave the rest of their belongings away except what they needed for travel. The only heirloom they kept was their grandfather's Tanakh. Ha-Rav had been right. They did know what to do.

Miryam came to know what she needed to do spiritually as well. She was embarrassed over her display of attachment to Rav Yeshua, despite Martha's attempt to console her. But inwardly Miryam knew that, though understandable and even admirable, such outward attachment was unbecoming and counterproductive to her spiritual aspirations and progress.

Even now she cringed at the memory of it. If she ever saw him again, she would keep a respectful distance from him emotionally. She wouldn't cling or become jealous of his affections for her siblings.

Easier to say than to do.

Rather than spread like wildfire, news of a spiritual teacher drifted across the countryside like a honey bee pollinating flower blossoms. The siblings inquired at every well and merchant's bazaar along the coast of the Sea of Galilee, every so often lighting up a face at the sound of Rav Yeshua's name. All the person could do was point in the direction the traveling storyteller had left their community. After a few weeks, they caught up with Rav Yeshua in a village called Cana. The siblings approached quietly from behind as he told a small gathering about a bridegroom who magically replenished the dwindling wine supply at his own wedding with nothing but water.

"The governor of the feast called the bridegroom and said, 'Everyone offers the best wine first, and once the guests are drunk, they serve the cheap wine. But you have saved the best till last.'" Ha-Ra stopped and looked at his small audience. "Does anyone know what the governor meant by this?" As he asked the question, he turned and caught site of his first students, Miryam, Martha, and Lazarus. Without breaking pace or changing expression, he said, "Miryam, tell us what is meant by this statement."

There was a twitter among the crowd at the shock that the speaker would call on a woman. No one was more taken aback, though, than Miryam. She stood slowly as she considered what to say, realizing she knew the answer. "Rav, the bridegroom in the story is a teacher of immense, divine stature. The governor of the feast represents the nefesh, the mind, which is beginning to recognize that the bridegroom is powerful. The wine is the Shefa, the Memra, and It never diminishes. It grows and deepens and intoxicates, allowing the neshama, the bride, to relax and trust and merge with the bridegroom, who will then take her to his true abode." When she finished this statement, she sat down again, barely hearing the gasps of the crowd at the sexual innuendo over the roar of the Shefa within her. Ayn, ever since initiation, the wine did indeed improve, becoming stronger and more delicious on every passing day.

Rav Yeshua finished his talk, and when he crossed to his students, his smile turned to a frown. "What are you doing here?" he demanded. He seemed angry with them. Miryam bowed her head, a bit shy about their sudden presence. Now she wasn't sure she should have come. She glanced at Martha who was equally self-conscious, and both women hung back as Lazarus approached their master.

"Your abba?" Rav Yeshua asked.

"Gone to his Abba," Lazarus answered.

"As it should be," Ha-Rav answered. "No one ever truly dies."

"Lo." Of course, Lazarus didn't know from personal experience, but he understood this to be Rav's teaching.

"What are you doing here?"

"We've come to be with you."

"For what reason?"

Miryam stayed a few feet away from her brother and her teacher, but she could hear their conversation. She knew that whatever his answer, it had better be a good one. Ha-Rav could not afford three heaven-struck misfits tagging along on his mission. She stepped forward when she saw Lazarus faltering as he thought about what to say. "Rav, please excuse us for intruding," she started. She no longer called him by his name, but addressed him with the respectful title due him. "We do not wish to become a burden. The Shefa grew so strong and powerful even after you left us that we are convinced it is real."

Ha-Rav put his hands on his hips. "Is this true, Martha?"

Martha then came forward. "Ayn. You told us that we would know what to do next. When father died, we talked about what to do with our inheritance, and we decided to share it with you and help you find the rest of your flock."

"And what do you want in exchange? You know that mammon won't get you into heaven."

"Lo," Lazarus answered. "We would like the privilege of staying with you and learning as much as we can."

"You have said the way back to heaven is impossible without a teacher such as yourself to guide us," Miryam said, trying not to beg or sound shrill. "You have told us that it will be many years before we can perceive you and your teachings within ourselves. So, how can we learn without being near you?"

Ha-Rav smiled more broadly this time and clasped each of their hands. They had passed their first test, Miryam realized. "What would a teacher do without students who yearned for his wisdom so much so they teach him how to teach? Ayn, you can stay. But I warn you that it will not be easy. There will be many tests and challenges, not just because you are an initiate of a true teacher, but also because you will be in his constant presence. You will be mocked by those who do not understand. You might even be in some danger. This is my Abba's work and not everyone will accept it."

The three of them remained silent, daunted by Ha-Rav's warning.

"And because you are with me and represent my Abba, I expect nothing but the highest behavior from you, exemplary behavior. You will get away with nothing. I will not have you treating my other students any differently than I would treat them. Do you have the ears to hear?"

They nodded.

"Good. Then, welcome!" Ha-Rav embraced each of them. "Come, meet your fellow students."

Miryam hadn't noticed until now the men who had stood nearby after the rest of the audience had wandered away. Among the students Ha-Rav introduced them to were the sons of Zebedee – Yakob and Johanan – and a man named Simeon. The men nodded and formed their lips into courteous half-smiles, not exactly certain of their standing with Ha-Rav or their acceptance of the newcomers, two who were women.

Even as the number of male and female students grew in the coming years, those of Ivrit heritage found it difficult to accept the women as true spiritual aspirants, especially the traditionalist Simeon. Miryam on the other hand found it difficult to share Ha-Rav's attention with anyone else, man or woman. No matter how much she attempted to keep it to herself, this unpleasant aspect of her lower being kept coming out. This was the mutual grindstone that polished the neshamas of both Miryam and Simeon.

The students sat at supper with Rav Yeshua one evening, Simeon sitting in his usual place next to him. Miryam ladled barley and lentil soup into the bowls in front of each man. When she came to Simeon, she saw such a smug look in his eye that she became distracted and inadvertently spilled some of the hot soup in his lap.

"Ayiii!" Simeon leapt to his feet to brush off the red and yellow mess from the front of his robe, fuming more on the inside than out. He pointed at her and shouted, "Rav, make Miryam leave. She is not worthy of the Life."

Ha-Rav remained calm, not as bothered by the eruption around him as the others. "Would you have me make her male so that she can enter heaven like you males?"

Miryam clinched her fists, stomped her feet, and ran from the porch. Rav Yeshua stood immediately and stormed after her, grabbing her arm when he caught up with her. "I love all my students equally." His usual smile was gone.

"What are you saying, Rav?"

"You mistreat the other students because of your jealousy."

"Lo, I don't."

"Spilling hot soup on Simeon was no accident. But other than that, I see how you speak to Simeon every day."

"He is *raca*, a fool! He doesn't understand your teachings."

"That is not your concern. He is coming along as fast as Abba can take him. You do not know what he is supposed to learn in this life or how far he attained in his last one."

"But ... ." Miryam was mortified. She had no place to go with this argument and she felt trapped. She let it out anyway in a desperate attempt to win. "You are constantly giving him special considerations and privileges. You let him sit next to you at meals. Where I was raised, that is the seat of power."

"You think you deserve the seat of power?"

"Why not? I am your first student."

"There are no special rights in Spirit."

"Well, it isn't fair that he can sit and learn from you while I have to serve."

"All my students are asked to do selfless service."

"Does not my funding your teachings earn any status?" As soon as she said it, she wished she could put it back.

"No amount of wealth will get you into heaven. I thought *you* understood my teachings better than that. This continues and I *will* ask you to leave."

Miryam looked at the face of her beloved and saw a sternness she had never before seen. She lowered her head and a hot tear burned a trail down her cheek. "Where would I go? There is no other place but with you."

"You confuse your love for a man with love for the Shefa and the Shechinah. You do not get special privileges because of this love or wealth or because you are my first student. Simeon was right; you must reconcile your womanliness. There is no place for it on the Way, just as there is no place for his overt manliness."

Rav Yeshua lifted her chin and wiped her eyes with the edge of his sleeve. "This all stems from your feelings of separation from Abba. Anger, lust, greed, attachment, and vanity all come from feeling separate, and they are a replacement for the higher love. This is all purposeful, for how else would you be able to tell the difference? I tell you this; you cannot go to heaven until you know the difference. You must also understand that even though you are burning from embarrassment and exposure, you are not perfect. You wouldn't be here if you were. Perfection is not expected, but you must recognize your flaws so that you can see the perfection of your neshama."

Ha-Rav softened his tone. "Your love for your teacher, Yeshua the man, is admirable. But the man cannot take you to heaven. You must create love for Ravi in here." He put his fingers on the center of her forehead. "Right here is your seat of power, not next to me on the rug. Ravi will take you to heaven, not I. Someday you and I will physically part, and then where will you be? Go and contemplate these matters. Remember, you are the apple of my eye." With that, Ha-Rav stood and left her to cry in the dust and heat.

Miryam stayed at the back of their caravan as they traveled to the next town, and she ate and slept separately from the others. She did not speak to Rav for days, nor did she even look at him. Martha tried to approach her, but Miryam swatted her away like a fly. Instinctively, everyone else left her alone to lick her wounds.

She did consider leaving. She still had a good portion of her inheritance in a bag under her robe, a gold coin that would set her up nicely. But where could a woman go alone? Women who lived alone were subject to all kinds of dangers, rumors, and ostracism. The more she rummaged through her thoughts, the further the Shefa receded, and that saddened her the most. She began to suspect that she had never felt the warmth and intoxicating joy of Abba's love within her at all, that she had been suffering from some mirage of feelings all along. Perhaps she had been blinded by her infatuation with Yeshua the man. All these years following a band of beggars now lost. She could have been settled in the safety of a new husband and children by now. Oy, the agony!

But what was truly causing the agony? The mere absence of Shefa was killing her. She had to go back to the beginning and remember all the times she felt the divine love flowing within her. There were those months when Rav Yeshua left them alone as the three of them settled their affairs – she felt Abba's love strongly then, even without Yeshua's presence.

Slowly she began to re-engage her love for her beloved Ravi, the master within her whose face was that of Rav Yeshua but who was eternal and all-powerful. She began singing to the Inner Rav her secret words of initiation, over and over again, with all the feelings of gratitude and awe she could muster. There was no response, only a dry, hot, silent pressure where once an invisible flame had danced. Just at the time she was about to give up, sitting on the bank of a creek on the Mount of Olives with her bare feet dangling in the water, the Shefa finally graced her. The Divine Flow entered through the crown of her head, flowed through the shepherd's gate in the middle of her forehead, and surrounded her heart, wrapping her in a robe of tingling lovesong from heaven.

Perhaps Ha-Rav was right, she began to admit – just a little. Perhaps my love for the man was keeping me from the higher love. *Ayn, I have been jealous of the others, I have been plagued with the demons of the nefesh.* With this small surrender to truth, another wave of Shefa swept through her. The wave of love was so tremendous, it knocked her backwards. She laid on the grassy bank all afternoon and gazed at Ravi's face behind her closed eyelids, all earthly concerns incinerated in His glorified body more radiant than the sun.

That evening as Ha-Rav ate on a rug surrounded by his students, Miryam walked into the room. Still in her Shefa daze, she kneeled on the floor before him. With tears streaming down her face, she washed Rav Yeshua's feet with oil – *ayn, Simeon, the expensive oil.* And having no spare cloth to wipe the excess oil from his feet, she used her own hair. Kneeling, her personal will had been brought to its knees and, in doing so, she inwardly felt her own vanity – havel – bend at the feet of her master. With nefesh receding, her neshama took the ascendance, and she began to sense her new identity.

"Miryam, please stand." Rav Yeshua said. "No one should bow at my feet." He took her by the shoulders and pulled her to her knees.

"I bow at the feet of the Inner Rav who you represent," she whispered.

He stared into her eyes a long time, sighing with so much love for her. He kissed her on her forehead and took her into his arms, whispering into her ear, "When you know that you bow to yourself is when you will no longer need me."

That was the last time most of the students had seen Ha-Rav before he was arrested and forced to leave them. How glad she was that he had taught her that final lesson, and how glad she was that she could thank him in her own way before it was too late. It was Paulos who had instinctively and innocently summarized the experience as being crucified to the flesh. And it was she – or, more accurately, her neshama – who had resurrected!

"Atta Miryam, have you made your decision?" It was Cerinthus, sheepishly peering down at her as she sat on the tree stump in the garden. "Will you tell me about Ha-Rav?"

Miryam's attention, which had been soaring on the inner while her physical body sat in the garden on Mount Koressos, focused on the boy. From this angle, he looked like a man. "Sit beside me. I want to tell you a story about a desert tribe who had never seen or heard about the ocean until a stranger arrived to tell them about it."

Nine

When Rav Yeshua spoke of Abba's house being filled with many palaces, he must have been referring to the complex of houses in the merchant's sector where Priscilla and Aquila lived, Miryam observed. Contained within larger houses that terraced up both Mount Koressos and Mount Pion, the residences shared common walls. Each individual doorway was accessible by steps off side streets and walks. Armed with directions from the rug shop, she easily found the residence marked by the ichthys where the Faithful gathered. The fish symbol was painted in red on the upper right-hand side of the door. Normally a Yehudi family would otherwise dutifully place a metal or wooden *mezuzah* case in this spot, which stated "Hear that Yěhovah is One" on a tiny piece of parchment. Few would notice such a subtle change.

Priscilla opened the door to Miryam, commanding a servant to relieve Martha's grip on Pegasus's reins and store him in a stable somewhere in the polis. "I'm so glad you arrived early," Priscilla said. "This will give us a chance to become better acquainted."

Before the sisters could utter agreement, for that had been the plan, Priscilla whisked them through a columned courtyard filled with plants, statues, and fountains. On the far side of the courtyard, they entered a great hall through a set of double wooden doors where servants were placing food on a long table flanked by benches. Beyond this room was a smaller chamber, though much larger than Miryam and Martha's own home and much more opulent than any the women had ever seen. A series of couches formed a wide semi-circle centered on a simple wooden table and three wooden chairs at the far end of the room. Each couch was covered in a rich red fabric that matched the red blossoms in the mosaic tiled floor. On the marble walls around the room, fresco portraits of Hellene men in togas provided an eerie feeling of disembodied spirits overlooking events below. Priscilla introduced them as the ancient philosophers, Plato, Socrates, and Pythagoras, who she'd been learning about of late. *If only they could talk*, Miryam mused. The wisdom they beheld and the secrets they've witnessed.

Priscilla seated the ladies on a couch nearest to Socrates, then brought a chair to sit in front of them. She was a good-looking woman of a complexion much fairer than most Yehudi. Her brown hair had just a hint of red in it and was intricately plaited and piled upon her head in Rhōmaioi fashion. Her white palla was plain, as was all women's clothing, but Miryam could tell the fabric was finely woven and likely expensive.

"This is where we'll be meeting," she finally announced.

"Here?" Miryam was astonished.

"Do you not think it's suitable?" Priscilla was genuinely concerned.

"It's perfect," Martha responded quickly. "We're unaccustomed to such beautiful surroundings. Ha-Rav discoursed on hillsides, next to rivers, on the roofs of crowded homes. Nothing like this."

"Aquila and I were fortunate to acquire this place from a Yehudi merchant who is well accepted in Ephesus. It's large enough and inconspicuous enough for our meetings. Ephesians can't afford to meet in the open for fear of being arrested if they come out too overtly against the local and imperial religions. Most of the Rhōmaioi authorities will think we're following our own religious duties or conducting business with the locals."

People were crucified in Yerushalayim for much less, Miryam thought, but she was surprised and also a little relieved to hear the ekklēsia would be cloaked in secrecy. "I thought Paulos preached openly, as he did on the steps of the Artemision or during his lectures in the Hall of Tyrannus."

"Ideas are freely circulated and entertained here but not exclusively embraced. Yehudi, under Rhōmaioi law, are free to worship their one God and practice their traditions as long as they keep to themselves. That's why Aquila and I are not scrutinized, and no one will notice if we shift from the laws of Abraham to the law of Christos. As a man, he might have been a threat, but no one can fight a spirit."

"I've warned Paulos about his public speeches, and when I saw him in action at the Artemision, I was frankly appalled by his boldness," Miryam said. "Is he purposefully trying to taunt the Rhōmaioi? Does he intend to martyr himself? I think he underestimates how severely the Rhōmaioi enforce their laws."

"Paulos must never speak of the Christos being greater than Julius Caesar in public," Martha added. "They'll surely execute him."

Priscilla opened her mouth, presumably to say something in Paulos's defense, then thought better of it, shaking her head. "He's passionate about the Christos, and he's protected by him. He knows his own day of ascension will come soon. He does not fear for his life."

"I'm still unclear on what Paulos teaches," Miryam said, using the opportunity to learn more about Paulos's gospel. "He's told me that the Torah is for fools, and that returning to the covenants goes against his gospel, yet he seems to promote some practices of purity."

"He's always modifying the vows of baptisma." Priscilla smiled uncomfortably as if unsure whether she should divulge all of Paulos's administrative woes. "Paulos wrote to the ekklēsia in Galatia to dissuade them from returning to the traditions, and now he is writing the Korinthians for the same reason."

"He said he has someone write his letters for him."

"He dictates, I scribe," she acknowledged.

Interesting, Miryam thought. Wasn't he against literate women?

"His hands are usually too sore to write," she responded, as if hearing Miryam's thoughts. "He gets so frustrated that he sometimes grabs the stylus from my fingers and scrawls out the letters himself. He suffers persecution for the Christos, and he expects the same devotion from his followers."

"Do you help give the letters form?"

She blushed and looked down at her own hands. "I interject some of the gems from his sermons into his letters. Sometimes he needs help with brevity and turn of phrase. The letter to the Galatians was so strongly worded, I've encouraged him to write to the Korinthians with love and gentleness rather than a rod."

Miryam wondered how much more influence the obviously educated and high-born Priscilla had over Paulos than she was willing to admit.

"You mustn't fault Paulos," Priscilla said. "He's an untiring servant of enormous talent. He's obstinate because he knows the time we have to complete our work is very short. He's strict with the ekklēsia because he wants them to be redeemed when the Christos returns."

"Paulos has told us about his mission," Martha said with neutral, polite expression designed to hide her true feelings. Miryam envied that skill.

"Not only is he concerned with the Faithful in Korinthos and Galatia, we've had our fair share of troubles in Ephesus too."

"I have no doubt," Miryam said, recalling the scuffle Paulos had with the guard on the steps of the Artemision.

"Someone arrived here before we did and baptized some people according to the immersion practices of Johanan."

Miryam hadn't heard anyone speak of Ha-Rav's own rav for many years. "I wasn't aware that Johanan's practices had reached so far from Yerushalayim. Did you know that Johanan was Rav Yeshua's teacher?"

Priscilla nodded. "The story told in Yerushalayim is that Johanan was controversial. The Pharisees thought Johanan too wild, purifying men in the river rather than the temple, eating locusts and wearing robes of woven camel hair. He made the cleansing available to all, whereas the temple priests only allowed immersion to those who made sacrifices to the temple. In the end, Johanan was beheaded, and his way became outdated with the resurrection. Yakob and Simeon have decreed that the Faithful be immersed in the spirit of the Christos rather than in water – and just the one time."

"Paulos did explain that to us," Miryam replied.

"Aquila and I re-baptized the Ephesians according to the new guidelines."

"Ah." Whether baptism by water or by spirit, it made no difference, Miryam thought. Both methods were merely symbolic of true initiation by a living rav ordained by Elah, and that was the missing component. Spirit could not be passed along from one to another like bees circulating pollen from plant to plant in the hope of nourishing the entire plant. There was only one Source for nourishment, and it could only be instilled by the channel for that Source, the true Living Water. *Should I try to explain this fundamental principle to Priscilla before she helps Paulos pen more erroneous letters?* Miryam knew that would be fruitless. She could no more convey the truth to Priscilla than Paulos could instill the Divine Flow in his followers. Besides, it wasn't her place to disturb Priscilla's beliefs as long as they were still sustaining her.

"We're so grateful for the invitation to participate in this private meeting," Martha interjected, confirming that now wasn't the time to argue.

Miryam nodded agreement. "Tell us, what can we expect to see today?"

Priscilla smiled, cheered by the new topic. "It isn't so much what you'll see as what you'll experience. Paulos will say a prayer inviting the Christos into our hearts. Then Aquila will serve as cantor and tell a story about ascending to the heavens, while we chant an ancient phrase meant to coax similar visions for the members."

Miryam raised an eyebrow and glanced at Martha. "An ancient phrase?" She was suddenly filled with fear that Paulos had disclosed Ha-Rav's secret words of initiation.

Priscilla wrinkled her forehead. "Ancient names that correspond to the five great rulers of the heavenly bodies: Cronus, Aries, Hermes, Aphrodite, and Zeus. I'm surprised you didn't know this."

Miryam shrugged, relieved but still quite concerned that Paulos had folded the Helene deities into a ritual involving Rav Yeshua's "spirit."

Priscilla continued. "Paulos will discourse on Enoch and whatever else the Christos wants to say through him. It can all be quite uplifting."

Again, how peculiar, Miryam thought. "Why Enoch? The Tanakh is filled with prophets rising to the heavens and transforming into angels."

"But not everyone who comes here is of Ivrit descent, and so Paulos uses the tale of Enoch precisely because it isn't in the Tanakh."

Enoch. Miryam vaguely recalled the story of Enoch and his allegorical ascent to the kingdom of Yĕhovah. "These stories are just *mashal*," she said. "How you say in Hellene ... parabolē? They symbolize truth but are not truth in and of themselves."

"I understand the word's meaning," Priscilla said, slightly taken aback. "Paulos has had his own visions of transformation, and he wants the believers to know they can have similar experiences with the ultimate *metamorphoō* taking place when the Christos returns for our salvation. What the Hellene find interesting is that the story of Christos is not a parable. It is truth. The anastasis of Christos had witnesses."

Miryam managed not to reveal her real thoughts, that the popular story of the resurrected Christos was a story imposed upon a real rav whose powers, invisible to the uninitiated eye, outweighed the myth. "And Paulos himself can testify to this truth?"

"Through his *apokalypsis* and *opstasia*, his revelations and visions."

"Which give him the credentials to lead the ekklēsia," Miryam said.

"Certainly Paulos would need the recognition in order to persuade the Hellene to follow him."

"Follow the Christos, you mean," Miryam corrected her.

Priscilla fluttered her eyelids, not fully realizing the error she'd made.

"You said that Paulos persuaded people to follow him, but don't you mean to say to 'follow the Christos?'"

"Will we be introduced to the group?" Martha asked, again changing the subject when she saw Priscilla struggle with embarrassment.

"We'll honor your wish for anonymity," Priscilla said. "We get visitors from other ekklēsia here, so your presence won't be all that unusual. Besides, they'll be more concerned about their own safety than about your identities. You're clearly not Rhōmaioi spies, but don't look for immediate trust from them. This is a private meeting, yet our mission is to bring in as many as can fit under Paulos's big tent."

"We're grateful for your understanding," Martha said with a slight bow of the head.

"But I do have to say, it's a shame you don't want to be known," Priscilla added.

"What do you mean?" Miryam asked.

"You play a central role in the story of Iēsous Christos."

"Why do you say that?"

"I'm surprised you don't realize the example you set, Miryam, how your love of the Christos above all others was noticed and admired by your fellow students."

Miryam blushed. "Ha-Rav inspired devotion, demanded it. Devotion to one's rav is the only way for the student to gain his in return. Spiritual growth through devotion happens by degrees. This is the key to transformation, to metamorphoō as you call it."

Priscilla smiled and nodded, impressed. "Perhaps you're unaware of your actions because of the acts of Theos working through you."

"What actions?"

"The story of anointing Iēsous's feet with oil always brings tears to even the most hardened of men."

Shocked, Miryam had no idea this story had been circulating and so far from Yehudah. "That was a private gesture. One that was deeply meaningful and moving to me alone."

The forcefulness with which Miryam said this caused Priscilla to sit back in her chair. "No one knows what you were experiencing, I assure you. But everyone saw it as a prophecy-fulfilled. Paulos refers to the Christos as the Last Adam, and many see you as the Last Chavah. Your anointing of Ha-Rav was a sign that he would ascend and transform into the son of God like Enoch, just as the First Chavah's tempting apple caused the First Adam's fall into the world." She raised a hand to her heart. "Don't be offended by this, be honored. You are the reason he is called the Anointed One."

Miryam exhaled to relax herself. "I apologize. But this story, you must understand, sounds like a parable."

"Are not all parables based in truth? Scripture says: 'I will open my mouth in parables. I will utter dark sayings of old.'"

"There is another proverb that says: 'Just as the legs of the lame hang weakly, so do parables in the mouths of fools.'" Ha-Rav had warned that pearls caste before swine would surely be trampled. She kept that to herself, though she had more to say despite feeling Martha flinch in such a way that was only perceptible to her. "I have one more question. Paulos said he taught to the elect as well as the immature. Which group will be gathering here today?"

Priscilla smiled to shield herself from what appeared to be an insult. "The discourse Paulos gave on the temple steps was a taste of his public lectures. Today's gathering will be much more private and therefore completely honest and open. I will let you decide on its level of maturity." She stood suddenly. "I must see to the meal we'll be having after our meeting. Everyone will arrive soon, and Paulos doesn't like to start late."

After Priscilla put her chair back in its place at the table and left the room, Martha leaned toward Miryam's ear to whisper. "What are you doing?"

"These falsehoods about Ha-Rav and his teachings need to be corrected."

"But were you seeing the Inner Presence and serving Him when you became angry over the teachings being misrepresented?"

Miryam paused, closed her eyes, and then opened them again with a sigh. "You're right. In the effort to save Him, I lose Him."

"Do you know who Priscilla reminds me of?"

Miryam shook her head.

"You," Martha said matter-of-factly.

"Me? How so?"

"She's curious and interested in being a helpmate to the master."

Miryam sighed. It promised to be an interesting day.

Before long, more than two dozen congregates, both male and female, filed into the room and took their places on the couches. The mix of Yehudi and Hellene surprised Miryam, although most were clearly of the merchant class or above. Some nodded to the sisters while others stole glances and politely looked away from them. Whispered conversations died down as one of the men lit candles and incense on pedestals around the room. A sweet-smelling cloud soon wafted around them. Miryam recognized the frankincense, myrrh, cinnamon, and tree bark typically burned by priests in the Yehudi temples. The effect created a sense of other-worldliness and caused the sisters to all but cough and choke. This was another departure from Rav Yeshua's casual meetings, which were more like conversations than ritual.

Paulos at last entered the room with the petite Priscilla and the ample Aquila following close behind. Priscilla carried a scroll, a stylus made from a split reed, and a jar of lampblack mixture, while Aquila carried two carafes, one filled with a clear liquid, presumably water, and the other filled with a greenish-yellow liquid that looked like olive oil. They stood in front of their straight-back chairs behind the table with Paulos between them.

Not knowing what to do, the sisters mimicked the others. They stood and bowed their heads in unison with the rest of the group, but not so deeply they couldn't peek at the people around them. Paulos closed his eyes tightly and raised his face to the ceiling in prayer:

> *Grant us Your mercy. Our redeemer, redeem us, for we are Yours. We came from You. You are our minds, give us birth. You are our treasure, open for us. You are our fullness, accept us. You are our rest, give us unlimited perfection. I pray to You, You who existed and preexisted, in the name exalted above every name, through Iēsous the Anointed, Lord of Lords, king of the eternal realms. Give us Your gifts, with no regret, through the human child, the spirit, the advocate of truth. Give us authority, I beg of You, give healing for our bodies, as I beg You, through the preacher of the gospel, and redeem our enlightened souls forever, and our spirits, and disclose to our minds the firstborn of the fullness of grace. Grant what eyes of angels have not seen, what ears of rulers have not heard, and what has not arisen in the heart that became angelic in the image of the Theos when it was formed in the beginning. I have faith and hope. And bestow upon us Your beloved, chosen, blessed majesty, You who are the firstborn, the first-conceived, and the wonderful mystery of Your house. For Yours is the power and the glory and the praise and the greatness, forever and ever. Amen.*

Paulos stood a few moments longer seemingly in deep prayer, wavering suddenly as if somebody or something had nudged him. He spread out his arms. "Thank you, Kyrios." As he slipped into his chair, everyone else seated themselves.

Without pause, Aquila began intoning the story of Enoch:

> *As I slept, there appeared to me two exceedingly large men such as never seen on earth. Their faces shined like the sun, their eyes burned with light, and fire came forth from their lips. Their hands were whiter than*

snow and their wings brighter than gold. I was suddenly seized with fear and terror. One of these men said to me: 'Have courage, Enoch, do not fear. The eternal Theos sent us to you, and you shall today ascend with us into heaven.'

"Ōr-i-mouth, Moun-i-choun-a-phōr, Tar-pe-ta-nouph, Chōs-i, Chōn-bal," Priscilla quietly chanted once Aquila paused, enunciating each syllable in perfect rhythm. Miryam assumed these were the ancient rulers of the heavens Priscilla spoke of earlier. Aquila resumed the story:

The angels took me on their wings up to the first heaven and placed me on the clouds. They showed me a sea greater than the earthly sea. They brought before my face the elders and rulers of the stellar orders, and showed me two hundred angels who rule the stars and services to the heavens.

"Ōr-i-mouth, Moun-i-choun-a-phōr, Tar-pe-ta-nouph, Chōs-i, Chōn-bal," Priscilla chanted, with the help of the participants, all whispering in syncopated unity. Aquila continued:

And those men led me up to the second heaven, and showed me darkness greater than earthly darkness. There I saw prisoners hanging, awaiting their boundless judgment, and angels weeping incessantly. I asked the men with me: 'Why are these prisoners so tortured?' They answered: 'These are apostates, who did not obey Theos's commands, but took counsel with their own will and turned away with their prince of darkness who abides on the fifth heaven.'

Again the group responded, slightly louder than before: "Ōr-i-mouth, Moun-i-choun-a-phōr, Tar-pe-ta-nouph, Chōs-i, Chōn-bal."

And those men took me up onto the third heaven, and I looked downward and saw all the sweet-flowering and fruit-bearing trees bubbling with fragrant exhalation. And in the midst of the trees of that life, in that place whereon the Theos rests when He goes up into paradise, was a tree of ineffable goodness, fragrance, and fire-like vermilion. It covered everything and bore all fruits, and its roots dug down into the earth. Two springs sent forth honey and milk, and their springs sent forth oil and wine, and they flowed down into the paradise of Eden between life and death, and returned.

"Ōr-i-mouth, Moun-i-choun-a-phōr, Tar-pe-ta-nouph, Chōs-i, Chōn-bal," the group chanted even more loudly. Upon mention of the third heaven, Miryam paid close attention, knowing that Paulos had told her several times that he had visited there. She wondered if this story was what he alluded to when he mentioned his experience. Aquila had more to say about the third heaven:

> *And three hundred bright angels kept the garden on the third heaven, and with sweet singing voices they served Theos throughout each day and hour. Those men said to me: 'This place, O Enoch, is prepared for the righteous, who endure all manner of offense from those that exasperate their souls, who avert their eyes from iniquity, and make righteous judgment, and give bread to the hungry, and cover the naked with clothing, and raise up the fallen, and help injured orphans, and who walk without fault before the face of Theos, and serve Him alone. For them is prepared this place for eternal inheritance.'*

"Ōr-i-mouth, Moun-i-choun-a-phōr, Tar-pe-ta-nouph, Chōs-i, Chōn-bal."

> *And those two men led me to the northern side of the third heaven, and showed me there a terrible place of cruel darkness and gloom, murky hot coals burning in a fiery river. Everywhere I saw fire and frost and ice, and angels chained mercilessly in thirst and shivering, bearing angry weapons. And those men said to me: 'This place, O Enoch, is prepared for those who dishonor Theos, who on earth practice sin against nature, who steal the souls of men and goods from the poor, and who themselves wax rich, who being able to satisfy the empty, cause the starving to die, who being able to clothe, strip the naked, and who know not their creator, bow to the vain soulless deities who cannot see nor hear, and who also build false images and bow down to unclean handiwork, for all these is prepared this place for eternal inheritance.'*

"Ōr-i-mouth, Moun-i-choun-a-phōr, Tar-pe-ta-nouph, Chōs-i, Chōn-bal."

Miryam was nearly entranced by the chanting, but more fascinated by the receptivity of all those who participated. There was a power in the story and the chanting that went hand in hand, however fantastic it all was. She felt warmth in the pit of her gut and a thumping in her chest. Just as quickly the chanting began to give her a headache.

Enoch was not a prophet written about in the Tanakh, but he was a figure popular with the Essenes, Miryam recalled. Simeon had been a member of the Essenes before he joined Rav Yeshua, and he used to describe ceremonies like this one in which Yĕchezqel, Yĕhovah, or Enoch ascended to heavenly palaces, or *hechalot*, usually in a chariot, or *merkavah*, to come "face to Face" with a white-bearded Yĕhovah on a throne. Miryam always believed that these stories were allegory of the real ascension in spirit, very much like climbing the rungs of Yacob's ladder to heaven – but within the self. Without a living master, the sects would chant to induce the effect of ascending through ever more resplendent heavens they could only imagine. Perhaps Paulos had reached back to the rituals of his own priestcraft to create a means by which his followers could imitate what they thought had happened to Rav Yeshua and to the prophets before him. Those who were not familiar with the truth did not understand that the heavens were within every living being waiting to be explored by those who had the eyes to see, just as the story itself suggested. The pathway to the heavens was not through the gut or chest or through a dream or vision or imagination, the pathway was not a set of steps one climbed to reach some beautiful paradise. The pathway was through the portal between the two physical eyes, where one meets the glorified face of one's master.

Most of the members in the room chanted with great passion and enthusiasm, and some were beginning to close their eyes and twitch as if being escorted upward right along with Enoch. The angels continued to carry Enoch into higher and more spectacularly gardened levels of heaven, as recited by Aquila, while the members continued to chant the names of the great rulers in between the verses in louder and louder tones.

At the fourth heaven Enoch saw the sun and moon, accompanied by thousands of stars and myriads of angels, as the celestial orbs rotated through a succession of twelve gates that regulated the seasons, the months, and the hours in a day. Enoch saw the withered-faced giants who renounced their vows with their prince of darkness, Satan, living in silence for eternity on the fifth heaven. He saw the seven bands of archangels who governed the kosmos and the world from the sixth heaven. He saw the troops of angels living on the seventh heaven who joyfully served Theos on the tenth heaven. Enoch shook with terror feeling quite alone until the archangel Gabriel lifted him up and placed him before the face of Theos. There he saw the circle of the twelve constellations on the firmament of the eighth and ninth heavens.

On the tenth heaven, Enoch saw the Glory of Theos's face, glowing and emitting fire and sparks like iron in the hot coals. Aquila recited:

I fell prone and bowed down to the Kyrios, and He said to me: 'Have courage, Enoch, do not fear. Arise and stand before my face into eternity.' The glorious servants bowed down to Theos, and said: 'Let Enoch go according to Your Word.' And Theos said: 'Go and take Enoch out of his earthly garments, and anoint him with my sweet ointment, and put him into the garments of My Glory.' Here the angels anointed and dressed Enoch, and the ointment smelled like sweet dew and shined like the sun's rays. Enoch looked at his reflection and was transfigured like one of the Glorious Ones.

By now the chanters were on their feet, clapping rhythmically and shouting: "Ōr-i-mouth, Moun-i-choun-a-phōr, Tar-pe-ta-nouph, Chōs-i, Chōn-bal! Ōr-i-mouth, Moun-i-choun-a-phōr, Tar-pe-ta-nouph, Chōs-i, Chōn-bal!" Miryam felt like putting her hands over her ears and running from the noise in the room. Aquila continued telling the story of how Enoch, now a deity himself, could enjoy the sport of creating the heavens and the worlds and everything in them, but the followers of Paulos no longer listened to his words, so caught up were they in the promise of their own apotheosis.

At last the story ended, the chanting died down, and the people returned to their chairs, their energy spent. Paulos stood and looked around the room a few moments without saying a word. Miryam could see the tremor beginning to take control of his hands as it often did when he became agitated or ecstatic. Paulos finally spoke: "I knew a man in Christos more than fourteen years ago who was carried to the third heaven, a paradise where he heard words that are unlawful to speak."

The members nodded and gazed tearfully at Paulos. Miryam assumed they understood that Paulos was speaking of himself, and that it would be unseemly for him to tell of his own experiences outright.

"Just as Enoch was dressed and anointed on the tenth heaven by the angels, you elect will rise from the earth and be clothed with the garment of life," Paulos continued. "In the presence of the Lord of Spirit, your garment shall not wax old, nor shall your glory diminish. For we know that if our earthly house is dissolved, we would have a house eternal, not made with human hands, but made by Theos in the heavens. We yearn to be clothed with our house in heaven, not because we do not want to be found naked, but so that our mortality might be swallowed up by eternal life."

That was quite profound, Miryam thought. The neshama, when taking on the human life, is in a sense clothed with an outer garment. But Paulos reversed the idea and suggested that the neshama isn't properly clothed until it rises and faces the Christos the way Enoch was clothed when he met his Lord in the upper heavens. In fact, according to the story, Enoch couldn't meet the Lord until he had been transformed with the heavenly clothing. She wondered if Paulos got this idea from their conversation over breadmaking when she drew circles portraying their heavenly bodies in flour on her kitchen table.

Paulos nodded to Aquila, and the latter recited more scripture:

> *After much tribulation, the sun will be darkened, and the moon will not give its light, and the stars will fall from heaven, and the powers in the heavens will shake. And then they will see the son of man coming in the clouds with great power and glory. And then He will send out the angels and gather His elect from the four winds, from the ends of the earth to the ends of heaven.*

"The son of man will be seen coming in the clouds," Paulos echoed Aquila's words. "He will send out the angels to gather His elect. Who are the elect?"

Paulos looked around the room. "You are! You. You will be raised aloft on the chariots of Spirit, but you must be transformed by renewing your soul so that you may prove what is the good and acceptable and perfect will of Theos. Just as Christos was raised up from the dead by the glory of Theos, we shall also walk in the newness of life."

Paulos stood and paced around the room, gazing from one set of eyes to the next. Miryam knew he worked best on his feet, creating drama as he waited for his next inspiration of words. He stood in front of Miryam and gazed into her eyes a moment. "Not all flesh is the same," Paulos began, now moving around the room again, looking at everyone yet no one in particular. "One kind belongs to humans, another to beasts, to birds, and so on. The sun has one kind of resplendence, while the moon and stars each have another kind. And even the stars differ from each other in their beauty and brightness. So it is with the resurrection of the dead. We are sown a temporary physical body and raised an eternal spiritual body. We are sown in dishonor and raised in glory. We are sown in weakness and raised in power."

Paulos pivoted on his heels. "How do we know this, you might ask? Long before the crucifixion, Iēsous led three of his apostles to the top of a mountain. Theos transfigured His only son in front of them, and his garments glistened with intense whiteness. After the crucifixion, his apostles saw him in his spiritual glory, as did the apostle standing before you years later."

Paulos pointed to a woman wearing a long veil around her head. "We are not like Moses, who veiled his face so that the children of Yisrael would not see his glory. To this day a veil still covers the Tanakh and the hearts and minds of those who read it. We reflect the glory of Christos with unveiled face like a mirror, and we are transformed into his same image, from glory to glory, through the Spirit of the Lord."

Suddenly, Paulos spread his arms and hung his head, mimicking the crucified body. The effect stunned his audience, and tears streamed down more than one set of cheeks. "Behold, I tell you a mystery," he shouted. "We shall not all sleep, but we shall all be changed, in a moment, in the twinkling of an eye, at the last trump. For the trumpet shall sound, and the dead shall be raised intact and for all eternity, and we shall be changed through Iēsous Christos!" He dropped his arms, but remained silent, letting his words sink into the minds of each participant.

"How are we transformed?" Paulos was now barely audible, and everyone leaned forward to hear him more clearly. "By renouncing the shame we keep hidden, by living in the Logos of Theos, by manifesting the truth, and by proving ourselves to every human being's conscience in the presence of Theos."

As Paulos paused, Priscilla scrawled his words out on papyrus as fast as she could move her quill, every once in a while stopping to redip it in lampblack or to quickly massage the stiffness out of her writing hand. Miryam admired the swiftness with which she wrote, and was particularly envious that she never spilled one drop of ink on her white tunic. Paulos may have tarried a moment longer than was necessary to allow her to catch up. When she lifted her face, beaming her satisfaction to Paulos, he nodded to Aquila for more recitation.

Miryam recognized the verse Aquila recited from the *Book of Daniel*:

And many of them that sleep in the dust of the earth shall awake, some to everlasting life and some to shame and everlasting contempt. The wise shall shine like the brightness of the firmament, and they who turn many to righteousness – the angels – are like the stars forever and ever.

Paulos had Aquila recite the verse, no doubt, to prove that this prophecy of resurrection had come true. She wondered if the Hellene followers accepted the Ivrit prophecy as their own.

"For even if our gospel is veiled, it is veiled in them that are lost," Paulos continued. "The powers of this world have blinded the minds of the unbelieving, that the light of the gospel and the glory of Christos shall not dawn upon them. For we preach not about ourselves, but that Iēsous is Christos, and that we are his servants. Light shall shine out of darkness on the knowledge of the divine glory in the face of Iēsous Christos, as it also shines in our hearts. We have borne the earthly images, and we shall also bear the heavenly images. Amen." With that, Paulos dropped into his chair behind the table. His hands still trembled, but more softly now, every last drop of emotion squeezed from his limp body.

Miryam thought the proceedings were now over, but Aquila stood and recited yet another verse, which she again recognized from scripture:

And Elijah went up to the top of Carmel, and he cast himself down upon the earth, and put his face between his knees.

Elijah, a champion of God, was another prophet who ascended into heaven, this time in a whirlwind. Following Elijah's lead, Aquila knelt on the floor and pressed his forehead on his knees. The onlookers, obviously expecting this action, followed Aquila's example and assumed similar positions on the floor. The heavier ones were unable to fold at the waist so that the forehead would touch the knees, but they did the best they could. Some of the women brought small rugs to kneel upon, thereby cushioning the knees and keeping their finery relatively unsoiled. Not fully understanding the purpose of the ritual, Miryam and Martha remained in their chairs, catching a few questioning looks from the others. Following Aquila's lead, the group sat up and bowed down to their knees again for a total of five times by Miryam's count, all the while reciting the names of the five great rulers as they had chanted earlier: "Ōr-i-mouth, Moun-i-choun-a-phōr, Tar-pe-ta-nouph, Chōs-i, Chōn-bal."

The group then stood and formed a single line at the table. Aquila mixed the water and oil in the large wooden bowl centered on the table. He lit fresh piles of aromatic bark, twigs, and leaves in the pots there and moved the candlestick closer to the bowl containing the oily water. One by one the men and women took turns staring into the mixture in the bowl and returned to their kneeling positions. With eyes closed, they bobbed or trembled as if enjoying their inner excursions. Miryam could only guess that the ritual had something to do with what Paulos had said about seeing the image of the Christos superimposed upon their own faces "as in a mirror," and perhaps each was searching for their own glorified transformation reflected in the liquid. She knew they were looking in the wrong place, but her curiosity got the better of her.

As the last man bent over the bowl to search for the image of Theos in his own reflection, Miryam got up to stand behind him, ignoring Martha's tug on her palla. She knew Martha would disapprove, but she had to know more about this latest distortion of Ha-Rav's teachings. As she stepped in front of the bowl, she was immediately struck by the smoke from the incense, and it made her feel light-headed and entranced. Bending over the water didn't help her dizziness, but she saw how the water and oil beneath candlelight indeed worked together to produce a faint, wavering reflection amidst the smoke, and for a split second she felt herself step outside of herself. She didn't like that sensation at all, so she quickly backed away from the table. As she did, all went black.

Miryam awakened flat on the floor, face up, staring into Martha's worried, disapproving eyes. Priscilla dabbed Miryam's forehead with a damp cloth. "This often happens to people their first time, especially after fasting," she said. "You have to build up your stamina."

Miryam struggled to sit up.

"Slowly," Martha warned.

Miryam looked around and noticed the room was empty. "Where is everyone?"

"They've gone into the banquet hall," Priscilla said. "We've been fasting in preparation, and now we break our fast as part of the ceremony. When you're ready, we'll go in."

"I'm ready now." Martha and Priscilla pulled her to her feet, but she rejected their arms offered for support. "I'm fine." The sisters followed Priscilla into the dining room.

The banquet table appeared to be divided between men at one end and women at the other. Paulos sat at the head of the male half of the table with Aquila at his right hand, and Priscilla seated herself at the head of the opposite, female half, with Martha next to her. Miryam took the only empty place at the center, and found herself flanked by men on one side and women on the other. Priscilla may have relegated her there by design, but at least here she would be afforded differing views from her dinner mates. She appreciated Priscilla's gesture once she thought about it.

Great bowls and platters of food covered the table, all typical of Ephesian fare in great abundance: seafood, lamb, pomegranates, melons, figs, olives, cheese, and nuts. If these people had been fasting, they must be ravenous, she thought, yet no one filled their plates, obviously waiting for the next phase to commence. Why they too didn't faint during that long, smoky, nearly oppressive session, she couldn't guess. Clearly the rituals filled them in some way.

With no fanfare, a male servant brought in a large tray of flatbread, followed by several servants carrying pitchers of wine. They stood silently next to Paulos, as if awaiting a signal from him to serve.

Paulos stood and all of the whispering quieted down. "I deliver to you that which I have received from Christos. On the night he was to be betrayed, Iēsous took bread, and when he had given thanks, he tore it and said, 'Take, eat. This is my body, which will be broken for you. Do this in remembrance of me.'" Paulos selected a flatbread from the servant's tray, tore it in half, and placed one half on the plates of the men sitting on either side of him. The servant then served previously-torn pieces of bread to each person sitting at the entire length of the table. The other servants meanwhile filled each person's goblet with wine.

Paulos lifted his goblet. "The Kyrios Iēsous said: 'This cup is the new covenant of my blood. As often as you drink, do so in remembrance of me. For as often as you eat this bread and drink from the cup, you proclaim the Kyrio's death until he returns.'" Everyone drank deeply from their goblets along with Paulos.

Miryam was instantly transported back to that evening of innocence, when master and disciples could still laugh together, learn together, ride the waves of Shefa together, even if for one last time. Ha-Rav did break bread and pour wine for everyone, reminding them that Ravi's very presence within each initiate was closer to them than had they actually consumed him. Ravi was the bread of life to them, and it behooved the disciples to partake of Him daily. When they ate and drank of the Shefa, the Divine Flow, they ate and drank of Him, yet not of Rav Yeshua, but of his Glory within them. For Ravi was the grapevine and the disciples were the branches: "Remain in me, and I will remain in you. A branch cannot produce fruit if it is severed from the vine, and you cannot be fruitful apart from me." *With Ravi, the eternal master within, we could bear much fruit, but without Him we are nothing,* she thought. Ravi was closer to them than their own heart beats, for He would stay with them even when their hearts ceased to beat.

Given the rituals and stories of that day, Miryam realized that everyone surrounding her ardently longed for this same Presence, whether aware of it or not, and they would never achieve it by the means demonstrated here. Not to the extent that she and Martha enjoyed when they lived with their "savior" and every day since then. On the other hand, Miryam could not deny that the believers who had gathered today had experienced something extraordinary. Tears welled up in her eyes, impressing those around her of how touched she was by their simple ceremony. They would never know the truth.

Suddenly she was done, and she was ready to go home. She looked down the long table and saw Martha serving herself and exchanging friendly banter with Priscilla. She finally realized she was famished, and when the woman next to her handed her a platter of lamb's meat, she transferred a slice to her plate.

"Are you new here?" the woman, obviously Hellene, asked.

Miryam wasn't prepared with an answer. "My sister and I have lived on Mount Koressos longer than I care to admit." The truth seemed to be the best approach.

"You're Yehudi," the woman said, despite the fact that Miryam's grasp of the Hellene language was nearly fluid.

"I'm from Galilee, actually."

She wrinkled her brow. "Have you been baptized?"

How to answer this question without giving myself away? "I have not been baptized. Paulos invited my sister and me to the ekklēsia to make our decisions later."

She arched her eyebrows in surprise. "That's never done. Visitors must be baptized before they can come to ekklēsia. One must make a commitment before witnessing or participating in the Mystery. He must think highly of you."

Miryam chuckled. "I'm not sure what he thinks. Have you known Paulos long?" She wanted to deflect the woman's attention away from herself.

The woman shook her head. "My husband and I were recently baptized, but I can tell you he's a very powerful man."

"What makes you say that?" Miryam accepted a bowl from the woman and spooned its creamy chickpea and olive mixture onto a pita.

"Paulos does not abandon those who are not baptized. He serves all, mostly by casting evil spirits from them. Folks around here collect his work aprons and cloths to rub on people who are possessed by these demons."

Oy! This reminded Miryam of the woman Paulos "healed" on the steps of the Artemision. That woman had also been fooled by Paulos's illusory power.

"He exorcised a demon from a slave girl in Philippi," the woman whispered in a gossipy voice. "Python possessed the young girl."

"Python?"

"Python was the dragon that guarded the oracle at Delphi and was slain by Apollo. The spirit of Python spoke prophecies through this girl. Her masters made a fortune with her, but Paulos changed that."

Miryam didn't doubt that Paulos forced himself on the situation, and she was sure the story would end with him being run out of town.

"Anyway, the possessed girl would follow Paulos and his companions when they went down to the river to pray, shouting: 'These men are the servants of the highest Theos, and he has shown us the way of salvation.' She did this many, many times. Finally, Paulos had had enough. He turned and faced the girl and shouted to the spirit within her: 'I command you in the name of Iēsous Christos to exit this young lady.' The girl was soon herself again."

"What happened next?"

"Well, her owners were not happy with Paulos because he'd rid the young girl of her prophecy-telling talent, and they felt robbed of their livelihood. A mob drove Paulos and his companions to the authorities in the agora, complaining that they were teaching customs that were not lawful for the locals to follow. The rulers commanded that they be stripped of their clothes, beaten, and put in prison." Miryam's table companion was wide-eyed and clearly in awe of Paulos as she told the story. "As Paulos and his men sat in stocks in jail, an earthquake broke open the doors and loosened the locked beams that bound their feet. The jailer, seeing that all the prisoners were freed, begged to be saved from their hands. Paulos told him to believe in the Iēsous Christos, and he would be saved."

"You believe," Miryam said as more a statement of fact than question.

"I believe. Don't you?"

Before she could answer, the men to the other side of Miryam, sitting opposite each other, said something that caught her attention. They had been discussing the ancient Hellene philosophers, toward which Miryam had bent an ear while she listened to the story about Python Girl. What caught her attention was one man asking the other: "Do you think Paulos shares Plato's ideas of the psychē?"

The other man pondered this question a moment. "I'm not sure."

"Here's what I don't understand. Socrates said that the psychē is immortal and cannot be destroyed after death, and yet Paulos says that only Iēsous Christos can raise the dead, and only through the Christos can Theos give the psychē eternal life."

"I see your confusion," the other man answered, resting his chin in his large hand. "You're saying: 'How can the Kyrios raise what is already alive?'"

Miryam sympathized with their dilemma and wanted to assert an opinion, but kept respectfully silent. She was here only to observe, as Martha had reminded her earlier, and not to challenge or clarify beliefs.

The second man continued: "On the other hand, in believing that our psychē is eternal, what hope do we have of eternal life in heaven without being raised by the Christos?"

"You make a good point, my friend," the first man said. "We have no proof that Socrates was right. He was facing death when he said this, after all."

"Precisely."

The first man ripped some lamb's meat from the bone with his teeth and chewed as he thought. "Plato said that the well-balanced psychē is divided into three parts. First there is the nous or mind, which develops the intellect of a philosopher king, then the *thymos* or emotion, which pursues acts of bravery – or acts of hubris if left unchecked. *Eros* drives the appetite and desires. I don't hear Paulos talking about these aspects."

"That's because he's Yehudi, a trained priest, no less, but the principles are the same. He speaks of the battle between the flesh and the spirit. I've heard Paulos say: 'For what man knows the things of a man except the spirit in him? And what man knows the things of Theos except the Spirit of Theos.' The common man cannot discern the spiritual things of Theos, for they consider them foolish. It is the mind of the Christos that bestows upon us the wisdom and knowledge of Theos."

The first man nodded. "When Paulos speaks of metamorphosis, what is changed, the soul or the body? He did admit that when he had his own visions, he didn't know whether he was in the body or out of the body, and yet I've also heard him say that we are temples of Theos and the spirit of Theos dwells within us. "

"Did he not say today that we are sown a physical body and raised a spiritual body, that we are changed into the image of the Spirit of Theos?" The man laughed out loud. "You raise good questions. We probably won't know the answers until the final trump sounds!"

These men were caught up in a conversation of the mind, and knew not the soul, and would never know it by just talking about it or striving to understand it, Miryam thought. They were not initiates of a true rav. But although she felt a certain sense of disdain for the men and their arrogant talk of the spirit, she was reminded again of how Ha-Rav's teachings benefited from association with the Hellene. The Yehudi had an ancient understanding of the Mysteries, but they were limited in how they could talk about it. The Hellene brought in new vocabulary and meaning. Just as the Hellene interpretation of the Word (Logos) filled out the Ivrit interpretation of the Word (Memra), Socrates and Plato and even Philo contributed a deeper appreciation of the soul. Philo attempted to bridge Hellene and Ivrit concepts, but Paulos was the glue that bonded them together and brought them to ordinary people. Even her own conversations with Paulos seemed to have gone into his sermon.

The rest of the meal became a blur as Miryam fought the urge to yawn and fall asleep in her hummus. She caught Martha's glance and silently conveyed her desire to go home. Now, preferably. Martha nodded and began the process of extricating herself from Priscilla's grasp without seeming rude. Priscilla cast a sympathetic look Miryam's way, making her realize that Martha must have expressed concern for her well being.

Miryam turned to the python-story lady next to her to say good-bye. She was so engrossed in a lively discussion with the women around her that Miryam couldn't get her attention. Just as Miryam stood to leave, she thought she heard the woman say something about Paulos burning books. Miryam was too tired to ask and gave the comment no further attention.

Now for the difficult part, Miryam told herself. She headed for Paulos to thank him for inviting them to such an interesting event, but she was stopped by a tug on her elbow from Martha. She shook her head and steered Miryam toward the doorway. Miryam didn't look back to see if Paulos had noticed them leaving. Once they were out of the banquet room and in the courtyard, Martha whispered, "It would be inappropriate to speak to Paulos while he is surrounded by his men."

"He continues to surprise me with his selective observances of custom," Miryam said under her breath. "This was not Rav Yeshua's practice."

"None of it is," Martha said.

Priscilla awaited them at the door. "I've sent for your donkey and wagon, and you will find them at the bottom of the steps, rested, fed, and watered."

"Again, toda," Martha said, grasping both of Priscilla's hands in her own. She subtly signaled to Miryam to do the same.

"Ayn, toda," Miryam said with a slight bow of the head. "You're to be commended for all the work you do. I apologize for not feeling well enough to stay longer."

Priscilla bowed her head slightly in like response, but kept her demeanor tight, obviously determined not to repeat their disagreements of that morning. "You will come again?"

The two sisters looked at each other, but only Martha could speak. "We don't come down the mountain too often."

"You lead quiet, contemplative lives and have no need for rituals, I understand. Perhaps we will meet in the agora someday." Priscilla smiled again, then quickly retreated inside.

The women stepped into the harsh reality of the midday sun and found their donkey and cart awaiting them as promised. They remained silent on their ride home, each digesting the strange sights and sounds of the day, each too stunned to talk about it. But that evening, as they dragged themselves to bed, Miryam could not help but ask Martha how it was that she wasn't affected by the chanting and the rituals.

"Through simple zakar," Martha said, as she blew out the candle on a table next to her bed. "I remembered Ravi, over and over and over. I knew that if I stepped away from His Face within, I would lose sight of Him and control of my senses."

Saying nothing, Miryam pulled a blanket under her chin. She sighed heavily, feeling the burden of her own failure in attention. She had soared above the agony of being separated from her beloved Rav Yeshua, and yet this single, harmless Paulos unnerved her.

Ayn, it is impossible to serve two masters at once, she thought. Paulos and the Faithful tried to replicate the inner spiritual journey with their chanting and storytelling, their incense and reflective water. No doubt some of them had achieved results, but what was ekstasis to them was sickening to Miryam. She could not participate in their outward rituals in their attempt to travel the heavens while also focusing on Ravi at the shepherd's gate.

She closed her eyes and whispered a verse from the *Song of Songs*: "Oh my dove, in the clefts of the rock, in the secret places of the mountain, let me see Your face, let me hear Your voice, for sweet is Your voice, and lovely is Your face." The dross of the day cleared instantly, allowing her to view Ravi's face again, all the while knowing He had never left her.

Ten

The sisters awakened in the middle of the night to shouting and abrupt banging on their door. "Atta Miryam! Atta Martha! Hurry!" Startled and dazed, Miryam threw a palla around her shoulders and carefully opened the door. Cerinthus was bent over with hands on knees, panting, clothes sweat-drenched. "Ran ... all the way. Wedding ... Ephesus. Paulos ... burning ... biblos."

The boy wasn't making sense. "Come in, come in," Miryam ordered. "Did you say that Paulos was burning books at a wedding in Ephesus?"

Cerinthus shook his head and in one quick gulp drained the bowl of water Martha handed him. "It's my cousin's wedding. The ceremony itself is in the morning." He presented his empty bowl to Martha for a refill, and collapsed on a bench at the table.

"Paulos was there?"

He shook his head. "One of his followers told my uncle that Paulos was organizing a scroll burning in the fields outside Ephesus. Or maybe it was inside the polis, I don't remember."

"Are you sure? How do you know?"

"I heard the man myself."

"What kind of scrolls?"

"Books on the magical arts, mostly."

"And how does he plan to gather them for burning?"

"The Faithful will surrender them freely to the fire."

Miryam thought about her own scrolls and wondered if she should hide them. She did not have any biblos on magic spells, but maybe Paulos would decide to burn other works as well. "When is this to take place?"

"Sunrise. There's little time."

"Why sunrise?" Martha asked.

"Don't know." Cerinthus shrugged. "People around here believe demons have the most power to cause disruption just before dawn and just after sunset," he offered. Then it hit him. "The festival of Artemis begins at daybreak with the procession of her statue through the polis!"

"Maybe he wants to show everyone that the Christos is more powerful than Artemis or any other spirit," Miryam suggested.

"Might even position his bonfire in sight of the procession," Martha added.

"Sounds like him." Miryam slowly shook her head in disbelief. "This public display will draw even more attention to his misinterpretation of Ha-Rav's teachings. We must try to stop him."

"Doubtful we'll succeed, Sister," Martha said, always the wary one. "And it could be dangerous for us if the locals or the Rhōmaioi don't like what he's doing."

"Ayn, but I don't see a choice." In the distance, she could hear an owl hoot as if sounding a note of caution. *What are you up to, Ravi?* She sensed no reply from the master within her.

After dressing quickly and grabbing a few supplies, the three of them soon bumped down the mountain in the donkey-pulled cart, their path illuminated by a full moon. The sun hadn't yet begun rising, but it wouldn't be long before the priestcraft, polis officials, and statue bearers began transporting a silver statue of Artemis from her temple to Ephesus. If Cerinthus could successfully keep Pegasus motivated, they would stay ahead of the slow, solemn foot parade as it made its way through the polis. It was doubtful Paulos would begin tossing papyri into the flames without benefit of the audience the procession would provide.

With the dawnlight brightening, the silhouette of the triple-arched Magnesia gate came into view. Cerinthus drove Pegasus toward the center stone arch meant for carriage traffic. A sleepy-headed Rhōmaioi guard leaning against the gate snapped his spear to attention and stepped in front of the cart. "The upper city is closed to non-residents until sunrise," he said gruffly.

"Please sir," Cerinthus said. "I must deliver my aunts to my cousin's wedding early this morning. My father will be cross with me if his sisters miss the wedding."

"Where is the wedding, and when does it start?"

"In the Embolos as soon as the procession passes. Timed for good fortune."

The guard eyed the three of them with skepticism. Cerinthus was still dressed in his wedding garb, though he was somewhat soiled from his midnight run up the mountain. Miryam and Martha had donned their best pallas for festival day, not wanting to look too out of place. It was still dark enough that the guard would not be able to see that their finest were rags compared to what a merchant's family could afford, though their peasant's cart should have been a dead giveaway. Where else would two women their age possibly be going at this time of day, anyway? What other motive? At least that's what Miryam was hoping the guard would be thinking. He sighed and stepped aside. "See that you get them to the house before the procession comes through. We need to keep the streets open."

Cerinthus nodded and, with a slap of the reins, encouraged Pegasus through the monolithic gate. A crow landed on the top of the arch and cawed to another crow on a distant building. The cawing sounded like laughter to Miryam.

As he steered Pegasus around the south side of the state buildings, the clouds above the eastern hills began to glow pink and yellow. They drove around the western end of the state agora and turned down Market Street through the Embolos where they'd attended Paulos's ekklēsia the week before. She wondered if Cerinthus's family lived in the same luxurious style here as Priscilla and Aquila did. She leaned forward to ask him if he'd like to be dropped off. He declined. The spectacle of Paulos's bonfire promised to be much more interesting than a boring wedding.

As they drove through the Embolos, householders were pouring onto their porches on the adjacent slopes to wait for the parade. Shopkeepers hurriedly swept out their stores and stacked goods to open once the procession passed. Several young ephebes, local teenage soldiers-in-training, arrived on horseback to patrol the streets. One waved Cerinthus out of the road just as he turned the wagon north onto the grand boulevard leading to the theater.

Miryam's pulse quickened, and her heart began to outpace the donkey's hooves as they hit the crushed rock. "Can't make this beast go any faster?" she asked, losing patience. Cerinthus slapped Pegasus again with the reins, and he in turn picked up some speed but then slowed to his original and most comfortable pace.

Ephesians crowded the theater sector of the polis, allowing themselves to be corralled by the ephebes beneath the covered colonnade lining the entire western length of the street that led to the colossal open-aired arena directly ahead. The massive commercial agora bordering Theater Street, with its periphery of shops and warehouses where the sisters shopped for staples, was uncommonly deserted for now, except for a few merchants opening their stalls. Cerinthus drove the cart past the agora, turned down the long avenue toward the harbor, and pulled to a stop.

"What are you doing?" Miryam asked. Intuitively she knew Paulos would be nowhere near Harbor Street, which would take them away from the procession.

"I thought it wise to get out of the way while we decide where to go next."

Miryam nodded her approval, but she was becoming anxious. She knew Paulos would have the havel of Abel, the hubris of Achilles, to burn scrolls in public, daring the authorities to lock him away or, worse, to kill him. Would Ephesians consider Paulos's bonfire an affront against their way of life? Intuition told her they would take offense, but just how extreme their reaction would be was difficult to foresee.

Miryam held mixed feelings about the burning. On the one hand, she could sympathize with Paulos's intentions. Very little spirituality was to be gained from casting spells or divining the future. And no one was exempt from practicing some form of magic upon another, from the Magi priests to the midwives, from the way spouses manipulated each other, or from the way the mind convinced itself to act detrimentally to the soul. Paulos was right. Magic was not the Way. On the other hand, Ha-Rav would never prohibit aspiring students from exploring everything the world had to offer before embarking on the Spiritual Way. But the more she thought about what Paulos was doing to Rav Yeshua's legacy, the angrier she grew.

Miryam struggled to control her anger with her secret words as she surveyed their surroundings. This sector of the polis, which began at the intersection of Harbor Street and Theater Street and extended north to the stadium, was oriented toward moving great numbers of people to areas where they could be entertained or could trade for the bounty that came in from the harbor. There were few government buildings, monuments, statues, and ornate private villas in this area except for the grand palace of the proconsul and smaller structures where the religious met for observances or listened to lectures. Beyond the theater stood the public stadium and the barrios, stables, and fields where most of the common Ephesians lived. If Paulos was inside the polis walls, he might be somewhere in that more open sector, with less obtrusive architecture blocking view of his bonfire.

"Let's continue north, Cerinthus. We're running out of obvious places to look."

Cerinthus nodded and turned Pegasus back onto Theater Street, heading north toward the stadium. Patrons and soldiers on horseback began to file into the street behind them, causing Miryam some concern. In the time it had taken them to zig and zag through the polis, the procession had likely already entered the Magnesia gate. Though Artemis and her entourage would advance slowly as it made ceremonial stops at various state buildings and the theater, Miryam began to feel an urgency. "Go, go, go!" she shouted, inspiring Pegasus not one bit.

"Maybe you didn't hear right, Cerinthus," Martha said. "Maybe he's not planning to burn biblos."

He shook his head. "I heard what I heard."

As they rounded the oblong stadium toward Ephesus's northeastern gate out of the city, Miryam spotted a bonfire against the city's northwestern wall near an ancient temple of Apollo. Cerinthus saw it too and automatically turned Pegasus toward the fire. Miryam wondered if Paulos had purposely chosen this location near the ancient temple as some kind of statement against the lesser deity.

Miryam and Martha scampered out of the wagon and ran for Paulos standing near the fire. Seeing them, he smiled his pompous smile. "You have scrolls to burn?"

"Paulos, what are you doing?"

He feigned innocence. "It's a purification, nothing more."

"What if the centurions see you?"

"What if they do? Is it against the law to have a small fire?"

"This is no small fire, Paulos!" she shouted. "Did you encourage this ... this performance?"

Paulos shrugged ambiguously. "I will not let happen in Ephesus what happened with my Galatia brothers."

Miryam sighed. She thought Paulos had reconciled the situation at Galatia by now. "The rite of circumcision?"

"It's more than that. Not knowing Theos, they bonded to that which by nature is not Theos." He nodded angrily toward the temple of Apollo. "But once they came to know Theos, or rather to be known by Him, they turned back again to the weak and miserable elements. They observed astrology and divined their fortune. They cast spells with their incantations. They paid homage and made sacrifices to their patron deities." Enraged, Paulos spat as he shouted. "I am afraid I have wasted my labor on them. Did they want slavery all over again?"

Only four women and two men huddled around the fire, all with empty hands. Miryam spotted the woman who'd sat next to her at the ekklēsia banquet table and told her the story of Paulos healing the python-possessed girl. She would expect this of her, but the rest were strangers. Curiously, Paulos's traveling companions and cohorts had wisely stayed out of sight.

The fire burned in a large hole in the ground about two meters in diameter. As Miryam approached it, she saw remnants of papyrus smoldering among the embers. *Too late*, she thought. *Whatever was written on these scrolls is now lost forever.* Paulos threw another log on the flames and they exploded into sparks. Miryam jumped backwards. Hearing him snicker, she glared at him.

"The Ephesians have seen the works of power, the healings with hands, the signs," Paulos said. "Many have confessed their evil deeds. They know they cannot drink from the cup of the Christos nor eat at his table while also drinking from the cup of demons and eating at their tables. These Faithful have decided on their own to burn these evil texts. Do you object?"

"Only that you're interfering with the rule in this polis."

"Christos would have interfered."

"If Rav Yeshua had thought we were casting spells, he might have gone on a rampage with us in private. But he certainly wouldn't have encouraged any of his students to cause a spectacle."

"Oh, fool, who has bewitched you?"

"I beg your pardon!" Paulos's verbal attack inflamed Miryam, but she as quickly regained control. "What if they accidentally burn the writings of Plato or scripture?"

Ignoring her question, Paulos climbed into a nearby cart and began shouting at her in Hellene as if she were his entire audience. "Cursed is everyone who does not observe and obey all these commands that are written in the Book of the Law. Christos has redeemed us from the curse of the law." Paulos had no centurion spear, shield, or helmet, but he looked no less fierce as he stood sentry over the proceedings.

Others meanwhile joined the bonfire a few at a time, some with just one or two scrolls in hand, others with an armload. A woman stepped close to the firepit, poised to toss her scroll into the flames, but Miryam clasped her wrist and grabbed the papyrus from her hand.

"Miryam!" Martha warned. "What are you doing?"

Ignoring her sister, Miryam unrolled the scroll. The lettering was foreign to her and looked nonsensical. "What's written here?" she asked the woman.

"A love potion," the woman said shyly.

"Did it work?"

The woman grinned slightly and pointed a thumb over her shoulder at the handsome man behind her. Miryam returned her smile and handed the scroll back to her. The man winked, showing her the scroll he meant to burn. "Anti-love potion."

"Didn't work so well for you, did it?" The man shrugged, and Miryam waved him on. The couple threw their papyri scraps into the flames.

Still standing in the cart, Paulos's eyes rolled up as if going into ekstasis. With head flung back, he began rattling off something about apostles preaching the Christos in Samaria: "Unclean spirits, crying with loud voice, came out of many that were possessed by them, and many who were palsied or lame were healed."

What would Rav Yeshua think about his students exorcising demons? she wondered as she moved through the growing crowd, unrolling scrolls one by one. Strangely no one resisted her. Most papyri included a few scrawled incantations, while others contained recipes for creating an assortment of potions, amulets, magical dolls, and antidotes for spells caste on them by evil spirits. Still other scrolls spoke of the casting of lots, dice, or coins for the purpose of telling fortune. So far, all of the scrolls were ordinary preoccupations of the hearth.

As Paulos began a story about a magician who practiced sorcery and bewitched the people of Samaria, Miryam herself was beginning to feel like the target of some magic spell. She felt light-headed, but she ignored it, attributing it to the early morning jaunt down the mountain in the cold without food or water.

The Faithful continued to pour into the area in increasing number. Miryam noticed that some of the rolls of papyrus were getting fatter and were not mere incantations. She asked permission to examine these as well. One explained the power of the celestial orbs in the sky and their influence over individuals on earth. Another described the demons and angels that represented the seasons.

Miryam unfolded the largest biblos she'd seen yet, a series of scrolls sewn together. "What's in here?" she asked its owner, a wrinkled old woman.

"Secret rituals for controlling certain powers, angels, and demons," she explained in hushed tones.

"Sounds dangerous."

"A person can influence the kosmos with this divine-working, for evil *or* good. Now that I have the Christos to mediate, I no longer need this book."

Miryam was incredulous. *Did this woman believe that the disembodied Savior would intervene between these powers for her with some magic of his own?* She flipped through the biblos, but the more she scanned the columns of letters, the dizzier she felt. Perhaps it was the smoke and heat from the fire that made Miryam feel dizzy and nauseous as she divided her attention between the scrolls and Paulos. She knew she should stop what she was doing and step away, but she couldn't help herself. Mortified by Paulos's behavior on behalf of her beloved master, she felt she must stop the arson before the Artemis parade neared the area.

"That's enough," Martha said, as she wrenched the papyri from Miryam's hands. "There's power in these scrolls. Not something you need to involve yourself in. Remember fainting at the ekklēsia last week?" Martha handed the biblos back to the woman and nodded toward the fire. The woman tossed the scrolls into the hungry flames.

Miryam ignored Martha's warning. By now the plume of smoke created by the burning papyri no doubt served as a beacon to anyone passing by, she worried. She had no idea how to go about stopping Paulos without simply kicking dirt over the fire herself, with or without Martha's help.

Something made her stop to listen to Paulos's ranting about the magician in Samaria: "Simon Magus marvelled at the works of power and signs the apostles did," Paulos shouted. "He saw the *Pneuma Hagios*, the Holy Spirit, appear when the apostles laid there hands on the Faithful. The Magus offered money, saying, 'Give me this power, so that I may also receive the Holy Spirit. But Simon Petros said, 'Your money will perish with you because you believe you can purchase the gift of Theos.'"

What does Paulos mean when he talks about the Holy Spirit, the *Ruach Hakodesh*, working through the hands of the Simeon and the other apostles? Miryam wondered. Perhaps to Paulos the two Simeons represented two conflicting powers: One power was the Holy Spirit, while the other power was demonic. The power of magic could be bought, while the Holy Spirit could not. But wasn't using the Holy Spirit to heal others similar to a sorcerer working his magic? Rav Yeshua never taught his students to heal others by laying their hands on them. If anything he spoke of a spiritual healing of the self whereby the Shefa liberated the neshama under his guidance. That was the supreme purpose of the true Holy Spirit. But Paulos was not initiated into the true Holy Spirit. He knew nothing of It. The holy spirit he spoke of was a form of magic itself, something that was merely the opposite of the demonic magic. Rav Yeshua had always said that using either power to change the external world was a misuse of that power.

Cerinthus suddenly called out, pointing to the long parade as it serpentined out of the theater and rounded the stadium to exit out of the city gate. Miryam could barely make out the faces in the procession, but she knew from watching previous parades that the megabyxus led, followed by the life-sized silver statue of Artemis, which was accompanied by the likenesses of fellow deities and their staff bearers, the cuertes priests and the melissa priestesses, and by dignitaries and their effigies. Miryam suspected her new friend, Phylaktos, would be in charge, though she could not see him and hopefully he could not see her. It would not do for him to see her involved in another one of Paulos's public spectacles.

The crowd around the fire soon swelled to a small mob. The Faithful continued incinerating scrolls, whether magical recipes or sacred literature Miryam could no longer see or care to see. Those who didn't have papyrus in hand squeezed into the crowd to see what was happening or to hear what Paulos was saying, as he chanted from his make-shift pulpit in the nearby cart. Miryam heard shouts protesting the burning, and she sensed the mood of the crowd shift from a simple ritual for the Faithful to imminent peril for her. Something told her to extract herself from the mob immediately, but she was trapped by the bodies wedged in around her. Panic set in. She wanted to shout for Martha, but she couldn't catch her breath. Just as she'd lost control over her attention during the ekklēsia rituals, she lost herself, her true self, again. She stopped immediately, and focused her attention on the radiant face of Ravi. Just as she was about to collapse, a strong pair of hands grabbed her around the waist and pulled her through the crowd to open safety.

Miryam breathed deeply and slowly regained her composure, even more slowly realizing that it was the young, slight Cerinthus who'd rescued her. She would never underestimate his strength after this. "Toda, Cerinthus," she said.

"He charged through the crowd to help you before I could stop him," Martha said.

The boy gave Miryam a leg-up into the back of the cart, then drove Pegasus to a safer distance so that they could survey their situation. "Lots of people followed the procession as it filed out of the polis through the Koressos Gate," Martha reported. "But there were so many that they couldn't all fit through the gate at once, so they had to wait for the crowd to thin out. That's when they saw the fire and the commotion and ran here to see what was going on."

Precisely the response Paulos had hoped for from local Ephesians, Miryam thought. He had captured an audience with this stunt. He was still standing in his cart preaching to what she thought might be hundreds of people by now, and not all of them liked what they were hearing, nor did they appreciate the burning. If she could hear him above the jeers and shouts, she doubted she'd like what he was saying either.

"We should let Cerinthus go to his cousin's wedding and take ourselves home," Martha urged. "We've had enough excitement."

Resigned to the inevitable, Cerinthus sighed and turned Pegasus toward Stadium Street. "Cheer up," Martha said to him, though she understood how he felt. "The festival begins tonight, and you'll be right in the heart of it."

By the time they reached Harbor Street, the parade watchers who'd followed the procession to the temple were now pouring back into the polis. Stadium and Theater Streets were teeming with pedestrian traffic so thick that the only route left for them was to turn down Harbor Street. "I'm sorry, Cerinthus," Miryam yelled to be heard above the din. "I'm afraid you're going to miss your cousin's wedding unless you try making your way there on foot."

"Let me first find someplace to stop and rest until the crowds disperse," Cerinthus yelled, jumping out of the cart. He carefully threaded Pegasus and the cart through the crowds down Harbor Street and into a lot behind a row of shacks where various trade guilds met. He tied Pegasus to the trunk of a lone shade tree to graze on the knee-high grass beneath it. Martha, with miraculous foresight, produced some apples, a half loaf of bread, and a ceramic jug of water. She spread a blanket on the grass for the three of them to sit and partake of the bounty.

This is absolutely the last time I leave the house without first sitting in my morning contemplation, Miryam said to herself and to Ravi within. Earlier there had been moments when she thought she might have blacked out again, so intense was the scroll burning ceremony. One should not leave the nefesh vulnerable to such attacks, both visible and invisible. *Paulos is right, damn him!* There are things in these worlds that are perilous and better left alone, she thought, and the only protection and guidance was the grace of Ravi. Miryam bit into her apple, savoring this tart, sweet morsel of truth.

Exhausted, Cerinthus collapsed onto the blanket and immediately began snoring. Martha smiled and laid down next to him, closing her eyes no doubt to go over the morning's events with the Ravi within her. Miryam started to lie down when she heard a loud, heated conversation brewing in the silversmiths's guild. She would've dismissed the ruckus had she not heard someone shouting something about Paulos. She approached the building and hunkered down in the alley behind it so she could hear what was being discussed.

One man in the building demanded: "Demetrius, just who is this Paulos?"

"My wife heard him speak once at Tyrannus Hall. Said he was the apostle of a powerful god named Iēsous Christos. Said this holy man was crucified by the Rhōmaioi and that he resurrected so that he could redeem those who believe in him. Paulos says he's an apostle of this man, this Theos, who is mightier than Artemis, Apollo, and Zeus."

"Blasphemy, blasphemy!" several chimed in.

"I once saw him stand on the Artemision steps and say that temples and trinkets can be destroyed and rebuilt, but his theos is not made by the hands of men," Demetrius continued. "You all saw the bonfire this morning? He organized that to burn biblos on magic he considers evil. He may come for the Artemis statues next, and then perhaps her temple itself."

"Won't be the first time someone would burn it down for fame," another man shouted.

Demetrius continued: "Not only is there a danger that our silversmithing may come into disrepute if Paulos continues, but Artemis herself may also be deposed from her magnificence."

"Are we to believe this Iēsous Christos has so much power that he can defeat Artemis and disrupt our livelihood?" another man demanded.

"We can't risk it," Demetrius responded. "We must confront this Paulos and force him to leave Ephesus before it's too late. Great is Artemis of the Ephesians!"

"Great is Artemis!" The group responded and continued chanting. "Great is Artemis!"

Without warning the guild house door flung open, and at least a dozen men poured into the alley, running straight toward Miryam with such speed and deliberation, she thought they meant to attack her for spying on them. The men filled in the tight spaces around her and began clapping their hands and stomping their feet, jostling each other to make room for everyone. An elbow caught Miryam in the side of the head, but its owner ignored it, obviously meaning her no malice. She was not the brunt of their protest, yet try as she might, she could not push her way out of the alley. She had done it to herself again. She had followed her nefesh, her mind, instead of Ravi.

The men continued their clarion call: "Great is Artemis!"

"Silversmiths, hear me," a heavy-set, swarthy man yelled. His baritone voice told her he was the one called Demetrius who'd just delivered his complaints inside the guild house moments earlier. He was clearly their respected leader. "Let us rally everyone on Harbor Street and force an assembly meeting in the theater!" Demetrius's proclamation received a cacophony of whistles and shouts from fellow smiths.

Within moments Miryam felt herself being whisked out of the alley into Harbor Street. She tried shouting for Martha and Cerinthus, to no avail. For a fleeting instant she could see Martha standing under the tree with hands on hips, shaking her head in exaggerated fashion.

By some miracle Miryam managed to stay on her feet in the stampede from lower Harbor Street to the theater. The festival that was to start that evening had already drawn in tens of thousands of people to Ephesus who'd come to shop, eat from the food stalls, get drunk, and find places to sit at the theater and the stadium to watch the games, plays, and contests. There was so little room to move freely in the streets that people filled rooftops, terraces, and adjacent hillsides. Onlookers shaded their eyes with their hands, trying to determine the source of the commotion building up in the street. As the protest marched beneath them, many climbed down from their perches and joined in, not fully understanding the purpose of the march. Utter confusion and pandemonium set in, and Miryam floundered in the thick of it. She began chanting her secret words though she could no longer hear herself, and she tried focusing on Ravi's radiant face, but she could no longer see Him. That's when real fear set in. Not for her personal safety insomuch as she was afraid that she had dishonored Ravi within – again! She'd failed her test three times now, and Ravi was allowing her to live in the circumstances she'd chosen. She had no choice but to follow it to the end.

The mob rushed with one accord into the theater and splashed up into the stone benches like a tidal wave. The rope on Miryam's right sandal broke, causing her to trip and catch a toenail on the first slab of rock. She couldn't look down to inspect the wound, but from the sting she knew the nail would be bent back and the nail bed bleeding. By some miracle, a couple of the smiths by her side lifted her up under her arms, carried her up to the top row, and left her next to a column. Just as quickly they disappeared back down the steps, presumably to sit closer to the stage. *I have forsaken You, Oh Ravi, but You have not abandoned me!* The Shefa cascaded within her.

She decided to stay put, knowing she'd be safe here until all the commotion passed. From her vantage point, she could see people still crowded in the streets trying to push into the theater like ants into the queen's underground home. She'd be here awhile.

Safe for the moment, and thankful for the shade provided by the colonnade overhead, she allowed herself to relax and inspect her bleeding toe. Wincing at the sight, she ripped a swatch of material from the bottom of her palla to tie around her foot. The blood would eventually seep into the material, but she did her best to slow the bleeding for now. Breathing more easily, she surveyed her surroundings.

Shaped like a near-complete bowl, the theater was built into Mount Pion on three levels, with two dozen rows of stone on each level for seating. Miryam had heard that it took sixty years to dig out the mountain just to create a level foundation. Dramas and contests took place on the round marble stage at the center of the bowl, backdropped by pillars and a two-storied stone building that concealed backstage preparation. The proconsul's expansive villa dominated the hill above and behind the theater in an overt display of ultimate power. A grand boulevard linked the theater to the harbor, the very street where Demetrius's protest march on the theater had just formed. The street was illuminated at night by a row of lanterns on both sides. From here, elite patrons were meant to view ships coming into the harbor, and passengers on board these same ships could also see the monumental theater from sea. This was where Ephesians met assorted financial patrons, government officials, emperors, and deities, and today where the absent Paulos had created the largest spectacle of his mission.

The assembly remained in disorder all afternoon, yet few people knew why they'd come together. Some thought it was to protest taxes, others to demand an even greater voice among the Rhōmaioi. Various officials took the center dais to calm the crowd, but quickly scrambled out of the theater ahead of flying stones and rotten produce. Demetrius entered the stage and re-enlivened the chant: "Great is Artemis of the Ephesians!" The mob, thinking this to be part of the festivities, answered with one voice.

The sun traveled across the sky, stealing the shade away from Miryam, now a puddle of sweat. She had a splitting headache, and her wounded toe throbbed. The stone all around her absorbed the sun's heat, and her dry mouth made her choke. She wondered where Martha and Cerinthus were, wondered if they were frantic to find her. There was no way out that she could see except to climb down the back of the stadium to the hillside behind it. The drop would kill her.

By mid-afternoon, Miryam's friend Phylaktos, the temple's chief guard, took the stage. Dressed in his brilliant violet toga, the crowd knew he was a temple official and quieted to hear what he had to say. "People of Ephesus, hear me. What man does not know that the polis of Ephesus hosts the Great Artemis who fell down from Zeus?"

"No one!" the crowd answered.

"That Artemis is mighty cannot be denied. Do nothing rash and listen to the clerk of Ephesus."

Another man joined Phylaktos on the stage. The purple border on his white toga signaled his station as a city administrator. Phylaktos put a hand on his shoulder as if to sanction him for the unruly crowd. "You fear that the Artemision will be destroyed and that the silversmiths will not be allowed to practice their craft and earn a living," the clerk shouted. An onslaught of whistles and applause interrupted him. "These fears have not come to pass," he started again. "No crime has been committed. If Demetrius and his fellow craftsmen have a matter against anyone, the courts are open, and the magistrates are on duty. You silversmiths are in danger of being arrested for inciting a riot if you do not cease and desist. I beg you, please, break up this assembly now, and go enjoy the goods and food in the agora."

Phylaktos and the clerk left the stage. There was nothing left to say or do. The crowd had spent its energy and drained itself of all emotion and anger during the past few hours of chanting. The protestors climbed down the stone rows and filed out of the theater in waves.

Miryam waited for the crowd to dwindle before she climbed down the steps and headed into the streets herself. Not knowing where Martha was, she hobbled in the general direction of the Magnesia gate on the reverse course Pegasus had taken them that morning. The rag wrapped around her sandalless foot had come loose and was shredding, exposing her wounded toe to scalding stones and street filth. On Embolos Street, she found Martha sitting on the wall of a fountain. Martha looked relieved to see her, as she eyed her torn palla and battered foot.

Miryam raised a hand. "Anything you have to say to me, I've already said to myself." She sat next to Martha and carefully peeled the remnants of her makeshift bandage away from her blood-encrusted skin.

"Don't judge too quickly, Sister. I was going to say that you had no choice but to follow this road to the end. And I have to also say that the road has not yet come to an end."

Miryam sighed. Her older sister was so wise. "Some debts are paid the hard way," she surrendered with a sigh. Removing the good sandal, she dipped both feet in the cool water. What a sight she must be, covered in blood, sweat, and dust, and she smelled like a campfire too. "Where is Cerinthus?"

"He is finally at his uncle's home. We've been invited to stay the evening. Can't make it home before dark, anyway."

Miryam nodded, defeated by her own mind. "Sometimes I wonder, Martha, why Rav Yeshua chose me instead of you to carry on his teachings. You have so much more control than I."

"We are in no position to judge our own journeys, nor should we compare ourselves to each other." She exhaled and smiled. "Besides, the Shefa is bold, and you are bold. We walk a path of purification, and you are so much more willing to put your feet in the fire than I am."

Miryam flung an arm around her sister's shoulders. "I can't tell you how much pain my feet are in right now," she said with a snicker.

Eleven

Returning to her contemplation room in her mountaintop home was like returning to a lover after a lengthy separation, though only a single day had passed since she chased Paulos and her own causes through Ephesus. Miryam abandoned the chair and sat cross-legged on the floor next to the hearth, where she could feel the firmness of the earth and warmth from the fire. She wrapped more tightly in her palla of familiarity, freshly washed, unlike the ripped and soiled town cloak she'd necessarily discarded.

She winced at the memory of Paulos, the scroll burning, and the riot. She wasn't here to lick her wounds, she reminded herself, but to dispassionately yet gently inspect them. Nevertheless, she wasn't quite ready to look at her own behavior. *Ravi*, she cried within herself with a deep sigh. *What did I do to myself?*

The response was immediate. A great flow of love poured through her and flooded her senses, a love greater than she'd ever felt before, and she marveled at this eternal spring, the Shefa flow, the way in which It just kept expanding without perceptible end. Her eyes closed, Ravi appeared within her more radiant, more glorious, more alive than the day she met him in his physical body, ever welcoming, ever beckoning her to Him. Part of herself, perhaps her neshama, wanted to shoot right into His face and there mingle with His essence forever. But something restrained her from doing so.

Paulos, the man who would be Christos, she said to herself as she fell into deep contemplation. She was instantly transported to the dark, stale jail cell in Ephesus where she'd visited Paulos the day before. On their way to the home of Cerinthus's uncle in the merchant sector, she and Martha had run into Priscilla and Aquila in the street. They'd been searching for the sisters to tell them that Paulos had requested their presence. He'd been arrested for creating a nuisance with his bonfire during the sacred procession of Artemis and for inciting the anger of the silversmiths. They explained that Paulos had heard about the riot and was on his way into the theater despite their pleadings when he was stopped by centurions at the gate. He announced that he was Paulos, the very man who had angered the people, and he had come to reap his adoration. Even negative worship was still worship to him. He was immediately removed from the theater's entrance. The mob might have torn Paulos limb from limb, Aquila said, had the centurions not taken him to the relative safety of jail.

Miryam bristled at the audacity of Paulos summoning her, but Martha whispered in her ear, "You've come this far, you might as well go the rest of the way." Rather than clean up, dress her battered foot, and rest at Cerinthus's uncle's home as they'd planned, she and Martha followed Paulos's loyal friends back the way they'd come, past the theater and the agora down Harbor Street toward the small prison on a shallow foothill of Mount Koressos. Miryam limped the entire way.

"You go in without me," Martha said to her once they arrived at the fortress where Paulos was imprisoned. "This is more your labor than mine." Miryam wanted to protest, but her elder sister was never to be disobeyed. The centurions on guard looked askance at Miryam's dishevelment yet nodded permission for her to enter. She obviously would not be able to free Paulos even if she wanted to.

"I have fought beasts in Ephesus," Paulos said to Miryam when she stepped into his dank cell somewhat fearfully. He sat on a floor of hay, his right foot in an iron cuff bolted to an iron chain that wrapped around a large wooden post, the chain's other end securely embedded in the wall. Several other prisoners were similarly tethered to their respective posts.

"I have fought beasts too, Paulos," Miryam said softly.

He turned to look at her, taking in her shredded palla, the charcoal smudges on her face from their mutual bonfire of vanity, her messed hair and bloodied foot. She in turn saw that the healed-over sores on his face were making their way back to the surface. "You have fought me and have found me a false martyr, and I do not understand why." His words seemed to rasp his already parched throat.

"Why?" Miryam said, raising her voice just a bit louder. "You have contrived an entire religion that can't be further from Ha-Rav's teachings." She caught herself when she noticed the other prisoners looking at her.

"My gospel is not so different from what Simeon and Yakob preach. Some of the branches were broken off so that I might be grafted in."

"They're wrong. They didn't understand Rav Yeshua's teachings either. It wasn't his intention to reform the old ways or to create a new way. He did not intend to put new wine into old bottles. Rather, he always said that he put old wine into new bottles, and that wine is far more ancient than that of Abraham."

"It doesn't matter what I proclaim or what Simeon and Yakob proclaim. What matters is that the Faithful believe what is proclaimed to them."

"Do you mean the fools or the elect?"

"Both." He shrugged. "By the grace of Theos, I am what I am, and the grace He bestowed on me was not in vain. I have worked harder than the other apostles. But if there is no resurrection of the dead, then Christos did not rise, and if Christos has not risen, then my preaching is in vain. If I have fought wild animals in Ephesus like a gladiator in a coliseum, what do I gain if the dead do not rise?" Paulos lifted an invisible goblet in the air in salute. "Let us eat and drink of the Christos, for tomorrow we die!" His fist fell in his lap and he slumped his shoulders. "I have no choice but to believe. I die daily, Miryam Magadan, but I will not die in vain." The bold gladiator of Christos, now reduced to a prisoner of his own making, began to sob.

In this moment, Miryam realized she was no different from Paulos. She was the gladiator of the Logos, the champion of Ha-Rav, and in doing so she'd become a prisoner of her mind, and it had made her vain and had torn her to shreds. She stepped toward Paulos and kneeled at his side, placing a hand on his head. "I, too, die daily. But I also rise daily. Everyone rises eventually. Nothing we do is in vain. And yet, all is vain."

There was nothing more she could do, nothing more she could say to convince him otherwise, for he wasn't initiated into the Logos, he wasn't meant to be initiated this lifetime, and he therefore would never understand. He was driven by a thousand horses, but as she had suspected all along, the horses were not all in his mind. Rather, they represented a divine movement to change hearts and prepare them for when they will meet their own masters in their own time. Paulos's stubbornness and zealousness would serve him spiritually, just as these identical traits had served her. Heaven, after all, was not for the meek.

"Love never fails," Miryam said, barely above a whisper, feeling the instruction of the Logos well up within her and spill out to Paulos as if It were a waterfall. "Prophecies fail, speaking in tongues ceases, special knowledge of the Elah vanishes, but love never fails. Without love we are nothing." As she spoke these words to Paulos, she knew she was speaking to herself. Ravi was the All-Love, and she was nothing without Him.

When she stood to leave, Paulos grabbed her hand. He opened his mouth to say something, but for once he was speechless. She looked into his eyes and cupped his cheek with her free hand. "Toda," she said, and squeezed his hand.

"For what?"

"For sharing your gospel with me. I learned more than you'll ever know." She smiled, let go of his hand, and turned to leave.

"Atta Miryam," he called.

"Ayn?" There was a glimmer of hope that he'd confess his ignorance and end the madness.

"Would you ask the guard to allow Priscilla in? I feel a need to dictate a letter."

She nodded and turned, realizing that Paulos would be imprisoned the rest of his life. She, however, felt wildly liberated.

She stepped into the clean sea breezes and breathed deeply, focusing on the radiant form of Ha-Rav within. When she opened her eyes, she found Priscilla and Aquila in front of her. "Where's Martha?"

Aquila nodded toward the harbor side of the hill.

A range of emotions showed on Priscilla's face. Miryam had known her to be a woman of rare calm, but she was obviously shocked by the riot and worried about Paulos's imprisonment. "He's been in trouble before," she said, as if reading Miryam's thoughts. "The Christos has always saved him."

"I expect so," Miryam said. It was no longer her first reaction to pass judgment. "He asks for his favorite scribe."

Priscilla smiled, eager to rise to her calling.

"And Priscilla ... ."

"Ayn?"

"Your dedication is commendable and you serve well."

Miryam skirted the lone prison building to find Martha facing the harbor. When her sister saw her, she pointed toward the water, smiling broadly. Miryam saw it herself: a flock of white swans on the water among the ships and fishing boats, bobbing, preening, diving for food, nudging their young. Some skidded along the top with their necks and wings outstretched in a manner that made them look like they were ascending to heaven, though they were merely defending their territory. Bumps pricked Miryam's skin, and she knew this to be a message from Ravi. All of the little ideas the crows within her had scavenged, pecked at, and ripped to shreds in their talons were now transformed into these majestic creatures. The ideas still existed, but they were somehow purified in the Living Water upon which the swans easily floated. She put an arm around her sister's waist. "I so appreciate your patience."

"Don't thank me, thank Ravi."

The sisters watched the swans until the sun set and the light grew dim. They began walking down the lantern-lit Harbor Street toward Cerinthus's family home. The shops and villas lining the Embolos were illuminated with small fires and candles. Even if it were pitch black, they walked in the safety of Ravi's light within.

Cross-legged on the floor in her room, Miryam didn't stir from her vigil, despite Martha's periodic movements through the room to stoke the fire or remove uneaten meals. The force that kept her inside herself was strong, and she felt herself in a constant state of ever-awakening. Last lights streamed through boarded western windows, only to reappear on the eastern side of the room. As the wheel of sun, moon, and stars spun in the sky over Ephesus, Miryam traveled an inner landscape, one filled with orchards of light, celestial orbs more brilliant and intimate than the physical sun and moon. There, a blue star on the firmament focused into the radiant face of her beloved master, Yeshua.

Miryam wanted to reach out to Ravi, but instead saw herself frantically riding a winged horse bareback through the polis of Ephesus. Cerinthus, Martha, and their real-life donkey were not part of this inner vision, just Miryam on the back of the steed over which she had no control no matter how tightly she pulled on his mane. Without his hooves touching the ground, they galloped past all of the statues and buildings, all of the stone-faced Olympians, emperors, and politicians, searching every corner for Paulos.

At last she saw a figure wrapped in a black cloak like a crow, standing on the edge of a great flaming pit, throwing papyrus scrolls over the side, scrolls she knew to contain the spoken words of Ha-Rav. She dismounted and started running for the cloaked figure, but the ground beneath her began to perilously rumble and shake and crack apart. On a hill opposite the crow and his fiery pit stood a glowing figure wrapped from head to toe in a white palla like a swan. She knew she would have just a moment to make a choice between reaching the crow, thereby saving Ha-Rav's works, or climbing the hill to the safety of the swan before the ground caved in beneath her feet. Thinking the white figure was her beloved Ravi, Miryam chose the swan. An instant later she found herself standing before the creature. She carefully unwrapped its palla, only to face another creature draped in black. Trembling, when she removed this dark palla, she found that the brown eyes staring back at her were her own.

The slow, steady gonging of a big bell transformed into the yearning sighs of a conch, and they in turn changed into the rhythm of pounding drum beats, pulling her deeper into the vortex, thrusting her up three steep mountain peaks to a luminous lake. Ravi floating above the water, beckoned to her, and she walked across to Him on sonorous wings of lyre music. They swam together in this ocean of pure, divine love for eons, face to Face, two as one – the true baptisma, that which washes away the seeds of indiscretion, not only from this lifetime but from all lifetimes. When Miryam emerged from the lake on the opposite shore, she was alone ... only one set of footprints in the sand, no longer carried by the power that was intertwined with her neshama, the soul, now realized as that Power. She sang the Song of Miryam, for beyond the convergence, she would become the Logos Itself, and beyond that ... her neshama would grow to encompass the Kingdom of Elah.

"Rav Yeshua, I saw you in a vision today," Miryam remembered saying once to Ha-Rav when they were physically together many years earlier.

"How fortunate for you that you didn't waiver at the sight of me," he had answered. "For where the soul is, there is the treasure."

"Rav, how do we see visions, through the mind or through the soul?"

"The vision is not important. Only your love for Ravi is important, for it is Ravi that will guide you to the Kingdom. It is Ravi you will become. The vision shows you how far you've come, how far you have to go."

"And when we hear the melodies of the Shefa, the Divine Flow, is it Elah playing the soul like a musical instrument?"

"It is the soul that plays the Song, Loved One."

Twelve

Cerinthus lowered himself into the steamy water of an Ephesian bath house, and with eyes closed he sighed deeply as he relaxed into the Shefa flowing through him. How he loved coming to the bath house so early in the morning when he could have the waters and Ravi to himself before the patricians arrived with their slaves in tow. He wasn't always aware of Ravi's Shechinah within him, but lately the Presence had grown much stronger, just as Atta Miryam had promised with continued daily practice. This had proven to be more difficult than it first sounded, for his mind was so inquisitive and so easily distracted. But these days he allowed himself to let his thoughts float on the water as he chanted his secret words.

"May I join you?"

The male voice was coming from the pool deck directly above him. Reluctantly he opened his eyes to see a naked man twice, maybe three times his age. "Plenty of room," he said in Hellene, though he didn't understand the human tendency to crowd another person when they had all the space in the world. Hopefully, the stranger wasn't one who expected the sexual company of men.

"Shlama," the man said as he slid into the pool beside Cerinthus.

"You sound like you're from Galilee," Cerinthus said, switching to Aramit.

"That I am. How can you tell?"

"My teachers were from Migdal Nunya."

"Ayn? My name is Johanan, son of Zebedee."

Cerinthus had heard the name from Miryam. Rav Yeshua had called him and his brother the Sons of Thunder, and he was also one of the Pillars, the leaders of the new Yeshua movement in Yerushalayim. "I'm Cerinthus. My teachers knew of a Johanan ben Zebedee. You might have known them: Miryam and Martha Binyamiyn, brother to Lazarus?"

Johanan's mouth gaped open. "Miryam the Magadan? Here, now?"

Cerinthus shook his head. "Sadly, they left Ephesus some time ago, but they did live on my family's land after they fled Yerushalayim. I used to work for them."

"Where did they go?"

Cerinthus shrugged, raising both palms.

"If you know who I am, you must know about Ha-Rav."

"Ayn." Cerinthus knew all too well.

Johanan stretched his arms and legs in the water a bit before resting his head against the poolside to relax. He closed his eyes, but obviously couldn't stop thinking about this chance encounter. "There are very few of Ha-Rav's students left. Most of us persecuted and killed in hideous ways, including my own brother, Yakob."

"Oy," Cerinthus flinched, feeling fortunate that he didn't have to live in Yerushalayim to follow the Way. "I once knew a man named Paulos, or Saulus as he was called then, who went after Rav Yeshua's followers before his vision of conversion."

"Paulos, oy!" Johanan clasped his forehead as if he had a sudden headache. "Such a nuisance. That's why Yakob and Simeon sent him away."

"He set up an ekklēsia here, but was jailed and then run out of Ephesus for being disruptive."

"So I heard. The ekklēsia is still in operation, much to his credit, though it's much less radical now and barely functioning. I'm here to give it a boost, perhaps settle down. I've been on the road too long." He closed his eyes and then opened them again. "It's interesting; the ekklēsia elders never talk about Lazarus or his sisters. Were they aware of the ekklēsia?"

"I believe the sisters attended once. And you're right, the practices of the ekklēsia were a radical departure from the way Atta Miryam described Ha-Rav's teachings."

"It is all different now," Johanan said, looking distant and a little sad. "They left Yerushalayim before everything started happening. I'm surprised

Lazarus didn't form a group of students here, but then again they didn't see the wonders that occurred after the crucifixion."

"They didn't feel that was Ha-Rav's wish for the students, to start an ekklēsia for new initiates, I mean."

Johanan snapped his head upright and looked at him. "How could you say that?"

Cerinthus didn't know how much he should divulge, but he was feeling brave. "They were aware of the story of the resurrection, the movement to attract new believers, of the baptisms, and the expansion outside of Yerushalayim. They didn't approve." He was sure Atta Miryam would say the same thing to Johanan's face if she were here.

"Didn't approve? Blasphemy!" Johanan hit the water once and created a splash. Some water hit Cerinthus's eye. "And yet, you were their student."

"Ayn," he said resolutely.

"Did Paulos baptize you?"

"I was initiated, but not by Paulos."

"Lazarus?"

"Lazarus wasn't here that much. The last time he came here, his sisters left with him."

"Surely, Miryam or Martha didn't baptize you. They're women."

"Atta Martha? Lo. Atta Miryam had Ha-Rav's permission to initiate new students once she was ready, but she never felt ready."

"Had his permission? I don't believe that. Well, if none of them initiated you, then who?"

Cerinthus felt he shouldn't answer the question, but he left the only obvious choice open. He watched Johanan's face as it slowly dawned on him what his younger bathing partner was implying. "You're raca! You're a fool if you believe that Ha-Rav, the messiah, initiated you himself."

Cerinthus remained silent, lifting a shoulder ever so slightly as if he didn't care what Johanan believed.

The older man stood and climbed out of the pool with so much vigor he nearly drowned Cerinthus in his wake. "I will not share water with lying demons!" He toweled off and wrapped himself in a robe, slipped on his sandals, and stormed out of the bath house.

Cerinthus splashed out of the pool, grabbed his clothes, and chased after him. He managed to pull the tunic over his head before following Johanan into the street. "Wait!" He quickly caught up with him. "Stop!"

Johanan stopped. "Make this quick, Demon. I'm expected elsewhere."

Cerinthus was slightly out of breath and dripping wet. He chanted his secret words to bolster his courage, at the same time suspecting why Ha-Rav called this man the Son of Thunder. "I know you don't believe me, and I'm not going to try to convince you. What does it matter? He could have appeared to me just as He appeared to you or Paulos or anyone else. I mean, that's not so hard to accept, is it? Isn't that what you preach?"

Johanan stood there in the middle of the street with hands on hips. Without provocation, Johanan yanked Cerinthus to the side of the road. "Hey!" Cerinthus turned around in time to see the back of a chariot driven by a centurion. The chariot would've hit him had Johanan not reacted so quickly.

"You must watch out for yourself."

Cerinthus paused a moment to catch his breath and check his bearings. "Would you like to see where they lived?"

Johanan exhaled loudly, then nodded. "I would, as long as I'm here."

"The house is near the top of Mount Koressos. It was Miryam and Martha's parting wish to keep it up in case any of Ha-Rav's original students should happen to need a roof over their heads. No one has occupied it since they left, although I use it sometimes for contemplation and study. Do you have time to go now?"

Johanan nodded. "Is it far?"

"Ayn, but Pegasus can take us," he said, grinning at Johanan's puzzled look.

Cerinthus was glad he'd brushed out the floors and stacked some firewood on his previous visit to his home away from home a few days earlier. He opened the door to Johanan.

"You're still maintaining the garden," he said, pointing to the cucumbers.

"Habit. Sometimes I stay for days and I need to eat. Come on in."

Johanan stepped through the door and stood a moment. "Did your family build this place?"

"Lazarus did." He opened the shutters over the windows to let in some light, revealing the stacks of papyri on the table. He then removed the lid off a hole in the floor, lowered a bucket through the hole, and quickly brought it back up filled with water. "There's a natural spring beneath the house."

"Wouldn't mind some of that. I'm parched."

Cerinthus ladled water into a bowl and handed it to his guest. "This is the main room for cooking, sewing, visiting. The sisters slept through that door on the left and studied in the other room through that door. Since it's only me, I've set up the library on the table here." He moved some of the papyri aside so Johanan could sit at the table with his drink. "Most of these scrolls belonged to Atta Miryam."

Johanan looked over the stacks of papyri with surprise. "She knew letters?"

"Learned from her saba, and she taught me to read the Tanakh in the Holy Tongue." Cerinthus seated himself opposite his guest. "I helped her with Hellene letters." He grabbed a stack of papyri and shuffled the sheets to the beginning. "See? Here we practiced writing our names, and here I copied some scripture. Here Atta Miryam did her own writing, but as you can see she crossed out the Ivrit and started over in Hellene on this page. It got confusing because Ivrit is written right to left and Hellene left to right. Here, see?"

Johanan accepted a sheet and turned it in different directions.

"You look bewildered," Cerinthus said. "Do you know letters?"

"Very few fishermen like me can read. But I do see it looks messy."

"This started out as a practice sheet, and then became more serious. I can read some of it to you." When the older man nodded, Cerinthus began: "At the Source is the Memra and the Memra is with Elah.'"

"Hmmm," Johanan said, resting his jaw in his hand.

"After Atta Miryam wrote that, she decided that Hellene conveyed the concepts more fully. Rather than Memra, for instance, she preferred Logos to describe the Divine Flow."

Johanan shook his head. "I had no idea she thought about such things."

Cerinthus beamed, clearly proud of his teacher. "That and so much more."

"What else does she think about?"

Cerinthus shuffled through the papyri and pointed to a section on one sheet. "Here she began recording some of Ha-Rav's parables and sayings, beginning with her favorite story of turning water to wine at a wedding in Cana. After she left, I scribed the stories and sayings she told me over the years to the best of my recollection."

At this prospect, Johanan's eyes lit up. "The ekklēsia have been starving for material such as this."

Cerinthus suddenly realized the error of his own actions. *Had he been boasting because of the way he reacted to Miryam being his teacher?* "Atta Miryam and I wrote these stories for our private use. I don't think she meant for others to read them."

"Why write them down if she didn't intend for others to see it? She had her memories. Obviously, she'd abandoned her own work."

"Point taken." In fact, Cerinthus had asked Miryam why she was leaving her writings behind.

"Why do I need the written word when I have Elah's Word inside me?" she had answered. "What truth comes through us does not belong to us."

"Then why did we work so hard to write all this down?"

"Many reasons." Miryam had stopped her packing, crossed to him, and clasped both his hands in hers. For most of his life, he was forced to look upward to meet her eye to eye. Now he was head and shoulders above her. He was no longer a child, but he would always measure himself against the height of his beloved teacher. Her long hair was nearly all gray, and her face was becoming wrinkled, but there was still a twinkle in those brown eyes.

"I suppose I needed to see that masters of the Logos have walked among the Hellene," she had continued. "What these loving souls contributed to the world has broadened my own growth. And I didn't know it then, but I needed to have a better grasp of their words to aid Ha-Rav in finding his own earmarked sheep among the Hellene and ministering to them." She gathered the papyri in a stack and handed them to Cerinthus, then cupped his cheek with her hand. "You keep this and work with it. Maybe that was Elah's intention all along. You are becoming the Logos yourself." These were practically her last words to him before she and Martha left Koressos Mountain forever.

"Truth that comes through us does not belong to us," Cerinthus told Johanan.

"What?"

"I will copy the work for you. In the meantime, do you want to stay in this house? You would be welcome."

"Long way from Ephesus."

"Not too far if you have Pegasus."

"I'll think about it." Johanan nodded and stood up. "I need to go back now."

"Shall I drive you?"

"I prefer to walk."

After bidding farewell to Johanan, Cerinthus stayed behind to pack away the scrolls, knowing the elder student of Ha-Rav would eventually accept the invitation to live in this place of safety and solitude. A feeling of melancholy suddenly swept over him. *The end of an era*, he thought, remembering the joy he faced every morning when he ran here to learn at the feet of Atta Miryam. Even after the sisters had left, he still had this place where he could sit with Ravi and read scripture.

Miryam had been reticent to initiate him, despite having Ha-Rav's written permission to do so. She worried that Cerinthus would be like Paulos and the other disciples who baptized anyone with a pulse and half a thought to be saved at the end of days. To her, that was not true spirituality. Furthermore, in her absence he might feel a need to create his own religion to fill the void the way Rav Yeshua's other students had. He promised he wouldn't do that after all he'd learned from watching Paulos. At last he wore her down, and she agreed to initiate him.

But on that very day, as Cerinthus sat in his usual place with Miryam at the table, a man crossed the threshold of their open door. The bowl Martha was whipping batter in crashed to the floor. Miryam looked up, and she flew into the arms of the stranger. Cerinthus instantly knew who this man was, or he felt he knew him. Astonished, he said it aloud: "Rav Yeshua!" Who else could it be? The facial features, the simple clothes, these could apply to anyone from Yehudah, but the Presence could not be denied, the brightness he radiated, the brightness those near him suddenly reflected.

"Ayn, Cerinthus. It is me." Rav Yeshua stretched his arms to him. "Shlama."

"Shlama," Cerinthus answered. "Do you know me?"

"I visited here with their brother, Lazarus. You were just a small boy when your parents brought you by the house."

"Ayn, I remember you!" The memory slowly unveiled itself in his mind. And without forethought or hesitation, he added, "I am ready for initiation." As soon as he said it, he felt his cheeks heat up, and he half expected Ha-Rav to laugh in his face.

"I can see you are ready," he said solemnly. He looked at Miryam. "Why haven't you initiated the boy?"

"I wasn't ready, Rav," she answered.

"You underestimate yourself. I know what you've attained."

She smiled sheepishly and looked at her hands. Cerinthus had never seen her succumb to a scolding from anyone before, however subtle.

"Rav Yeshua, if I may say something … *you* are my rav. I know you. I see you in my dreams. It is you I talk to, not Atta Miryam."

Rav Yeshua laughed out loud. "You are bold. In three days, I will initiate you."

And so it was done.

Cerinthus stepped into the bare room where the sisters once slept. The straw used for bedding had long been swept out, but he wanted to make sure all was tidy before Johanan came to stay. There was little to do but to clean up mouse droppings. He walked into the next room where Atta Miryam's writing table and two chairs were still shoved against the wall. All that remained on the table's surface was the leather tubing that had held Philo's manuscripts. He felt guilty when he saw it, for he'd never returned the works to Phylaktos, though, granted, the temple guard had never asked for them either. He decided he'd deliver the volumes to the new Celsius Library in Ephesus at his first opportunity. That had been the old guard's original intent.

He took the empty tube back into the main room and began assembling Philo's scrolls. Standing the tube on end, he slid the thickly layered papyri down into it – but they wouldn't fit. Something blocked the bottom. He turned the tube upside down, and a small slip of papyrus fluttered out of it to the table. He read it with astonishment. The note was from Ha-Rav declaring that Atta Miryam was to take over his teachings in Yerushalayim when he died. Of course, she hadn't accepted the mantle because he hadn't yet died. Reunited with Rav Yeshua, she had left it behind, for it was no longer useful to her. Perhaps she'd hidden it knowing Cerinthus would one day find it.

I should burn this, he thought, and he started to stack wood in the pit for a fire, but then stopped himself. Instead he would keep it as a memento of his upbringing under this great woman's careful, loving eye. He would keep it safe, along with the original scroll of her writings, smudges and all.

He decided he would continue scribing the stories and sayings Rav Yeshua had told, which Miryam had conveyed to him over the years, and most likely he would also pass these along to Johanan in time. The parables he was privileged to hear were much truer than the stories of the resurrection in circulation now. They were Ha-Rav's public teachings, the ones told "in open eye." Surely, he was beginning to have the eyes to see and the ears to hear Ravi's inner teachings.

Oy, how he missed all of them, the sisters and Ha-Rav. Eyes moist, he stepped into the garden, chanting his words until Ravi's Presence exceeded the heaviness of being alone. "And Elohim said, 'Let there be light, and there was light,'" Cerinthus recited out loud, remembering his first conversation on spirituality with his teacher. He kneeled and plucked some weeds, at the same time realizing the power of the Logos in his own life. "No crows in the garden today, Atta Miryam," he said, laughing to himself, knowing how proud of him she would be.

Part Three

Freedom Here and Now
Denver, Colorado, 2003

You search the scriptures because you think they possess eternal life,
but they only bear witness to [the Logos].

— John 5:39

One

Alyson Sego looked up from her laptop screen to see her apartment manager, Evan Hartman, on a stepladder hanging a freshly filled hummingbird feeder in the tree outside her window. Sunshine on his blonde hair produced a halo effect, and he smiled and waved innocently. Alyson approached the window, gave him the *namaste*-prayerhands gesture, and then abruptly dropped the Roman shade. *What next, a candygram?*

She suspected Evan of trying to charm his way inside her apartment to inspect Professor George Goodnight's translation of the papyri scrolls that had been sealed in an ancient jar she inherited from her Aunt Ruth. Alyson had given a copy of the so-called Logos Notebook to George, the husband of her old college roommate, Stephanie, several weeks earlier, and she'd restlessly waited for the result. As soon as the professor's commentary dropped into her e-mail inbox, she shared her excitement with Evan, and then she asked him to give her time to absorb everything she could from the codex.

For this was her inheritance, her journey, a message in a ceramic jar from Mary Magdalene directly to her. Evan was so well-read, she didn't want his or anyone else's opinions barging in on her impressions. If she could just sit in solitude with the writings for a while, she felt she could start to strip away two thousand years of religious indoctrination crammed into her very DNA. She wanted to see what she could see for herself.

Alyson read through the translation from beginning to end, hungrily devouring every line as she read. At the end, she felt the same way everyone feels when they eat too quickly – bloated and craving for more. She decided she needed to re-read more carefully. After spreading the photographs of the original papyri across the dining room table, couch, and coffee table,

Alyson printed out the translation in 14-point font and set each page next to its corresponding photo. This way she could allow her intuition to lead her through the pages less linearly, if she felt the urge to do so.

Alyson knew going in that the codex wasn't an essay or gospel narrative. By definition it was a scrapbook of esoteric thought. Yet what struck her as she hovered over the pages was that the codex wasn't necessarily random, either; there was a scope and sequence to it, a series of divinely orchestrated revelations that seemed to unfold as the author or authors discovered new information and insight. Maybe that was conjecture on her part, but it was one she hoped would come to a glorious conclusion of relevance to her own spiritual search. Perhaps the revelations would divinely unfold for her as well.

As the professor had mentioned weeks earlier, the codex began with the names of two people, Miryam and Cerinthus, each written several times in both Hebrew and Greek as if for practice. Because the codex was accompanied with a legal writ by a Jesus from Nazareth willing his ministry to a Mary from Magdala, she felt it safe to assume that the two Marys were one and the same. The signatures on the codex would serve as fingerprints for handwriting experts to determine who wrote what, but she knew in her heart that Mary was the primary author. Whether she truly was or not, it didn't matter. Alyson wasn't after the sensation of discovering a Magdalene text – she simply wanted some relief from her pain and insight into her next spiritual step.

The first three verses from Genesis followed the signatures, and according to the professor the Hebrew characters were carefully yet crudely formed as if their very writing had also been an exercise. Alyson skimmed through the verses:

> *... In the beginning God (Elohim) created the heaven and the earth. ...*
> *And God said, 'Let there be light, and there was light.'*

"Okay, nothing too exciting here," Alyson said, until she read the next passage of Hindu origin, written in Aramaic, strangely enough. The professor noted that the first line came from the *Rig Veda*, the oldest religious text in India. The last couple of lines came from the *Upanishads*, written some five hundred to a thousand years before Jesus. *How did Mary Magdalene get hold of these verses?* she wondered. The first verse had a familiar ring:

> *In the beginning was Brahman, who was with the Word (Vak), and the Word was the Supreme Brahma.*

> *The Word is Aum. Aum is speech, man is speech, and so man is Aum. One must meditate on the Aum to understand the laws that govern Creation, and also to feel fulfilled in all desires.*

Following the Hindu verses came what sounded like the opening to the Gospel of John, also scribed in Aramaic. As Professor Goodnight demonstrated in his translation, the author had struck through the lines and later rewrote them in Greek on another page. This verse, it appeared, was an original composition:

> ~~The Word (Memra) exists at the Source. The Word exists with God (Elah). God created everything. Nothing exists that is not in the hand of God.~~

Alyson skipped to the page where Mary had rewritten the verse in Greek, thereby replacing the word Memra with Logos:

> *The Logos exists at the Source, and the Logos exists with the One, and the Logos is the One, and the One is the Source. The One makes all, and nothing exists that is not in the hand of the One. From the One comes life, and the life is the Light of the world. And the light shines in darkness, and the darkness comprehends it not. The Logos is made flesh and dwells among us, and we behold His glory, the glory as the son of the One, full of grace and truth. In Him is life, and the life is the Light of all souls.*

Obviously, at least to Alyson, the Word verse was modeled after and perhaps inspired by the Hindu verses entered just above it. Alyson recalled Professor Goodnight saying that although the Word translated into Memra in Hebrew and Logos in Greek, the two words had completely different meanings. The Hebrew definition referred to the utterance, action, and instruction of God, while the Greek Logos referred to an overriding reason or pattern of the universe. Just for fun, Alyson searched the Hindu verse on the Internet and discovered that *Vak* is understood to be the Word that brought all of creation into existence as an emanation of thought. By switching languages Mary had changed the definition, or perhaps had even merged all three concepts, Hindu, Hebrew, and Greek. She smiled, wondering what Christians would say if they knew they had common roots with the Hindu and, more importantly, that Mary Magdalene had been influenced by them.

Just as she picked up a page of Greek sayings, Noche, the black and white cat, jumped upon the dining room table right in the middle of the print outs and began play-clawing and scratching them wildly, scattering some to the floor. Before he could do more damage, Alyson corralled both him and his sister, Luce, into the bathroom with food, water, and litter box. "Why is it that whenever you want to do something important, the universe starts causing a ruckus?" she asked out loud. She exhaled slowly, realizing it was really her own fault for forgetting about Noche's paper fetish. She picked up the stray pages from the floor and re-inserted them into order with the ones on the table. She then trudged into the kitchen and returned minutes later with a triple-shot latte to concentrate by.

Alyson began where she'd left off: with the sayings by Heraclitus, a pre-Socratic Greek philosopher who lived in Ephesus around five hundred years before the time of Jesus. She learned that Heraclitus had written more than a hundred such sayings, but for some reason, Mary had chosen just these three:

> You could not discover the limits of the soul, even if you traveled by every path in order to do so; such is the depth of its meaning.

> Although the Logos is common to all, most men live as if they each have a private intelligence of their own.

> Listening not to me but to the Logos, it is wise to agree that all is one.

Next came a few excerpts from the extensive works of Philo of Alexandria, a Judeo-Greek scholar whose life overlapped with those of Jesus, the apostles, and Saint Paul. Professor Goodnight provided sources for each excerpt, although he noted that most had been paraphrased into the codex. During her first read of the translation, Philo's gift as a writer and his passion for the Word impressed Alyson. She had no idea that people entertained such ideas back then. The language, style, and subject matter of the Bible seemed so much less sophisticated by comparison. Whereas the Bible cloaked mysticism in short bursts of allegory, Philo was much more open. The first passage was in keeping with the theme of the power of the Word, or the Logos, in creating the cosmos:

> *For God, while He spoke the Word, He did at the same moment create. He did not allow anything to come between the Word and the deed, and if one may advance a doctrine which is nearly true, His Word is His deed.*
> *– On the Sacrifices of Cain and Abel*

The focus of the next passage switched from the creative power of God's Word to what that power can do to rectify soul's dilemma:

> *The soul falls in with a scorpion exiled into the wilderness. The thirst of the passions seizes on the scorpion until God sends it the stream of His own wisdom, and induces the soul to drink of its immortality. ... As it drinks it is filled with the most universal manna, for manna is the primary source of everything. – Allegorical Interpretation II*

If there was any question about what that soul's divine elixir might be, a description from Philo followed:

> *And who can pour over the happy soul which proffers its own reason as the most sacred cup, the holy goblet of true joy, except the cup-bearer of God, the master of the feast, the Logos? Not differing from the draught itself, but being itself in an unmixed state, the pure delight and sweetness, and pouring forth, and joy, and ambrosial medicine of pleasure and happiness, if we too may, for a moment, employ the language of the poets.*
> *– On Dreams, that They are God-Sent*

"Wow," Alyson whispered simply to herself. "Is there a chance this soul-drink is real?" She had to assume that Philo was still talking about the Logos, but judging by the poetic force with which he had written the passage, he seemed to have had personal experience with It. Was he merely talking about the ecstatic lather only religious fervor could produce or some kind of a ritual involving wine and opiates? He was a Hellenized Jew living in Egypt, and this ambrosia of pleasure and happiness might have come from the Greek wine cult of Dionysus or local Egyptian cult rituals, for instance. Whatever the case, the Logos was obviously a universal concept, one which Mary Magdalene, presumably of Jewish heritage, had also related to and personally experienced.

The next passage by Philo continued with the theme of the exiled soul, along with a clue as to how the Logos could be obtained:

> Some souls, having descended into the body as into a river, at one time are carried away and swallowed up by a most violent whirlpool, and at another time strive with all their power to resist the river's impulsiveness. At first they swim on top of the river and afterward fly back to the place from where they started. These, then, are the souls of those who have been taught some kind of sublime philosophy, meditating, from beginning to end, on dying as to the life of the body in order to obtain an inheritance of the immortal and eternal life, which is to be enjoyed in the presence of the unmanifested and everlasting God. But those souls, which are swallowed up in the whirlpool, are the souls of those other men who have disregarded wisdom, giving themselves up to the pursuit of unstable things regulated by chance alone ... rather than to the dead corpse connected with us, that is, to the physical body. – On the Giants

To Alyson, Philo's depiction of the soul being thrown into the deep end of mortality to sink or to swim sounded neither Jewish nor Greek. In fact, "flying back to the beginning" sounded like reincarnation and karma – to the extent she understood these principles – which seemed more Hindu or Buddhist. "Dying as to the life of the body in order to obtain an inheritance of the immortal and eternal life" echoed the crucifixion and resurrection symbolism of Jesus, and yet Philo's writings may have pre-existed that final chapter of the Jesus story. All that aside, Philo had stated most eloquently that the souls of those who died as to the life of the body had been taught some kind of meditative technique. But before Alyson could dwell on what that technique might be, she read the next passage, which this time had been copied from Plato's *Phaedo*, as explained by Socrates:

> The soul will calm passion by listening to the Logos within and by always being in it and by beholding what is true and divine and not the

object of opinion. And being nurtured by it, the soul will seek to live in this way for as long as she lives, so that when she dies, she will enter that which is kindred and similar to her own nature, and be freed from human ills.

Alyson's inner being began to rev up as she read this passage from Plato. *Now, we're onto something,* she thought. She walked back to the papyrus that held the statement from the Upanishads and read: "One must meditate on the Aum to understand the laws that govern Creation, and also to feel fulfilled in all desires." She then compared that to a similar statement by Heraclitus: "Listening not to me but to the Logos, it is wise to agree that all is one." A pattern was beginning to form, and the anticipation of discovery exhilarated her.

In the way Philo described it, the Logos wasn't merely a message from God. Nor was it cold, dry reason – it was an intoxicating goblet of Spirit. To get drunk on this wine, one had to drink it in some way. *Can't run down to the grocery store for this kind of wine,* she thought. Those who meditated on the Logos dwelled in It as if It were ... dare she say it ... a God-like sensation that, according to Socrates, had the power to calm passions and desires. Alyson sensed that the Word provided even more than a balm. Otherwise, what would be the point?

Mary Magdalene must have looked to the sacred documents of her own tradition for evidence of the meditative technique to summon the Logos, Alyson reasoned. Perhaps she could not find anything akin to the philosophical method of "listening to the Logos" per se, but she did find a few spiritual directives that, upon closer examination, might also achieve Philo's "inheritance of the immortal and eternal life." Professor Goodnight said the following excerpts came from the Tanakh, upon which the Old Testament was based:

The desire of soul is to repeat the Name in remembrance of God. – Isaiah 26:8

I call to remembrance my song in the night. I commune with my own heart, while my spirit searches diligently. – Psalms 77:6

I rise early at dawn, and I wait for Your Word. My eyes open before the night-watches, that I might meditate on Your Word. – Psalms 119:147-148

Dwell in the garden with the Comforter until you can hear His Voice. – Similar to Song of Songs 8:13

Stand in the gate of the Lord's house, and proclaim there this Word. – Jeremiah 7:2

Let me know the way wherein I should walk, for I lift up my soul unto You. – Psalms 143:8

Had these verses from the Tanakh not been in the context of the Logos by other authors, the casual reader might have missed the direction subtly stated there, Alyson thought. But it was clear to her now that the ancient Jewish mystics practiced some form of meditation or active prayer that may have included a mantra. What that mantra was, she couldn't say.

Alyson turned her attention to the final section containing text from the New Testament, mainly the Gospel of John accompanied by a couple of lines from Paul's epistles tacked on toward the end. She assumed that Mary had recorded these sayings from her remembrance of what Jesus had said to his students. As she read, she noticed how like the *I Ching* these verses were, now that they were separated from the narrative of the gospel, and they were clearly full of mysticism:

That which is born of the flesh is flesh, and that which is born of Spirit is Spirit. Unless a man is born of Spirit, he cannot enter the Kingdom of God. – Similar to John 3:3 – 7

Spirit blows where it wishes, and you hear the Logos thereof, but you cannot tell where it comes and where it goes. So it is for every one that is born of the Spirit. – Similar to John 3:8

The Kingdom of God is not of this world. The Kingdom of God is within you. – John 18:36, Luke 17:21

The light of the body is the eye. If therefore your eye be single, your whole body shall be full of light. – Matthew 6:22

It is the spirit that quickens; the flesh profits nothing. – John 6:63

Ask, and it shall be given you; seek, and you shall find; knock, and it shall be opened unto you. – Luke 11:9

He who reaps is rewarded and gathers the fruit of life eternal, so that both He who sows and he who reaps may rejoice together. – John 4:36

It is sown a natural body; it is raised a spiritual body. There is a natural body, and there is a spiritual body. – 1 Corinthians 15:44

Love never fails. Prophecies fail, speaking in tongues ceases, special knowledge of God vanishes, but love never fails. Without love we are nothing. – Similar to 1 Corinthians 13:8

You search the scriptures because you think they possess eternal life, but they only bear witness to the Logos. – Similar to John 5:39

The last line rang true for Alyson. *I am searching the codex because I think it holds the key to my happiness,* she thought with exasperation. She scanned through the remaining sayings and parables, which continued on with the theme of the Logos. When she was finished reading, she took her empty coffee mug to the kitchen. She rinsed it out under running water until it ran cool and clear. Refilling the mug with water, she took a long swig until it was empty. Reading between the lines of the Logos Notebook made her thirsty and mentally antsy.

She should have felt elated that she'd broken the code, and if not broken it, at least she had put a large dent in it. Yet she still felt unfulfilled. Why wasn't Mary clearer about the meditative technique? Was she that afraid to convey the secrets? Maybe Evan would understand these passages, and she thought about breaking her vow of silence to consult him. She decided to forward him the translation, with a post script to please give her another night.

A million questions still swirled in her head. She thought about the authors, Mary and Cerinthus. How old were they? What was their relationship to each other? If this was the infamous Cerinthus, the so-called Gnostic heretic of the second century that drew the vitriol of bishops, he must have acquired his convictions from Mary herself.

More questions arose: Did Mary and Cerinthus write the Logos Codex in Ephesus near where Aunt Ruth had purchased the earthenware jar that contained it? With the presence of Paul's verses in the codex, did this mean that he spent time with Mary in Ephesus, and if so, how much influence did they have on one another? Alyson read somewhere that Valentinus, a noted Gnostic of the second century, was a follower of one of Paul's students, and essentially considered Paul to be the grandfather of Gnosticism. That meant that the Gnostics identified with Paul's esoteric leanings, and if that were the case, then Paul may have been influenced by Mary.

Were there women scholars in the days of Jesus? The New Testament shows that Jesus had women followers. Some sources say that there were literate Greek women during that time period. If Mary Magdalene stood in line to inherit Jesus's ministry, then she was an evolved and formidable soul in her own right. What's more, she had survived the Jerusalem that had supposedly killed Jesus, and she clearly enjoyed enough leisure time to contemplate such heady topics as the Logos.

The golden thread throughout the codex was the Logos. Maybe the written word had some special power. It was a stretch, she knew, the product of so much fiction and film, but there had to be something about this Logos that was so enrapturing to have inspired prophets and philosophers alike.

Alyson read the codex again for a third time, slowly this time, even more deliberately and without analysis, hoping to achieve that state of pure delight and sweetness that Philo mentioned by the simple act of reading the words. Nothing happened. The strain gave her a headache. Maybe she was supposed to work with the concept, see it emerging in her life, write about it in her own journal. Weren't there already about a zillion self-help books on similar exercises? That seemed pointless.

Growing frustrated, Alyson shoved the photographs and translations aside on the couch and flopped down. Here she had the knowledge that Mary Magdalene existed and that she had created something uncanny, and yet it did nothing for Alyson's own spirituality. She yearned for Mary Magdalene's life experiences that occurred between the lines.

From the moment the earthenware jar shattered on her dining room floor and gave birth to the papyrus scroll, Alyson had held onto the promise that the codex would lead to her salvation. Now that she knew the truth, that promise was beginning to wane. The translation only inspired more questions. "Beware of answers, for they may be a form of death," Aunt Ruth had warned before she died, and, yes, Alyson felt a part of her had also died a little. As intriguing and stimulating as it all was, she didn't feel that peace she craved within herself. She didn't feel the codex inspired her to embrace Christianity or a modern version of Gnosticism or even Hinduism for that matter. She felt as removed from these religions as she did from the Logos Notebook authors themselves, now two thousand years dead. *Beware of answers, for they may stop your search cold*, she thought.

Feeling weary and let down, Alyson fed the cats and dragged herself to bed. She slept fitfully most of the night. In the early hours of the morning, she dreamed she floated through the ethereal palace she vaguely remembered from another dream weeks earlier when she first opened the earthenware jar from Aunt Ruth. She came to the great hall where the blue and yellow compass had pointed toward "home" in her previous dream. This time the original papyrus sheets of the Logos Codex were spread out across the floor of the compass room. The pages were shaped like giant jig-saw puzzle pieces. She picked up one of the pieces and set it next to another, turning it around and around, failing to match up their edges. She picked up another, then another, forcing them together, but they wouldn't fit into a cohesive image she could recognize.

Finally, she pulled the pieces together into a stack and sat down to ponder the dilemma some more. She mouthed the words, "Please, please, tell me your secrets," as if politeness would help. "Now!" she shouted, using the strength of her will. Magically, the pieces vibrated and levitated one by one to form a stairway, twelve papyrus steps rising on an incline to a door at the top. Bright golden light shined through the door jamb and key hole. Feeling invited, she tentatively stepped onto the first stair, and when she felt it hold her dream-body weight, she stepped onto the next one and ascended toward the door as on an escalator. She heard the words from the Logos Codex: "Ask, and it shall be given you; seek, and you shall find; knock, and it shall be opened unto you." Gently, she knocked on the dream door. It didn't open. She knocked again, more loudly this time. Nothing. She grabbed the handle and turned it, pushing against the door. It wouldn't budge. She needed a key, she realized, but she couldn't remember where it was. As she turned to descend the stairs, the papyrus steps collapsed beneath her feet. She fell in slow motion, and as she fell, she saw Evan kneeling on the floor below her stacking the pages.

Alyson awakened abruptly and sat straight up. She realized now that she hadn't read everything the day before when she attempted to penetrate the Logos Notebook with her mental laser beam. There were a few passages that she vaguely remembered reading on her laptop, but during her read of the printout, she hadn't come across them again. She ran into the dining room and started rifling through the papers, but she couldn't find the missing pages. She got down on hands and knees and looked under the hutch next to the table. "Ah, here you are," she said, pulling two pages out from under it. Must have slipped under there during her cat's wild fit, she thought.

The first page contained two more entries by Philo:

... The most universal of all things is God, and in the second place the Logos of God. – Allegorical Interpretation II

And the Father who created the universe has given to His highest and most ancient Logos a preeminent gift, to stand between the Creator and that which He Created. And this same Logos is continually a humble petitioner to the immortal God on behalf of the mortal race, which is exposed to affliction and misery, and is also the ambassador, sent by the Ruler of all, to the subject race. And the Logos rejoices in the gift, and, exulting in it, announces it and boasts of it, saying, 'I stood in the midst, between the Lord and You.' – Who is the Heir of Divine Things?

The second page contained the verse Mary Magdalene had rewritten into Greek and expanded upon. As Alyson reread, she realized that the verse naturally flowed out of Philo's previous inspirational excerpts about the Logos and Its power, which mediated between God and humanity:

The Logos exists at the Source, and the Logos exists with the One, and the Logos is the One, and the One is the Source. The One makes all, and nothing exists that is not in the hand of the One. From the One comes life, and the life is the Light of the world. And the light shines in darkness, and the darkness comprehends it not. The Logos is made flesh and dwells among us, and we behold His glory, the glory as the son of the One, full of grace and truth. In Him is life, and the life is the Light of all souls.

"Enter Jesus Christ," Alyson said out loud. "The one who died and was reborn to redeem the sins of the world." *Back to allegory*, she thought, *drenched in romanticism, veiled by symbolism.* If this were a testimony for the same-old same-old New Testament stuff, she was quitting.

"But maybe it isn't that cut and dry," she said a moment later when she calmed herself. Jesus was not mentioned at all in the notebook; there was nothing of the beloved teacher being nailed to the cross, nothing of the miracles he performed in the New Testament written here. The codex was all about the power of the Logos, and the miserable position of the exiled soul that could somehow take advantage of that power. Hadn't the philosophers and ancient religions quoted in the notebook mentioned the mediator long before Jesus even existed?

Below the Logos-made-flesh entry, Mary had included three simple verses, which, according to Professor Goodnight, were pre-cursors to those found in the Gospel of John. These final verses indeed implied that there was a universal master to help transfer the Logos to the soul:

Whosoever drinks of the Living Water shall never thirst; the Master is the Everlasting Water. – Similar to John 4:14

For the bread of the Father comes down from heaven and gives you life. He who eats that shall live forever. The Master is the bread from heaven. – Similar to John 6:33 - 51

He who enters the sheepfold not by the door, but climbs up some other way, is the same as a thief and a robber. But he who enters by the door is the shepherd and the sheep know His voice. The Shepherd is the door. – Similar to John 10:1 - 9

These three verses were all relevant to the previous passages by Philo in the codex. The living water was the divine elixir of the Logos and the bread was the universal manna. The last statement, "the shepherd is the door," called to mind the dream of climbing the papyrus stairs to a door with light around it. The door wouldn't budge when she knocked. Of course, the door wouldn't budge. The door was the master and she didn't have a master. For without the shepherd, she was nothing but a thief and a robber herself.

Suddenly she knew where the Logos Key to the door was hidden. She ran to her bedroom and changed into a sweatshirt, jeans, and running shoes. She scooped up all the transcripts strewn around the house, and ran out of her apartment toward Evan's door.

Two

Evan opened his door before Alyson could knock. Clutching the photos and papers in her fist, she waved them haphazardly in the air. "You know what this means!" It was more an accusation than a question.

"Yes." The boyish smile was gone and in its place a steadiness she'd not witnessed in him until now. "I read the transcript you e-mailed me yesterday."

"When were you going to tell me?"

"You said not to bother you."

He opened the screen door to let her in. As she stepped inside, she saw he was dressed in black slacks and dress shirt. "Where are you going?"

"I have a spiritual meeting this morning – *satsang*, it's called."

"I'm intruding."

"No, I have a couple hours. Got dressed early just in case you wanted to talk." He led her to the living room. "I'm afraid all I have is Folgers, but I can steam some milk in the microwave." He disappeared into the kitchen, knowing what her answer would be. A caffeine junkie would take anything in a pinch.

As she headed for the couch, the bookcase behind it caught her eye. Can you judge a man by the books on his shelves? She thought about her scavenge hunt the previous year, rotating through pulp fiction and pop metaphysics. Her books were not a representation of current beliefs. Rather, they were the exoskeletons of ideas she had impulsively donned and as quickly shed. Without an intervention, the Logos Notebook was in danger of becoming just another book on her shelf.

Evan's shelves appeared to be more a cohesive statement on his current state of being. Just as she suspected, he'd found what he'd been looking for and was content to spend the rest of his life immersing himself more deeply into it. Yet the shelves displayed a seemingly broad range of spiritual thought. She expected the books on modern theology, some of which he had loaned her, as well as the books on the Gnostic gospels. She also expected the volumes on Taoism and Greek philosophy, but not the poetry by Rumi, *Delicious Laughter*, and Hafiz, *I Heard God Laughing*. She'd never heard of Nanak, Kabir, or Kirpal Singh, but their books seemed consistent with such titles as *The World is Sound*, *The Music of Life*, and *From Light to Sound* by modern authors. She didn't know what to make of the two shelves of books by a single press in India called Radha Soami, each book bearing a different, pastel-colored jacket with no illustrations. She was spellbound.

"These books are all about the Logos." Evan explained when he entered the room with two mismatched mugs. "Also called the Unspoken, Unmanifest Word, the Light and Sound, or *Shabda Dhun* in Sanskrit, and dozens of other names in various languages. Light and Sound is at the root of most religions, and yet the teachings transcend all religions."

"I'm beginning to see that." Something inside Alyson was churning and knocking at her door from within, and she had a feeling that this might be it. Evan was a scout from the last frontier, and she was about to be shown the way. She took the larger mug from him and sat on the couch, thinking about how he never ceased to surprise her. She trusted him, yet she knew nothing about him, where he came from, what he did besides read and watch cable TV and fix her plumbing. "Just who are you? Much, much more than an apartment manager, I'm willing to wager."

Evan drew an imaginary line with his finger above his breast pocket, mouthing the name *Evan* that would be there if he was wearing his work shirt. "I am nobody, really. I was once somebody, I once achieved about nine and a half minutes in the spotlight, but now I'm happy to report that I'm nobody. You have to be somebody before becoming nobody."

"You're speaking in Zen *koans*."

"All right." He leaned forward. "You want to know who I am? I taught comparative religion at a Midwestern university."

"I knew it!" Alyson exclaimed.

Evan didn't smile. "Before I could get tenure, Gulf War One happened, and because I had enlisted in the National Guard years earlier to pay for college, I was deployed to Iraq. By the time I got back, I found that my house had burned down from an electrical short and all of my lectures and books and papers with it. In the meantime, the funding was cut for my job. Did I mention I didn't have tenure?"

"That's terrible!"

"It was okay. Really. I didn't see a lot of action in Iraq, just sand dunes and burning oil wells. It was so surreal, I felt out of place. Being sent to a foreign environment against one's will is like being an increasingly aware citizen on planet earth. You kinda feel like you don't belong here anymore. I needed to believe in something greater than the planet, something greater than myself."

"I can relate to that. A stranger in a strange land."

"Exactly. I realized I didn't know who I was or what I believed in. All I had were borrowed religions; nothing of my own."

"What did you do when you got back from Iraq and found everything gone?"

"Moved to Denver, to this apartment. The first time I went to the grocery store for supplies, there was a flier on a bulletin board announcing a Light and Sound seeker meeting that very weekend. I met my master within twenty-four hours of arriving here."

"You didn't want to tell me about your spiritual path because you didn't want it to end up on my bookshelf with similar rejects."

"No, that's not it." He smiled. "Well, yes, you're right, but you had to have your own miracles to lead you to that door."

"Miracles? Not yet. Unless you count a couple of ironic dreams." She looked up at him shyly over the brim of her mug as she sipped, not wanting to disclose to him how integral he had been to her spiritual search. Then she winced at the memories of her own past that had brought her to this moment. She drew in a deep breath. "I haven't had it so easy either. A couple years ago, my daughter had a drug episode that led to a crime. She went into rehab, and my husband and I ... well, I guess you can say I drifted away and he didn't stop me. I haven't seen either of them since." That wasn't as difficult to say as she had feared it would be, she thought, and kept going. "Went on a two-year binge of self-indulgence. Did a lot of reading, mostly about spirituality in the end, but I couldn't find a path that interested me enough to pursue it. Couldn't focus on my job throughout that whole time, which is probably why I got fired."

"Divine discontent."

"What?"

"Think about it. Sounds like an oxymoron, but what you have gone through is what most would-be saints go through before they start yearning for Home. Just like me, your crisis propelled you into a spiritual quest. You tried to quench the pain with everything you could think of. And after you tried everything, you found there was nothing left to yearn for. All that's left is the desire itself." He gulped down some of his coffee. "That intense feeling is God yearning for you. He – or I should say It – must want you back badly. Moved heaven and earth to get that codex into your hands."

Alyson hadn't thought of it that way. She wrapped herself in the blanket thrown over the back of the couch. Yes, yes, she did feel a strong desire for *something* she couldn't quite name. "I feel I've arrived in your proverbial strange land, and I don't speak the language. I need help deciphering the message."

Evan sat in the overstuffed chair opposite the couch. "Where do I start?" He knew what she wanted.

"The Logos?"

Evan closed his eyes a moment and sat very still. When he reopened his eyes, he looked as if he had taken a quick nap; his face was smooth and rested. "The spiritual path I'm on has existed through time, and there has never been a time when it didn't exist, just as the codex says. God is too great to exist within Its creation, and the Logos is the divine power and love of God that enables a person to return to It through self and God realization. That's it in a sound bite."

"Now tell me the rest of the story."

"Okay. You've heard the phrase, 'In my Father's house are many mansions?'"

"Yes." She again flashed on her dream of running through a heavenly palace.

"Many belief systems refer to multiple heavens or worlds. The Light and Sound teachers say the mansions metaphorically represent ascending levels of consciousness that are all contained within the human body. You unconsciously operate as if thoughts, emotions, and sensations are within you. Well, heaven is within, God is within, soul ... all of it exists within the house of your own self, but they exist beyond the mind, and the mind, over the course of many, many lifetimes, has become thick and dry and jealously protective of what it thinks of as its own power. The mind has lived off the God energy that is passed down through soul to the point that soul is barely operative. The imagery of the crucifixion, the empty tomb, and the resurrection all suggest the soul reclaiming its inheritance from the mind by rising above the body consciousness."

"Where does the Logos come in?"

"The task of regaining residency in the spiritual realms is to slowly take back that power by contemplating on the Logos."

"Yeah, yeah, the codex is all about that." She thumbed through the translation of the codex and randomly selected a passage. "Take this, for instance, from the *Song of Songs*: 'You dwell in the garden with the Comforter until you can hear His Voice.' Is that contemplating on the Logos?'"

"Yes, the Voice would be the Logos."

"But who is the Comforter?" She already knew the answer, but she wanted to hear Evan's response.

His face brightened. "That's the million-dollar question, and the answer is difficult to accept in America."

"Beware of answers, for they may be a form of ... ."

"Out of the mouth of the dying. But death to what? What has to die before you can live in soul?"

"Mind ... ego?"

"Exactly. And who would you trust to help you with that? The very mind and ego that have taken control?"

"No, that doesn't make sense, I guess."

"You would need someone who has already transcended the mind and ego and has already gone home. To go home is to be God realized in *Sach Khand*."

"Sock ... conned?" Alyson copied Evan's pronunciation.

"Sanskrit for the fifth spiritual region from which soul originated, according to the Light and Sound Teachings."

She reflected upon this a moment. "Mary's Word made flesh – that's the master?"

"The Shepherd, the Door, the Bread, the Living Water – someone who has mastered the journey. And not just any master. One you can trust, one who has a long résumé and lots of experience. It isn't an entry level job, and the path isn't an invention of his – or sometimes her – own mind."

"And you have such a Word-made-flesh master?"

Evan nodded. "We call him the *Sat Guru*, or True Guru."

When the student is ready, a teacher appears, she thought. She must be on the verge thereof, if such a being indeed existed that wasn't after one's money and other sordid things. "Are you implying that your master is on par with Jesus?"

"You say that because all you have to go on are the trumped up miracles that were written for a different audience at a different time. There have been many masters, many more will come. Why would there only be one savior in two thousand years, and none the previous fifty thousand? Why not now?"

"Wouldn't that be something?"

"Yes, Al, it is something," Evan whispered. His face brightened, and he suddenly seemed much younger and much older at the same time.

"Have you achieved God realization?"

"Me?" he asked, clasping his chest. "Are you kidding? No. I've been on this spiritual path for about a dozen years, and I'm just now barely beginning to see some of the antics of my mind, but I am also beginning to have experiences of switching over to the soul-side."

"Really? How are you able to do that?"

"By contemplation on and through the Sound and the Sat Guru."

"Right." Alyson nodded. "I get that now. What differentiates him from, say, a yoga teacher or a Buddhist monk or the guy teaching a workshop on the laws of attraction at the community center?"

"The teachings state that God realization requires a physical master who is divinely associated with a form that appears within the initiate."

Alyson wrinkled her brow. "Sounds so sci-fi."

"Not when you think about it. Followers insist that Jesus, Buddha, Yogananda, or any 'ascended master' that is dead, can teach or appear to the student in spirit, but their teaching is subject to the mind's interpretation even if they left behind their writings. Others can teach in the physical form through lectures and books, but initiates also need guidance within their beings where all consciousness occurs. Both avenues are needed."

"Sounds weird. There's nothing about that in the Logos Notebook."

"Ah, but there is. The Logos made flesh refers to both the inner and outer masters. The Inner Master is the eternal power of the Logos, or Shabda, that manifests at the third eye and bears the face of the physical, historical master. In the Bible, when Jesus takes several of his disciples up the mountain and reveals his glorified body to them, that is a metaphor for seeing the radiant form of their master at the junction between the mind and the God worlds within their consciousness. The New Testament is filled with such metaphors. Of course coming to the point of being able to see the Radiant Form at the third eye takes many years of practice and personal revelation."

"So, your master *is* on par with Jesus."

"All of the Light and Sound Masters are."

If only it were true. "If you know all these things, Evan, then why were you so interested in the scrolls?"

"I can tell you're a journalist."

Alyson smiled. "Has to come in handy sometime."

"Well, okay, fair question. I love a good mystery. Doesn't really change anything for me, except verify that the authors may have been initiates of a Light and Sound Master, and that Jesus was such a master. Clearly, there is more to the New Testament than meets the eye. I also wanted to see where the codex led you and see if I could be of any service in that regard. But I didn't want to push."

"You think Socrates was a Light and Sound Master?"

"It would appear so, along with Plato."

Alyson scanned her pages. "Socrates and Heraclitus talk about listening to the Logos as well."

"Scholars debate whether that is a cerebral or a spiritual exercise. I prefer the latter."

"So you think the Logos is real?"

"Yes, in my experience, the Logos, or Sound, is a real vibration within. God's vibration. The more the students progress within themselves, the more refined yet powerful the vibration becomes. The masters liken these vibrations to a big bell, a conch, a lyre, drumbeats, and bag pipes, in that order, but they're metaphors for the increasingly powerful vibration of the Sound."

"What does it mean to contemplate on the Sound?" Alyson flipped through her translation until she found the verses she was looking for and handed the page to Evan. "The codex might have been hinting at these exercises in the excerpts from the Tanakh."

He nodded, "Yes, like this one from *Psalms*: 'I rose early at dawn, and I waited for Your Word. My eyes opened before the night-watches that I might meditate on Your Word.' To me that sounds like the basic practices of *simran*, *dhyan*, and *bhajan*. Sanskrit words meaning to constantly remember and repeat the secret words given upon initiation, to lovingly contemplate the inner form of the master, and to listen to the Sound. The Sound pulls one inward and upward in consciousness."

"How does that work, in practice?"

"Well, you focus your attention on the third eye and sense the Presence of the Inner Master there through contemplation on the works of that Master. There are many nuances to these practices, and it takes years of devotion to develop them."

"How is this different from Zen Buddhism or other forms of meditation?"

"Meditation focuses on outer sounds like chanting, bell ringing, and the like – or on no sound at all – for the purpose of stilling the mind. But these practices do not involve *the* Sound. We're not talking about actual noise here. Sound is what I can only describe as Omniscient Love, which feels like a vibration and has the power to perform miracles within you.

Meditation can't do that. The best that can happen with meditation is cosmic consciousness. Some paths talk about self-realization, which is a step toward God realization, but I suppose it depends on their definition. Self-realization is not simply unity with the creation of the lower worlds; it is the realization, perception, and control of the self as soul."

"I think I understand what Sound is. I mean, Philo said that the Logos is a God Power that can't be heard with the physical ears but can be heard and seen internally."

"That's right."

"But I don't understand how you get hooked up to the Sound."

"By initiation," Evan said succinctly. "When a Sat Guru initiates one into the Light and Sound, he re-enlivens the Sound Current that has been lying dormant within one all these eons. It's like lighting a pre-existing candle within the individual with the divine flame. From that point onward, the Shabda is constantly flowing at the third eye. The initiate begins to experience the Sound as a subtle vibration or some kind of heightened awareness or changes in one's daily life. It's different for everyone. Some experience nothing and yet feel compelled to continue on the path."

"I would hear the Sound right away?"

"It takes years to hear it, if at all. It's not important to actually *hear* the Sound, but to *feel* what is called the *bhakti*, the God Love that the Sound represents. It is a very real energy."

Alyson nodded, yet nothing in her experience allowed her to relate to what he was saying.

"Hearing or feeling the Sound is not the end game anyway."

"What do you mean?"

"How can I explain this?" Evan stared at the ceiling a moment to collect his thoughts. "It's a life-long process. When one successfully practices simran, one's scattered energies in the body rise, thus allowing one's attention to stay centered in the third eye and dwell there in the Shabda for longer and longer periods until it becomes a permanent seat of consciousness. There are many times when one isn't practicing simran and isn't centered, and the Shabda comes anyway, just as a loving reminder of the Presence. It's not an altered state of consciousness, but a state of heightened attention and bliss that is repeatable and sustainable and grows stronger with each passing year. Eventually, the initiate builds up so much Shabda that the third eye opens, upon the will of the Inner Master, and the initiate's higher consciousness is allowed to move up through the Pure God Worlds."

"Philo called it the 'intoxicating ambrosia of pleasure and happiness.'"

Evan nodded, and his eyes gleamed as if he were feeling the ambrosia now.

"When you speak of the Light and Sound, what is the light?"

"Light is knowledge," he answered. "Alone, light doesn't return the soul to it's origin."

"Knowledge as in the Greek word gnosis?"

"Yes, but it's difficult to tell what was meant by that word. Adam and Eve fell into the physical world because they ate from the Tree of Knowledge. Yet 'to know' another person is a biblical euphemism for merging, which is part of the process of ascending in consciousness. So, gnosis may have referred to the soul merging into self and God realization, or it could have referred to cosmic consciousness, which falls short of self-realization. Not only that, the Gnostic literature is missing the necessary component of having a living master. They talk about the Christ figure, but he was long gone by the time Gnosticism developed its Christian doctrine and, as I said, an ascended master can't deliver a devotee into self and God realization. But getting back to your question, a Light and Sound Master makes use of the light, or the outer teachings, to illuminate the path within the initiate."

"New Age paths talk a lot about the light as the means to, well, enlightenment."

"And they miss the essential components of the Sound as well as a bona fide Sat Guru. Reading the works of a Light and Sound Master doesn't get you any closer to God realization. Without the Sound, all light does is stimulate the mind and leave one hungering for more."

"I think I know what you're saying," Alyson said. "I feel the same way about the Logos Notebook. Don't get me wrong. I'm thrilled to know what's in the codex, but I have to admit that part of me is disappointed."

"Why?"

"Because no matter how monumental it is that Jesus willed his teachings to Mary Magdalene, and that we have what are possibly her unedited and uncensored writings, I want what she's got. I've tried penetrating the words, but I get nothing." She wanted to tell Evan about her experience after meeting Professor Goodnight on the CU campus in Boulder when she felt that her soul had briefly awakened and peered through her eyes, but she hadn't repeated the experience, and it seemed too farfetched now.

"Isn't that the point of the Logos Notebook?"

"What do you mean?"

"In the beginning was the Logos, the Word. The author was trying to convey that the Word, with a capital W, is different from words on papyrus, even if those words were divinely inspired. The Word – in quotes – is the God Power that exists at the Source and created everything and is everything. The Word then is splintered into light and darkness, or into permanent duality. You can't ascend into the God Worlds while still being controlled by duality. You can only ascend by becoming One, and that is only possible through the Logos, which is singular. Says it right in the Logos Notebook: 'If therefore your eye be single, your whole body shall be full of light.'"

"You're losing me."

"Right, well, there's a lot to learn."

She thought about it a moment. "I think I know what you're saying. The Logos doesn't exist on this plane." She swiped the space in front of her with both hands. "You have to be initiated in the Sound Current to experience it."

"Yes!"

He seemed genuinely elated that she was catching on, and that pleased her, but she felt she wasn't totally getting it. "But you were saying earlier that you could contemplate on the spiritual works to build up the Logos, or Shabda?"

"Yes, an initiate of a Sat Guru might find that contemplating on the works of that guru is more expedient than meditating. But I was trying to explain why the written word alone can do nothing for you. In Sanskrit, the Logos, the Sound, is called *Dhunatmik*, and the light is called *varnatmik*. A true disciple needs both to ascend. But many religions, not just Christianity, treat their sacred book as if *the book itself* is God by proxy. Take the Sikh religion. Their holy book is the *Adi Granth*, which they call *Guru Granth Sahib*, the Tenth and Final Guru of a long line of Light and Sound Masters. The ninth guru chose not to pass the mantle on to a living master, because possibly none were ready to take it on, and so he declared the sacred writings themselves to be the 'guru.' Followers treat Guru Granth with all the same adulation and ritual they would give Guru Nanak Dev, the founder of the movement that became Sikhism, as if he were there in person. They carry the holy book into their religious gatherings above their heads, and the devotees bow to it as it passes by."

"What's in the Adi Granth?"

"Writings from the previous nine gurus, collectively called *Bhagat Bani*, or 'Word of the Devotees.' Sometimes it is simply called the Word of God."

"Imagine that. Not unlike the Bible."

"Or other holy books. What's ironic is that the Adi Granth also speaks of contemplating on the Word or the Unstruck Melody, which they call *Naam*, and yet the followers of the Sikh religion no longer have a living master who can initiate them into the Naam. The Adi Granth is quite profound, as is the Holy Bible, the Torah, Koran, even your codex, full of awe-inspiring descriptions of the soul, spirit, guru, and God. By the way, Pythagoras, Lao Tzu, Rumi, Hafiz, not to mention a dozen masters in India who are not so famous to the West, are all thought to be Light and Sound Masters. Their writings are stunning. And yet there is nothing in these works that would reveal your soul to you right now, because mere words, however beautifully or truthfully written, do not possess the power to do so. The soul is not the mind; it is not the emotions, not the personality, not sensations, not intuition, not even your most virtuous trait. Even if the codex revealed the truth about your most burning questions, you would be no closer to realizing the true nature of God or your soul."

Evan focused his eyes at some invisible point in front of him. "It is precisely that intensely burning quest for truth that will bring you answers, but not through the 'light.' Rather, your desire will only be quenched by merging with Truth itself, *within* yourself. Spirituality is like marriage. You have to enter into it to know what it is."

"I don't think I can make such a commitment to a spiritual path I know nothing about."

"You're right," he said, leaning forward. "But you can commit provisionally, and you can test the principles as if you believe in them. If a path can't deliver the goods it promises, then it is nothing more than a cult. With the growing familiarity of Sound in the world, there will be many pseudo gurus and counterfeit teachings. But how would you ever know unless you try them out?"

That made sense, Alyson thought. "One last question, and I know it may be the death of me."

"But in a good way, right?" Evan smiled.

"How does the Logos work for you in practice?"

Evan thought about it for many moments. "At every stage along the Light and Sound Path, as one ascends, there is an aspect of the self that is introduced to the initiate and purified. So my answer would always be different depending on what I'm entertaining spiritually in the moment."

Alyson was disappointed by his answer. "But generally, what does it do for you?"

Evan nodded, exhaling. "There's a Sanskrit word, *jivanmukti*, or spiritual freedom here and now, meaning that in any given single moment an initiate of a True Master can transcend the body consciousness no matter what the problems of the day are, no matter how angry one might be. The Sound *changes* a person without even trying."

"Still too complicated," she said.

"Let me make it even simpler, then. Every single day when I awaken, I know I have something to live for, and I can feel loved by the Sound flowing through me from within."

She was feeling inspired, yet skeptical at the same time. "I'm seeing the light, as it were. If only it were true."

"I will tell you this," Evan added as an afterthought. "When you embark upon a true path of Light and Sound, your life is rearranged to support your spiritual undertaking. All your problems are resolved, exposed as the illusions they are, or just plain forgotten about. At least eventually."

"Seek first the Kingdom, and all else will be added unto you."

"That's the prime directive of spirituality. But it doesn't mean that life becomes hassle free from here on out. The Inner Master re-dispenses karmic events for the purpose of letting you see many of the attitudes and propensities you have tucked away in your psyche after eons of lives. The difference is that now, once seen, the Master Power unwinds the problems."

Alyson nodded, trying to take in everything Evan had to say. She felt herself going into a daze. Another part of herself was feeling heightened and dancing on top of her skull. She had never felt that sensation before. She liked it.

"I can see I've said too much. I don't mean to proselytize. This path is not for everyone."

"No, no," she said emphatically. "I asked. I wanted to know all about the Logos." She placed her empty mug on the coffee table and stood up from the couch.

Evan stood and faced her. "I guess you'd like to ponder all this. Hope I haven't scared you."

"Nope, I need to get ready."

"Why, where are you going?"

"I'm going to satsang with you to see for myself."

Surprise crossed Evan's face. "Are you sure? Don't you want to read some materials, think about it? Contemplate it?"

"After all I've been through? Are you kidding?" She thumbed through her stack of photocopies from the Logos Notebook. "This is the first time I've felt an inner nudge – no, it's a kick in the hind end – to take a step forward. In fact, the more I think about it, the more I'm convinced this is my next step. The timing can't be ignored." She started toward the door. "I mean, it's a little scary, but if it turns out to be a fraud, I can at least write the story." She fumbled for the door knob, and all her papers fell to the floor.

Evan was there in an instant on one knee to scoop up the papers. He handed them to her with a smile and a nod. *Just like my dream*, she thought. But this time he looked like he was proposing, and in a way he was.

Standing, he nodded and looked at his watch. "You have about half an hour."

Three

Alyson flew back to her apartment, barely feeling her own feet beneath her body. She quickly showered and pulled on a simple dress complete with heels and nylons. Her heart raced and her hands trembled as she put on some make-up. Checking herself in the mirror, she barely recognized the person she saw there. She had been stripped of her entire life – her daughter, her husband, and her job all consumed by a black hole she may have created herself. The Logos Codex and the prospect of meeting Evan's master were the only two things she had left in her life for now. She worried that even this venture would come to naught.

No, I have to get hold of myself, she thought. She realized that this might be another dead end, but she would never know unless she investigated it. With that, she was able to relax. Just as she did, she felt a kind of quickening inside her forehead, between and behind her two physical eyes where the legendary third eye was said to be. There was a real energy building there – not a full-bloomed lotus exactly, but a tiny rosebud opening toward the sun.

Evan drove into the parking lot of a hotel near the Denver International Airport and pulled into the first empty space he could find. With Alyson's last-minute decision to attend satsang, they were running late despite her attempt to dress quickly. They rushed through the double doors that led toward the ballroom where the seeker meeting was to be held. Alyson didn't have time to feel the jitters of the unexpected. She felt giddy and full of anticipation. Not quite a bride on her way to church just yet, more like a young person heading for a first date.

The great entry hall to the ballroom was empty except for two women sitting alone behind a table at the far end. "You'll need to sign in with them, but be quick. I think they're about to start."

"Right," she said and hurried toward the table. The older woman was a tall, silvery blonde, stunningly lit with a spiritual grace. Oh, how she hoped she would look like that one day. But once she glimpsed the younger woman, she stopped cold in her tracks. She didn't recognize her at first, for absent were the neon pink hair dye, the facial piercings, and the pink and black clothes. In their place were a plain black skirt, black pumps, and white sweater. As she approached the table, Alyson started trembling.

The young lady looked up with the pleasant smile she must have given all previous seekers who'd checked in. Her mouth gaped open when she recognized Alyson. "Mom?"

"Kendra! Where ... what ... ?"

Kendra embraced her mother for a brief moment, and then she stepped back to look her in the eyes. "There's time for all that later. We should go in now."

Kendra took Alyson by the arm and ushered her toward the ballroom. Evan opened the door to a crowded room of quiet devotees seated theater-style. In the same moment, she heard, or rather sensed, a deep rumbling. At least she thought she did.

"What's that sound?" Alyson asked Evan.

"What sound?"

"I must be hearing things," she whispered.

He smiled at her knowingly, as they followed Kendra to two empty seats in the back.

Just as they sat, a thousand voices sang aloud and in harmonic unison: "Huuuu." Alyson closed her eyes and let her mind and all the tension in her neck and shoulders flow into the waves of the Hu chant as the devotees sounded the single, drawn-out syllable several times.

At last a silence fell across the collective body as Alyson imagined each person listened to the reverberation of the chant echoing within them. She felt still and elevated at the same time. When she opened her eyes again, a tall, slender man of Nordic heritage, dressed plainly in black slacks and a blue v-neck sweater over a tan dress shirt, stepped onto a platform at the front of the room. He folded his hands in front of him and slowly gazed at his students from one side of the ballroom to the other. Alyson knew in this moment that this was her master, and she could relax at last. For the first time in years, a single tear rolled down her cheek.

Glossary

In most cases, the glossary attempts to compare the exoteric, or historical religious, meaning to the esoteric, or spiritual, meaning in the context of the Light and Sound Teachings.

(A) = Aramaic, (G) = Greek, (H) = Hebrew, (S) = Sanskrit or Hindustani

Abba (A) - Father; term of endearment for one's Holy Man; how Jesus referred to God.

Abraham (H) – Originally Abram, or exalted father; became Abraham, father of the multitudes or nations.

Adam (H) – Red or ruddy, from the root word *adamah* meaning earth or dirt; the archetypal man created in the image of God. Esoterically, Adam represents the soul's descent from the Pure God Worlds. The soul embarks on a return journey to the proverbial Eden with the help of a True Master.

Agape (G) – Brotherly or universal love, good will, charity.

Ahab, Ahavah (H) – God's love toward humankind or individuals; human love toward partner, family, etc.

Anastasis (G) – Resurrection; to be raised again; likely developed from a Persian concept by survivors who lost loved ones in battle. The Old Testament laments about the soul being raised from the grave, but there is no Hebrew equivalent except possibly *techiyah*, meaning to revive. Esoterically, the resurrection is an inner stage of spiritual attainment that follows the crucifixion of the mind and ego, in preparation for further ascension into higher levels of consciousness.

Apokalypsis (G) – Revelation; to lay bare or make naked, to expose as the truth; esoterically, Divinity revealed within the Self.

Apotheosis (G) – The ancient Greek and Roman tradition of elevating an emperor to the rank of the gods; esoterically, a metaphor for God Realization on a Light and Sound Path.

Aramit (A) – Aramaic, meaning "exalted"; the Semitic language of the Arameans in Syria, or Aram, and the preferred language for much of the Middle East; everyday language of Jerusalem during the time of Jesus.

Atman (S) – Breath; in Hinduism the core essence or soul of the individual as well as the world said to be fully identical to *Brahman*. In the Light and Sound Teachings, the *atma* is the soul in its formless state as a pure particle of the Divine.

Aum, Om (S) – The creative vibration that gives energy to all matter and life. Meditation on the Aum can bring one's consciousness into unity with the lower-world creation, but no higher.

Ayn (A) – Yes.

Ayn b'gla (A) - Literally "in open eye"; an Aramaic idiom meaning public disclosure.

Baptisma (G) – To cleanse by submersion in water; to wash away all sins through the Holy Spirit; based on the Judaic ritual *tevilah*. Esoterically, *baptisma* is a metaphor for initiation into the Living Water, or the *Logos*.

Barukh Haba (H) – Welcome; blessed is he who comes.

Basileia Ouranos (G) – Kingdom or rule of heaven; likely a translation of a Jewish concept since the Greeks formerly did not have a concept of heaven per se, except perhaps the mythological Mount Olympus or the Elysian Fields. However, the idea of the immortal soul most likely came from Greek philosophy. See *Malchut Hashamayim*.

Beit HaMikdash (H) – House of Sanctity or Holy; the Second Temple in Jerusalem destroyed in 70 CE.

Bereshit (H) – The beginning, origin, source, summit, upper part; first book of the *Torah* called *Genesis*.

Bhajan (S) – Worship; the spiritual practice of listening to the Sound Current; the third phase of contemplation in the Light and Sound Teachings.

Biblos, Byblos (G) – Book, scroll, writings; the Phoenician city that exported papyrus materials made from reeds that grew in the Egyptian delta; root word of bible, bibliography, etc.

Brahma, Brahman (S) – Brahma is the Hindu creator god and ruler of the lower worlds; one of the three supreme Hindu gods; high priest; Lord God of all traditional religions. Brahman is pure consciousness in the Hindu religion. See *Dēmiourgós*.

Chata, Chet (H) – Sin; a Judaic-Christian concept meaning to miss the goal or path of right or duty, just as the archer can miss the target. See *Torah*, *Hamartia*.

Chavah, Chavvah (H) – Life; to breathe or make known; Eve, the archetypal woman created from Adam's rib. Esoterically, Eve is the energy that brought the soul into the lower worlds through the Tree of Knowledge. On the return journey back to it's origin, the soul reunites with this aspect of the self.

Chokmah (H) – Wisdom of God; the sense of justice and wisdom of King Solomon in the *Tanakh*; understanding the ethics of the so-called "Wisdom Literature," i.e., *Kings*, *Proverbs*, and *Psalms*; esoterically represents divine understanding of the Light and Sound Teachings. See *Sophia*.

Chowb (H) – Debt; used here to convey the principle of *karma*, or the law of cause and effect. The New Testament gives some clues that Jesus may have taught about *karma* privately to his disciples.

Christos (G) – Christ, the Anointed One. See *Mashiyach*, *Sat Guru*.

Davar, Ha-Davar Elah (H, A) – The Word, the Word of God; the written or spoken word; in early Judaic-Christian terms symbolizes Jesus Christ as the messenger of God. See *Memra*, *Varnatmik*.

Dēmiourgós (G) – Demiurge, common worker, or artisan; in Plato's works, the name of the creator of the visible world; in Philo of Alexandria, a mediator between heaven and earth and likely the forerunner to the Christian Word made flesh; in Paul's epistles, a subordinate power, heavenly-ordained mediator, or devil that is ruler of the world. Gnostics, taking their cue from Paul, regarded the demiurge as being both good and evil, which has parallels to the Sanskrit word *kal*, meaning time, the power that creates, sustains, and destroys the lower worlds through both positive and negative powers. Kal opposes the soul in its return journey to God Realization according to the Light and Sound Teachings. Also equated with *Brahman* and the Judeo-Christian concept of God, as opposed to the Nameless Pure Consciousness above duality.

Devakut (H) – Cleaving or being attached; devotion; from the word *davak* meaning glue; communion with God in Jewish mysticism, much like the beatific vision. In the Light and Sound Teachings, devakut approximates the ongoing practice of *dhyan*.

Dhunatmik (S) – The inexpressible and formless Voice or Language of the Nameless One; can only be perceived with the spiritual faculties of soul; *Logos*, *Shabda*, the Word, Light and Sound.

Dhyan (S) – Contemplation; holding one's focus and devotional love on the form of the master or the *Shabda*; the second phase of the spiritual contemplation in the Light and Sound Teachings.

E'Alma (A) - All creation, the heavens and earth, all that exists, cosmic world order; esoterically, everything that is manifested or given form, as opposed to the Unmanifest Realm of the Nameless One.

Ekklēsia (G) – A gathering or meeting of early Christians in private homes as a forerunner to the church; *kehillah* in Hebrew.

Ekstasis (G) – Ecstasy or ecstatic trance discussed in the Acts of the Apostles in the New Testament, most likely brought on by rituals prominent in Jewish, Egyptian, and Greek mysticism of the times.

Elah (H) – Awesome One.

Elohim, Elohiym (H) – God or gods; El means Strong One.

Enoch (H) – Great-grandson of Adam who did not die but "walked with God." The books describing Enoch's ascension into the upper echelons of heaven were not part of the *Tanakh* or Old Testament, but were associated with the Essenes as evidenced by the Dead Sea Scrolls.

Ethnos Apostolos (G) – Messenger to the nations or all peoples; what Paul of Tarsus called himself.

Euaggelion (G) – Gospel, triumphant news, the Christian Word or message of Christ as Savior.

Galut (H) – Exiled; those living in the Diaspora, referring to the multiple expulsions of Jews from the ancestral homeland.

Goyim (H) – Anyone who isn't Jewish; the uncircumcised; Gentile.

Hagios Pneuma (G) – Holy Spirit or Ghost; originates from the Jewish term *Ruach Hakodesh;* refers to being filled with the inspirational Presence of God. In Christianity, the Holy Spirit corresponds with the resurrected Christ, although the concept of the Holy Trinity (Father, Son, and Holy Spirit) didn't develop until the Fourth Century CE. Esoterically, the Holy Spirit without the Christian symbolism is another term for the *Logos.*

Hakshavah (H) – Jewish practice of listening with attention and heeding the instruction one hears; esoterically, is used in this story to refer to the practice of *bhajan*, or listening to the *Logos* in the Light and Sound Teachings.

Hamartia (G) – Sin; to miss the mark, to err, to violate God's law. Sin developed into a religious construct that engenders guilt, fear, and repression, promoting the idea that soul is impure by the very fact that sin has to be washed away. See *Karma.*

Ha-Rav (H) – A formal title or proper name, i.e., *The* Master. See *Rav, Ravi.*

Harmaronia Universalis (G) – Universal Harmony, the Music of the Spheres; the theory of the workings of the universe put forth by Pythagoras in the Sixth Century BCE; esoterically a metaphor for the *Logos.*

Havel (H) – Vanity; breath or vapor; Abel, the son of Adam and Eve.

Hechalot (H) – Palace, temple, hall; divine abodes of heaven, usually five to seven in number to match the ruling powers of the planets that could be viewed in the sky; God sat on a throne in the highest heaven. Jewish mysticism from Talmudic times, 200 and 500 CE, respectively, developed writings and meditative practices that drew upon the books of Ezekiel, Isaiah, and Enoch to depict visions of ascent through the heavens guided by angels, though the practice may have originated in Second Temple times to emulate those written adventures. Paul may have referred to such an experience when he said he knew a man who had been taken to the third heaven. Esoterically, this symbolizes the initiate's ascent through progressively rarefied regions of consciousness on the Path of Light and Sound. See *Merkavah.*

Hellene (G) – The name the Greeks called themselves, originating in the works of the Greek poet Homer.

Hu (S) – The Divine Presence issued into form as an audible vibration; chanted as a mantra to collect scattered attention at the third eye and enable the lower self to be more spiritually receptive.

Ichthys (G) – An ancient word for fish; a symbol of two intersecting arcs used as an early secret symbol for Christianity; a Greek acronym for Jesus Christ Son of God Savior.

Ivrit, Eber (H) – Meaning 'other-sider' because Abraham came from the other side of the Euphrates; refers to the Hebrew language and descendants. In the times of Jesus, the Jewish (*Yehudi*) religion and identity had not yet coalesced as we know it today.

Jivanmukti (S) – Spiritual liberation for the entrapped soul from the cycle of life and death. Association with a true master of a Light and Sound Path can produce such freedom in the moment of surrender at the third eye.

Johanan, Yochanan (H) – Yĕhovah has graced; either John the Baptist or John of Zebedee of the New Testament. John of Zebedee is the accepted author of the Gospel of John, among other New Testament works.

Karma (S) – Law of cause and effect; one's stored karma drives the cycle of life and death, or reincarnation; the debts and credits derived from one's desires, perceptions, and actions. Jesus may have taught the principle of karma when he said, "As you sow, so shall you reap."

Kosmos (G) – Cosmos; the lower worlds and its inhabitants, the universe, the circle of earth, a harmonious arrangement, order.

Kyrios (H) – Lord, messiah, master, God.

Light and Sound Teachings or Path – The God-made path to liberation imprinted on the soul and revealed by a true master through inner guidance and outer instruction. Also called *Sant Mat*, the original teachings of the saints, or *Surat Shabda Yoga*, the practice of merging the soul into the Sound Current. Not an outward, man-made religion.

Lo (A) – No.

Logizomai (G) – To reason, contemplate, listen; esoterically, to listen to the Logos akin to the contemplation practice called *bhajan* in the Light and Sound Teachings.

Logos (G) – Word, reason, discourse, thought; first coined by Heraclitus in Ephesus around 600 BCE to mean the higher-order principle that governs a changing universe. Definition broadened through Christianity to mean the Word or Message of God manifested through Jesus the Christ as the Word made flesh. Esoterically, the Light and Sound matrix or system that matures the soul and returns it to its origin. See *Memra, Shabda Dhun*.

Malchut Hashamayim (H) – Kingdom of Heaven, so-called in the New Testament because Jesus the Christ was seen as the ruler of this kingdom. Esoterically, the Pure God Worlds. See *Shamayim*.

Mammon (A) – Money, wealth, riches personified.

Mara Ha-Memra (H) – Master of the Word; in the Jewish religion, a rabbi or someone who can interpret the *Torah*; esoterically, the Word made flesh, the *Sat Guru*.

Mashiyach, Mashiach (H) – Messiah; Christ, the Anointed One; to be anointed with oil, particularly as a sacred rite in death or when being inducted into office such as king or priest. In the story of Jesus, some say he was anointed by Mary Magdalene as part of his process of becoming the messiah. See *Sat Guru*.

Mayim Chayim – Living water; the natural or running water the priests used to purify by immersion, which evolved into the Christian baptism; title given to Jesus the Christ because of the idea that Christians would be baptized in his spirit rather than being plunged in water. Esoterically, symbolizes the *Logos*, *Shabda*, or the Light and Sound.

Memra, Ma'mar (A) – Utterance, voice, speech, command, promise; in the *Tanakh* or Old Testament, the creative or directive Word of God manifesting His power into the matter and mind of the world. With the help of Philo of Alexandria (c. 20 BCE – 50 CE) and the emergence of Christianity and Judaism, Memra evolved to assimilate the Greek concept of Logos, paralleling the concepts of Wisdom and the Divine Presence to become the "Word made flesh."

Merkavah, Merkabah (H) – Winged chariot or heavenly throne mentioned in the *Tanakh* forty-four times as the metaphoric vehicle that made ascension into the heavens possible. Following the destruction of the Second Temple in 70 CE, Jewish mysticism sought ecstatic states and visions through ritual, purification, and prayer, with the caveat that one could possibly lose their mind if they attempted this without proper guidance. Modern scholars suggest that Paul, as a former Pharisee, had sought *merkavah* experiences. See *Hechalot*.

Miryam the Magadan (H, A) – Mary Magdalene; Miryam means rebellious toward God; Magadan refers to the unique fish storage towers in Magdala, or Migdal Nunya on the Sea of Galilee.

Nefesh, Nephesh (H) – That which breathes; in the Old Testament, referred to as that spark of consciousness in all living beings that animates and sustains the body while living, and thus has appetites, desires, emotions, passions.

Early Christians confusingly translated nefesh as the soul, but esoterically, nefesh refers to lower states of consciousness that are not the soul, i.e., the mind and emotional body, which have to be transcended in order to reveal the soul, the *neshama*.

Neshama (H) – Spirit or breath of God; that part of the consciousness that is inextricably connected to God. The Jews in the time of Jesus thought of the spirit as being the higher part of the human, but that the soul (the *nefesh*) was the part that animated the body in life and stayed in the grave in death. Through interaction with the Greeks they developed a more complex concept of the soul. *Neshama* is used in this story to represent the soul, one's divine essence or higher self, consciousness, and attention, the active aspect of self that experiences the *Logos* and the Presence of the Divine.

Nevuah (H) – Prophecy; much of the New Testament was written to portray the prophecies of the Old Testament as being fulfilled by Jesus.

Nous (G) – Complex or ambiguous philosophical term for mind or intellect; Divine Mind; the higher powers of the soul, the faculty of perceiving divine things, of recognizing goodness and of hating evil.

Orach Chayim (H) – The Path of Life, a term from *Psalms* in the Old Testament; used in this story to refer to the teachings of Jesus.

Palla (G) – An ancient Roman mantle worn by women, long and rectangular in shape, fastened by brooches.

Panim El-Panim (H) – Face to the Face of God; to come into the Presence of God in the highest heaven, possibly during a *merkavah* ritual or vision. Exoterically, refers to meeting the God of the lower worlds, but esoterically could refer to God Realization.

Pharisees (G), **Perush, Perushim** (H) – Separate; a school of thought focusing on the *Torah*, which flourished in Jerusalem during the five hundred-year reign of the Second Temple. After the destruction of that temple in 70 CE, the Pharisee order re-emerged as Rabbinic Judaism of modern times.

Philosophía (G) – Philosophy, the love of Wisdom. See *Sophia*.

Pleroma (G) – That which is filled; a term used by Paul to convey perfect cosmological timing; Christian believers being filled with the power of God and Christ.

Pneuma (G) – Breath, vapor, spirit; the Divine Spirit, a simple essence devoid of all grosser matter, possessed of the powers of knowing, desiring, deciding, and acting. Paul used this word for the Hebrew *neshama* to portray the mature elect, or the higher aspect of one's consciousness as soul. See *Psyche*.

Pneumatikos (G) – Spiritual; a term Paul used to describe the mature, rational believers who were filled and governed by the Spirit of God through wisdom.

Polis (G) – Ancient Greek city-state.

Psychē (G) – Breath of life, the vital force that animates the individual; the seat of feelings, desires, affections, aversions; the soul as an essence, which differs from the body and is not dissolved by death. Though Heraclitus, Socrates, Plato, and Philo used the word *psyche* to represent the soul, Paul saw it as the lower self, the immature person who sought signs in order to believe in Christ. Paul's use of *psyche* parallels the Jewish word *nefesh*.

Psychikos (G) – The living, breathing, perishable, sensuous, "natural," or physical; the immature believers or fools according to Paul.

Rav (H) – Great, revered; teacher, master; lord. Rav is the root of *rabbi*, and is used in this story to differentiate from the conventional idea of a Jewish rabbi, which didn't develop until after the destruction of the Second Temple.

Ravi (H) – My master or teacher. Ravi is used here as a name for the Inner Master in the tradition of Light and Sound Paths. An Inner Master is the Eternal Power that works through the Outer Master, or *Sat Guru*, within the realms of the initiate as a projection or channel of the *Shabda,* or *Logos*.

Ruha (A), **Ruach** (H) – Wind, breath, air, spirit; creative Spirit of God; the primordial or primitive divine essence of the individual. See *Nefesh, Neshama*.

Sach Khand (S) – The changeless realm, the fifth spiritual region existing within the individual consciousness; the abode of soul and God realization.

Sadducees (G), **Tzaddukim** (H) – Righteous; a school of thought that thrived during the Second Temple in Jerusalem; tended to be more Hellenistic and willing to cooperate with the Romans.

Sat Guru (S) – True Master; Word made flesh; one of the requisites of a genuine Light and Sound Path. A Sat Guru is self and God Realized and can re-enliven the latent Sound Current within the initiate as well as guide one through the levels of consciousness within their being. Ultimately, it is the Sound Current, the *Shabda*, or *Logos*, that is the Sat Guru.

Satsang (S) – Union or association with Truth, while in the presence of the *Sat Guru* during physical discourse of the teachings or among fellow *satsangis*; communing with the *Shabda* during contemplation and eventually merging with It.

Sefer (H) – Book or scroll.

Shabda Dhun, Shabda, Shabd (S) – The expression of the Divine as pure spiritual consciousness that creates and sustains all life; a river of divine love experienced in the initiate as an audible vibration, presence, or perception with increasing magnitude; the means by which the soul returns to its origin.

Shamayim (H) – Heaven, the visible sky and its celestial bodies, the abode of God personified. The *Torah* doesn't discuss an afterlife, and the idea of the resurrection for all souls was a developing concept. The phrases "world to come," "a new earth," and "Kingdom of God" likely referred to Christ's Second Coming and an apocalyptic heaven on earth, as Paul promoted. The idea of heaven as an afterlife developed over the first few centuries of Christianity. Esoterically, the Second Coming is viewing the Sat Guru at the third eye. See *Sach Khand*.

Shechinah, Shekhinah (H) – Divine Presence, inspiration; symbolized by a pillar of cloud and fire, for instance; used in this story esoterically to describe the inner presence of the Divine within one's own consciousness.

Shefa (H) – Divine Flow, grace; seemingly corresponds to the Sanskrit word *Shabda*, the Sound Current.

Sheol (H) – Hell, grave; the place where souls in death go in the Jewish tradition, both good and bad; originally, a landfill.

Shlama, Shelam (A), **Shalom** (H) – A greeting or farewell wishing the other person peace and wellbeing.

Simeon Kephas (H), **Simon Petros** (G) – One who hears or is heard; Jesus called Simon "kephas," or "petros," meaning "the Rock"; traditionally one of the founders of the Christian movement.

Simran (S) – Remembrance of the Sat Guru or repetition of one's mantra; the first phase of spiritual contemplation in the Light and Sound Teachings.

Sophia, Sofia (G) – Wisdom of God; a central theme in Greek philosophy, theology, and mysticism; figures prominently in the New Testament where it mixes with the symbolism of the Hebrew *chockmah*. In Gnosticism, the feminine *sophia* personified the soul and was seen as the bride of Christ as well as the Holy Spirit of the Trinity. Later Jewish mysticism likened *sophia* to the Divine Presence, or *Shechinah*.

Sound Current, Audible Life Stream, Light and Sound – See *Shabda Dhun*.

Spermologos (G) – One who sows seeds; a bird or crow that scavenges; a talkative person or babbler; term given to Paul by Stoics and Epicureans in the Acts of the Apostles.

Talmid, Talmidim (H) - Student(s), disciple(s); used here to refer to Jesus's ministry.

Tanakh (H) – The Hebrew holy book, called the Old Testament in the Christian Holy Bible; an acronym for *Torah* referring to the books and laws of Moses, *Nevi'im* refering to the books of the prophets; and *Ketuvim* meaning writings, which includes *Psalms* and the Books of Job and Daniel.

Tevilah (H) – Immersion; a ritual bath in running or "living" water in a specially constructed pool called a *mikveh*; precursor to baptism. The Living Water thus became a metaphor for Jesus the Christ; esoterically a metaphor for the *Logos*, or Light and Sound.

Tera (A), **Thyra** (G) – Gate, shepherd's gate; Christian metaphor for entryway to heaven. In Sanskrit, the *til* is esoterically the gate or doorway between levels of consciousness with the *tisra til* being the third eye.

Theos (G) – Supreme Divinity, a general name for gods and goddesses, adapted to mean God and the Trinity in the Judaic-Christian movement; the root of theology, theory, etc.

Toda (H) – Thank you.

Torah (H) – Teachings, instruction, law; the five books of Moses, which purport 613 commandments or laws to follow; from the root word *yarah* meaning hitting the mark, as opposed to *chata* meaning missing the mark, or sin. See *Hamartia, Karma.*

Varnatmik (S) – The written word, the "light" in the Light and Sound Teachings; can be divinely inspired but is esoterically not a substitute for *the* Divine. See *Dhunatmik.*

Yakob, Ya'akov (H) – The supplanter; James the son of Zebedee, brother to John (Johanan). In Paul's letters, there was some confusion as to whether this James was one of the Pillars of Jerusalem who made decisions for the early Christian movement, or another James who was the half-brother of Jesus.

Yĕchezqel, Jehezekel (H) – Ezekiel; the prophet-priest of Babylonian exile whose visions described in the Old Testament book by his name are the starting point for Jewish mysticism. See *Merkavah.*

Yĕhovah, Jehovah, Yahweh, YHVH (H) – The existing one; the unspoken personal name of the one true supreme God in the Jewish religion.

Yehudi (H) – The people from Yehudah, or Judea, the Kingdom of Judah, who eventually became known as the Jewish people.

Yehudah (H) – See *Yehudi, Yisrael.*

Yerushalayim (H) – Jerusalem; teaching of peace; also called the City of David.

Yĕshayah (H) – Isaiah; the Book of Isaiah prophecies the coming of the Messiah and Israel's true king for Jerusalem and Judah. Isaiah's vision of God on a throne gives rise to subsequent mystic literature and Christian imagery. See *Hechalot*.

Yeshua, Joshua (H), **Iēsous** (G) – Jesus, from Yĕhowshuwa meaning Yĕhovah Saves. Esoterically, Jesus is considered a "historical Master" of the *Logos*, or the Light and Sound. See *Sat Guru*.

Yiray-Elohim (H) – "God Fearers"; typically non-Jews or Arabs who believed in the One God, as opposed to the Greek Parthenon of lesser gods and spirits, but didn't wish to participate in the laws of purity and other commandments of the *Torah*; likely the group Paul proselytized to and who would be the most receptive to his message.

Yirmĕyah (H) – Jeremiah; One who God has risen or appointed; a prophet of the Old Testament or *Tanakh*. The New Testament quotes the Book of Jeremiah to demonstrate that Jesus fulfilled its prophecies.

Yisrael (H) – Israel, from God prevails; name given to the northern kingdom consisting of the ten tribes under Jeroboam; the southern kingdom was known as Judah, or Yehudah. Paul said everyone who believed in Jesus as savior were all Israel, or Children of God.

Yob, Iyov (H) – Job, meaning hated or persecuted; a major topic of the Book of Job in the Old Testament is the ultimate mysteries of God's existence.

Zakar, Zechar (H) – To remember, to do in remembrance; repetition; similar to *zikr* in Arabic. See *simran*.

CPSIA information can be obtained
at www.ICGtesting.com
Printed in the USA
LVOW07s1403210817
545800LV00004B/252/P